# DUKE GRANDFATHER SAVES THE WORLD*

## JAMES MAXSTADT

*OR AT LEAST A SMALL PART OF IT

Duke Grandfather Saves the World*
*or at least a small part of it

Printed in the United States of America

First Printing, 2018

ISBN-13: 978-1985160279
ISBN-10: 1985160277

James Maxstadt

Cover art: SelfPubBookCovers.com/ DawnyDawny

Visit at jamesmaxstadt.com

# Titles by James Maxstadt

## The Duke Grandfather Saga

Tales of a Nuisance Man

Duke Grandfather Saves the World*
*or at least a small part of it

Duke Grandfather Hears Voices

Duke Grandfather Unleashes Hell

## The Lilly the Necromancer Series

Death Lessons

Work-Death Balance

Death, Love, and Happiness

## The Fall

Shriven

Bereft

## The Travels of Solomon

Solomon's Exile

Solomon's Journey

Solomon's Odyssey

## Black Friar Quest

How to Trick a Demon

## Box Sets

Duke Grandfather: The Whole Story

Life with the Dead, Lilly the Necromancer, the complete story

The Travels of Solomon

## Anthologies

Rejected Worlds: A Short-story Anthology

Dying Earths (various authors)

To Mom and Dad, who never discouraged a weird kid from being weird, and always encouraged an imagination.

# Contents

## THE START OF THE STORY

In the middle of Capital City, or near enough that it makes no difference, sits a house. It's an unassuming place, neatly maintained and cared for, but with that lived-in look that comes of seeing generations born and raised there.

There are secrets inside this house. Not of the bad kind, or even the good kind. And maybe secrets isn't the right word. Maybe the right word is…stories.

The young man who approached the house thought that would make a nice opening. He'd already written several of these stories down, so that people would know who lived here, and what they had done. But there were more. A lot more.

Stories from long lives and two remarkable people who lived them. They were his grandparents, and he knew them his whole life, but that didn't make them any less incredible. Actually, for him, it made them even more so.

"Granddad!" he called, letting himself in. "Are you here?"

"Oh, what now," came a voice from further inside. It was the voice of an old man, but still strong and steady.

"Hush, Duke," a woman's voice answered. Her voice wavered slightly, but it brooked no nonsense or backtalk.

There was a soft chuckle, then Duke's voice. "Come on in, boy. Let's go look upstairs."

The young man hurried into the house, stopped to say hello and kiss his grandmother, and then ran up the stairs to the trophy room. Or at least that was how he thought of it.

It was a room that was lined with shelves, and several tables scattered around. Various items crowded the surfaces, and they were all mementos of his grandfather's time as a Nuisance Man, those men and women who helped keep Capital City safe. Duke was the most famous of those, and his grandmother, Lilly, was still spoken of with reverence in the City Watch.

"What are you doing with all this, boy?" Duke asked when the young man entered the room.

"I told you, Granddad. I'm writing it down, and making a book out of it. People love it."

"I'll have to be more careful what I tell you then. Now, everyone knows we have a basement that's become a Brownie colony."

"Yes, but no one cares. And if anything, it makes you and Grandmother safer. Who in their right mind would want to try to break into this house?"

"Heh. If they could get by your Grandmother, they'd have a chance against Petal too. She's still got it, you know." His voice softened as he looked off in her direction.

"I know," the young man smiled. "And so do you. Now, is there anything you want to tell me about?"

The old man waved his hand dismissively. "Take your pick. It's all good."

The young man walked around the room looking at the variety of items. He came upon a scroll, slightly yellowed with age, and tied with a still bright, red satin ribbon. He held it up for his Granddad to see.

"What's this?"

Duke walked over and took it out of his hand. "Something I haven't looked at in a long time. But something I'm proud of, and so's your Grandmother. It will make a good tale."

He began to walk from the room, still holding the rolled-up scroll.

"Wait," the young man said. "I don't even know what it is."

"Good," Duke's voice came back to him as the old man started down the stairs. "Come down and get comfortable. This is a long story, the longest I've told you yet. Then, when it's over, I'll show you what this says."

The young man smiled. His grandfather was ever the showman. He ran down the stairs after him, eager to get started.

## THE SOUND OF THE FURY

"What are we doing this weekend?" Lilly asked me, over breakfast. The day was bright and sunny, and was shaping up to be beautiful. Lilly needed to work at the Watch, and I was going to go in and take a peek at the Nuisance Board.

Truth to tell, it wouldn't have bothered me much if there wasn't anything on it. There was a new place, "The Draugr's Garden", which I was looking to try. It supposedly had an area behind the tavern, with long wooden tables to sit at, and quaff gigantic mugs of ale, three times the size of a normal one. Jessup told me of it, and it seemed like a perfect day to try it out.

But first, I'd need to at least take a look at the Board, then I could get an ale with Jessup. Or two. Maybe three, but definitely no more than four. Those things were huge, and prudence was required.

"Not sure," I replied. "Why? Have something in mind?"

"Mmmm…no, not really, I guess. I was thinking of the Crown Street Bazaar. But I know you don't really like it…"

Ah, my clever Lilly. She did love to shop, and knew that no, it was not my favorite thing to do. However, the Crown Street Bazaar was the site of our first "date", although neither of us realized that's what it was at the time. By reminding me of that, she wrapped me around her finger. As I said; clever.

"We can do that," I said, trying to muster enthusiasm for the prospect. "Maybe spend the morning there, and then go get some lunch or something."

Aha! Turnabout is fair play! If I didn't end up at The Draugr's Garden today, I still had a shot at it this weekend.

Lilly smiled as she picked up her coffee cup, knowing full well what I meant.

"Let's see if the weather is going to be nice enough to sit outside."

I smiled back. She may have played me like a fiddle, but there was one thing about my Lilly. She did believe in fair play.

We finished breakfast, cleaned up and left the house. It was like leaving a quiet oasis, and we were suddenly surrounded by the hustle and bustle of our city, as people of every race went about their business.

One of the things that I've grown to truly love about Capital City over the last several years has been the diversity. Oh, I admit, that when the King first opened the borders and the other races flooded in, I was right there with all those who claimed that it was unfair to those of us already here, that they were going to take our jobs, and so on.

But, I was also very young, and foolhardy. Here I was, yelling about an imaginary lack of jobs, and I hadn't even decided what to do with my own life. Eventually, of course, I turned that around into becoming a Nuisance Man, and ended up with quite the career. It wasn't until much later, when age, wisdom, and circumstance caused me to change my views on what was going on in our fair city, that I began to appreciate our differences.

Now, I was friends with a dwarf, who wielded an axe almost as deadly as my own gun. I lived with a basement full of Brownies, who could cause my arms and legs to magically fall off without breaking a sweat. And, most amazingly of all, I somehow acquired a live-in girlfriend.

Ever since we came back from her sister's wedding, Lilly was spending more and more time at my house, and less and less at hers. To be honest, Lilly's house was much nicer than mine, and in a better neighborhood, being tucked into its own little dimension, populated only by the other necromancers that work for the Watch. But mine was where Petal and her people ended up, after we helped free her and her large family from the clutches of an evil Elder Being a short time ago. Since they then needed somewhere to stay, they set up shop in my basement, and have since taken over the whole space. It's kind of nice when you visit, if a little nerve wracking at times. Brownies are tiny, and no matter how well we get along, I'm always afraid that the nice will wear off if I step on one.

Lilly tells me that I'm being silly, and spends a good amount of time down there. She loves them, and they seem to love her. She always tells me that her magic and theirs are entirely different things, but I swear she must be getting pointers. Then again, what do I know? Magic has always been a headscratcher to me.

As I was saying though, the diversity in Capital City was something that I truly appreciated. There was something refreshing about walking down the street and seeing something new every day, even if that meant there was the occasional bit of trouble as well.

Like when we turned a corner and I was suddenly run into by a man, staggering down the street. I grimaced, as the thought of getting that looped, that early in the morning, was too much for even me. Not that there was any shortage of that sort of thing in Capital City, but it still always surprised me when it was shoved in my face.

"Whoa, there, friend," I said, holding on to his arms and guiding him around me. "Take it easy, pal. Might be a good idea to find a place to sleep it off."

I smiled as I said this, to let him know that I meant him no harm. He looked back at me, an expression of utter incomprehension on his face. His eyes searched mine, flickering wildly back and forth as he tried to focus, and his mouth hung open. A garbled noise came out of him, and he pulled back away

from me. Finally, he tore his gaze away, and continued down the
street, stumbling and bumping into other people as he went.

"Ugh, he was a mess. Poor guy. I wonder what he was into?
Ale doesn't do that to you."

"No," Lilly said, standing next to me, her hand in mine and
watching the drunk move further away down the street. "I don't
know what does. There was something else, too."

"Really?" Lilly was always more observant than me. It's how
we ended up with a basement full of Brownies in the first place.

"Whatever it is he's on, it made his ears bleed too. I wonder
if he could even hear you."

I looked over at her and saw the concern on her face.

"Do you want me to follow him?" I asked her. "Make sure
he's alright?"

"No…no, it's okay. I'll ask around today, see if the wizards
know about anything new on the street."

We watched until the drunken man moved out of sight, and
then continued on toward the watchhouse.

"Hey, Sarge," I said as we walked in.

"Duke. Lilly."

I'm not sure that he even looked up from the newssheet he
was reading. It was commonplace for me to walk in with Lilly now,
and Sarge mostly ignored us. I knew better. It was an act. Sarge
thought Lilly was good for me, although he also thought she could
do much better. I thought Sarge was right on both counts, but I
wasn't about to tell him that.

Lilly kissed me on the cheek and walked behind the counter
and through the door that led to the necromancers' offices, down
in the lower levels of the watchhouse.

"Anything good today, Sarge?" I asked.

"Look for yourself, lover boy," he replied.

I sighed, and walked over the Board. Somedays, Sarge was
like a regular guy, ready with a friendly quip, or to point out an

item of interest in the news. Other days, he was withdrawn, almost grumpy. I learned to respect his different moods, even if I didn't always appreciate them.

Luck was not with me today, and it looked like Jessup would be visiting the Draugr's Garden without me. There were plenty of nuisances on the Board to choose from. I looked them over carefully. The Watch had become much better at verifying that the individuals posted on the Board actually deserved to be there, but some innocents still slipped through every now and then. There were still no human faces, of course. Those ended up on the Board at the NHLF headquarters, where Brindar and a select few others took care of them.

One other way that I changed in the last couple of years was in my preference for which nuisances I would take. In the past, it was all about which one would pay me the most money for the least amount of effort. I liked to believe that I still thought that way, but in reality, I tended to go for ones that truly had it coming. Those that preyed on the weak, the very young, the old, or the helpless, were a particular favorite of mine.

Today was no exception.

The notice was posted by a group of elderly ladies, all who resided in the same house. You got that sometimes, here in the city. A certain group would get together, pool their resources and buy a place to live. It was mostly those who didn't want to be on their own for whatever reason. A lot of the times, it was financial. But sometimes, which could be case with these ladies, it was because they were all elderly and alone, and found common ground that way.

The notice showed a large, upright, dog-like creature, with huge, slathering jaws. It must have been a picture of the thing at night, because during the day, it would look like everyone else. This werewolf was hanging around at night, threatening the ladies and their pets, which mostly consisted of tiny dogs with bows in their hair. If it didn't get money, or food, it would grab the pet, and get fed that way. This was making a lot of little, old ladies, very, very upset.

But the werewolf made a major mistake. It picked victims with financial resources, and the fee they were offering for removal of this nuisance showed it. It meant I needed to work tonight, after the sun went down, but for someone who truly needed help. Plus, it was damn good money.

The other upside is that it gave me the day free, so my plans to visit with Jessup and a mug or two of ale were good to go. I would definitely have to exercise some caution today if I was going to be any good tonight, and limit myself to only one, maybe two of those giant mugs of ale. Three, tops.

Right before sundown, I pulled myself together and left the house, aware of Lilly's wry expression as she watched me go. I had done well though, and only drank two mugs of ale. Not that I couldn't have drank another, mind you, but…priorities.

The elderly ladies who put the werewolf on the Board were located in a reasonably priced, very nice, area of the city, called Tradesmen Circle. Carpenters, masons, seamstresses, bakers and other trade folk and their families lived here, forming a tight knit community. No frills, no great palaces or fancy coaches, just solid, well-built houses, neatly maintained.

How a werewolf managed to move in on anyone in this neighborhood was beyond me. Usually, neighborhoods like this took care of their problems on their own.

When I got there, the sun was about down. I knocked on the door and waited patiently as the yipping from inside was hushed, and the door opened, no more than an inch. A bright, blue eye peered out at me, the whites slightly yellowed with age.

"Yes?" a voice quavered through the opening. "Can I help you?"

"Hello ma'am," I said, trying to put on my most respectful voice. "My name is Duke Grandfather, and I'm here about your werewolf problem."

"Who's grandfather? You don't look old enough to be a grandfather!"

"No, no. I'm sorry. My *name* is Grandfather. Duke Grandfather," I said, a little more loudly, and slowly.

The eye blinked at me.

"No one's grandfather is here, dear. Just a bunch of old grannies in this house. You must have the wrong address."

"It's my name!" I practically yelled it at her. "I'm a Nuisance Man! I'm here about the werewolf!"

The eye blinked again, and I thought she was about to repeat that I was too young to be a grandfather, when there was another voice on the other side of the door.

"Oh, for Pete's sake, Emma! Stop messing with the man and let him in!"

There was a snort of laughter, and then the door opened fully, exposing a short, grey haired woman. She was dressed in simple trousers, a frilly shirt, and surprisingly, a pair of slippers with bunny ears on her feet.

"I heard you the first time, Mr. Grandfather," she said in a perfectly clear voice. "You have to allow the elderly their little games. Keeps us feeling young."

The change was so sudden and so dramatic that for a moment, I could only stand and gawk. Then, my sense of humor regained its control, and I chuckled.

"Well played, Mrs...?"

"Reynolds. Please do come in, Mr. Grandfather."

The place was pretty much as I was expecting. Nicely decorated, a little old-fashioned, but clean. Mrs. Reynolds led me into a parlor, where three other elderly women sat in comfortable chairs and sofas. There was the smell of flowers and soap in the air, and all four women looked at me expectedly.

"About time, Emma," said one of them. She was a stout woman, dressed in a black dress, floor length, which reminded me suspiciously of a witch's gown. "We don't have all night to fool around. That damn wolf will be back any minute. You saw the notice, Grandfather. You're here, so I'm assuming that means you're in."

"So rude, Gertie," Mrs. Reynolds said to her. "Allow the boy time to get his breath. Would you like a cup of tea, dear?"

She directed this last to me, but I declined the offer and turned to Gertie instead.

"Yes," I told her. "I'm in. Although I have to say that I'm pretty surprised that a werewolf is in this neighborhood, and that some of your neighbors haven't already handled it."

The four women exchanged uncomfortable glances.

"Ah," I said, as understanding came over me. "He's from the neighborhood, right?"

"He was a bad seed to begin with," Gertie said. "Even as a young boy. Now I don't blame the family, mind you, but when you spare the rod…"

"Alright, Gertie, that's enough," Mrs. Reynolds said. "There's no use in going on about all that. The Carvers are a perfectly decent family. It's not their fault that young Ronald got mixed up in the things he did."

"Hmph." Gertie crossed her arms and looked away.

I cleared my throat. "I can understand why no one around here wants to do anything about it, then. But, here's the thing. There's really only one way to deal with a werewolf. They don't see reason, and I'm not going to be able to talk to it. If I do this, it's going to have to be removed, permanently."

"We understand, Mr. Grandfather," Mrs. Reynolds said quietly. "As do the Carvers. Do what you must, and we'll deal with the aftermath, together as friends and neighbors. As it should be."

I nodded, and took my leave. This wasn't quite as cut and dry as I hoped it would be, but sometimes, things need to happen the way that they're going to.

I went back outside and parked myself on a bench down the street from the house. The moon was full tonight, a fact which was going to make the werewolf his most powerful. I took out my gun and whispered "werewolf" to it, setting the little, metal ball that came out to whatever would do the most damage. In this case, I was guessing that meant silver.

I didn't have long to wait. Down the street, a figure was coming this way, long legs eating up the distance quickly, as it moved from one pool of light from the street lamps to another. It moved rapidly, at times dropping down to run on all fours, then rising again, and loping along on two. It didn't hesitate as it approached the women's house, but jumped up the stairs leading to the doorway and banged on it savagely.

He was huge, fully eight feet tall, and powerfully muscled. His legs had an extra joint in them, so that when he went on all fours, he could run even more quickly than on two legs. Gray fur covered him from head to toe, and there was a bushy tail growing from his rear. A long muzzle, filled with large, sharp teeth, thrust out from his face, and his pointed ears twitched on top of his head.

"Hey," I called out, standing up and throwing my cloak back over my shoulder. "Ronald!"

The werewolf spun around, lips pulled back from his muzzle and a low growl rumbling up from his chest. He looked me over, his eyes roaming up and down, and he leaped off the steps and started toward me, moving slowly, stalking me.

"You might want to stop," I said, knowing full well that he wasn't going to listen to me.

He didn't. He threw his head back and unleashed a howl that echoed off the buildings lining the block. I didn't see anyone peer out of a window to see what was going on, not that I took my eyes off of Ronald for long. They knew. Word spread through the neighborhood that a Nuisance Man had been called in to take care of one of their own, and although they might not like it, they knew it was necessary. Some problems are too big to handle alone.

I raised my gun and sighted along it, aiming at Ronald's heart. Werewolves were big, fast, and brutal. If you're going to put one down, you better do it quickly, or else it might be you hitting the street.

"Last chance, Ronald."

No change. Instead, he charged, and I was out of options. I squeezed the trigger and with a bang the little, metal ball flew out and took Ronald directly in the chest, right where his heart was. The werewolf froze in his tracks, a surprised look on his face, and then he started to turn, as if to run away.

Instead, he crashed to the ground, and lay still. A moment later he started to shrink, the fur melting off of his body and the muzzle becoming a normal nose again. In a few seconds, there was a perfectly normal, nude man, dead on the ground.

Doors opened along the street, and people began to come out. I saw a middle aged couple, distraught and holding on to each other. Gertie, Mrs. Reynolds and the other women from their house came out, as well as other neighbors.

"Thank you, Mr. Grandfather," Mrs. Reynolds said to me, her voice quiet, and tears shining in her eyes.

I was about to walk away, not wanting to be an intruder on this scene any longer than I needed to be, when Gertie spoke up.

"What the hell was that?" she said.

Glancing over at her, I saw that she was looking around, a frown on her face.

"What, dear?" Mrs. Reynolds asked.

"That noise. Like...I don't know, like some crying, or wailing, or something."

I looked around. It wouldn't have surprised me if Ronald's mother was letting loose, but the woman was still huddled within the protective circle of her husband's arm, both of them weeping quietly.

"I don't hear anything," Mrs. Reynolds said.

"How can you not? It's coming from right over there!"

Gertie raised her arm and pointed across the street, but there was nothing there. Nothing that I could see anyway, and like Mrs. Reynolds, I couldn't hear anything either.

"You're tired, dear. It's been a long day."

Mrs. Reynolds crossed to her friend and took her by the arm, steering her back to their house. Gertie let herself be led, but continued to stare at the spot that she had pointed at. I stood and watched, already forgotten, and then turned and made my way home.

Sometimes, my job really sucks.

One of the nice things about being a Nuisance Man, which I've mentioned before, is the flexibility. I did the werewolf job, and although I understood the necessity of it, it still left me feeling down, so I took the next few days off. Lilly understood, and as long as I wasn't out totally wasting every day with Jessup, she didn't have a problem with it.

But, as all things do, the feeling passed, and the money started getting low, and it was time to consider going back to work. I accompanied Lilly back to the watchhouse, meaning to check the Board again and see what was on it. I didn't have to take a job yet, and was only planning on it if there was something truly worth it. Someone who the world would be better off without.

"Hey Sarge," I made my normal greeting as we entered.

"Duke, Lilly. I was hoping you'd be in today. Come on over here. I've got something I want to show you."

Huh. Usually when Sarge calls me over like that, it means that he has something pretty big. Last time it was to combat the gargoyles that were terrorizing the city, but I wasn't aware of anything like that going on.

He slid a paper across the counter to us. It was the same form that was used to post a notice on the Board, with room for a picture, a description of the supposed crime, and the contact information for the one posting it.

This one was done differently. Instead of a nuisance, something that needed to be eliminated, it was a picture of what looked like a victim. The man in the picture was most assuredly dead, but he died with a look of extreme horror on his face. His eyes were wide and staring, and his mouth locked open as if he was screaming in his final moments. And there were dark stains running from his ears to the collar of his shirt.

"Is that...?" I asked, bending closer to get a better look.

"Blood," Lilly said. "Duke, what does that remind you of?"

I shrugged my shoulders and looked at her. "No idea. Should it remind me of anything?"

"Think back a few days, to the last time you walked me to work. The same day you took the werewolf job."

For a moment, I didn't know what she was talking about, but then it hit me, and I remembered the man who ran into me that morning with the same wild-eyed expression and blood running from his ears. I looked at the posting again, and it was definitely not the same man, but the similarities were remarkable.

"He's not the only one, either," Sarge said, sliding two more notices across the counter. The people in them, one male dwarf, one female human, looked the same. Like they died terrified and screaming, with blood flowing from their ears.

All three notices were posted by the same person. Someone who truly cared. Father Magnus. He submitted them with the plea that if anyone had any idea what could be doing this, to please contact the Watch, and then see him at the Temple of the Good God for their reward. No mention of what that reward would be, but with Magnus, you could trust that it would be fair.

"Huh," I said. "This is a new one on me. What about you, Lilly?"

"Not sure either," she said, and then hesitated. "But…I may know of something…let me do some research. Don't take anything off the Board right now, and hang around nearby. I might have something shortly."

"I guess we're going to investigate this?"

"It's Father Magnus. What do you think?"

She marched off to her office and I stayed put with Sarge, looking at the horrified faces on the notices.

"Looks like a weird one," he said after a minute.

"Yeah, plus Father Magnus is involved. Well, not involved, but concerned. Maybe I should go speak to him."

"Sure, sure," he said, nodding. "That's a great idea. Head on down there so that when Lilly comes up looking for you, you won't be here. I may not know much, but I do know this. When you've got someone like her that's willing to accept such a ridiculous last name as yours, you shouldn't piss her off."

"What? What do you mean accept my last name?"

"Open your eyes, Duke," he snorted.

I was flabbergasted. Still, his point was well taken. I was fine on my own before I ever met Lilly, but now that I was with her…well, yeah.

"Tell her I'll be right around the area when she comes back," I said, "I'll keep checking back in, too."

"That's the boy. Smarter than you look, even when you need to be beaten over the head with it."

Well. What could I say to that?

I hung around outside, people-watching, until I got bored and went into a few shops, browsing and looking at some finely crafted weapons, but finding nothing that could come close to my gun, and avoiding the taverns in the area. It was too early for that, even for me.

Finally, after what seemed like hours, Lilly came back up.

"I think we figured it out," she said, without preamble. "But it's not good."

I looked at Sarge, who was paying no attention to me, eyes focused on Lilly.

"I think we're dealing with a banshee," Lilly said, with the type of gravitas a person says, "He was crushed beneath a boulder."

This time when I looked at Sarge, I saw the same dumb expression that I was sure was on my own face.

"Ooookay," I said. "Next question. What's a banshee?"

"Really?" She looked from me to Sarge, and then back again. "Neither of you?"

We both shook our heads, causing her to sigh heavily.

"Fine. But you should know that it's caused quite a stir downstairs. We think that a banshee is a spirit, but we're not sure. And honestly, no one knows if it's good or evil. See, if you hear it, it means that you're going to die. Now, the reason that we don't know if it's good or evil, is because we don't know what the scream means. Does hearing it cause you to die? That's one theory. The other is that the banshee only shows up if you're going to die anyway, and it's meant as a warning."

"And it's not like anyone can ask one, right?" I asked.

"Right. As far as I, and anyone else down there, can find, no one has ever even seen one, or heard it, except for those who die."

"Wait a minute," I said. "If no one has seen or heard one, than how do you know they exist?"

"Because the victims, if that's what they are, have a few days. They'll talk about hearing the scream, and seeing a woman, and then, when they die, they stare at something that no one else can see, in horror. So, we know *something* is doing it."

Suddenly, Gertie's insistence that she could hear a scream the night of the werewolf popped into my head.

"Crap," I said, heading for the door.

"Where are you going," Lilly called after me. "We're not done!"

"I'll be back! See what else you can find out. See if there's any record of someone hearing it and not dying!"

I ran out, already knowing in my heart what both Lilly and I would find.

I wasn't wrong. There was a black bunting hung across the door frame of the house that the elderly ladies lived in, and I could see it in Mrs. Reynolds face when she opened the door. Gertie was gone, and after some gentle questioning, I learned that she never gave up on insisting that she heard something scream that night. She became progressively worse, saying that a woman kept showing up and screaming, until she was almost mad from it. She made it until this morning. When they found her, there was a terrified expression on her face, and blood running from her ears.

I gave my condolences, and made my way back to the Watchhouse.

When I got there, Sarge told me that Lilly wanted me to come on down to her office, which always made me a little nervous. Like I've said many times, magic gives me the creeps, and the type that the necromancers do, even more. No matter how many times Lilly has explained it to me, magic that deals with death at its core still makes me really uneasy.

"Where did you run off to?" she asked me when I opened her office door.

I told her what I found out, including Gertie insisting that she was hearing a scream the other night, even though no one else could.

"Why didn't you tell me?" Lilly said.

"Didn't seem important, at the time. I thought it was some old lady being…well, you know. But it wouldn't have really mattered, right? Unless you found out anything else."

"No," she sighed. "I haven't. I can't find any reference to anyone saying that they've heard the banshee and then not dying. It really does seem like if you hear it, you're as good as done for."

"Well, why is it here then? You would think that if it was always around, we'd have heard about it before."

"I don't know that either. My theory is that it came now because of all the new races flocking here. Maybe it came in with one of them. But that's really only a guess."

We sat in silence for a few moments, each lost in our own thoughts of what was going on, and what it could mean for the city.

"If this thing is evil, and has come here to kill, it can get to an awful lot of people," I said.

"And as far as I can tell, there's no way to stop it, either," Lilly said

"On the other hand, if it's warning people...well, there's no shortage of people dying in this city either."

"No, there isn't. But, Duke, can we take that chance?"

"Do we have a choice?"

"Duke! Lilly! Wonderful to see you both!"

When Father Magnus said something like that to you, you really believed that he meant it. That he truly did find it wonderful that you showed up on his doorstep. The thing was, we were here to try to help this time, but it would have been the same reaction if I came begging for money.

"Hi, Father," I said. "We're here about the postings that you put in at the watchhouse."

"Ah, those," his face fell. "Horrible, isn't it? Those poor people dying and looking as if they'd been scared to death. Death is a normal part of life, and will come for us all, but if we can ease a soul's passage from this world, so much the better."

"We think we know what's doing it," Lilly said. "The problem is that we're not sure how to stop it, or if it can be stopped."

Magnus looked quizzical, and then stood aside, motioning us to come inside the temple. It was cool in there, with large stone pillars holding up what I knew was a second floor. There were long benches, with a few people, human and otherwise, scattered about, either in prayer, or gazing about. At the front was the symbol of the Good God, and an altar below that where either Father Magnus, or one of the other priests of the temple, performed services.

We sat in one of the benches at the back of the temple, and Magnus took the one in front of us, turning so that he faced us over the back of it. We talked in hushed voices, so as not to disturb those who had come in to worship.

"Well then," he started. "What do you suspect is doing this?"

"I think it's called a banshee," Lilly answered. "But I don't know much more. We don't know where they come from, or really what they even are. All we know is that no-one can see them, or hear them, except for a single person. And when that one does, they die a few days later, with a terrified faces, and usually blood running from their ears."

"I see," Magnus paused and considered. "Is it your opinion that it's an evil spirt, or a magic being of some sort, or….what?"

"I really don't know. As you know, my specialty is the realm of the dead, but if banshees exist there, I've never heard of it. I don't think it's a spirt. A part of nature, maybe? Or maybe you're right, and it's a magic evil being of some sort."

"Regardless," I cut in, "we're going to check into it. If it's something that is actually killing people, we'll find a way to stop it."

Magnus sighed. "In the meantime, I'll put the word out and tell people that if anyone hears this thing, they can come here. Maybe we can help make their final moments less frightening."

Over the next several days, more cases of those that heard a mysterious wail cropped up, and word spread that relief could be found at the Temple of the Good God. As usually happens, the story morphed and changed with each telling, until soon, people began showing up expecting that Magnus could fix it, and that if they went to him, they or their loved one, wouldn't die.

It was a credit to the man, and to the other priests who worked there with him, that they were able to stop the inevitable disappointment from turning into rage and violence. Instead, they took the doomed in, stayed with them, and talked with them through their final days and hours. It must have been grueling, and when Lilly and I went back to check on things, we could see the toll that it was taking on them all. None more than Father Magnus, who refused to get solid rest himself, in his need to take care of others.

Lilly spent more time at the watchhouse, meeting with other necromancers and wizards, trying to find an answer, but they came up empty. At home, she spent several evenings in the basement, talking with the Brownies, who heard of the banshee, but never been bothered by one, and didn't have any ideas for how to stop it either.

We came to feel that the thing was indeed an evil force of some kind, although we didn't know that for sure. But some of the people who heard the wail seemed to be perfectly healthy, and showed no signs of illness or disease. Of course, those people could have all been slated to fall victim to an accident, but that seemed more and more unlikely, especially when they were kept in safety at Magnus' Temple, and they still died.

Those that did die in the temple did it the same way as those in the streets, or in their homes. They all stared at something that no one else could see, they all lost focus and would stop responding to anyone else around them, and they all died with blood running from their ears and horrified looks on their faces.

For me, it was frustrating. We ran into some horrible things before, but never anything that we couldn't plan for and defeat in time. But with the banshee, we didn't even know where to start.

It was a warm evening when Lilly and I decided that we needed a break from it, and went to dinner. We returned to

Pierre's, which was the site of our official first date, and ate a great meal. Lilly looked gorgeous, as she always did, and even I cleaned up for the night. We tried our best to talk about other things, but our conversation often turned back to the banshee, or Father Magnus, or how we could fix things. Then we'd purposely swing to something else to try to give our heads a rest.

The walk back home was pleasant. The crowds on the streets were lighter these days, as people thought that if they stayed inside, they'd be safer from the banshee. It didn't seem to matter, but people would think what they were going to. The air was warm, but not oppressive and I was with the woman I loved. In spite of everything else, I was happy.

I suddenly realized that while I was wool-gathering, Lilly was talking.

"Sorry," I said. "I was off in a fog. What did you say?"

Lilly repeated herself, but she must have been annoyed, because whatever she was saying, it came out in a mumble, and I couldn't make it out.

"I said I was sorry," I said. "Come on. What were you saying?"

Lilly stopped and pulled me around so that I was looking at her. She didn't look angry or upset, or even like she was playing a game. She was looking at me with concern, and I could see her mouth moving, but the words coming out were muffled.

Well, actually, when I thought of it, it wasn't that they were muffled. It was more like her voice was being overridden, and there was another noise drowning her out. I shook my head, but instead of going away, it came clearer.

It was a high pitched, wavering noise, but low, almost to the point of my not being entirely sure that I was hearing it. It was on the edge of my hearing, but gaining in strength now that I recognized it, and it was drowning out Lilly's voice and any other sounds around me.

My heart started to hammer in my chest, and a sweat broke out on my brow. I could see Lilly looking at me, asking me what was wrong, but I couldn't answer her.

Instead, I looked around wildly, not seeing anything, but that noise was making me feel disoriented and dizzy. I stumbled slightly, and Lilly grabbed me, holding me steady.

Across the street, I saw her then. There was a beautiful woman watching me, her mouth moving slightly, as if she was singing softly. She wore a pale blue gown that flowed to the street, covering most of her form. There was a bluish tinge to her face and long hair, and she seemed somehow…unsubstantial. As if she wasn't really there.

I tried to pull my gun from my belt and set it to "banshee", but I didn't even clear it when the world started to spin. Lilly's cry of "*Duke!*" penetrated that horrible noise and then the world went dark, I felt something hard hit me, and that was the last thing I remembered.

When I woke up, I was home and lying in my own bed. Lilly was sitting in a chair nearby, an anxious expression on her face.

"You're awake," she said, and now, I could hear her easily.

"Yeah. Sorry about that."

"Don't be an idiot, Duke," the words sounding harsh, but I could hear the tears that she was holding back. I hated it, so I held my arm out to her, telling her silently to come over to me.

She crawled up on the bed next to me and snuggled in.

"You heard it," she said, her voice quiet.

"I did. I saw it too. Have to say, she was pretty hot stuff." I smiled as I said it, and Lilly took it for the joke it was meant to be and punched me softly on the arm.

"I said not to be an idiot."

We lay silently for a few minutes. She felt nice, lying there with her head on my chest, breathing. Hell, just breathing felt nice at this point. I wondered how much longer I would do that?

"You know what this means," she said, not looking at me.

"Yep. But we're not finished yet. Maybe we'll find an answer."

"Maybe. How are you feeling now?"

"I feel fine. Some buzzing in my ears, but it's low. I can hear and I don't feel dizzy or anything anymore. Want to get up?"

"Not yet," she said, and turned her face to mine.

The next morning, we were up and moving, heading to the watchhouse to see if anyone came up with anything overnight.

"Hey, Sarge," I said.

"Duke. Doing alright?"

· News travels fast.

"I'm good. Be better if someone comes up with an answer."

"We're all trying, Duke. There're a lot of resources being thrown at this now. Hell, even some of the other Nuisance Men have asked if there's anything they can do. If there is an answer out there, we're going to find it."

"Thanks, Sarge. I'm a little surprised at how fast the news has gotten around."

"Really? With Lilly as your girlfriend? She grabbed a couple of guys passing by off the street to get you home, and then contacted one of the other necromancers here. Don't ask me how. But the call went out right away, messengers sent around. Did you expect anything less?"

I was touched, not only by Lilly's actions, but by Sarge's words, and by the support from all the others. But, being the tough Nuisance Man that I was, I swallowed that and forced a light tone into my voice.

"Well, thanks, Sarge. Let everyone know that I appreciate it, but not to worry. I'll still be around to annoy everyone for a while."

"You got it, Duke."

I followed Lilly down to her office and took a seat, ready for a long day. She was insisting that I wasn't to be out of her sight for long, and since I wasn't about to spend what could very well be my last few days arguing with her, I went along.

All day, she flew in and out of her office, while others entered and left. I heard voices raised at times and once I heard what I could have sworn was Lilly pleading with someone, but I really wasn't sure. Sometimes, it was hard to tell what was going on. I didn't want to tell Lilly, but that buzzing in my head was starting to get louder again.

Not only that, but it was changing, turning back into that same type of undulating wail that I heard the night before. The world dimmed around me, as if I were looking at everything through a heavy, dark fog. Lilly's blonde hair and red robes took on a washed-out appearance, and even though she was talking, I couldn't really focus on what she was saying. It sounded like she was speaking through a thin tube, from very far away.

Then there was a bright spot that cut through the fog. Along the wall of Lilly's office directly across from where I sat, a light appeared. A small dot at first, but then it started to grow. The cry that I could hear grew louder still, and then she was there again; the woman in the pale blue dress.

Only now, she wasn't as pretty. There was something harder, more angular about her face. Where last night she was almost pure and innocent looking, she was now much more severe. Her eyes were darker and bored into mine, leaving me feeling like she was looking into my soul, judging me, and finding me wanting.

I shrank back, pushing my chair until it slammed into the wall. I wanted to get away, stop her from looking at me, or at least to turn my gaze away. But I couldn't. She held me with her eyes, and all I could do was try to beg her to stop. But I couldn't speak either, my voice was frozen in my throat, and all that came out was a pitiful mewling sound. With a feeling of shame, I realized that tears were freely rolling down my cheeks.

Suddenly Lilly was there, in front of me, cutting off my view of the woman. She was shouting, but I couldn't make out what she was saying. She turned her head, looking in vain for what only I could see.

Finally, the light that was behind her started to fade away, and the wailing dropped down. It didn't get as quiet as before, and remained very distracting. It also didn't sound like a buzzing noise anymore, but distinctly like a woman screaming over the loss of a child, or something equally as bad. I shook my head, trying to clear it, so that I could respond to Lilly.

"I'm okay," I was finally able to croak out. "It's gone."

"The hell you are!" Lilly cried. She threw her arms around me and started sobbing. All I could do was hold on to her, and try to ignore the noise in my head.

What can I say? The rest of that day was pretty much the same. I failed miserably at trying to ignore the sound. When it seemed to fade, I would start trying to focus on it, to hear if it really was getting quieter, or if I was imagining it. It would definitely get louder at times, causing me to close my eyes, and try to shut it out, which never worked.

Twice more the banshee showed up, and each time it was worse. The wailing got louder and more desperate sounding, and the woman got more and more vile looking. She was hideous to see, and there was no feeling of good or love in her. It was like looking into the face of pure evil, and every time, I couldn't turn away. I was forced to stare at her and every loathsome thing I ever saw came back to me, every vile thing I ever did was repeated, and even every unclean thought that ever passed through my mind was paraded in front of me again. No wonder all of her victims died with horror on their faces. It wasn't only at the sight of her, part of it was at the crystal-clear glimpse at the unpleasantness inside of us.

The third time that she came, I ended up on the floor, staring at the wall vacantly, unable to respond to Lilly's frantic cries. Not to reassure her, or to ask for help, or to beg her not to leave my side. After that, I didn't know anything else. The dark came down over my vision like a heavy curtain, and that was it for a while.

When I finally woke, it was only to come back to more misery. I was now lying in my bed, how I got there, I wasn't sure. I guessed that Lilly had some of the Watch members bring me home, and even through the noise and the pain, I was grateful for that.

I didn't see Lilly anywhere, but I also didn't have much of a chance to look. My eyes were only open for moment when that blue light appeared on the far wall, and then there she was again. Gone was the beautiful, young woman in the blue dress. Now, she was old, ancient, with a withered smile and blazing, hateful eyes. Her hair still had the pale blue tinge to it, but it writhed around her head like snakes, or blind worms found deep in caves. She was huge now, obese and moist looking, and the pale blue that infused her skin earlier had turned the color of old bruises.

Still, I couldn't turn away. She opened her mouth, revealing sharp teeth, bits of rotted flesh stuck between them, and screamed. It was as if every loss, every pain, and every fright in the world were all bundled together and let loose at once. It was terrifying, saddening and maddening, in equal measures. I pushed my head into my pillow, trying to force it to come up around my ears and block out some of the sound, but it didn't work.

I thought I would go mad. My mind was slipping away, eager to escape the pain and the terror. I was whimpering shamelessly, but I had no idea how loud. There was no other sound in the world other than that terrible wail coming from the banshee.

And then Lilly stepped in front me, at the foot of the bed. She looked at me with such sadness, and such love that if I wasn't already weeping, I surely would have then.

She carefully mouthed the words, "I'm sorry", and raised her hands, sparks dancing around her fingers. Her hair stuck out around her in a wild tangle and her eyes turned completely black.

I could see her chanting, but couldn't hear the words, not that I would have understood them anyway. There were tear tracks down her cheeks, and she pointed at me.

A spear of black light sprang from her fingers, striking me in the chest. It felt like I was hit by a bolt of lightning, and I cried out. There was a horrible pain in my chest and my vision went black.

And the noise faded.

When I could see again, everything was foggy. Not only the banshee, like when I first saw her. But everything. Lilly, the bed, the room itself, and me. There I was, my body sprawled on the bed, while I stood to the side of it looking down.

I became aware of a noise, but it was faint and far away. Glancing over, I saw the banshee, looking at my body in confusion, her song slowly fading. Lilly was still standing at the end of the bed, her face in her hands, shoulders racked with sobs.

I very much wanted to go to her and tell her that it was alright, I was still here. But surely, she should know that. She was a powerful necromancer, skilled in death magic. If she cast the spell to free me from the banshee's evil, she must know that I was still here, watching.

After a moment, she stopped crying and looked up. There was the Lilly that I knew and loved. Her face was a mask of determination, and she started spell casting again. It was hard to pay attention to it though. It somehow didn't seem all that important. Neither she nor the banshee, still there and screaming again, with more and more force, really held my interest.

There was something beyond them. I couldn't see it, but I could feel its pull. It felt like home. Someplace that was more home than I ever knew. Someplace with no nuisances, no Nuisance Men, and no pain or fear. All I needed to do was start walking that way and it could all be mine.

I took a step, but then felt a tug, as if I was still tied to my body somehow. Like a string was stretched between the lifeless husk lying in the bed, and where I was now. I could break it. All I needed to do was pull. If I did there was no going back, but I wasn't sure that I cared.

A new noise broke into my thoughts, and I realized that it was Lilly, chanting louder and stronger, making me look at her again. This woman, who I loved so much, was doing something that was obviously very difficult. The strain of it showed on her face, and in her whole body language. I didn't know what it was that she was doing, but I didn't like it.

The pull of that place of peace wasn't as strong now. Why would I want to go there, when Lilly was in need? No, I needed to stay, to be by her side, to fight another day, and all that other stuff. There was no one, and nothing, that was going to keep me from her.

I moved forward, stepping further from my body, but closer to Lilly, and I *felt* the step. I could feel the floor beneath my feet, and the temperature of the room. Everything was coming clearer, like the fog was dissipating.

The wail from the banshee was gaining strength again too, but it lost most of its power now. It still sounded horrible, with all the pain of the world rolled up in it, but now it sounded like a trick. Something that showed all the terrible, mean parts of the world, and left out all the good, the love and the joy.

I looked down at myself, amazed at how solid I was, including all of my clothes, and the gun at my belt. My gun. My Ultimate Weapon.

I casually pulled it free, said, "banshee!" in a clear voice, stepped around Lilly, and shot the banshee at close to point blank range.

The little, metal ball that came out this time looked like a ghost ball, clear and with a vaporous cloud behind it. It struck the banshee directly in the mouth, and the wail was cut off immediately.

The banshee exploded. In a soundless flash, it flew apart into several pieces, passing through the walls, the ceiling and the floor without any resistance. Some passed through Lilly and some flew threw my bodies, both the one standing and the one still lying in the bed. There was no feeling from it. It was as if the banshee was really nothing after all.

Lilly was still chanting, the strain showing horribly on her face, while I felt stronger with every passing second.

I put my hand on her shoulder and said, "It's over, Lilly. You can stop."

She jumped and looked around, her eyes not finding me, but the chant dying on her lips. Then she straightened, and lowered her hands, her hair settling back onto her shoulders. The tug from the string on the bed grew stronger, and I let it pull me back, moving faster as I neared my body.

There was darkness again, I not sure for how long. I felt like it was only moments until I opened my eyes, blinking rapidly as the light flooded in.

Lilly was sitting next to me on the bed, her face drawn and gray. I reached up and stroked her cheek, still wet with her tears.

"What did you do?" I croaked, suddenly aware of how parched my throat was.

"I found an answer, or hoped I did. Your gun, that thing that's done so much, *could* kill it. But it needed to find it first. The only way to do that was for you to be dead, but still have the strength of will to draw the gun in with you."

She stopped, and bowed her head. Her voice sank to a whisper.

"I killed you." She stopped, and I pulled her to me to let her cry it out. She sobbed, clinging tightly to me.

"I'm still here," I said. "Whatever you did, it worked. The gun did come with me, and I was able to kill it. It's gone."

"I needed to hold you here," she said. "I had to make it so that you would be dead, but still here enough to do the job."

"I know. You did wonderful."

Then, a terrible suspicion came over me.

"Lilly," I said. "How, exactly, did you do that? How did you give me that strength?

"It has to come from somewhere..." she whispered.

That was why she looked so tired and worn out.

"What did that do to you?"

She shook her head, not looking at me.

"Nothing," she said. "I mean, if I didn't, we wouldn't have any more time together. This way..."

"This way, what?"

"This way we still have a long time. Just maybe a couple of years less."

"You gave up some of your own time? For me?"

She nodded, still avoiding my eyes.

I put my hand on her chin and gently turned her face to mine.

"Don't you ever again...," I started, but then stopped.

How could I say that? I would lay down my life for her. She gave us more time together and saved how many others in the process?

"You're an amazing woman, Lilly," I said. "All the time in the world won't be enough."

We stayed quiet for a few minutes, lost in our own thoughts.

"There's something else, Duke," Lilly said.

"Oh? The banshee wasn't enough?"

"We found an old text, buried in the library in the wizard's area. It told us something."

"Go on."

"According to that scroll, banshees don't simply show up on their own. They have to be sent."

I sat up straighter and looked at her.

"What do you mean?"

"They're like some kind of hired killer. Which means someone, or something, sent it here."

The implication of that was frightening.

"Sooo...?"

"So, we don't know. The Watch is aware, and the Palace Guard and the Royal Family have all been informed. Something, or someone, is targeting Capital City."

Great. As if we didn't deal with enough already.

I thought back over the last couple of days. The fear and anguish that so many people went through. Father Magnus' charity and caring. Lilly's sacrifice.

The more I thought, the angrier I got. Sure, there were problems here, what city didn't have them? But there was an awful lot of good, too.

Still, what could I, a lowly Nuisance Man, do about it? Well, plenty, really. Show me who or what it was, and I had a little, metal ball with their name on it.

In the meantime, I learned another lesson. Life was short, and it could come to an end at a moment's notice. You needed to hold on to what you had, enjoy your time here and not waste it.

"Your father still say we have his blessing?" I asked Lilly.

She pulled away and sat up, staring at me with wide eyes.

"Duke, are you…"

"Yeah, I am."

I was about to say more, but she was kissing me then. I took that as a yes.

## PARADISE DEFERRED

Being killed sucks. There's no two ways about it, even if the reason you were killed is a perfectly good one. But there are after-effects that linger when you come back to life, even if you didn't go too far toward the other side.

One of those, I was finding, was a lack of satisfaction with the world around me. When I was dead, even for those few minutes, I experienced the promise of a place of peace. A place where all the cares of this world would be forgotten, and all you would know would be contentment.

I could have gone, if I chose to. It was right there, within reach. All I needed to do was pull a little harder and the cord that still tied my spirit to my body would have snapped, and I could have entered paradise. It was very tempting, and I almost did it.

But there are things here in this world that make life worth living, and one of those was doing everything in her power to save me. Even against the pull of paradise, Lilly stood out to me. I didn't want to enter that place without her, and more, I wanted more time with her here. So, I ignored the draw, did what I needed to, and let myself be pulled back into my body.

It's not a decision that I regret. I'm happy to be alive again, and happy to be with Lilly, who over the last few days has gone into full-blown wedding planning mode. I know a lot of guys get annoyed with that whole thing, but I'm getting a kick out of it. She's been talking to her sister, and to friends, and I swear she's accosted random strangers on the street to ask questions about colors or flowers. The one person she hasn't really asked is me. It's probably better that way.

No, my life with Lilly was great. What I'm having a problem with is everything else. Nothing that I do, that I usually enjoy, is bringing me happiness. Jessup has noticed, and remarked about it the last time I was with him. My drinking game was off, and I didn't even try to match him mug for mug as I usually do. I called it quits early and returned home, midafternoon, well before I needed to. The ale didn't taste that good, the conversation wasn't holding my interest, and the tavern, a local favorite called The Barman's Choice, seemed rundown and seedy. Understand, rundown and seedy is the way I prefer my taverns. Usually.

And what did I do when I got home? Nothing. Nothing at all.

I sat in a chair, staring out the window, watching Capital City flow by. Not paying attention, not noticing anything in particular, or even enjoying all the different lives I saw. It didn't feel important.

When Lilly got home from the Watch, she found me in that same place. I told her I was tired, and inferred that I drank more ale with Jessup than I really did. Not that I wanted to lie, but I didn't want her to worry.

Since then, I've gotten better at hiding what was going on in my head. I was sure I'd get over it, but in the meantime, there was no reason to give Lilly anything to fret about.

Still, it was hard to get the memory of that perfect place out of my mind.

"Are you going to work today?" Lilly asked me as we ate breakfast.

I shrugged. "I guess. I'm actually getting kind of tired of sitting around the house all day, so I might as well."

"Are you sure you're up to it?" Ever since the attack by the banshee, Lilly was keeping a pretty close eye on me, which made acting as if everything was normal a little tougher.

"Sure. I feel great. You know me. If I don't have to work, I'm not going to. But it's time."

I smiled at her over my cup of coffee, and she seemed reassured. A short time later, we walked through the door of the watchhouse together.

I kissed her goodbye, and walked over to the desk.

"Hey, Sarge."

"Duke. Glad to see you back up and around. Close call last time."

"Yeah. But we got it. No more banshee."

"No," he agreed. "No more banshee. But, we still need to figure out who sent it. There's all sorts of noise being made about that. From way up on the hill."

"Above my station," I said. "If anyone comes up with anything, let me know. If I can help, you know I will. But until then, I guess it's business as usual. Anything good today?"

"The normal. Nothing crazy, run-of-the-mill creeps and miscreants. By the way, congratulations."

"Thanks, Sarge. I'm a lucky man."

"You are that, Duke. But also, I'm happy for you. Nice to see something good happen to a friend."

"Damn, Sarge. You'll make me blush."

"Don't get used to it," he growled. "Now get to work. Loverboy."

I laughed, rapped on the surface of the counter with my knuckles, and strolled over to the Board.

Sarge was right; there was nothing out of the ordinary on there. There wasn't even anything particularly challenging. There was mostly a bunch of goblins, as usual. Goblins, as a group, are pretty stupid, but don't know it, so some of them think they can become criminal masterminds; but in reality, they make dumb mistakes, choose the wrong victims, and are horrible at covering their tracks. I'm convinced that if all there ever was on the Board were goblins, the NHLF would never have been born.

A couple of bug-bears and a gnoll rounded out the group, and that was it. No minotaurs, no golems, no band of orcs, nothing like that. On most days, I would say my goodbyes to Sarge and go find something else to do for the day. Goblins were strictly entry level stuff, and the bug-bears and the gnoll weren't much better. But today was different. Today, I thought, might be a good day to ease back into the game.

I took down one of the goblins, who went by the name Gallowswing Woundbringer. Even for a goblin, that was obviously a made-up name, and he probably thought it made him sound fierce. He was apparently mugging folks, but being a goblin, wasn't very good at it. So far, according to the notice, he stabbed a man in the back of the leg, causing some pain and bleeding but no serious harm, and chased a group of school kids with a knife, presumably after their lunch money. That was bad enough, but not worth being put on the Board for.

No, our friend Gallowswing upped his game when the kids got away from him. He went after a man and woman walking home from an evening out, minding their own business. When he threatened them with his knife and demanded their money and jewelry, things went south. The man refused and stepped forward, ready to defend his wife. Gallowswing panicked, lashed out, and caught the man just right. He bled out a few minutes later, while both the wife and Gallowswing stood over him, looking on in horror.

Gallowswing took off after that, leaving the wife plenty of time to get help, and describe him to the Watch. And now here he was on the Board. Stupid yes, but now he was going to have to pay for his crime.

"Kind of low level for you, isn't it?" Sarge asked when I brought the notice over.

"Usually. I don't know, guess I'm bored. Plus, this creep deserves what's coming to him."

"Well, happy hunting."

Gallowswing turned out to be fairly easy to find. I headed for the Stews, that area of Capital City that's been settled by a lot of different races, with more arriving by the day. Most of which are law-abiding folk, trying to get by and provide for themselves and their families. But of course, some, like Gallowswing, threatened to ruin it for everyone.

Which was why almost everyone I talked to was happy to point me in the right direction. It wasn't long before I stood outside a run-down flop house, exactly the type of place that someone like Gallowswing would run to.

I walked in the door and to the reception desk, if you wanted to call it that. There was an orc sitting behind a thick pane of glass, who barely glanced up when I approached.

"2 ingols an hour," he croaked out, his voice muffled behind the glass. "12 to stay for the day. Anything gets broken in your room, that isn't already, will cost you another 20. Cash up front."

"I'm not looking for a room," I said. "I need some information."

Now the orc looked up, his eyes taking in the boots, the cloak and especially the gun at my belt.

"Nuisance Man?" he asked.

"Got it in one. I'm looking for a goblin who calls himself Gallowswing Woundbringer, if you can believe that."

"What makes you think he's here?"

"Because everyone in the neighborhood says so. Look, he's a creep, and he's going to bring a lot worse than me down on the area if he's not taken care of."

The orc considered this, and I let him think. The fact that he was sitting in this dump, with its peeling paint, cracked floors and unidentifiable odors, told me that he was one of the Unhoused.

One of those orcs that either willingly left his family, or was driven out for some reason. Either way, odds were that he wasn't exactly an upright citizen himself, and having attention from the Watch focused nearby wasn't going to be good for him. I figured that he would come to the right decision, and soon enough, he did.

"He's upstairs. Room 312, but you know how goblins are. Good at hiding, but I haven't seen him come back past here."

I didn't put a lot of faith in that. Goblins were experts at hiding and sneaking, and the orc was barely paying attention to anything. Still, it was as good a place to start as any.

Sometimes with goblins, it's best to move quickly and try to get a jump on them, before they can sense you coming. I ran up the two flights of stairs as quickly as I could, and burst into the third floor hallway. It ran straight to the other end of the building, with 3 doors on each side.

I passed door 301, then 307, 391, and 348, in that order. Don't ask me why. Someone obviously didn't have the knack of counting, or stole the room signs from other buildings and used what they had. The last door on the right was room 312.

I tried the handle, but as I suspected it would be, it was locked. I raised my fist, and pounded hard and fast on the wood.

"Open up!" I yelled. "Gallowswing, I'm here for you!"

Melodramatic, I know. But I was trying to startle him, and it worked. The door didn't open, not that I expected it to, but there was a high-pitched squeal from inside, and the sound of someone skittering around.

I backed up a step, and kicked the door with the bottom of my boot, near the handle, as hard as I could. The building had seen better days, and hadn't been taken care of, so the door sprang open. I could have kicked it half as hard and it still would have opened right up.

It hit the wall behind with a crash and started swinging back, but I was already moving through it, drawing my gun as I did. I said "goblin" in a loud voice to make sure it heard me, but kept my eyes moving around the room, looking for where Gallowswing could be hiding.

It turned out that I didn't need to bother. He was standing in plain sight, near the window, which he was trying in vain to open. I didn't know if it was painted shut, stuck because of years of accumulated filth and grime, or nailed closed, but it was resisting his best efforts.

He turned when I barged in, and held his hands out in front of him.

"I'm sorry!" he squeaked, and I grimaced. At the best of times, goblins' voices grate my nerves raw, but when they're begging, it's even worse. "I didn't mean to kill him! I only wanted the money!"

"Too late for that now, Gallowswing," I replied, bringing my gun up and aiming. "You should have gone into a different line of work."

I prepared to pull the trigger, but...there was something stopping me. Not physically. I could pull it, if I wanted. But I was having a hard time wanting to.

The thought of that place of perfection, that paradise, was suddenly in my mind, and it didn't feel right to sully it. Like if I pulled the trigger and the little, metal ball flew out and killed Gallowswing, I was somehow betraying the memory of that peaceful kingdom that I glimpsed.

But this was my job, and goblins like this needed to go. There was no place for them in our city, and if I let him off, he would do it again for sure. His remorse would turn into relief, which would morph into pride, and he would end up believing that he was the terrible scourge that he wished he was. He wouldn't be, and someone, somewhere, would show him how wrong he was, but in the meantime, some other innocent person was going to get hurt, or worse.

He needed to go.

I took a deep breath, and steeled myself. But I still couldn't do it. There was simply no way that I could bring myself to kill him.

I lowered the gun, and stood there, my head bowed, breathing deeply.

"What is this? Some sort of cruel game?" Gallowswing whined.

I couldn't answer him. My mind was whirling, fighting against itself. I wanted to pull the gun back up, pull the trigger and end him, but every time I readied myself to do that, the thought of paradise stopped me.

Slowly, Gallowswing moved away from the window and worked his way around me, staying close to the walls. When he reached the door, he turned and ran, his footsteps echoing in the hall, down the stairs and gone.

I had failed. I couldn't do it, and now someone, somewhere, was going to pay the price.

And what did this say for my future as a Nuisance Man?

That night, I fessed up and told Lilly what was going on with me. She knew I took a goblin off the Board, and was surprised. News travels fast around the watchhouse. I told her that I was bored, and wanted to get back in the game, but that it didn't worked out that way.

I asked her to sit and listen, while I told her what happened and why. I told her about the way I'd been feeling since that evening with the banshee, and how I failed to kill Gallowswing today, and what was in my mind at the time.

When I was done, Lilly sat quietly for a few minutes. I hoped she was taking it all in, rather than thinking of ways that she could get herself out of this, and away from a Nuisance Man who was now useless.

"It's understandable," she finally said. "I should have thought of this."

"Why would you have?"

"Because you're not the first person to be brought back. There have been others, although it's rare. It's hard to do, and, well, you know the cost."

"Others have reported the same thing? A glimpse of paradise?"

"Some," she said. "Not all. Some talk about seeing exactly what you're saying. A place of peace and contentment. Others report a place of agony and despair that they were being pulled toward, no matter how hard they resisted. That's actually more rare, though"

"Then there are more of us destined to go a good place than to a bad one?"

"Not necessarily. The procedure doesn't always work. Sometimes, the necromancer isn't strong enough, and can't hold the spirit near the body. It's thought that the pull of the bad place is strong enough to overwhelm a lot of spirits wills, and they get taken, which is why we don't hear about it as much."

"But you have no way of knowing that."

"Not really, but we can make a pretty good guess. One of the main things that the procedure has been used for is to extract information from a really bad person, when nothing else has worked. You know, the type that kills someone, and then keeps playing games with the family, refusing to say where the body is, or leading them on wild goose chases. Every now and then, someone has enough, and a necromancer gets called in to do this. They get paid well for it too. They'd have to, or the cost to themselves would be way too high. And no one ever does it more than once.

"The creep gets shown a glimpse of what's waiting for them and, if they come back, is usually more than willing to talk. But they tend to get lost more often. The worse the person is, the bigger the chance that they're not coming back. No great loss to the world, but not much information gained either."

As I've mentioned before, Lilly is seriously scary people when she wants to be. She lives and works in a realm that I can't even begin to imagine. It's a wonder that she's the woman she is.

"Well," I said when she was finished, "what do I do about it? How do I go about getting over this? Take another nuisance and force myself to finish the job?"

"No, definitely not that. First, I'm not sure that you could. If it's affecting you that way, you might not be able to pull the trigger no matter what. Then you'd be in serious danger, especially if word got around that Duke Grandfather couldn't kill. Second, if you did manage to do it, it could break you. I think the remorse you'd feel would be too great. No, we have to find another answer. Let me work on it some."

My answer for now was to wait and see, which isn't my strongest quality. When she came home the next evening, Lilly didn't have anything new, but did say that they were working on something.

"Be patient," she said. "We'll get this solved."

But since I was also never a very patient man, the next day, I walked Lilly to work, and then turned to the Board when she went to her office. I took less time than normal about selecting a target, because as soon as I walked up, whom do I see? My friend Gallowswing, of course.

I took the notice down, and showed it to Sarge on the way out the door. He looked like he was going to say something, but stopped himself. I smiled as I left, to let him know that everything was fine.

There was an anger brewing inside of me, and it was directed at Gallowswing. It happened exactly as I thought it would, only quicker. This time, he didn't killed anyone, but he did cut a kid, pretty badly too. He was simply too stupid to stop on his own.

I tracked him right back to that same flop house, and didn't even bother with the orc at the desk as I went up the stairs. As I've mentioned, goblins are stupid, and Gallowswing probably thought he was being clever by staying in the same place.

This time, I didn't knock or announce myself. Slamming into the door hard, I burst through it, gun already drawn and loaded for goblin. Only there was no Gallowswing, or anyone else, in the room. The window was still down and looked like it hadn't been disturbed since the other day.

I turned, scanning the room, but not seeing anything. At least until I remembered that goblins are expert hiders, and started looking closer. The room was filthy, and there wasn't much in the way of furniture. No one was under the bed, or hiding under the threadbare blanket thrown on top. No closet, no cubby hole of any kind.

Which only left one thing. I turned quickly, realizing as I did that the door didn't hit the wall hard like the other day. He was already coming out from behind it, knife at the ready, but still a few paces away. There was plenty of time for me to get the gun up and shoot him.

Except that I couldn't. I got the gun up and lined up for a quick shot that would stop Gallowswing in his tracks, but I still couldn't pull the trigger. I don't know if I had more time, as I did the other day, if I could have made myself or not. But in the fractions of a second that I had now, I simply couldn't.

The knife took me in the stomach, cutting deep. I felt a searing coldness, followed immediately by intense pain, and then a wetness as the blood flowed out of me. I grunted and doubled over, striking out with my gun, and connecting with his chin. Gallowswing yelped and fell back.

I straightened up as much as I could, glaring at him.

"Come on," I spat out. "Let's go."

An ambush was one thing, so was attacking a child. But facing a fighter, even a wounded one, was beyond what Gallowswing was ready for. Instead of charging in again, he repeated the performance of the other day, edging around the door, and disappearing down the hallway.

I was relieved. In spite of my words, I was in no condition to fight anyone, not even a kitten. I sank down on to the bed, and grabbed the filthy blanket, rolling it up and pressing it against my wound. It would help to slow the bleeding down, at least until I could get somewhere to get stitched up, but I hoped it didn't give me any nasty diseases as well.

I made it back to the watchhouse, moving slowly and keeping the blanket pressed tight, ignoring the stares of those on the streets. Once there, I gave way to the blackness that was flickering around the edges of my vision. I think I finally managed to surprise Sarge, when I keeled over in the doorway.

Lilly was not pleased. To say that she was not pleased might be an understatement. It might be the understatement of the year. For a while, I wasn't sure if she was angrier at Gallowswing or me. After I bit, I was certain that it was me.

"You're an idiot!" she said, for what had to be the hundredth time. "I told you that you weren't ready! But you had to go and get yourself almost butchered! What were you thinking?"

I opened my mouth to reply, but she was already moving on.

"What am I supposed to do, Duke? Tie you to the bed? Oh, shut up!" she said, before I could get out any sort of wise ass comment.

She railed for a while and then, with a visible effort, calmed herself and sat in a chair near the bed.

"Duke, I can't stand to see you get hurt. Not when it's so easily avoidable. I get that it's sometimes part of the job. But not right now."

"It was stupid," I admitted. "But I can't sit around here day after day. I need to be able to do my job."

Listening to myself, it sounded like someone else talking. I needed to be able to do my job? I spent all the time that I possibly could trying *not* to do my job. But, that was when I could whenever I felt the urge. Now that it was a distinct possibility that I might never do it again, it changed things.

Lilly, to her credit, seemed to understand.

"I know, Duke. I do. Give me another day or two."

I agreed, of course. Partly because with the wound in my stomach, I wasn't going anywhere for a couple of days, but also because I really did feel that I had put her through enough. I could be patient.

Patience is over-rated. I was bored out of my skull over the next two days. I read a book, cover to cover, which isn't something I do often. I watched the world go by through the window that I could partially see from my bed. I slept…a lot.

And I thought. Even though I didn't want to, I kept thinking about that glimpse of paradise. The thought would then come unbidden that a little deeper, a little harder, and the cut that Gallowswing gave me would have sent me back there. I didn't mind that thought, when I was lying there alone. Then Lilly would come home, and the desire to stay here would take over again.

After two solid days of this, she came home with two bottles of liquid. One was a bright blue, and it sparkled as it moved within the bottle. The other was in an amber colored bottle, so I couldn't see what color it was.

Lilly set them down on the table. "We're going to fix both problems."

I raised an eyebrow at her.

"The first being that you're too enraptured by the sight of paradise to do your job. The second is that gash in your stomach. I can fix them both."

"Well, good," I said. "What do we need to do?"

"The first is going to fix your head," she said. "The other one is going to take a couple of days to work, so hopefully we can make it easier for you while you're still laid up."

"Sounds great. Let's do it."

There was a slight bit of hesitation on my part. Yes, I wanted to go back to normal, and function again as a Nuisance Man. But there was a tiny part of me that was loath to give up the memory of what I saw. It was perfect, how could I want to forget it? But the more rational part of my mind prevailed and to have any chance at a happy life again, it needed to be done.

Lilly poured the liquid from the amber bottle into a mug and handed it to me, the contents giving off a slight bit of steam.

"Straight down," she said. "No stopping. Drink it all in one go."

No problem, or so I thought. After all, I could down a mug of ale in less than ten seconds flat if I wanted to, so what was this?

A lot, as it turned out. The taste was vile and bitter, and it burned. As soon as it touched my lips, it felt like I had kissed a campfire. The searing went into my mouth and straight down my throat until it hit my stomach and stayed there, burning away my insides. But I already ignored Lilly once, to disastrous results, so this time, I was determined to obey her.

I did it, as hard as it was. I gasped when I was done, wiped the sweat from my brow and grabbed the mug of water that she held ready for me. The coolness helped some, but not much. The fire still raged in my belly, and I still felt like I had eaten hot coals.

"That was horrible," I croaked out.

"Yeah, I thought it might be. But it should help. It won't make you forget that glimpse of the other side, but it should help you keep it in perspective for a while. Long enough for it to fade on its own, anyway. Ready for the next one?"

I took a deep breath, nodded, and held out my hand.

She gave me another mug, this time with the blue, sparkly liquid in it.

"You can take your time with this one," she said.

I raised the mug hesitantly to my mouth and sipped at the potion.

Ahhhh! Sweet relief! It calmed the flames still dancing in my mouth and felt like cold, clear water in my throat. It hit the inferno in my stomach and damped it down. It didn't go away entirely, not at first, but it was such a balm that I didn't mind.

And it tasted like the finest candy. It was sweet, but not disgustingly so. It was the best thing that wasn't ale that I ever drank, and when it was gone, I was left wishing for more.

"Thought that might help," Lilly said. "That was the other reason for drinking them in that order. The second one is going to make you sleep, and when you do, you'll go out. I'd be amazed if you woke up before I went to work tomorrow, but when you do, you should be feeling a lot better. Not well enough to go out yet, but better.

"Take tomorrow, rest, and by the next day, you should be good to go. By then, hopefully your head will be in a better place too, and then we can get start getting back to normal."

"I'd like that," I said. "I'm sorry that I put you through all this."

"You didn't. It was that damn banshee and whoever sent it. We're going to find out who that was too, and then there'll be hell to pay."

I couldn't have agreed with her more, but she was right about the potion making me tired. I could barely keep my eyes open, and vaguely remember Lilly bending down to kiss my forehead before I was off into dreamland again.

She was also right about me not waking before she went to the watchhouse. I woke myself with a massive yawn when the sun was already climbing high into the sky. As I blinked in the sudden light, I took stock and considered how I felt.

Overall, I felt pretty good. The wound in my stomach wasn't aching anymore, and when I took a look, it was sealed together and healing over already. I poked at it, and although it was still tender, it didn't really hurt. Lilly said it would take a couple of days for me to heal, but I seemed to be ahead of schedule.

That didn't surprise me. I always was a fast healer. She should have known that about me.

Well, just because Lilly was wrong about something *again*, didn't mean that I needed to stay here waiting around. There were things to do, and one of them, was to get my revenge on that little bastard who cut me. Gallowswing was going to be in for a surprise when I found him.

A short time later, I was back at the flop house. I couldn't believe that the goblin would be that stupid a third time, but then again, he was a goblin. I walked up to the desk and that same miserable orc on "duty".

"He here again?" I asked.

"Don't know who you mean," the orc said, not even looking up at me.

I glanced around and saw the door that led to the inner office where the orc sat, thinking he was safe behind his thick pane of glass. It didn't withstand more than two kicks before the lock busted and was left hanging. By that time, the orc was on his feet, putting his chair between him and I.

"Hey!" he sniveled. "I don't want any trouble. I know who you are now."

"Too late for that," I growled.

I shoved the chair out of my way, pulled my gun, and smashed it into the side of the orc's jaw. He dropped like a puppet whose strings were cut, and I planted a boot into his gut. Twice, to make sure he got the message, and then once more, because it felt good.

I squatted down next to him, ignoring the foul breath that was panting out of him.

"Now," I said, my voice calm and reasonable. "Let's try this again. That little creep, Gallowswing. Is he up there?"

The orc nodded, which I believe was all he could do at the moment.

"Good," I said. I considered giving him another shot for making me come in here, but since I didn't want any more of his filth on my boot, I let him be.

Calmly and slowly I walked up the stairs. When I reached the top of the second set, I started calling out to Gallowswing as I walked down the hall.

"Galllllooowswing. Galllllloooowswing. I'm back. Where are you?"

I kept my voice friendly, knowing that he would be cowering in his filthy room, hiding like the rat he was.

This time, I didn't even try the handle. I kicked the door in, and let it swing back on its own, stopping it with my foot. Then I walked in, looking around carefully. He was there, standing perfectly still near the window, trying to blend in with the filthy wall.

I laughed, raised the gun and shot him. The ball was still set to goblin and it did a horrible amount of damage to him. He was dead before he hit the floor, but I shot him again, because I could.

Scratch one goblin, and welcome back Duke!

Later on, I walked into the watchhouse and dropped the notice on the desk in front of Sarge without saying a word.

"Lilly got you fixed up, huh?" he said.

"If that's what you want to call it," I replied. "Although I think I would have healed fine on my own. I don't know, maybe it helped some. Who can say?"

Sarge looked at me strangely. "I think we can. You were hurt pretty bad, Duke. From what I hear, Lilly and some others worked hard on those potions."

"Yeah, well, that's their jobs, right? Speaking of, anything good on the Board?"

"I'm not sure you should be taking anyone right now. Lilly says you should still be resting today."

"Lilly says, Lilly says. Well, Duke says that he's taking a job and shooting someone."

With that, I walked over to the Board and looked. Not much, or at least not much that was worth my time and attention. Although, there was one...

I grabbed the notice and walked out, not even bothering to glance over at Sarge again. Let him stew if that's what he wanted. I had better things to do.

Who or what was on the notice doesn't really matter. I never even looked at what the complaint was. I grabbed it, found the complainant, and went to work. A half hour later, I had the cash in hand and blood on my mind. A short time after that, the job was done, and I was feeling better than ever.

It was getting late by then, so I decided I would go back to the watchhouse the next day, and pull a few more nuisances to rid the world of. In the meantime, I was thirsty, and ale was the next thing on my list. I didn't feel like going home, and didn't really feel like listening to Jessup ramble on about some meaningless crap. I wanted to go somewhere fresh. Somewhere I knew, but wasn't too familiar with. Somewhere that I was liked and admired.

I ended up at The Witch's Kettle.

The last time I was there was to be the butt of a joke. It was a good one, and no harm done, except to my pride, and Raven's too. I laughed again thinking of his face that night, but then sobered when I remembered mine. Well, no tricks this time.

The witches owed me. They could start making up for it by buying me a round or three.

I walked in like I owned the place, ignoring the looks, and slapping away a questing hand or two. Nasty, old crones who thought they had the right to lay their bony hands on my person. There were a few squawks and hurt looks when I did that, but they'd get over it.

Making my way to the bar, I looked around for a familiar face, and who should I spy, but Camelia Rosenblatt, the girl who once used me as her patsy. She was the perfect person to start paying me back. She noticed me at the same time, smiled, and worked her way through the crowd toward me.

"Mr. Grandfather!" she said. "What are you doing here?"

"Giving you the opportunity to make good, toots," I told her. "Open up the purse strings, and start buying. I'd rather drink with you than most of the old crones in here. Speaking of that, where's that other one? What was her name? Minerva, or something like that? She owes me a few too."

It was almost worth the price of admission to see the look on her face. Almost. A few mugs of ale would go a lot further toward making amends.

"Excuse me," she said, her smile faltering. "but I'm afraid I don't understand."

"What's not to understand? You used me a while back. I never got paid for it, so now's your chance. Belly up to the bar, sister. You've got a few ales to buy. But make sure none of these nasty old bats touches my rear again. I don't like it."

"Are you alright, Duke?"

"I'm perfect! Number one Nuisance Man, how could I not be? Now how about that ale?"

My voice rose as I was speaking, and I didn't immediately notice that the place had fallen silent. Not quiet, like when I was in here before, but a silence so heavy that you could cut it with a knife.

"I think you should go, Mr. Grandfather," Camelia said quietly. "It might not be safe for you here."

I snorted, and laughed, loudly, right in her face.

And then I was moving, not of my own volition. My feet were sliding across the floor and I was moving faster and faster directly at the door, which opened as I reached it. When I went through it, it was as if a rug was jerked out from under me, and I went sprawling into the street. As a final humiliation, a bucket suddenly appeared out of thin air above my head, and I was dowsed with ice-cold water.

The door to The Witch's Kettle slammed shut, and I could move on my own again. I jumped to my feet and ran at the door, determined to get back in and collect on what was owed me. But when I reached it, I was repelled, violently, and tossed unceremoniously back into the street again, narrowly missing a passing carriage.

I howled my rage and frustration and threw myself at the door again, with the same result. And again. And again. By the time I landed in the street for the fifth time, I was sore, and it was beginning to sink into me that I wasn't getting back inside.

Picking myself up, I dusted off the dirt and filth as best I could, and headed home.

Oh, the dramatics when I got there. Where were you? What were you doing? Why are you all wet?

It gave me a headache. I growled something about being wherever I felt like being, and went to bed. Even with all the yammering going, on, I managed to fall asleep.

When I woke up the next morning, the sun was already climbing high into the sky. I had slept late, even for me. Well, what of it? If anyone deserved a rest, it was me, after all the times I saved this stinking city. Let me take some time for once, and let the city move on without me. I'd be out there soon enough, saving it from itself.

I got up, but Lilly was gone already, back to her supposed "job" with the Watch. I snorted, amused by the thought of someone being tied to the same place day after day, rather than free to do whatever they wished, like I was. Lack of ambition was the only reason I could think of that would account for it.

My day stretched ahead of me however, and I mulled over what I should do with it. Yesterday was fun, and I thought of going back in and getting a few more nuisances from the Board. But really, why should I do that? Why limit myself to what the Watch felt was reasonable, or to waiting for someone to work up the courage to post a complaint in the first place?

There were plenty of nuisances walking around the street every day, waiting to be put down. I could use the gun on the first one, and then if the next wasn't the same race, they'd find out that I was a pretty good swordsman too.

That plan was sounding better and better when I heard the door open. I sighed and prepared myself for a lecture, assuming that it was Lilly coming home to check on me like I was some sort of baby. I turned, arms already crossing, ready for the worst.

But it wasn't Lilly. Instead, the man who came in was taller than me by a good three inches, but thin to the point of being lanky. He wore his hair long, down to his shoulders, but it was always clean, and he would toss it to try to get a girl's attention. It worked more than you would think, too. As always, he was dressed in the latest fashion, from his boots to the silk shirt, tucked into the wide leather belt at his waist. He wore a sword, a light dueling model, but I wasn't even sure that he knew how to use it.

"There you are," he said.

"Jessup," I replied, letting a hint of frost into my voice. "What are you doing here?"

"Came to find you. I thought maybe Lilly finally neutered you all the way."

There was a little flicker of red in my vision when he said this.

"What the hell is that supposed to mean?"

"Oh, come on, Duke," he laughed. "Let's face it. You've been off your game for a while now. Working more often and even when you're not, you hardly ever come to the tavern anymore. I think you've let her get to you."

"Not all of us were born with silver spoons in our fat mouths," I told him.

He laughed at me again. "Say what you want. I only came to see if the mighty Duke Grandfather was still alive. Now that I see you are, sort of, I'll be going. It's almost lunch time, and I've got a mug of ale with my name on it. See you around, Duke."

He sneered at me and turned to go.

I reached out, grabbed his arm and spun him back around to face me.

"Let's go then, tough guy," I told him. "Right now."

He looked down at my hand on his arm, then around the kitchen that we stood in.

"I don't see any taps, or a serving girl for that matter."

"What are you talking about?"

"You didn't think I was going to fight you, did you?" He laughed again, and shook his arm loose. "I'm not that stupid, Duke. I'm sure you'd beat me. That's your lifestyle, not mine. But the Duke Grandfather I know would have given me a good run downing ale, although I still would have prevailed. With what you've turned into? Domesticated? Not even a contest."

If there was one thing that Jessup was good at, it was throwing out the insults. My fist was curled and it was taking a lot of self-control not to unleash a haymaker right onto his pointy chin. But what would that prove? He already admitted that I could out fight him. Not that I was ever in question about that. But to imply that I couldn't out drink him as well? And never could?

No, some things, as a man, you have to prove.

"Let's go," I growled. "You run the tab. Whoever goes down first pays it off."

"Sure you've got the money?"

I growled at him, and he laughed at me again, but turned and led the way to The Barman's Choice. I followed along behind, aware that he was secretly laughing at me and, I was equally sure, mocking me to everyone he passed. Soon enough, he'd learn to regret that.

In all the years that I've known him, Jessup has never worked. He came from a wealthy family, one of several children. I don't know how many siblings he has, and I don't think he does either. His father is perfectly content to put money in an account for him, as long as he stays out of the newsheets, and doesn't embarrass the family; which he accomplishes by staying in taverns most of the time.

I used to find him amiable and good-natured, but now I could see him for what he was; a simpleton, who let his family's money rule his life, which he was wasting away. After I showed him who was the better man, my relationship with him was done, and he could sit in the corner and rot for all I cared. I had better things to do with my time.

I took a corner seat at the tavern, chasing away an old man who was already there. My fame and prestige came at the cost of making enemies, and I didn't want any of them sneaking up on me here. Plopping down, I waited while Jessup summoned over the serving girl, some floozy that he obviously knew, and told her to bring us two ales, and then keep them coming until one of us slid out of their chairs.

She laughed, sounding like a crow if you asked me, and went to do as she was told.

We sat silently, staring at each other, while we waited for our drinks. I glowered at him, trying to intimidate him, but he looked back at me with a slight smile playing about his lips.

Finally, the drinks came. We both picked up our mugs, he saluted me with his, which I ignored, and we drank. The first one was easy, and I was on a mission, so it was gone in a matter of seconds. Jessup lowered his first, and watched me with a bemused expression.

"Wow, something to prove?" he asked.

"Shut up and drink," I said.

He smiled, picked his mug back up and drained it. Then we waited for the serving girl to bring us another, and then another after that.

After the fourth mug, the call of nature began to get insistent. Not that I would tell Jessup, but he was better than me at holding off, so I got to my feet first, steady as a rock, despite the gentle swaying that the room was doing.

"Be back in a minute," I said. "Get two more. At least."

I lurched my way to the back, used the facilities, and then found our table again. There were two more mugs of ale waiting, and Jessup was already into his.

"Couldn't wait, huh?" I mumbled. "Fine. I'll catch up."

I picked up my mug and took a swig. It was beginning to lose its flavor, but I wasn't about to tell him that. Jessup looked stone sober, no sign of the ale affecting him. I was horrified when I realized that it was starting to hit me pretty hard, and that I could lose this match. I needed to do something drastic if I was going to have any chance, so I picked up my mug and drained the whole thing in one go.

"Let's see you do that, you big dandy," I said.

He shook his head, that same bemused, mocking smile on his face, only now it seemed different. Somehow…sadder maybe. What he had to be sad about was beyond me, but whatever it was, it was his problem.

The room was definitely swaying now, and starting to spin. I barely registered it as Jessup looked up to the door, and nodded. I saw a flash of red, like a robe, and maybe some blond hair, and then the world went away.

I seemed to be spending an awful lot of time in bed lately, but this time when I woke up, I wished I hadn't. My head was pounding like a troll was in there beating on the doors of my brain. My stomach was queasy, and I wasn't sure that I wasn't going to get sick if I tried to move.

But, I needed to get up, and…and what?

I really wasn't sure. I could go to the watchhouse, and see about some work. Or even better pop in on Lilly and see how…

The events of the last two days became clearer in my mind, and I sank back into my pillow. What had come over me? My thoughts seemed like they belonged to someone else, that I was reading about some two-bit villain in a melodrama.

Lilly. With the things I had said I was sure that we were done. The best thing that ever happened to me, and I blew it by acting like a total ass.

And Jessup. I knew the man for years, but after the things I said to him, and the way I treated him, I was sure that friendship had gone the way of far too many others in my life.

There was a noise from the hallway, and I turned my head to see Lilly come into the room, carrying a plate with a few pieces of toast on it.

"I didn't think anything more than this was a good idea," she said, setting it down near me. "It's going to be a long day for you, but you'll get through it."

Then she looked at me and smiled. I couldn't return it. I couldn't even trust myself to look at her. I looked down at the blanket covering me instead.

"Lilly, I…" I started.

"Hush," she interrupted. "Potions don't always work the way they're supposed to. Healing is an art, not a science. I guess we went a little heavy with the brimstone in yours."

"What?" Now I did look at her.

She laughed gently, and sat down on the side of the bed.

"Do you really think you suddenly changed into such a jerk without some outside help? It was the potion. It was supposed to tamper down the memory of what you experienced, but it was too strong. Instead of helping, it tipped you too far over in the other direction. We needed to even you out, so I enlisted Jessup to help me."

"The ale."

"Yep. He held on until you left the table, then he dumped another potion into your mug. We knew you'd refuse to take it, with the state you were in, so we needed to trick you."

I stared at her.

"That was pretty risky, wasn't it?" I asked. "What if Jessup couldn't have lasted?"

"That wasn't that hard," another voice said, and Jessup himself came into the room. "I know the serving girl, Shireen. She's a sweetheart. Every other mug she gave me was a small bit of ale and mostly water."

He laughed again, but now, I was glad to hear it.

"Not that I couldn't have beat you anyway," he said, and this time I laughed with him, which set off fireworks in my head.

"Like I said," Lilly said, noticing my wince, "it's going to be a long day for you. But by tomorrow, you'll be fine."

"What then?" I asked.

"Then, it's back to normal. Or almost, anyway."

"Almost?"

"You've got one stop to make. The Witch's Kettle. I convinced them to let you in. But I'll leave it to you to explain to Camelia exactly what happened."

That was fair. I had acted like a complete ass to several people, and she was one of them. I'd make amends there, and then start getting back to the important things in life.

We still had a lot of wedding plans to make, and someone was still out there, targeting Capital City.

## THE PIPES OF WRATH

It turned out that the important things in life mostly revolved around wedding plans. Who knew there were that many flowers that could be used to decorate a place? Not only types, but colors! And not *a* place, but a couple of them; one for the ceremony itself and one for the party after.

I asked Lilly if she wanted to get married at her parent's place, outside of the city. She told me that she appreciated it, but knew that I hated going outside of the walls if I could help it, so no, we would find a place here, in the city. I suggested a couple of nice taverns, but her look quickly told me that they were not viable options after all.

Thank all the gods for her sister and her friends. Most of the burden of planning fell to them, leaving me time to pursue my other interests. That was mostly drinking with Jessup, of course, who drank for free the next time I saw him as a thank you for the help he gave Lilly when I was out of my mind. I worked some too, of course. But I knew I was back to my old self when that took its rightful place in my priority list. Way down, near the bottom, slightly above "do the dishes" and "walk the dog", which we didn't even have.

But there were guests that were going to be coming in from out of town. Bryer and Iris, Lilly's parents, of course, were coming, but so was Wally Worthington, her father's business partner and his family. While they were all staying in one of the fancier hotels that Capital City had to offer, they would certainly visit us here at home as well. That meant the place needed to be cleaned and tidied up, and even though the wedding was still weeks away, we apparently had to start now.

"Ugh," I said, as I moved a sofa away from the wall so that the floor underneath could be cleaned. "How did those get there?"

It was a crime scene. The bodies were strewn across the floor like there was a massacre. Some were old and dried up, obvious victims of a long-ago crime, but others were fresh, recently killed.

Lilly came and looked over my shoulder, letting out a shriek that went through my head like a headman's axe through a fat man's neck. (Pardon the graphic image, the carnage under the sofa put me in that mood).

"Ewww! Duke, get them out of there! That's disgusting!"

"Oh, come on." I stirred the lifeless husks with my toe. "It's just a few roaches."

I was a little grossed out myself, but you don't live your life in one of the biggest and busiest cities of the world without encountering a pest or two. True, this was more than a couple, but then again, I probably hadn't moved that sofa since I moved in and found it there. It was one of the things that I was amazed Lilly hadn't gotten around to changing out yet. In a sense, this was *her* fault.

When I turned to share that amusing observation with her, I saw her face and decided that the prudent course of action was to keep it to myself. Instead, I turned back to the task at hand.

"I'll get the broom. They'll be gone before you know it."

"Good," Lilly said. "Then move all the rest of the furniture and check there too!"

Yep, I had a feeling that was coming. Sighing, I set to work.

Later that evening, we sat in one of my favorite taverns, "The Untapped Keg". I loved the name of the place, so full of mystery and potential. Plus, it wasn't quite as much of a dive as a lot of places I frequented, had good food, and Lilly kind of liked it too.

It was her suggestion to come here for dinner, after a full day of cleaning and sweeping up dead bugs.

As we sat and ate, and drank, we half listened to the sound of the city from outside the windows. It was a nice evening, warm, but not oppressive and a gentle breeze. I requested a table near the window, which was thrown open so that the patrons could enjoy the night air.

You could hear fragments of conversation as people passed by, the sound of children playing in the next street, and occasionally, bits of music wafting through the air. It was pleasant, and even though I hated cleaning the house, both Lilly and I were relaxing in the glow of a day's labor, neatly accomplished.

"Oh," she suddenly said, looking around, "I love this song."

I listened and could hear a jaunty tune being played on a pipe, the high pitched notes skirling away into the evening. People along the street stopped and looked around, smiles on their faces as the man responsible came into view.

He was a young man, thin, with straw colored hair that stuck out from beneath a peaked cap, set rakishly on his head, with a large feather stuck into it and bobbing along with him. He wore bright yellow pants, and a lime green jacket over a shiny, purple shirt. His thin lips were pursed as he blew for all he was worth across the mouthpiece of his pipe, but he still had the presence of mind to wink and smile at those he passed, especially the young ladies.

I never heard the song in question, but I had to admit that it was catchy. It had the sort of rhythm that set your foot to tapping and if you weren't careful, would sweep you up and set you to dancing, or some other such foolishness.

The player stopped directly across the street from our window, so we got a good view of him. He set himself and then really let go. The catchy tune that he was playing got even more rambunctious, and he twirled and danced around as he played. Others joined in, and before long, there were several couples, and not a few individuals, whirling like dervishes in the street along with him.

"Come on!" Lilly said, rising to her feet, and holding her hand out to me.

"Come on, what?"

"Duke Grandfather! Get your butt out of that chair and dance with me. Or do I have to go ask one of those nice young men over there to do it?"

I was fairly certain that she was bluffing, but I also wasn't willing to risk it.

"Fine," I grumbled. I rose to my feet, took her hand, bent over, and brushed my lips across the back of it. "Milady, may I have the pleasure of this dance?"

She laughed, which always made me smile in return, and we hit the street, joining the others in the fun. More people showed up, and the impromptu ball grew larger. The piper finished his song, bowed in acknowledgment of the applause, and launched into another.

He was good. Very good, in fact. His songs fit the mood of the crowd, and kept everyone up and moving. Those few who didn't, sat and tapped their feet in time, or beat their hands on their thighs. When a few more songs were played, the piper lowered his pipe and smiled at us all.

"Thanks, folks," he called out, his voice smooth and steady. "That was great fun, but I need to be moving on now."

There were assorted groans and cries of dismay at this, but he only smiled.

"Don't worry! I'll be back around soon! I promise! And then we'll all dance again!"

Now the crowd cheered and clapped, and Lilly and I joined in. With a flourish of his hat, the piper moved off, raising his pipe again and leaving us with one last tune, a slow, calm measure, which settled us down gently.

We were sitting back down at our table, out of breath and laughing, when we heard the sudden, startled scream, and then nervous laughter. Before we could react, a mouse ran past us, and out the door, heading off in the same direction that the piper went.

"Looks like he wants more music, too!" someone quipped, and everyone shared one final laugh, before returning to their private conversations.

"Thanks, Duke," Lilly said.

"No problem," I replied. And it wasn't. When Lilly looked at me like that, nothing I could do for her was a problem.

"Ahhh! Duke! I thought you cleaned under here!"

After the great night we had, that wasn't how I envisioned being awakened in the morning. It was back to being a work day, so Lilly would be heading off to the watchhouse soon, and I was going to walk with her, figuring that it was a good day to take a job myself. Before I got up, I lay there with my eyes shut, trying to figure out what she was talking about. I had moved literally every piece of furniture in the place yesterday, I was sure of it.

Grumbling to myself, I climbed out of bed and staggered out to the living room to see what Lilly was upset about. My favorite chair was pulled back away from its normal spot near the fireplace, and she was pointing at the floor where it had sat.

"Look!" she said.

I shuffled over and did as instructed.

"Huh. Weird."

"Huh, weird? That's all you have to say? If my parents saw that, they'd be sure I was making a mistake."

Well, that was hurtful. Bryer liked me, I was sure of it, and not only because I did him a huge favor a short time ago. We were a lot alike, apart from the money and breeding. Still, I could see Lilly's point. I wouldn't want to move a chair and see a bunch of dead roaches under it either.

"I did clean under there yesterday, Lilly. Promise. But it's all good, I'll take care of it."

"Thank you. And check under the rest too." She moved off to get ready for her day.

"I don't have time," I called after her. "I was going to walk in with you today."

"Uh-uh. You stay here and make sure we got them all this time."

"But…"

"No buts. I'm a big girl and you don't have to take a job yet. Do it tomorrow, but today, get rid of all of those roaches, wherever they are! Then make sure they can't get in again!"

"How am I supposed to do that?" I asked.

"Figure it out," her voice floated out from the bedroom. "You're smart. Most of the time."

I did figure it out, and used my head to do it, too. After I moved every single piece of furniture in the house, again, and gotten up all of the dead roaches again, I went to see Petal. Brownie magic is ridiculously powerful, and a lot of it is nature based, or at least that's what Lilly has told me. I had no idea what that meant, but roaches are animals, so they're a part of nature. A nasty, icky, gross part of nature, to be sure, but part of it nonetheless.

Petal talked to the rest of her people and they assured me that they would fix it so that no more roaches, or any other pests, would get into the house. Not only for the duration of our expected visits from family, but for good. They raised their voices in song, which was totally unlike the music of the night before, with a hypnotic quality to it, and my mind drifted off for a few moments.

I wandered among fields of the funniest flowers, which burst open as I passed, revealing perfectly cooked steaks, roasts, pies and other foodstuffs. The stream that wandered through this meadow flowed with the brownest, tastiest ale ever brewed, and the grass was soft and comfortable, perfect to settle down into, and contemplate life while sipping cool, frothy brook ale, and gnawing on a delicious flower steak.

Then, the song ended and I was back to the real world, standing in my basement which was being converted into a town fit for six-inch high magical people. Petal and the rest were staring at me with open amusement.

"Nice," I said to them. "Anytime you want to send me back there is fine with me!"

Their laughter was high-pitched and rapid, but there wasn't a shred of ill-will in it. It was infectious, and I joined in before saying my good-byes and heading back upstairs.

The cleaning done, for today at least, I decided to head for the watchhouse anyway. If there was something good on the Board, maybe I'd take it and either get it done today, or get an early jump on it tomorrow. No later than 11:00, or soon thereafter, I promised myself.

"Hey, Sarge," I said, when I came through the door.

"Duke," he replied, as was our custom. "Heard there was a 'civil disturbance' in your neighborhood last night."

"What? What civil disturbance?"

"You tell me. Rumor is that a bunch of people were seen gyrating and convulsing on the street. One man in particular was seen in the company of a beautiful, young woman, far too good for him. The fear is that he's delusional, as well as horribly uncoordinated."

"Been working on that one for a while?"

He smirked. "Ever since Lilly came in, all beaming and told me about your fun last night."

"You're a pip, Sarge. Anything good up there today?"

He shrugged. "You ask me that all the time, Duke. What do I always tell you?"

"See for yourself," I said. "I know, but one of these days you might shock me and end up being helpful."

"Now that's just mean."

I rapped on the counter and walked to the Board. There was some good stuff on there, including an actual harpy. That was exciting and gross, all at the same time. Winged creatures are always more of a challenge, due to the fact that they can simply fly out of range, but they usually carry a bigger pay-off because of that. And harpies in general are disgusting. They're essentially huge vultures, with the heads and breasts of old ladies.

Not the sort of old lady who gains wisdom and sophistication over the years, but the type that you envision shoving innocent children into ovens inside cabins made of candy. And they still eat roadkill and carrion, so they stink to the high heavens. I know nothing about their "culture", if they can be said to have any, but they are somewhat intelligent. They talk, even if what they have to say is mostly curses and foul language.

What was strange, other than there being one in Capital City, was that there was *only* one. Like most birds, they flew in flocks, so there should have been several. This one was hanging out around a fountain on Silver Tree Lane, one of the high-brow areas of the city. It was leaving its droppings and the remains of its meals around, and the denizens of the street wanted it gone.

They could, and did, pay well to have nuisances removed from Silver Tree Lane. Luckily for me, I was the first one to grab it off the Board.

"I'll take this one," I said, walking over to Sarge and showing him the notice.

"Good one. Pay is nice, and who doesn't want to shoot a harpy? Even the NHLF couldn't have a problem with that one."

"You wouldn't think so," I said, and took my leave.

According to the notice, the harpy was around pretty much all the time. During the day, it came and went, screeching and verbally abusing whoever came within earshot. At night, it slept on top of the statue, but slept lightly enough that any attempts to sneak up on it resulted in its flapping off, aiming its discharge at its would-be attackers with remarkable accuracy.

The person who posted the complaint was a nice old gent name Roland Remington, the Fourth. If he was the Fourth, it was the most current edition of a story filled with money and success. His house made most of the other houses on Silver Tree Lane seem shabby. I was sure he could afford to move to one of the really posh neighborhoods higher up on the hill and closer to the Palace. But, maybe he liked being where he was the biggest fish in the pond, or, maybe I was being too harsh, and he wanted to stay where he had grown up. Whatever the reason, the ridiculous amount of money that he was offering to get rid of the harpy probably didn't even dent his daily tea and crumpets budget.

"It's around the corner, Mr. Grandfather," he told me. A tall, distinguished man, with silver hair and a truly, epic brushy mustache, he stepped out onto the porch of his home to greet me himself, rather than letting a servant do it. That alone gave him a few credibility points in my book. "It perches on top of the War Memorial Statue and makes a mess of it. A perfect disgrace if you ask me."

"You can't even see it from here," I said, looking up the street in the direction that he indicated. "Why do you care?"

"I like to take my morning walk there, and sometimes in the evening, Mrs. Remington will accompany me. It's bad enough having to hear the vile thing when I'm on my own, but I simply will not allow my wife to be subjected to it. Besides that, it's fouling the statue, and, well, perhaps you'll understand when you see it."

That was good enough for me, although with the amount he was paying, he certainly didn't owe me an explanation. I took the money, shook his offered hand, which was another check in the plus column, and went after my prey.

On my way up the street, I reflected on Mr. Roland Remington, the Fourth. He obviously more money than any ten families could burn through in a lifetime, but his demeanor was of someone who still knew its value, and didn't look down on those that weren't born as fortunate as himself. In that way, he reminded me of Bryer, Lilly's father. I wondered if they knew each other.

When I turned the corner and came to the square, I saw immediately why Roland was so adamant that the harpy be removed. First, it truly was leaving the place a mess. Second, it was fouling a statue that must have meant a great deal to him. The man it depicted was surely Roland's ancestor, and he was a dead ringer for it, right down to the mustache. I have no idea which of many wars it was supposed to commemorate, or what the man had done, but it was an obvious source of pride.

The harpy was there, perched on top of the statue, surveying what it surely believed to be its kingdom by this point. It saw me coming and let loose with a string of profanity which was even offensive to me, and I've been in bars where ogres drink.

"Nice mouth," I said. "Do you kiss your mother with it?"

The harpy replied by telling me what it did to my mother, what I could do with her, who else was doing it, and on and on. I actually hesitated in raising my gun, stunned at the creativity of the thing.

"Wow," was all I could think of to say as I shot it off the statue. Not quite in the same league as the harpy's verbal assault, but the little, metal ball that took it out made my point for me.

The smell that lingered after I shot it was horrendous. I gagged and turned to go, but as I did, I heard a sad note played on a pipe. The man came around the corner, playing what could only be described as a funeral dirge. He wasn't the same guy as the night before, but was dressed much the same, in a bright, mismatched outfit, with a peaked cap and a feather.

He continued to play as he came up to me, and then stopped, looking me right in the eyes.

"Now why did you have to go and do that?" he asked. "Was she really all that bad?"

"You're joking, right?" I asked.

In answer, he smiled, began blowing his pipe again and sauntered on down the street. I watched him go, not quite sure how I should take his question. Shaking my head, I turned my gaze back to the square and fountain. The people who lived around here would have to come clean the place up themselves, since that wasn't a service that the crown provided for. Having met Roland, I didn't think he'd have too many problems convincing others to join in.

They should hurry though, I thought. Already the rats were coming, dragging bits of offal to their underground lairs, now that the harpy was no longer there, happy to prey on them also. I shuddered, never having seen so many of the things at one time. They must have been gathering, waiting for their chance.

Yuck. I turned my back on the scene and went on my way.

Lilly came through the door that evening, stepping quickly.

"What is going on around here?" she asked.

I looked up from the book I was reading. "Hmm? I don't know. What are you talking about?"

"The roaches! They're all over the place out there! It's like something drove them all out of the sewers or wherever they usually live. You can't walk two feet without stepping on one."

"Really? I didn't notice. I don't think it was like that when I came home."

"Well, see for yourself. I feel gross. I'm taking a bath. And no, before you ask, you can't join me. But please tell me you got them all out of here, anyway."

"Of course. And I went one better." I told her about asking Petal and her folk to magic the house to keep the pests out.

"Good idea!" she said. "I don't know why I didn't think of it. Really good, with whatever is going on out there."

She shuddered, and then disappeared, bound for hot water, suds, and glass of wine.

For my part, I wanted to see what she was talking about, so I went to the front door and opened it. It wasn't hard to spot. Roaches were everywhere, crawling in the street and over the face of buildings. People walked hurriedly, wearing expressions of disgust on their faces as their footsteps made a crunching noise more often than not.

I was gratified to see that our house was clear of attack by the nasty little things. As I watched, one scuttled across the street, straight for our steps. When it came within a few inches, it veered away, and disappeared from sight.

"Gross," I said to myself, and shut the door, sure that whatever was causing the problem would be over with by morning.

It wasn't. Lilly's cry of disgust when she opened the door told me that as sure as if I saw it for myself.

"How am I supposed to get to work?" she said.

"I guess you either take the plunge or stay home," I said, not very helpfully.

"You're coming too," she told me. "Something is going on."

The tone of voice left me no choice. I put on some older boots, perfect for roach stomping, and went out the door with her.

A few streets over, the roach infestation died out. There was no sign of them here, only several people looking back apprehensively at the areas they crossed where the nasty things were. Lilly wore the same expression and I'm sure that I did too. Turning back around, I spotted another of those pipers with the loud outfits, playing softly as he leaned against a wall. When he saw me looking, he smiled, and touched his cap as a greeting.

I half lifted my hand to him in return, uneasy about seeing another one of these fellows here and now.

"Hey," I said to Lilly, indicating the man with a tilt of my head. "Have you seen these guys around a lot?"

Lilly looked.

"He looks a lot like the guy with the music the other night. Only it's not the same guy, is it?"

"No, he isn't. As a matter of fact, he's the third one I've seen. The other one was hanging around where I killed that harpy last night."

"Really? Ugh. Maybe his nose was broken and he couldn't smell."

"Maybe. But it seems weird."

"It's probably some publicity stunt for a bunch of guys trying to get their music heard. You know how minstrels are. Always trying to get attention."

The piper watched us talking about him, but then straightened off the wall, turned his back to us, and walked away, his tune growing louder but following him as moved off. Soon, we couldn't hear him at all any more.

At the watchhouse, Lilly and I walked to the desk to speak with Sarge.

"Have there been reports of any weird things?" Lilly asked. "Things like a large number of roaches or anything?"

"Weird question," he grunted. "I should have known you two would be involved."

"Hey," I protested. "We're not involved in anything! But we have a huge number of pests outside of our house. It seems weird."

"It is weird, but why would you ask me? What do I look like, an exterminator?"

I was about to reply when Lilly cut me off. "Alright, I know you two boys like to antagonize each other, but I don't have time for it right now. Sarge, as a member of the Watch, I'm asking. Anything?"

"Ah, I hate it when you pull rank, Lilly," he said. "Yeah, there've been some. Some like you're saying. Lots of roaches. But we've also gotten complaints about rats, mice, and flies too. Like huge numbers of them. Worse than that though, check the Board."

Ah. There were the rest of the harpies. There must have been at least 20 of them, rewards being offered on their removals from all over the city.

"Those are the ones that are left. Raven was in earlier and took three of them, although how he's going to get to something that flies is beyond me. A few of the other guys, too."

"This is crazy," I said. "Do we have a sudden increase in the amount of garbage around or something? I mean, something must be causing it, right?"

Lilly looked thoughtful.

"Go kill a few harpies, Duke," she said. "I'll see you at home tonight."

There was a knock at the door that evening, but instead of Lilly, there was a messenger there when I opened it, who told me that Lilly wanted me to come back to the watchhouse as soon as I could. Having nothing better to fill my time with, I followed the messenger right away.

Lilly was in a large room on the second floor, where the wizards keep their labs and libraries. A long, wooden table, with several comfortable chairs around it dominated the space. It looked like a room where a lot of people could gather at once for a meal, or to discuss business if need be.

The room was unoccupied except for Lilly and an elderly man, seated at the far end of the table, talking quietly. He was human, and was one of the oldest living people I ever saw, but when he looked up, there was still a gleam in his eye that said the lights were most certainly still lit.

"Duke," Lilly said, "I'd like you to meet Herr Schmidt. He has an interesting story to tell."

"Yes, well, I don't know if it's interesting, or even true, but it's what was told to me," the old gent said.

I took a seat. "Go ahead."

"I grew up in a town far from here, way to the north, where winters get very cold. A lot of pine forest and mountains. Life wasn't easy, but the area was beautiful, and as a boy, I was happy. I had no concept then, of course, of how hard life in a place like that could be for parents, and I was sad when they moved us here to the city.

"Before that, there was a legend in my town, about a man in bright clothing who played the most beautiful songs on a pipe, and could bewitch men, women, children and animals at will. We were told that if we misbehaved, this piper would come and play at us, and he would take us away, never to be seen again.

"But he wasn't always an evil man. He was said to have helped towns who were overrun by rats, or mice, or locusts, as well. He could drive the pests away with the same music that he would use to lure us children. Was he good, was he evil? Who could tell?"

I stared at Lilly while Herr Schmidt told us his tale.

"It is these clowns with the pipes," I said.

"Could be. It'd be a pretty big coincidence for them to show up at the same time as all these pests, wouldn't it?"

"Sure would. Herr Schmidt, do the tales tell of anyone who stood up to this guy, or how they might have gotten him to go away?"

The old man shook his head. "No, the tales never said that. Only that he would come and take you if you were bad. I never met anyone who actually saw him."

"You have now," I said.

Lilly let her bosses know what she discovered, and the word went out to be on the lookout for the pipers dressed in the multi-colored clothes. Several were seen, but when the Watchmen went to arrest them, the pipers played a tune, and the Watchmen woke up later, with the piper long gone. In the meantime, the plagues of roaches, rats, mice and other pests continued to get worse.

"How did you even find that Herr Schmidt guy?" I asked Lilly, later on.

"It's amazing what you can find in a library," she said. "And the Watch has some pretty big resources."

"Now what?"

"Now we need to figure out how to get rid of them. In the meantime, we're eating at home!"

I resolved to keep my eyes open and if I found one of the pipers, I was going to lean on him, hard, until he told me what I wanted to know. But, since the Watch were onto them, they no longer lounged against walls, or started impromptu dance parties outside of taverns. Now, they stayed hidden, only being noticed when someone heard the sounds of their pipes, and that was usually immediately before the area was overrun by something disgusting.

All I needed to do was wait around to hear people start screaming in disgust and horror. If I was quick enough, I might catch one in the act, and then I'd find out what I needed to know.

I learned a long time ago that standing around waiting for something to happen is boring work. But at the moment, I didn't have a better idea. If the pipers were really causing these outbreaks of pestilence, then that was my only lead. It could take days for me to be in the right place at the right time, although you wouldn't think that people dressed like they were would have that many places to hide without standing out. Maybe they changed clothes when they weren't serenading rats.

While I waited, the city started to spiral down into panic mode for the second time in a few short weeks. Unlike with the banshee, people weren't afraid that they were going to die, they were just too disgusted to attend to their normal affairs. At one point, a whole flock of harpies descended on the Royal Palace, and made a huge mess before the Guard could drive them off with crossbows and slings. Word was that His Highness was not at all happy about it, and who could blame him.

I even visited the NHLF headquarters, to see if Brindar had any news, but like me, he was mostly waiting around, hoping to find one of the elusive pipers to question. From what he alluded to, it appeared that he was spending a lot of his time underground, where the dwarves were expanding, and running into pockets of their own types of pests. I didn't ask too many questions, but the fact that dwarves were busily tunneling under everyone's feet was interesting.

Finally, after more than a week, I got lucky. It was late in the afternoon, and I gave up for the day. After walking for miles and listening in vain, I was ready to hit a tavern, have an ale or three, and then go home to my beautiful bride-to-be and call it a night. My head was hung pretty low as I walked along, making my way back through the Stews, and feeling dejected.

The melody was playing for a moment or two before I even realized it. It started to rise through my subconscious, until I could hear it plainly. It was a weird, haunting melody, and sounded like it came from more than one pipe at a time. I got a cold chill thinking of what they could be calling to them if there were indeed more than one piper, but I followed the sound, until I realized it was coming from an alley in front of me.

I stopped, pulled out my gun and made ready to set it to...to what? Human? I guessed the pipers were human, but was what they were doing worth killing them over, human or not? Maybe they were practical jokers who got a kick out of grossing everyone else out. And despite the old man's story, I hadn't heard any reports of children being led to their dooms, so as far as I knew, they hadn't actually hurt anyone.

I needed to take one alive, and find out what was going on, so I put my gun back into my belt, and loosened the sword that I still wore. A whack with the flat of the blade upside a piper's head wouldn't kill him, but it would put him down. I looked up, and saw that the buildings on either side of the alley were only two stories, although in this part of town, they probably housed several families of goblins, gnolls, or even ogres, in each one.

The music was still coming from the alley in between the two, and there was now a distinctive squeaking noise rising from all around as well. Great, this one was calling rats. Other people on the street were beginning to take notice, and I heard a couple of startled yelps and screams from inside the houses as well.

The nearest alley other than the one the piper was playing in was several houses back, which all ran side to side, with no gaps between them, from that one to this. I turned and ran back to the other one as fast as I could, and using skills developed long ago, made my way up the side and onto the roof. I ran across the rooftops until I reached the gap between the buildings, the alley that piper was standing in playing.

Making my way cautiously to the edge, I leaned out slightly and looked down. It was a scene out of nightmare. The piper, still dressed in those ridiculous bright clothes stood in the middle of the alleyway, legs astride, pipe to his lips. That haunting melody came out, and the rats came to it like it was free cheese. They gathered around him, climbing over and among each other, bunched near his legs so that you couldn't even see his feet. More and more arrived with every second, milled around, and left the alley, to run into the street, or to squeeze through cracks in the walls.

I looked around, and found something I could use. A lot of the buildings in the Stews had been there for long time, and a lot of them weren't kept up as well as they should be. Chimneys deteriorated over time, and some of the bricks on the tops were loose. I took one, walked back to the edge, took careful aim, and let fly.

A moment later, I was rewarded with the satisfying sound of it connecting with flesh, an "oomph" sound, and the sudden cessation of the music. As I made my way down from the roof and into the alley, the rats were starting to disperse, which was nice for me.

He was out cold when I got to him, but to be safe, I picked him up by the front of his shirt, and socked him a good one in the jaw. His feathered cap fell into the grime of the alleyway, and I gladly let it lay where it landed. I took his pipe and stuck that into my belt, sure that Lilly would want to see it. I didn't know if the magic belonged to the man or the instrument, but I would let the experts work that out.

I hefted the unconscious piper onto my shoulder when I heard more music. It was faint at first, but definitely getting louder. One of this guy's buddies was coming to rescue him. Well, they'd have to catch me first.

Running with a body over your shoulder isn't the easiest thing to do, but then again, neither is trying to run and play a tune on a pipe either. There were times that the song would start to get into my head, urging me to slow down, to stop running, to dump my prisoner, but then it would hit a wrong note, or there would be a heavy breath, and the compulsion would disappear, only to start to build again. Every time, it grew a little stronger, and a little harder to resist.

I heard yet another pipe start up, and there was no way I could make it to the watchhouse. The new sound started between me and the direction I needed to go in. They figured out where I was going, somehow communicated it, probably through that infernal music, and made a plan to cut me off.

But they didn't realize one important thing. I wasn't headed for the watchhouse. I was headed for home. Let them try their magic pipe playing there, where Petal's folks were. My money was on the Brownies.

By the time I hit home, I was sweating, and not only from the exertion of carrying the piper. The song telling me to quit was getting harder to ignore by the second, and if I hadn't had enough of someone else playing with my mind, I might have succumbed to it. But the more I thought of not being in control of my mind again, the angrier I got, and that helped to shield me.

I pushed the door open, stumbled inside, dropped the piper on the floor and sank down, panting heavily. Outside, I could still hear the music, but it lost its power in here. I didn't know if that was due to the Brownies, or because I was home, but either way, I was safe.

The music stopped, and I crawled to the window, rising up enough to look out, but ready to duck back quickly if needed. There were two more pipers out there, their pipes no longer raised to their lips, regarding my house with quizzical expressions on their faces. They looked at each other, then raised their pipes back up, and walked off in different directions, their music floating through the air behind them.

I sighed deeply and turned back to my captive, who was beginning to stir.

"Buddy, you better hope you tell me what I need to know before Lilly gets here. Trust me."

He groaned, and I don't think it was a thank-you. Some people have no sense of gratitude.

When Lilly did come home, I was in the kitchen, sitting in a turned around chair, my hands crossed over the back of it. The piper was in front of me, bound to another chair, but ungagged.

"Ummm...what's going on, Duke?" she asked.

"I caught one," I said, not taking my gaze off of the piper.

"I see that. But why is he here? Why didn't you bring him to the watchhouse?"

I told her about the other two, and the fact that they knew he was here, and about the compelling music and how it lost its power in the house. She nodded as I finished.

"Yep, I guess that would work. Let me see that pipe."

I gave it to her and she took it farther away from the piper while she looked it over. She set it down, raised her hands over it and said some words in what sounded like a nonsense language to me. Sparks flashed on her fingertips and her eyes turned black.

The piper stared at her in horror while this was going on, a fact which wasn't lost on her. I'm sure she threw in a few extra dramatics for his benefit, but I couldn't have sworn to it.

"Interesting," she finally said. "Have you gotten much out of him yet?"

"Nope, he doesn't want to talk. I was going to lean on him some, but I know you get upset with blood on the kitchen floor, so I thought I better not. At least not until you were here to say if it was okay."

"Sweet of you. I don't think that will work though. I don't think he really cares if you beat him to a pulp, do you Mister Piper?"

The piper was still staring at Lilly in horror, although now I noticed that his eyes kept flickering back and forth between Lilly's face, and the pipe that she held in her hands.

"No, beating him up wouldn't do anything," Lilly mused. "But, if I was to do something to this pipe, like, oh, I don't know, set it on fire..."

"No!" the shout burst out of the restrained piper, and he jerked against the rope in a futile effort to get free.

"That's what I thought," Lilly said, quietly.

"What?" I was lost, again. That happened a lot when Lilly got rolling. "I don't get it."

"They're one and the same, Duke," she replied, but her eyes weren't on me, they were boring into the piper. "The pipe and the man, they're the same thing. One can't exist without the other. Oh, we could kill him, but eventually the pipe will find someone else to play it, and then that person will become part of it. But...if we destroy the pipe..."

"Please," the piper begged, "don't. Please."

"Then I think you better start talking," Lilly said, still holding onto the pipe.

"What do you want to know?"

"Why are you guys around?" I asked. "I mean, what's in it for you?"

"Money," he replied. I was disappointed. Why is it always something as simple and base as greed? It seemed like it should be some sort of nefarious plot, not that someone was paying them to…. to what exactly?

"Why?" I asked him. "Why would someone pay you to come here and bring rats and roaches and stuff like that?"

"To cause chaos in the city, keep you all on edge," he said. "At least, that's what we were told."

"By who?"

He opened his mouth to reply, but then clamped it shut again. Well, well. Maybe enough money does buy loyalty, for a little while anyway.

"Dumb move, my friend," I said.

Lilly stepped in front of him, the pipe held up in one hand and raised the other. Sparks again snapped and popped between her fingers, giving off an acrid odor.

"I can't!" the piper wailed. "I physically can't say!"

"Are you saying there's a spell on you?" Lilly asked him, lowering her hand.

"Yes," the man's head was down, and he was panting, glancing at the pipe in Lilly's hand with desperation in his eyes. "I can't say, and if I'm forced, it will kill me. All of us, we all had to agree to that to get paid."

"You must have been paid an awful lot for that," I said.

"We did. But we would have done it for less."

"What's that supposed to mean?"

"Capital City," he snorted. "Everyone here thinks they're so high and mighty. Greatest city in the world. So enlightened. What a load of manure."

"Wait," I said. "You're telling me that because you don't like our city, you're willing to spread chaos and destruction here?"

"Don't think we're alone," he sneered. "We're just one of the first waves. There's worse coming. You're all dead, you just don't know it yet."

"I've heard enough," Lilly said, stepping forward again.

She raised her hand, and the piper looked at his pipe and whimpered. But Lilly waved her hand, moving her fingers in a strange way, and he went to sleep. Or at least, I hoped he was asleep. Lilly being a necromancer, you could never really be sure.

"We'll take him to the watchhouse," she said. "See what the wizards can do about that curse that's on him, and what more they can tell us about this pipe."

"How are we going to get there?" I asked. "The other ones, at least two of them are out there waiting."

"It's not that hard, really. Forewarned is forearmed."

A short time later, we turned the sleeping piper over to the Watch, and removed the wads of cotton from our ears. If the pipers had tried to get to us, Lilly stymied them by the simple trick of making sure we couldn't hear.

Since I wasn't part of the Watch, I was left on my own when Lilly was summoned to a meeting on the second floor. She told me that it could be awhile before she was done, so maybe I should go piper hunting, but not to forget my ear plugs. I agreed with her.

Whoever it was that had it in for Capital City, they were devious. First, they made people fear for their lives, and now they've made it so that no-one even felt safe in their own homes. Whatever was coming next was sure to be even worse. We could only hope that the wizards would break the curse placed on the piper and get some answers. Then the king could send the Guard after them and end this whole stupid affair.

"I'm off hunting," I told Sarge. "Let Lilly know I'll see her at home, would you?"

"Sure, Duke," he replied, "be careful. Those rats can bite pretty hard."

"Glad to know you care," I said, ducking out the door.

I didn't have to hunt too far. They were out there already, looking for me apparently. I don't think they liked the fact that I took one of their friends, and were out for a little payback.

I saw the first one almost as soon as I left the watchhouse. He was standing across the street, in plain sight, watching the door. As soon as he saw me he scowled, pointed at me, and then turned and walked away. Of course, it was a trap, these things always are, but what were they going to do? Play music at me that I couldn't hear?

I followed this piper for a few more streets, until it opened up in a square. I recognized it as the same place that Raven and I first tried to corral Camelia's broom. The rest of them were there waiting, lazing on the walls of the fountain, pipes held casually. Six of them in all, which meant we had the seventh, if that's all there were.

One of them lifted his pipe to his mouth and started to play. I stood there, and smiled at him, unaffected by the music. He stopped, and pantomimed taking something from his ear. I laughed and said, "No way," my voice sounding strange in my head.

He held up his hand, and carefully set his pipe down next to him on the wall. The others all did the same.

I could play along if it got me more information. I pulled the cotton from my ears, but held it up, at the ready, in case there should be another piper around.

"We need our brother back," one of them said, the same one who started playing when I came into the square.

"We need you guys gone," I said. "Out of our city. Then maybe, but no guarantee."

"No, you don't understand," said another. "This isn't a negotiation. Up to now, we've been nice."

"Nice? Really? By scaring everyone half out of their wits?"

"No, by only bringing the little beasties," said a third.

"You've got an hour to release him, all unharmed. Or we all play, together. Now run on your way, messenger boy, and tell your lords and masters that."

With that, they picked up their pipes, and I shoved the cotton back into my ears. But they didn't play, they all cast one final glare at me, and walked away, each going their own way.

Messenger boy?

The hour passed and no one was going to release the piper from the Watch's custody. As a matter of fact, several of the Palace Guard came and got him. It seemed that His Highness wanted a word with him, one on one. Lilly's reports of the threats he made to Capital City reached the ears of those in the highest places, and they wanted answers.

"I don't think they'll get them, though," she said to me, as we watched the Guard, plugs of cotton firmly in their ears, lead the piper away. "That spell on him is powerful. And it's set to kill him if it's tampered with. Whoever this is, they're playing for keeps."

Eventually, we needed to leave the watchhouse if we weren't going to make it our new home. Sarge offered to have several of the Watch accompany us, but we turned it down. The day that I couldn't deal with a few pipe playing misfits, especially with Lilly by my side, was the day that I hung up being a Nuisance Man.

For a while, there was no sign of them on the way home, but we kept our cotton ear plugs ready. And then, of course, the music started.

They were smart, these pipers. However it was that they were communicating, they had us surrounded already. The music rose up all around us, not gradually like the last time, but with a sudden blare, and it was insistent. "Give up," it screamed. "Relax. Don't resist." And on and on.

But they weren't counting on wills like Lilly and I possessed. We'd been through a terrible time together, and we weren't about to fold that easy. Both of us managed to fight through the compulsion and get our cotton plugs into our ears, blocking out the music. It didn't take it away entirely, but it quieted it down enough that we could continue on our way.

I was fairly certain that they wouldn't physically approach us. Like most minstrels, none of them were particularly intimidating. There was no doubt in my mind that even if Lilly couldn't blast them, I could take them all out fairly easily.

Which is why I was so surprised when one of them stepped out from an alley in front of us, pipe raised to his lips and a nasty smile on his face. I turned my head and saw others coming up from behind. A quick count showed me that all six of the remaining pipers now stood around us, and none of them looked nervous.

I pulled my gun, but Lilly put her hand on mine and shook her head. I shrugged and pulled my sword instead. Guess it was time to do this the old-fashioned way.

Lilly took a pose beside me, her hands coming up and her mouth moving, although I couldn't hear the words through the cotton in my ears, and over the music that the pipers were playing.

But they never hesitated, they played louder instead.

Then the ground started to shake, a tremor at first, but then harder. Cobblestones began to pop out of the street, flying into the air, and the ground itself swelled up in a huge hump. The dirt underneath the stones rose, falling off the thing that rose through the earth.

I really wish I never knew that things like that existed. It was one of those horrible bugs that you find in your bathroom from time to time, long, slim, with about a million legs, scuttling around too fast to catch and squash easily. Only, this one was larger than the common variety. Much larger.

It was huge, as a matter of fact. Longer than a coach drawn by four horses, and bigger around than a beer keg. Its many legs were as thick as young trees and ended in a single sharp claw, bigger than a dagger. Its jaws opened and it screamed, the noise cutting through the cotton in our ears, and piercing into our brains. No teeth showed inside its maw, but the liquid that fell from it smoked and sizzled on the ground.

I pulled my gun again, and said...nothing. What the hell was that thing? I didn't even know what its smaller cousins were called, so what was I supposed to tell my gun to kill? I looked over at Lilly, who was as wide eyed as I felt.

She recovered and started a spell, one I saw her use before. A ghostly image of the giant bug would start to separate from its physical body, but then would suddenly snap back. She was trying to pull the life force from the thing, but it was resisting. How, I have no idea, but it must have been some sort of natural protection to magic.

I fired my gun anyway. The little, metal ball that came out wouldn't be designed to do maximum damage to this thing, but that didn't mean it wouldn't hurt it. The ball hit one of the legs, a lucky shot, and sheared through. The leg dropped away and the thing swung toward me, moving incredibly fast, the missing leg not bothering it all.

Lilly changed tactics, and started to summon something. It was also horrible to look at, but given the two, I'd take Lilly's creature. Pitch black and vaguely man-shaped, it stood about eight feet tall, with muscles on top of muscles. Lilly pointed and it threw itself on top of the thing in front of us, and began punching, its fists sinking through the insect's shell with every blow.

The bug screamed again, and rolled, a long sinuous curve, crushing the black shape beneath it. There was a sudden blast of wind, and the shape disappeared. I heard a cry and saw Lilly collapse to her knees, a fierce look still on her face.

Damage had been done to the creature, though. There were gaping holes where Lilly's shadow man punched through the thing's armor. A plan formed in my mind, crazy and probably useless, but still, better than nothing.

I ran directly at the thing, and it spit at me. A blast of that liquid from its mouth caught me in the arm, and it burned through my cloak, the sleeve of my shirt underneath, and into my skin. I screamed, loudly, because it hurt like the devil! But my cloak and shirt must have taken the brunt, since my skin turned a nasty red color and blistered, but that was all.

Lilly hit it with a force bolt of some sort, something that looked like the absence of light when she threw it. It hit the creature and sank in, causing it to be outlined in a black fire for a second. It writhed on the ground, stunned for a moment, but then started to recover. But that was the chance I needed.

I ran right up onto it, passing between the legs with a shudder. At the first hole in the carapace I came to, I stuck my arm right inside it, ignoring my revulsion, and pulled the trigger on my gun as fast as I could. The gun went off, and those little, metal balls tore up its insides horribly. It jerked and convulsed and I was thrown off my feet, holding onto it by grabbing at the edge of the same hole in its shell that I shot into. Pulling myself up, I slid to the next one, and repeated the whole act.

This time, it did the trick. I shot as many times as I could before the thing rose up with a horrible scream and keeled over, taking me for a ride with it. I rolled clear as it collapsed, and came up with my gun at the ready, but it wasn't needed.

It was dead, and lay there in the ruins of the street dripping a foul-smelling ichor onto the stones and the dirt. Lilly came up, panting and exhausted, and leaned against me.

There was no sign of the pipers.

We never did find out what happened to the piper that the Palace Guard took away, but the other six took to their heels and fled the city. Reports came from Watchmen posted at the gates of hearing music, falling asleep, and then waking a few minutes later. It was assumed that the pipers all fled that way, now that we were on to them.

"Bugs are gross," Lilly said to me over dinner.

I nodded, too tired to do much more.

"Who do you think is behind this?"

"I don't know," I said. "But I think I'm going to get some of the others together. Maybe compare notes on some recent nuisances, and see if there's anything else that's funny. Like that lone harpy. Maybe there's more going on here than we realize.

"Good idea," she said. "Let me know what you find out."

I nodded again, not really listening, but watching a spider build a web in the corner of our kitchen ceiling, too tired to do anything about it.

# BRAVE NEW UNDERWORLD

One of the first people that I tried to contact, against my better judgment, was Raven. While I couldn't stand the guy, I had to admit that he was an effective Nuisance Man, and he did get involved in an awful lot of stuff.

Sarge told me that he hadn't been in for a couple of days, so he was expecting that he would be shortly. I hung around, mostly annoying him, until the man walked in, dressed head to toe in deep black, as was his annoying custom.

"Grandfather," he sneered, when he saw me. Raven used professional level sneers, and I tried hard to copy them.

"Raven. We need to talk."

"What for? I can't imagine what you could possibly have to say that would interest me."

I sighed. This was going to be harder than I thought.

"Look," I said, "it's no secret that we don't like each other, but when we've needed to, we've worked well together. I'm not proposing anything of that magnitude, at least not yet, but I am saying that we should exchange information."

He looked down his nose at me. "About what?"

"About what's been going on in the city. We're under attack. You must realize that, right? The banshee, the pipers. They were sent by someone, or someones."

Raven furrowed his brow as he regarded me. "Not all of us have your inside information, Grandfather. What are you talking about?"

I realized that even if mine might ran deeper, the dislike for Raven was pretty widespread and no one filled him in. I took the opportunity to do that now, and told him about what Lilly discovered.

"I see," he said. "And you suspect me of having something to do with this. Is that it?"

"No! Well, actually I hadn't thought of that. You don't, do you?"

"No!"

"I didn't think so. No, what I thought was that I would see if you had encountered anything out of the ordinary, more than normally, I mean. Maybe it would help point the way toward whoever is responsible."

He simply stared at me for a moment, then, "No, I can't say that I have. It's been business as usual, except for those harpies the other day, vile things. But you knew about them already. Other than that, it's been simple nuisance removals."

I hadn't really expected much else, since word did tend to get around, but you had to start somewhere.

"Well, if you notice anything, leave word with Sarge. I'll get in touch with you then and we'll compare notes. In the meantime, you haven't talked to Brindar, have you?"

"The dwarf? Why would I have?"

Ah. For a moment there, Raven almost seemed like a decent human being. But the tone of his voice when he asked me that, told me that I was mistaken.

"Never mind," I said. "But let Sarge know if you find anything that you think could help."

I shook my head as I walked away. Not that I was always a paragon of equal rights for everyone, but we were both witness to Brindar's valor. It was a shame that Raven so steadfastly refused to change.

A while later, I walked in to the NHLF headquarters. It was out of there that Brindar worked, so it was where I hoped to find him. I looked around as I entered and saw their version of a Nuisance Board. It wasn't much different from the one I was used to, with various nuisances on it from all different races; Unhoused orcs who were shaking down local businessmen, goblins wanted for arson, or gnolls for mugging. But, unlike our Board, these notices were posted by non-humans. By honest dwarves, orcs, and ogres who wanted to earn a living, raise their families and be left in peace.

And also unlike ours, there were humans on this Board. At first, these notices caused the hairs on the back of my neck to stand up, but then I started reading. Yeah, I knew it was the case, but here it was in black and white. The other races held no monopoly on criminal and abhorrent behavior. We did plenty of it too. And after reading some of the things these particular humans did, I started to feel that I should visit this Board to take a few of them for myself.

"Ah, Mr. Grandfather," a voice said.

I turned, to find Ivar Ivarson, the founder and head of the NHLF. He was always unfailingly polite, even when he first confronted me in that alley those years ago. His voice was rich, deep and cultured, and spoke of an upbringing of civility and education. An upbringing that he used to bring the greatest change to Capital City that occurred since His Majesty opened the city to one and all.

"Ivar," I said, sticking out my hand. "It's good to see you again."

His hand shake was firm and strong, hinting at a strength that would easily top mine if he wanted it to.

"And you," he replied. "What can I do for you?"

"I'm actually looking for Brindar. I thought he and I could compare notes on recent events."

"Ah. The attacks on our city, yes." Why was I not surprised that he was in the know on this? The NHLF had become a force to reckon with, and being at the head of it, I imagined that Ivar had some pretty high-up contacts.

"Exactly," I said. "I've run into a couple of really odd things lately, even for Capital City. I know he had his hands full during the incident with the pipers, and I'm wondering what else he might have noticed."

"Good idea, Mr. Grandfather. Unfortunately, I don't know that I can help you. You see, I haven't seen Brindar in several days. And from what I hear, neither has anyone else."

"What do you mean? Where did he go?"

"He was in the Underworld, or at least that's where he was headed when last heard of."

Now it was my turn to furrow my brows. I hoped it looked better than when Raven did it.

"What's the Underworld? I've never heard of it."

Ivar smiled. "It's dwarven territory, Mr. Grandfather. The rights of which were given to the dwarves by your very own king, in return for certain trade rights and other concessions."

"Then I need to travel to get to it? Back to the mountains I assume?"

"No, Mr. Grandfather. All you need do, is head down."

I was confused, I'm not afraid to admit it. If you talk to Lilly, she'll insist it's my normal state of being, but that's not true. I just have other things to occupy my mind a lot of the time.

It turned out that Ivar was speaking literally. The dwarves had been granted license to excavate beneath parts of Capital City, and create an entirely separate city beneath the streets. It was young yet, and only underway for the last year or so. But as anyone who knows dwarves can tell you, they are nothing if not industrious.

The Underworld, as they called it, was ruled over by a coalition of three dwarves, all from different guilds. One was the mining guild, another was the construction guild, and the third was the militia guild. All decisions about Underworld was made by them, with two out of three being in agreement enough to settle disputes. Dwarves, as a rule, are remarkably pragmatic, so when the dissenter was overruled, he or she immediately dropped it, and cooperated fully with the other two.

Ivar explained to me that while Underworld was self-ruling, it was still governed by the laws of Capital City. What was a crime up here, was a crime down there. It would not be a haven for criminals to escape to, and the citizens that lived there were answerable to both the ruling three of Underworld, and to the crown.

"Isn't that kind of against what you've been fighting for?" I asked Ivar.

"In some ways, perhaps," he said. "But humans, or anyone else, are allowed to visit, and even to live there if they wish. But there are not too many other races willing to live with solid roofs of stone over their heads every moment of the day."

"I can see that. What about orcs though?"

He smiled at that. "We have some who have come and set up shop there. But the orcs that have moved to Capital City have proven remarkably adaptable, don't you think? Witness their warrens of buildings converted to their own uses. They have no need, no desire, to spend their resources on going underground. No, it is mostly the dwarves who long for the comfort of stone surrounding them."

"Well, I can't say I've ever really been somewhere like that, but I really would like to find Brindar. So, off to Underworld I go. One question first."

"Yes?"

"How do I get there?"

Ivar gave me directions, and I left the NHLF headquarters, which was located near the docks. From there, I headed inland, back into the warren of buildings that make up the bulk of our city.

The dwarves, like a lot of races, mostly settled in a few areas. The First Quarter was one of them. It was called that because it was one of the first places that you reached if you got off a ship at the docks and headed in a direct line toward the palace on the hill. Not that many people did that, but at one time, it may have been a thing. There was once a large thoroughfare that led from the port, in a straight line, to the castle. But over time, it was encroached on, covered over, and generally obliterated until it only existed in isolated fragments spaced throughout the city today.

But once upon a time, the First Quarter was home to the latest and greatest in fashion, food stuffs, weapons, and anything else the rich and powerful would have a yearning for. Those shops suffered as the tides of time changed the area. They were replaced or closed outright over the years and then the Quarter fell on truly hard times and became a nest for unsavory types and criminals.

Then the dwarves moved in, and in a brief time, the bad element was pushed out. Now, it was full of dwarven businesses, and becoming known again as a place to go for the best in weapons, armor, cookware and several other items that required careful craftsmanship. The proximity to the docks was again a boon to the area, as the dwarves imported material, and turned it into goods that were becoming essential throughout Capital City.

It did my heart good to walk through the area, even if there were some suspicious looks in my direction. The social revolution that Ivar started didn't only find opponents on the human side. There were plenty of folks in all races who didn't see everyone as being equal. Time would tell if the idea ever truly became universal.

It turned out to be pretty easy to find the entrance to Underworld, once you knew it was in the First Quarter. There was a large stone arch, the street that ran under it disappearing down into the ground, and large letters spelling out "Underworld" carved into the top of it. That was a pretty clear clue that I was on the right track.

I moved along the road, marveling at the size and artistry of the arch as I passed under it. If there was one thing that dwarves did better than anyone, it was stone work. The air coming up from the hole that the road dipped down into was decidedly cooler, and as I got closer I hoped that there were torches lit. I realized then that I had no idea if dwarves could see in the dark, but hoped that since Ivar said that others were welcome there, light had been provided for.

There was a guard booth next to the road, with three, sturdy, heavily armed and armored dwarves standing nearby. They talked among themselves, but kept a watchful eye on the foot traffic passing in and out of Underworld.

"Hi fellas," I said as I approached them. "I'm hoping you can steer me in the right direction."

The three of them fell silent and stared at me from beneath bushy eyebrows and caps of steel. None of them said a word.

"Let me try this again. I'm looking for Brindar, and I understand that he was last seen heading down there." I indicated the road leading underground with a tilt of my head. "Who wants to tell me where I could find him?"

Still nothing, but one of the dwarves said something to his companions in their own language, which sounded like a bunch of rocks being crushed by a hammer. They all looked back at me and laughed.

"You guys are hilarious," I tried again. "But here's the thing. Brindar is a friend of mine, and a colleague. Maybe you've heard of me. The name is Grandfather, Duke Grandfather. You can either tell me what I want to know, or I can head out of here and see if Ivar can straighten you out."

As threats go, it wasn't much. But I wasn't trying to start an inter-species war here, just get some information. If me saying that I was Brindar's friend didn't work, maybe dropping Ivar's name would help.

To my surprise, it did. Well, a little anyway.

"If you're his friend, why don't you know where he is?" one of them challenged me. His friends all looked as if they thought he scored a point.

I was starting to get tired of this, so I stepped right up to the dwarf and bent to put my face close to his, our noses almost touching.

"In case you hadn't heard, *friend*," I growled, "I was busy saving the city from those pipers, like Brindar was doing here. And what were *you* doing?"

I straightened up as the dwarf looked embarrassed.

"Deep," he said. "The last time Brindar was seen, he was heading deep, chasing something."

"What's that supposed to mean?" I asked.

"Follow the road. Keep going. When it's not a road anymore, keep going anyway. That's where he was last."

"But you're dwarves. If he went deeper, why haven't you found him already?"

The three guards looked at each other, then down at the ground.

"It's forbidden," a different one said. "Where he went, it hasn't been cleared yet."

"I don't understand. What do you mean it hasn't been cleared yet?"

They all shuffled their feet, and refused to answer any further questions.

"Stop at the Guild office on your way," one finally told me. "They can answer your questions, or not, as they see fit. You can't miss it if you stay on the main road."

"Thanks for the information," I said, and started to walk down the street. One of them called me back.

"Wait a second," he said, and ran inside the guard shack. He came out a moment later with a lantern that held a round, black stone inside of it. "Here," he said, handing it to me. "Down in the lower levels, there isn't always light. I hope you find him. We need Brindar."

I looked at the black stone dubiously, but I had been around long enough to know that things weren't always as they appeared. I thanked him, told him that I would do my best, and headed down, under the earth, into Underworld.

Underworld was an interesting place. I suffered a moment of panic as I walked out of the light of day and into the cave, but it passed quickly. The place was huge, and the size of it made it impossible for all but the most serious claustrophobe to feel closed in. There were lamps shining brightly everywhere, and the dwarves had cunningly placed reflective surfaces in strategic areas to make it seem even brighter.

In my experience, dwarves tended to be stolid, taciturn people, not given to idle chatter or playfulness. While that may hold true up above, here in Underworld it was different. Children ran and played, and weren't hushed by their parents, who looked on with watchful, but lenient, eyes. People said hello to each other as they passed, and even to me.

In addition to dwarves, I saw at least one business, a clothes cleaner, being run by orcs, who seemed on good terms with their dwarven neighbors. Everywhere I looked, I saw nothing but smiles, friendliness, and prosperity. It seemed as if the dwarves really had built themselves an ideal place.

But if that were the case, then why were they here in Capital City in the first place? Why didn't they stay in the mountains, in their own cities, which were said to encompass entire mountains? That was a mystery, but it was for another day. Today, I wanted to find Brindar.

Not only to compare notes on our last several days, but because something didn't feel right. No one had seen him, and the guard up above said that he went deep, and implied that he was missing. Now, Brindar and I were friends, or at least I thought so, but we weren't real close. But if I was concerned, then why wasn't every dwarf in this city going crazy trying to find him?

I walked along, musing on this, and marveling at the size and complexity of Underworld as I went. It was only a little over a year, and they had constructed something truly remarkable. The houses and buildings blended into the stone walls behind them, like they had been there for centuries. The streets were wide, well paved, and clean. In addition to the main thoroughfare, several smaller streets branched off, leading to side caverns where more lanterns glowed and flashed in the distance. The air was cool, but moved nicely and didn't feel stuffy in the least. All in all, it was a very pleasant, cosmopolitan type place.

The Guild office was pretty far down. The road turned a few switchbacks as it descended, grew steeper in some areas and leveled out in others. I walked for a good thirty minutes before I saw it, and the guards words came back to me. There was no way I could miss it.

The building was huge, dominating the cavern that it was housed in and set right across the road, so that by following it, you had no choice but to enter the building. There was something else about it, something that felt different from all the other buildings around. It took me a moment to realize what it was, but when I saw it, the answer was obvious.

This building was old. Not built to look that way, or built to blend in with its surroundings. It was ancient. The stone showed signs of erosion, and there were water stains on some of the walls where the cavern ceiling overhead dripped. Looking closer, there was moss and lichens growing in the cracks of the carvings which decorated the façade. It was as if the dwarves dug out this immense area for their new city, and ran right into the ruins of an old one.

The road ended at a set of immense stone steps. There were ten of them, each wide enough for two carriages to drive up side by side, and still have room to spare. From there, the building arched over a passage, several stories high, and the road looked like it continued on, through the building and out of the other side.

On each side of the arch, there were large doors that led into the building, made of intricately carved stone, but standing open at the moment. Windows covered the front of the building, revealing that there were seven floors inside. All in all, it must have had room for several hundred dwarves to comfortably work, without feeling crowded.

I walked up the stairs, still marveling at the sheer size and sense of age of the place, and at the complexity of the carvings in the doors, and the statues and gargoyles on the face of it. It was a true work of art.

Inside, it was no different. Stone, polished to a high gleam, shone from every surface. Dwarves walked about, with the intent looks of people engaged in serious business on their faces. Several paces across the floor was a raised area, with a large, circular desk in the middle of it. Chairs were set along the wall nearby, with a few dwarves sitting in them, glancing every now and then at the female dwarf attending the desk.

I walked up to the raised platform, mounted it, and approached the desk.

"Hi," I said, trying to keep my voice cordial and friendly. "I was told to come here by…"

"Do you have an appointment?" she asked me, interrupting me.

"An appointment? Well, no, I didn't know I was coming here. See, the guards up at…"

"Take this," she said, shoving a thin piece of wood with a paper form attached to it at me.

"What's this?" I asked.

"Form 1087-BN. Application for an ad-hoc appointment. Fill it out and return it to me here when you're finished. Make sure you've marked which Guild you're here to see."

"But I'm not here to see any Guild," I protested. "I was told to stop here to find out where…"

She reached out and took the board away from me and pushed another into my hands.

"Fill this out instead, please. Form 1269-DK. Request to file an inquest. When it's complete, drop it in slot C, near portico A12. Someone will get back to you within five weeks. At that time, your question can be presented and sorted to the correct Guild for answering. Thank you for visiting the Guild Hall, and have a pleasant day. Oh, and please bring the clipboard back to me when you've finished. I lose more of those things…"

She turned away and began rummaging through papers on the other side of the desk, dismissing me as if I was no longer even standing there.

I looked down at the form in my hand. It was filled with small writing, several lines on which I was apparently supposed to write, and a whole lot of boxes to check. Shaking my head, I set it back down on the desk, and walked off the dais and away.

Well, if there was no one here to help, then there was no choice but to continue on my own. The guards said that Brindar went "deep", whatever that meant, and to keep going even when the road no longer looked like a road. To me, the way was simple. All I needed to do was go back out, and follow the road under the Guild Hall, and down to wherever it led next.

I stepped back out, turned and walked along the front of the building and came back to the road. I walked along it, looking up at the underside of the Guild Hall arching far above me, a many candled lamp hanging down from it. It was so far up that I wondered how they managed to light the thing, let alone change the candles in it.

Then, my eyes were drawn to what was in front of me. Apparently, when the guard up top said that it was forbidden to go on, he meant that literally. There was a large iron gate across the road, locked with a gigantic lock, and guarded by no less than six of the largest, most heavily armed dwarves I ever saw.

Given the initial reaction to my presence from the last guards, I didn't have high hopes as I approached these.

"I don't suppose you guys are going to let me go through there, are you?" I said.

They all looked at me with bored expressions on their faces.

"No, sir, entry is forbidden to one and all, unless they have special orders signed by the head of the Militia Guild," one of them said.

"And to get that letter?" I asked.

He pointed back the way I came.

"The Guild Hall, sir."

"Thought so," I sighed. "I don't suppose one of you guys know a quick way to get those orders, do you?"

Nothing.

"I'd really like to get through there. I'm looking for Brindar, who I'm sure you've heard of, and last he was seen, he was down that way."

Still nothing, although a couple of them looked at each other out of the corners of their eyes.

"I don't understand you guys," I flared up. "Brindar is my friend, and he could be in trouble down there. To you guys, he should be a national hero! If you're not going to go yourself, why are you stopping me?"

Suddenly, the six dwarves snapped to attention and stood looking straight ahead.

"Mr. Grandfather," a voice said. "If you would step over here, please."

I turned to see a large dwarf approaching. He was stouter than most, and his beard was one of the most magnificent I had ever seen, snow white, and flowing down to his belt, where it forked and was held by two ties. He had piercing blue eyes that told of a man who missed very little, and the mental capacity to match.

I stepped off with him, and he walked slowly with me until we were out of earshot of the guards.

"Allow me to introduce myself," he started. "Grundir Grimshornson, head of the Militia Guild. We got word that you were coming."

"From Ivar, I'm assuming?" It must be, since he was the only one who I'd told I was headed this way.

"Indeed. He implored us to let you through the gate, to go deep, as it were, although I must confess, I have my hesitations about it."

With the refined way that this guy spoke, he could have been Ivar's long lost brother.

"Let me through," I said, "and I'll find Brindar, bring him back, and everyone will be happy."

He stared at me with those knowing eyes.

"I've heard of you, Mr. Grandfather," he said. "I heard of you back before Ivar started his movement. You were a cautionary tale to our youth, and a story to frighten each other with around a fire in the deep of night. The Nuisance Man with the Horrible Gun is how we referred to you. You can imagine my surprise when Ivar not only spoke on your behalf, but named you friend."

I was actually surprised by that myself. I had a great deal of respect for Ivar, but I didn't know that he considered me a friend.

"He told me of your saving of the NHLF headquarters from the War Golem, and of the mutual respect built between Brindar and yourself. Still, I find it hard to let a human, let alone a human who used to consider us no more than animals, into what lies beyond those gates."

"Look," I said. "I don't really care what's beyond the gates. I want to see if I can find Brindar, help him out if he needs it, and if not, compare notes on what's been going in the city. That's all." I stopped then, and glanced over at the iron gates, noting for the first time that beyond them, the paved road stopped, and became a rough stone passage. There were also no lanterns, so although there were what appeared to more buildings, they were shrouded in darkness a few paces inside.

"But, uh…so I know…what *is* beyond those gates?"

Grundir regarded me for a moment, considering whether to answer my question or not, I was sure.

"We call it the Deep," he finally said. "And it's not what we expected to find here."

"The Deep? The guard up at the top said that Brindar went deep, but I thought he meant that he went deeper into Underworld."

"Underworld stops here, Mr. Grandfather. Or right before here, if we're being technical. The Guild Hall is the first of the buildings to be reclaimed from the Deep. It very well may be the last."

He walked around me, looking past the gates, into the darkness beyond them.

"When we sought your King's permission to build Underworld, we had no idea that we would stumble onto a legend of the dwarves. The Deep was one of our oldest cities, lost to time and memory, and only spoken of in old songs that few today remember. But as we dug, and built, and expanded on the caverns that we found here, we came upon this building, looking out into the darkness as it had for centuries. We uncovered the road beneath it, paved it with our cobbles and began to go further."

He stopped and sighed.

"And then we lost men. A lot of men. Most who ventured further down the road simply never came back. Those few who did, spoke of whispers, and shadows blacker than night gliding through the darkness, beyond the reach of the lanterns. They descended into madness soon after. Any attempt to move past this building, deeper into the ruins of the ancient city beyond was met with disaster.

"Our scholars were called in, and they examined what they could see, and proclaimed that we had uncovered the Deep. The city that dwarves once called great, but were driven from by forces unknown.

"We sent in Militia forces, of course. To the same result as the workers. They were lost, or returned to us mad. We put up the gates, expanded Underworld in other directions, and have tried to forget that it is here. Until Brindar chased one of the pipers into there, several days ago now. He hasn't been seen or heard from since, and we fear that he is dead.

"So, Mr. Grandfather," he concluded, turning back to me. "Hearing all of that, do you still wish to enter the Deep?"

I looked again at the dark, abandoned city beyond those huge gates and swallowed hard. Really, what choice did I have?

"Unlock them," I said, hoping that my voice sounded more sure to Grundir than it did to me. "I'll find him."

As soon as the gates clanged shut behind me, I could feel the oppressiveness of the place bearing down. Unlike Underworld, the Deep had a dark, forbidding feel to it, like I wasn't welcome and the stones themselves were watching me. It was a horrible feeling.

I had to give it to the piper. He entranced the guards to unlock the gate, and then fled down here on his own. That showed either a great deal of fortitude on his part, or it showed how fearsome Brindar could be. Either way, I was amazed that he didn't turn around, flee back to the gates and throw himself on the dwarves' mercy.

The air was thick and heavy, the way it would be in a house that was closed up for years on end, only worse. The ventilation that was in place for Underworld obviously didn't spread this far, and my footsteps sounded dull as I walked along, gun in hand.

I had nothing to set the gun to, of course, since I had no idea what I was walking into. But it could still do a lot of damage to most things. My sword was loose in its scabbard as well, as a backup measure in case I needed it.

The buildings down here were old, older than anything I ever saw before. They stretched out before me, looming suddenly out of the darkness into the light from my lantern. Grundir had shown me how to light the thing, and it was more than it appeared. The black stone glowed softly, but could be made to shine more brightly simply by blowing on it. Once it was blazing, it would continue to for hours, fading slowly until you blew on it again. Each time, it consumed a small piece of itself as it lit the way, but Grundir assured me that I had hours before it would be completely gone. Still, he advised me to keep it as dim as I could, since the brighter it glowed, the faster it used itself up.

Behind me, the light from Underworld, and that massive chandelier hung under the Guild Hall disappeared, and I was alone in the dark. I blew on the rock in the lantern, enough to get a little more light and see the entire road from side to side. Then I stopped, to fight off a sense of despair and uselessness.

The Deep was a massive place, with buildings piled on top of each other, lanes running between them, and roads that suddenly opened into large empty areas. It led from cavern to cavern, some with wide passages leading from one to the other, and others with narrow, constricting ways, obviously meant to bottle up an attacker and provide the place with a defense.

Brindar could be anywhere in here. My only thought was that the piper would have been feeling the same sense of bewilderment as I was, and therefore, he may have stayed on the main road, to try to avoid becoming lost in the dark warren. Hopefully, Brindar would have thought the same, and followed the road himself.

I was walking for a good hour or more, time was hard to keep track of here, when I heard the whispers. On the edge of my hearing, like children trying to win at a game of hide and seek, only these voices sounded sinister.

I laughed, my voice ringing out into the gloom of the Deep, and I wondered how long it was since that particular noise was heard here. But I couldn't help myself. Grundir told me that dwarves who came here and returned spoke of these whispers, and were driven mad by them. That very well may have been true; they were unnerving. But those dwarves never heard and survived the cry of a banshee. In comparison to that, they were simply annoying.

My laughter cut them off, and they died off without another sound.

"If that's the worst you've got," I said aloud, "then you may as well call it quits."

There was no answer, so, with my spirits suddenly buoyed, I continued on.

I passed another large, ancient building on my right. Not nearly the size of the Guild Hall, it looked as if it could have been someone's palatial estate when the Deep was a city of renown. Now, it stood empty, its dark windows opening onto only blackness. Or at least that's what it looked like at first glance. But as I walked along, I saw what looked like a darker shadow move in one of the ground floor windows.

I raised the lantern and walked over, but whatever it was, if anything, it was no longer there. There was nothing inside, showing in the pool of light, but blank walls and an empty stone floor. Stepping back, I looked up, and sure enough, now there was a figure in one of the upper floor windows, barely visible against the darkness within. It appeared to be watching me, even as I looked at it.

After standing there for a moment, the figure showed no sign of moving. I stepped back, keeping my eye on it the whole time. It still didn't move and I began to doubt that I was truly seeing what I thought I was. Since it appeared to be no immediate threat, if it was there, I turned and continued on my way. If whatever haunted the Deep used ghostly whispers and dark apparitions as its weapons, then I would have no problem other than finding Brindar in this maze. I had seen worse.

Which is always the type of thought that leads to the greater threat arriving, just so that the universe can laugh in your face and show you how little you really know.

Behind me came the sound of a door creaking open. The doors in all the buildings were carved from stone, the medium of choice for the dwarves. As such, it didn't creak as a long neglected wooden door might. Instead, it made a grinding noise, sounding like bones being crushed beneath a wheel.

I turned, and that black shape from the window, or one like it, was coming out. Now I could see it more clearly, and while I wasn't comforted, I also wasn't overly worried. It looked like a dwarf. He was short, only coming up to about four feet, and stocky, with thick, powerful arms and legs. Other than that, I couldn't tell much else, as he was still in silhouette, except for the war hammer that he carried. The head of it gleamed from the light of my lantern, large, heavy looking, with a flat crushing surface on one side, and a wicked looking spike on the other.

I pulled out my gun and said, "dwarf", brought it up to aim, and fired. The report was loud in the cavern that we were in, but the little, metal ball flew straight and true, and took him squarely in the chest. There was a puff of dust, the dwarf staggered back a step or two, and then continued to come at me, showing no ill effects from the shot.

"What the…" I began, then raised the gun and shot him again. To the same effect. And again. And once more. Each time, the same small puff of dust telling me that I hit him, the same step back, and the same relentless approach.

Now it was within range of my lantern, which I still held in my left hand, and I could see that what I thought was a silhouette was actually how it looked. It was shaped like a dwarf, and carried a dwarven weapon, but it was utterly, completely black. Dark eyes glinted in the light of my lantern and it chuckled evilly as it came near.

I stuck my gun back into my belt and pulled my sword. Whatever this thing was, it wasn't a dwarf, and since the little, metal balls didn't do it much harm, it was time to see what sharp edged steel could do.

It came close, hefted the hammer and swung, but I was already moving. I dodged the swing and moved in myself, sword flashing out and caught the thing on the right shoulder. My blade bit deep with a sound like an axe hitting wood. But it did damage. The thing hissed, black crooked teeth showing when its lips pulled back, and a black liquid oozed from the cut.

It pulled back, reset itself and tried another swing with the hammer, this time aiming the spike at my foot, trying to pin me to ground. I jumped back, let the blow fall, then lunged in again, chopping down on the hands holding the hammers shaft. It hissed again, dropping the hammer and backing away, cradling its damaged hands to its chest.

Whatever it was, it wasn't much in the fighting department. That one may not have given me much trouble, although the viciousness of its swings did speak of a horrible strength. But now, I could hear others, all around me. The soft whispers as they spoke to one another in a language I didn't understand and suspected was long dead. The grinding of stone doors opening and the rasp of weapons being dragged along the streets.

A good fighter knows his limitations. Without my gun doing much good, I was severely outnumbered, no matter how good a swordsman I thought myself to be. It was time to do the only thing that made sense, and run.

It's not easy to run through a dark, underground city at the best of times. The lantern swayed as I ran and caused the shadows to lengthen and shorten crazily around me. It was very hard to try to stay oriented, but I thought I was mostly staying on the main road. It did cross my mind that maybe I should take a side street, or duck into one of the buildings, but I didn't want to get lost, or hemmed in, so I stuck with what I was doing.

Then I tripped over the foot. When I say a foot, I mean exactly that. It wasn't a foot attached to a leg that was stuck out to trip me up and cause me to lose my balance. No. This was a foot, clad in a bright, green boot, that ended in a ragged stump shortly above the ankle. It was laying there, right in the middle of the road, and in my haste, I never saw it. Not until I went sprawling, barely holding on to my lantern, but losing my sword, and turned to look.

I've seen a lot of horrible things in my life, including body parts that were no longer attached to their rightful owners. But there was something about that foot, laying there, in its bright colors, down here in the Deep that got to me. Cold shivers ran down my spine, and I bent down and groped blindly for my sword, my eyes glued to that foot like I was afraid it was suddenly going to come to life and start hopping toward me.

And then something grabbed my hand, and the lantern went out. I made a noise, I'm not afraid to admit it...well, actually I screamed. A high pitched, warbling scream like a little girl whose doll came to life and asked her to play in a scratchy old ladies voice. It rang out, echoing off the buildings and definitely giving my position away.

"Damn it, Grandfather, shut up!" a hoarse voice whispered, and a thick hand clamped down over my mouth, silencing me.

I got control of myself and stopped the racket I was making. "Bbbuunnnrrr?" I said.

"Yeah, it's me," Brindar whispered. "Now keep quiet and follow me."

"I can't" I whispered back. "I can't see a thing!"

He sighed. "I forgot. Humans and their eyesight. Never mind. Here, put your hand on my shoulder."

He took my hand and placed it on his broad shoulder, and we started away. I couldn't see a single thing down there. Not a building, the street beneath my feet, Brindar's back, or even my own hand. I'm not sure how long we walked, moving slowly to try to keep the noise to a minimum, but it felt like it was hours. The blackness, for that's what it was, pure blackness, pressed in on me, and I flinched and hesitated with every step, sure that I would walk smack into a barrier, or tumble down a pit into the abyss.

Finally, I heard a door being opened, Brindar helped me step over a threshold, the door closed, and a light appeared. I gasped with relief, my eyes drawn to the softly glowing stone of my lantern.

Brindar stood in front of me, solid and dependable as ever, except for the dirty bandage wrapped around his head. I was glad to see him, but I have to say, I was even more glad that my mission was accomplished and now we could get out of here.

"What are you doing here, Grandfather?" he asked me.

"Looking for you! I came to find out if you had seen any other odd events occurring in the city, hoping that it might help lead to whoever's been attacking us. But then I was told you chased one of those pipers down here and that was it. No one had heard from you since."

"Yeah, well, you saw what happened to the piper," he said. "So, no worries about him. Why you though? Why did you come?"

I shrugged, suddenly uncomfortable.

"I don't know," I mumbled. "You know, you're a Nuisance Man, we have to stick together, and friends and stuff…"

"Hmmph, well, yeah. Thanks then. For coming, I mean…"

If it was possible for a situation as dire as ours to become more awkward, it had.

"Anyway," I said, forcing more levity into my voice, "I found you, so we can go. Let's get out of here."

"That's not going to be that easy. There's a lot of them out there, and they're smart. They know our only way out is back to the gate to Underworld and they've got us cut off."

"Great. Well, there are two of us. I hurt one with my sword, so I'm thinking that big axe of yours can hack right through them."

"It can. But the one you hurt? Did it make a hissing noise?"

"Yeah, and it dropped the hammer it was holding. Why?"

"It wasn't hissing in pain. It was laughing. They're tough. And yeah, Biter can take pieces off of them, but they can take a lot of damage before they're down for good. There's too many of them for me to get them all before they swarm me."

"That's not good," I said, pausing to think it over. "What are those things anyway?"

Brindar moved away and sat with his back against the wall. I suddenly felt how tired I was, and copied him, sinking down against the opposite wall.

"They're called Dokkalfar, and they're as much of a legend as this place is. Some say they're related to us, but I'd hate to think that was true. Regardless, they live down here, deep in the earth, deeper than we go even, and they never go up into the sunlight. I don't know if that would kill them or if they just hate it, but they're made for the darkness and the deep places."

"But what are they doing here? Did the pipers call them up too?"

"I doubt it. I think they were what happened to the Deep all those centuries ago. They attacked and drove the dwarves out. Over time, the memory of this place, and the Dokkalfar kind of faded. Who would want to remember them?"

"Until you guys accidently uncovered them."

"Looks that way. Now what?"

"Now I still think we need to get out of here. Any chance of sneaking past them?"

He shrugged. "Doubt it. From what I can tell, they can see in the dark like it's bright daylight. And they have excellent hearing too. We can try, but neither one of us are exactly built for stealth."

I resented that! I was pretty lithe and agile, if I do say so myself. As long as I didn't trip over something in the dark, like an errant appendage for instance.

"Alright," I conceded. "Sneaking isn't going to work. Still, we can't stay down here until they find us, or we starve."

The squealing noise of a sharp blade being dragged along stone silenced us. It sounded like it was still down the street, but it was moving this way. Brindar reached out and cupped his hand around the stone in the lantern, extinguishing it. Neat trick, that.

We sat silent and stiff as the noise came closer, growing in volume as it did. It paused for a moment, outside the door to the room we were in, and I slowly eased myself up the wall, my sword in my hand. The door latch rattled briefly, and then stilled, and the noise started up again, moving away.

I breathed out a sigh of relief and sank back down. Brindar blew the stone back to life again, and gently set Biter back down beside him.

"Those things are seriously creepy," I said.

He nodded, his gaze cast down on the floor in front of him.

"What happened?" I asked, indicating the bandage wrapped around his head.

"A couple got too close. I took them, but one got through with his own axe. Nothing serious, a scalp wound, but you know how they are. I was half blinded by the blood before I could get away."

We sat in silence, gathering our thoughts, before Brindar spoke up again.

"What about your gun? That should do some damage to them."

"Maybe, now that I know what they are. But I can't re-set it until tomorrow."

He looked quizzical at this, and I realized that he didn't know how my gun worked, or the limitations of the thing. I filled him in, on how it would do the maximum amount of damage to whatever I set it to, but that I could only do it once a day.

"What's it set on now?" he asked.

"Dwarf," I replied. "Because that's what I thought was coming at me. If I knew it wasn't, I would have left it unset."

"It needs to be a full day after you set it?"

"No, right after midnight. Theoretically, I could set it to bugbear say at a couple of minutes before, shoot one, and then reset it to goblin a few minutes later. But then I'm stuck on goblin for that whole next day."

"So after midnight, you reset it to Dokkalfar and we start hacking and shooting our way out of here. You take out as many as you can from a distance, I handle them when they get close."

"Sounds great," I said. "The only problem is that I don't know when midnight is. I can try, but I have no way of knowing if it worked until I shoot one. The gun doesn't give me any sign."

"You forget," and here he smiled, "you're with a dwarf. We might not be quite as comfortable underground as these bastards, but we're still pretty good. Midnight isn't far away. A couple of hours. Let's wait a few to be safe, and then we'll come out blazing."

I nodded. "Sounds good. Rest up in the meantime, I guess."

He settled back and regarded me.

"How'd you get that thing anyway?" he asked me.

"It's a long story," I replied. "I'll have to tell you another time. What about yours?"

He glanced over at the huge axe propped against the wall next to him.

"Biter? It was handed down to me. But yeah...long story too."

I nodded, understanding. Sometimes, it's not the right circumstances.

I dozed off occasionally over the next few hours, each time jerking awake to the sound of one of the Dokkalfar passing by. On those occasions, Brindar would extinguish the light from the lantern and we would sit silently in the dark until they moved on.

Finally, it was time.

"Here's the plan," Brindar said. "We'll leave the lantern off and go as quietly as we can, hugging the walls. I'll lead you. I can't see down here as well as they can, but well enough. If we come up on any, I'll take them out with Biter quick, before they can warn the others. Eventually, they're going to see us, light or no. Then, we'll turn the lantern up as far as it will go. Those things go pretty bright, so we'll be able to see for a good distance. It will draw them to us, but you start taking them out as soon as you spot them. We make a break for it then, and hopefully, we make it through."

I took a breath, and said, "Dokkalfar" to my gun, hoping that Brindar was right about the time passage. I wasn't thrilled with the idea of walking through the dark, being led along like a child, but Brindar's plan had merit. The longer we could go without drawing them all down on us, the better.

He extinguished the light and I wrapped my hand into his cloak, getting a good grip on it so that I wouldn't fall behind. In the event that he needed to move quickly, I would let go, and stay near the wall of whatever building we were in front of until he finished. Then, he'd collect me and we'd move on again.

From the moment the light went out, I hated the plan. I felt helpless and couldn't stop straining my ears, trying desperately to hear one of the Dokkalfar approaching. As we moved out, I saw the flaw in our plan. Brindar was in the lead, could see, and knowing him, I was sure that he was attentive and vigilant, looking in all directions at once. But what if one of them came up behind me? Would he see them in time, or would he only know when I pitched forward into him, with an axe blade buried in my spine?

My back itched and burned the whole time we walked, waiting for the blow. I kept turning my head, trying to get my ear pointed in the right direction to give me some sort of warning. The further we walked the more the feeling of dreadful anticipation increased, until I thought I might go crazy if there wasn't light soon.

Suddenly, Brindar stopped, and putting out a hand, moved me to the side until I was pressed against a wall, my eyes staring sightlessly out into the darkness. He left me then and I heard a soft grunt, a sound like a knife cutting into cold meat, and a thud. A moment later, and he was back, taking my hand and putting it on his shoulder again.

"One down," he whispered. "But I think there's a bunch more of them up ahead."

"I'm almost relieved. I don't know how much more of this darkness I can take."

"Hang in there."

He moved off again and I followed, still sure that my back was about to be split open at any moment. We only went a few paces when he stopped.

"Shit," he said quietly.

"What is it?"

"You're getting your wish. There's about ten of them up the street from here, and no way to get around them. If I didn't know better, I'd think they knew we were here."

Then we heard the noise behind us, closer than we would have liked. It was a soft, hissing noise, the same sound that Brindar told me those things made when they were laughing.

"Jigs up!" he said. "Keep your eyes averted!"

He drew in a deep breath and blew as hard as he could on the stone in the lantern, which flared into a sudden brilliance. It was like a god dropped down into the Deep carrying a sun with him. The world exploded into light and the Dokkalfar that was coming up behind us threw his hands up in front of his face and let out an unworldly howl.

Brindar moved faster than me, and his axe took off the things head in mid-howl. The noise was cut short, only to be picked up a moment later by the ones up the street, and echoed back from others further away.

But I did exactly as Brindar said and kept my sight focused away from the lantern as it flared up, so I wasn't blinded by the intensity. It was horribly bright and threw the shadows back for a long way up the street. I could clearly see the Dokkalfar starting toward us, but almost wished I couldn't.

They looked like a gross parody of the dwarves. They were the same size and general shape, short, but wide and solidly built. But they were completely black, from head to toe. Their hair was greasy, ebony waves that lay flat and unmoving on their heads, and hung from their faces in tangled beards. Their eyes were flat and black, and reflected the light from the lantern so that they seemed to glow a sickly gray color. When they looked at me and howled, I could see black tongues moving like slugs over blocky, black teeth. They were horrible to look at, and I didn't wonder that they chose to stay deep underground, hiding in the dark.

But now they were between me and freedom from this place. I raised my gun, sighted on the one closest to me, and pulled the trigger. There was a loud bang, and a glow as the little, metal ball sped off, round and blazing with a brilliant light of its own.

It hit the Dokkalfar in the chest and the effect this time was much more satisfactory. Instead of the puff of dust, there was almost an explosion, and the dark thing only had time to look down at the smoking hole that punched completely through it, before it crumpled to the floor, dead before it hit.

The others paused when the first one fell, and I took advantage. I pulled the trigger again, and again, and two more dropped, their bodies ruined by the luminescent balls that hit them. I began to laugh, feeling that now we were home free, and nothing would stop us from getting to the gate. Certainly not the Dokkalfar, now that my gun was set to kill.

The spear came in from the darkness, which was quite a way off. It was only that fact which saved me, I'm sure of it. If I had forgotten, I was suddenly reminded of the strength of these things.

It was an amazing throw, and only missed me by a fraction of an inch.

It was enough for me to turn, scan the darkness and fire off a shot. I missed, but by the light of the passing metal ball, I could see one of them scrambling behind a building down a side street.

"Great," I said, "they throw things! Let's go!"

We took off running, which wasn't great for aiming the gun, but was better than staying there to be sitting ducks. As we fled, Dokkalfar would jump from windows, or out of streets or doorways that we passed. Brindar cut them down whenever one was close and I shot them from a distance. We could hear the sound of pursuit getting closer, since we needed to constantly stop to fight and the ones chasing could keep coming.

It felt like we ran and fought for hours, and I lost count of the number that we killed, yet they kept coming. They blocked our way, and we barreled into them, slaughtering them and taking wounds ourselves. They threw spears, knives, and axes, and we dodged and took more wounds. They jumped onto us from overhead as we passed beneath windows and we threw them off, killed them, and took more wounds.

If it wasn't for Brindar, I wouldn't have made it out of there. I like to think he would say the same about me, but in the end, I know I was leaning on him more heavily than he was on me. I thought we were done for when we saw a light ahead. The gate was within sight. Our breath heaving in our throats, we fought on, knowing that soon we must be heard by those beyond the gate, and surely, they would come and help us.

They did. I saw the gate open and a horde of dwarves pour through it, led by a large figure. Moments later Grundir grabbed me and was pulling me back toward safety, while two other dwarves did the same with Brindar.

"Easy, lads," he rumbled. "You've done enough. We'll stop them here."

In the end, it was a close thing. Without my gun, and Brindar's axe, it was a much harder fight. Axe and hammer blows only slowed the Dokkalfar down, while their weapons did horrible damage to the dwarves. They were pushed back, taking causalities, until it looked like they would be overrun.

But when the first Dokkalfar crossed into the pool of light cast by that enormous chandelier hung in the Guild Hall arch, it all changed. The candles flared up, brighter by far than the lantern had down below. The Dokkalfar screamed, threw their hands up and ran, back down into the Deep. The dwarves rallied, and followed, cutting them down as they fled, but going no further than the light thrown by the chandelier.

When the last Dokkalfar fled, the light slowly faded, and the dwarves withdrew with it, until they were all safely back through the gate, and it was securely locked once more.

Brindar and I were slumped against a wall, watching the battle unfold, trying to ready ourselves should we be needed if the Dokkalfar breached the gate. When it was over, and we weren't needed, we glanced at each other and smiled tiredly.

"We still have to compare notes," I said to him. "Something is still out there."

He nodded. "I know. Ale first. Then maybe a bandage or two. Then talk."

"Yeah," I agreed. In spite of everything that happened, his words got me thinking. What exactly did dwarven ale taste like?

## LOOK HOMEWARD, DEATH ANGEL

It turned out that dwarven ale was pretty good. It tasted a lot like the ale I was used to, only stronger, and earthier. I enjoyed it a lot, but only drank a couple, since I needed to get back home and let Lilly know that I was still alive.

Brindar and I compared notes, but he hadn't seen anything out of the ordinary either, other than the banshee and the pipers. That made three of us, when you included Raven, which I was pretty sure meant that those were the only attacks that had been launched. I was equally sure that they wouldn't be the last.

When I finally got home, it was to that weird mix of emotions that always happens when you've worried someone, but they're glad that you're safe. Lilly was furious that I was gone for so long, and been worried about what could have happened to me. She knew that I went into Underworld, which she was apparently already aware of, and that was it. But, when I told her what happened and how I helped get Brindar out of a jam, I was forgiven.

"I know this is your job, Duke," she told me. "It's dangerous, like mine is. But I wish we had a better way of keeping in contact."

I nodded, agreeing, but only half listening. It was still early in the day, but I was exhausted, and needed sleep badly. I kissed Lilly, told her that I promised I would talk to her more about it in a few hours, and was out before my head hit the pillow.

Those few hours turned into the rest of the night. By the time I woke up, it was early morning, for the world and not only for me, and the sun was barely starting to shine on the streets. I opened my eyes slowly, glad to be home in my own bed, and lying next to Lilly, who was still sleeping peacefully next to me.

She looked beautiful, as she always did, and not for the first time, it struck me how lucky I really was, and what a remarkable woman I had. My mother thought I was destined for greatness, thus the name Duke, and I don't know if this was what she had in mind, but if not, I think she would have been proud and happy to have Lilly for a daughter-in-law anyway.

Speaking of, I wasn't even sure where we were in terms of the wedding. We were three weeks away at this point and everything was still the same. I felt a twinge of guilt at that. Sure, I was told to stay out of the way and let the women handle it, and I was good with that. On the other hand, I didn't want to shirk my responsibilities either. Not for this. For other things, sure, no problem, but failing on this felt too much like failing her.

I slipped out of bed, tip-toed out of the room and down the stairs. Coffee was calling my name, and I was bound and determined to be a good host and answer it. Soon, I was installed in my favorite chair, near the hearth, sipping the hot brew and enjoying life.

Lilly came down a short time later, and since I heard her moving around, I had a cup ready and waiting for her when she did. She sipped it while she watched me preparing breakfast.

"You're up early," she said. "And making breakfast, too. What's the occasion?"

"No occasion. I thought you might like it."

She nodded, and moved to the table where I brought her a big plate of eggs, sausages and toasted bread. Taking a chair next to her, I tucked into my own plateful.

"Not bad," I said, my mouth still full, "if I do say so myself."

"Not bad, Grandfather," she said. "Who knew you had it in you?"

"Hey, I had to eat before I met you, you know."

"I thought you lived on ale and fried potatoes."

"No. Sometimes I made eggs too."

"It shows," she said, and wolfed down the rest of them.

Later on, we walked into the watchhouse together, even though I wasn't planning on taking anything off of the Board quite yet. Although my journey into the Deep didn't pay anything, I still got beat up pretty badly, so I was going to take a day or two to heal up.

"Sarge," I said, as we entered.

"Duke, Lilly," he answered. "Geez, Duke, you look like you've been run over by a carriage. What'd you do, piss off the wrong goblin again?"

"Good stuff, Sarge," I said. "That's why I come here. The sparkling wit. I leave here and go use the same jokes as part of a comic act. It kills them in the sticks."

"You two have fun," Lilly interrupted, giving me a peck on the cheek. "I'll be home later."

She started to walk off when a messenger came running full bore into the Watchhouse, and skidded to a stop in front of the desk. Whatever he had to say looked awfully important, but he couldn't get it out. Instead, he panted and wheezed, bending at the waist with his hands on his knees.

"Whoo…geesh…man oh man…"

And so on. The three of us watched him in amusement for a moment, and then Sarge spoke up.

"Alright, son. That should about do it. Deep breath, straighten up, and say what you came to say."

The messenger did as he was told.

"Yep, sorry," he was still out of breath, but was making a visible effort to pull it together. "Here it is. The guards at the gate are requesting that a senior officer come down with all haste."

We waited, but the messenger didn't say anything else.

"That's it?" Sarge asked, one eyebrow raised. "Send an officer down to the gates? Nothing else?"

"That was all, sir. It was all that I heard anyway. The Watchman shouted it at me, so there may have been more. I couldn't really tell. That's why I ran, you see. It sounded important."

"Wait a second," Lilly said. "Why did he shout it at you? Where was he?"

"He was in the guard shack, ma'am."

"Oh, then where were you?"

"I was right there, ma'am. Standing near the doorway, if you see what I mean."

"I don't," she replied. "If he was in the guard shack, and you were right near him, why did he shout?"

"He didn't at that time, ma'am. That came later. When he was running away."

The three of us looked at each other.

"Running away?" Sarge said. "What do you mean he was running away?"

The messenger shrugged. "Can't say, sir. It may have something to do with the knight at the gates, demanding entry. He was a big fellow, and scared me half to death too, I don't mind saying."

"I'm going down there," Lilly said. "Let's go, Duke."

She didn't have to tell me twice. I was pretty sure that this was going to be attack number three. Normally, I would have said that it was nothing to worry about. If Lilly was going there personally and I was there with her, then the problem should be easily dealt with. But I had seen enough recently to know that that probably wasn't going to be the case.

The trip from the watchhouse to the gates isn't a long one, and under normal circumstances, we could have made it in about fifteen minutes. Today it was taking longer, since we needed to fight through the throngs of people that were flowing in the other direction, fleeing from the area around the gates to get deeper into the city. Another sign that something was definitely amiss.

"Oh, forget this!" Lilly said, and fired up her magic. Whenever she does this, a transformation comes over her. Her hair will frizz out and stand up in a cloud around her head, sometimes almost seeming to move on its own accord. Her eyes go completely black, so that they are dark orbs in her face, no sign of the whites at all. And most disturbingly, sparks begin to dance among her fingertips, leaving the impression that if you weren't careful, you'd be in for a nasty shock.

Even in their fear, few people could ignore the sight of a necromancer in full display of their power, and today wasn't the exception. They parted before us like a huge invisible hand came down and pushed people to the side. Adults grabbed the hands of children and pulled them away, to not attract the attention of Lilly.

I was perfectly happy to stay right behind her and let her take the lead all the way to the gates. As it turned out, she didn't need to keep it up for that long. After a few more blocks, the crowds thinned out. Apparently, most of those that were going to flee already did.

Finally, we made it to the gates, which were closed, the portcullis lowered and locked. The Watchmen that should have been at the gates were no longer there, and their shack stood empty and abandoned.

"Dereliction of duty," Lilly said. "I'm going to have to report them."

"Sure," I replied. "But before that, can we maybe see what it was that scared them that badly?"

There were stairs that led up the inside of the wall, so that you could get to the top and have a look around. Normally, they were open for anyone to climb, and a lot of people did exactly that, to see the local scenery and show their out of town relatives the sights. You got a pretty good view of the city from up there.

But, if the gates were closed, you could also see straight down and tell who or what was at the door.

The day was bright and the sun beat down on the walls and the ground below, warming everything up nicely. If you looked up into the clear, blue sky, you'd swear that there couldn't be a thing wrong in the world. A day this perfect wouldn't allow it. Somewhere, the flowers were blooming, water sparkled in streams, and the lovers of the world mooned over each other in bliss.

And then you looked down, at the figure near the gates to the city, and it all changed.

The flowers in your mind wilted, died, and rotted in seconds, leaving a slimy, foul smelling mess. The waters in the brooks stilled, stagnated and dead fish floated belly up, fouling them even further as they too rotted. The lovers' expressions of devotion to each other faded, became leers and snarls, and sharp knives were fingered behind their backs.

All of that and more ran through my mind as I looked down. Whatever it was, it was scary. Looking at Lilly, I saw that she was pale, her eyes large, and she was trembling. I moved closer, and put my arm around her.

"What is it?" I asked, unable to tear my eyes from the armored figure.

"A Death Knight," she whispered. "By the gods, Duke, it's a Death Knight."

I didn't know what a Death Knight was, and didn't think I wanted to. He sat on a black horse before the gates, clad completely in plate mail armor, also painted black. He wore a huge helm that covered his entire face, shaped like a snarling beast with huge, curled horns at each temple. At his side hung a long sword, and a morningstar hung from his horse's saddle, within easy reach.

But those weren't his most potent weapons, I could tell that. Not by a long shot. His most lethal weapon was fear, and he used it like an expert swordsman wielded their blade.

He must have felt us staring down at him. He looked up, directly at us, two glowing red spots shining through the eye slit in his helm.

"Open the gates," he boomed, his voice was deep, hollow and very loud. "Open the gates so that I may return to my home."

There was nothing in the world that I wanted to do less than to open those gates and let that thing into the city. And yet, I felt a strange compulsion to do exactly that. My legs almost started moving of their own accord.

"Not a chance," Lilly responded. In comparison to the Death Knight, her voice sounded high and strained, with a slight waver to it. Still, she refused him, and that act alone gave a little more steel to my spine.

"Open the gates," the Death Knight boomed out again. "Open the gates so that I may return to my home."

"Get bent!" Lilly yelled, and started casting a spell, her hair frizzing, eyes blackening…I moved away before the sparks came.

"Three times must I ask," the Death Knight said. "Open the gates. Open the gates that I may return to my home."

Lilly didn't bother responding this time. She chanted out nonsense words, to me at least, and a black globe, shot through with veins of gold, formed between her hands. She moved as if she was molding it, forming it into a perfect sphere. Then, she raised it above her head, spitting and crackling with magical energy, and prepared to hurl it onto the Death Knight below.

The Death Knight looked up, raised his left hand, with two fingers extended up, the rest curled into his gloved palm, and spoke a word. The word hurt. It flew from his lips into my ears and I thought that my head was going to split in two. My vision blurred and went red, and I sank to my knees. And I only got the edge of it.

Whatever the spell was, it hit Lilly like a ton of bricks. She gasped, and the orb she held above her head winked out of existence as if it had never been. Gasping, she collapsed to her knees, retching and heaving.

Below us, another word came, in the same foul, dark language as the first one. There was a rumble, and a crash, and the gates fell to the ground, followed by the portcullis, its iron bars twisted into a tangled heap of scrap.

I yanked my gun from my belt, croaked, "Death Knight" at it, and raised it as the Death Knight appeared through the ruins of the gate on our side of the wall.

He looked up again, only this time, his gaze was focused on me. It was all I could do to continue to look at him, to try to aim and pull the trigger.

"Ah," he said, and his voice was quieter now, more like a groan coming from something buried, but awake, inside a crypt. "Griefmaker. There you are."

He raised his hand and said another word, and I pulled the trigger.

Nothing happened. The gun didn't fire. Never, in all the years that I owned it, did that happen. Not once. I pulled the trigger over and over, desperate now, and still nothing happened.

The Death Knight laughed, a sound that sent more shivers through me, and turned his back and rode on. As he moved away, he became cloudy, and then started to fade, until he disappeared from sight entirely. The noise of his horse's hooves faded slowly away as well, until it was as if he was never there. The only evidence that he had been was the ruined gates, and the vile feeling that persisted from when he looked at me.

"What the hell was that, Lilly?" I asked, feeling like I was on the edge of panic.

"I told you," she groaned, leaning back against the parapet. "It was a Death Knight. This is bad, Duke. Really bad."

No kidding, I thought, but chose not to say it out loud.

We collected ourselves and slowly made our way down the steps inside the wall. The gate lay in total ruin at our feet, and there was no sign of the Watchmen, or anyone else, returning.

"Lilly," I said. "Did you hear what that thing said? When I tried to shoot it?"

"No, I was busy trying not to heave my guts out. What'd it say?"

"It said, and I quote, 'ah, Griefmaker, there you are'. Then he said another word in that scary language, and my gun didn't work."

She stopped walking and turned to me.

"That's not good either, Duke. Nothing has stopped your gun, not even the Fomorii. Does it work now?"

"Good question." I pulled it from my belt and turned back to the ruined gate. When I pulled the trigger, there was a loud report, and the little, metal ball sped out, kicking dust up from the ground where it hit.

"Yep, it works now. But he did something to it. And he called it, or me, Griefmaker, like it was a name."

"I'm pretty sure he wasn't talking to you, Duke. No offense, but I don't see why he would have been. No, he recognized your gun, and had a spell ready to deal with it."

"That's very disturbing," I said. "And what was up with that having to ask three times and wanting the gates open to come home stuff?"

She shrugged. "I have no idea. Honestly, Death Knights are like bogeymen for necromancers. Something that's used to scare us. I didn't believe they even really existed until now."

"Not something that you're going to banish back to the netherworld, then?"

"No, I don't think so. I think he's stronger than I am. A lot."

"Now what?"

"Now we go back to the watchhouse. You let Sarge know what's going on, I'll talk to my bosses."

Sarge wasn't too happy to find out that two of his officers deserted their posts, but after listening to what I told him, and filling him in on what Lilly said, his anger cooled off. He sent some men out to see if they could find the deserters and to spread the word to be on the lookout for the Death Knight, but to be aware of how dangerous it was and not to attack it.

For her part, Lilly disappeared down the stairs to the necromancer's area immediately. But it wasn't long before she came back up, fuming.

"Those idiots!" she stormed. "Unbelievable!"

"What's going on?" I asked.

"They don't believe me! They think it must have been something else and that I'm covering for getting my butt kicked. There was even some suggestion that I take a few days off!"

I was stunned. Lilly was always fiercely loyal to the Watch and had risked her life on several occasions in the performance of her duties.

"How could they say that?" I said. "Don't they know the things you've done?"

She deflated.

"Thanks, Duke. But you have to say that. Plus…I guess I can kind of see their point. They don't *want* to believe that a Death Knight is loose in the city. They wouldn't know how to deal with it."

"I believe you," Sarge said. "And we'll watch for him. But from what Duke has told me, it's going to be more than my folks can handle."

"Don't let them approach him!" she said. "Not even close. If they see him, you have to get word to me. I don't know what I can do either, but I'll be working on something."

When I heard Lilly talk like this, and heard the iron in her voice, I didn't know if I should be more worried about her, or the Death Knight. Then I recalled the ease with which he destroyed the gates, taken us both out, and shut down my Ultimate Weapon. I was definitely more worried about Lilly.

We said our goodbyes to Sarge and walked out, intending to go home, get some rest and hope that our headaches would pass. But we didn't go more than a block when we heard the noise of horse hooves walking slowly past on the cobblestone street. There was nothing there, no sign of an actual horse, just the sound of its passing. It started out quietly, but steadily increased, until it rang out as clear as a normal horse.

The air seemed to shimmer as we watched, and the Death Knight slowly came into view, appearing from nothingness. He didn't so much as glance at us, instead, he rode straight on, directly toward the watchhouse.

He stopped his horse there and dismounted. It was only then that I really took note of the beast for the first time. Black, with a black saddle and reins, it was a large horse, the Death Knights helmet only coming to his jaw. But that wasn't the most disturbing thing. The horse was obviously dead, and had been for some time. Its eyes were gone, leaving two empty holes in its skull, covered over by tattered flesh. The teeth showed through the side of its jaw in places, and bones showed clearly through the thin skin along the rest of its body. Yet it stood strong and tall, the remnants of a once proud steed, animated in a mockery of the life it once had.

As for the Death Knight, he turned to the Watchhouse and raised his arms, his voice starting a chant, low and hollow from inside his helm.

"Not happening," I heard Lilly say, and she raised her own hands, the sparks dancing, the hair flying, and her eyes black orbs.

The Death Knight paid no attention to her, so his back was turned when Lilly unleashed her own spell. It sped away from her, invisible, but with a buzzing sound as it cut through the air, like a swarm of angry hornets. It hit the Death Knight in the small of the back, causing him to stumble forward, his arms coming down and his chant interrupted.

But that was the only effect. He turned and looked at us, and again, all thoughts of anything pure and good in the world were corrupted and turned to filth.

"I was hoping that would do more," Lilly said. "It would have cut right through anyone else."

The Death Knight simply regarded us for a moment, and then laughed, that same mocking laugh he used before.

"Little wizard," his voice boomed out. "You think the realm of death is yours to command, but you are wrong. Now witness the power of a true master of death."

He pointed at Lilly, and said another word in that horrible language. I lunged, trying to get to her, tackle her to the ground and out of the path of whatever spell was coming. But it moved too fast.

Lilly gasped and bent over, as if she had been punched in the stomach. That was all. She didn't fly through the air, or start bleeding, or vomiting, or anything. But when she straightened, I could see a horrible loss on her face.

"Lilly," I said, trying to keep my voice calm, "what is it?"

"It's gone, Duke," she whispered, her eyes wide and staring, returned to their normal blue.

"What's gone?"

"My magic. He cut me off. I can still feel it, but it's out of reach…like a tease…"

The Death Knight laughed and turned from us, dismissing us from his thoughts. He raised his arms high, and started chanting again.

What the hell, I needed to try. I pulled my gun and aimed, squeezing the trigger as I did. Nothing. Again, nothing happened, and the gun refused to fire. I didn't expect anything else, but it was worth a shot.

Instead, it was time for sword work. I stuck the gun back into my belt, drew my sword and charged. I fared no better than Lilly's spell.

The Death Knight stood with his back to me, and I ran in, swinging as I came. My sword whipped around, and crashed into the side of his helm, a blow that should have knocked him sideways at the very least, and removed his head if I was lucky. It did nothing of the sort.

Instead, I yelped as my sword stopped dead, as if I swung it as hard as I could at a large stone, only with less effect. There were no chips or splinters that went flying, and in the brief glimpse I got, I didn't so much as put a scratch on him.

But there was an effect on me. After my blow fell, there was a flash of light and I was thrown back, landing in a heap several paces away. I picked myself up, groaning, only to see that my sword was now a smoking ruin, the metal pitted and corroded, like it had been buried underground for decades, and then burned in a forge.

"Stop, Duke," Lilly said, moving to my side. "We can't beat him. Not like this."

It infuriated me, but she was right. Instead, we could only watch as he continued his spell casting.

The watchhouse started to change, as well as the buildings that surrounded it on either side. The walls turned to stone and grew, forming towers on each end. All up and down the block, the buildings that held the Watch, businesses, taverns and homes were swallowed up, or replaced, and a dark keep formed in their places.

Where the watchhouse once stood, was now the entrance to the keep, the gates dark wood, thick and sturdy. They opened at the Death Knight's gesture, and I could see a courtyard beyond, where once other buildings had been. It was a dead place, with weeds and skeletal trees growing, and a fog hovering above the ground. A cold wind came from there, like breath from a suddenly opened tomb.

The Death Knight mounted his horse, rode forward without a glance in our direction, and entered what we could only imagine was his home. The gates swung shut behind him, and all was still.

A new keep suddenly formed in the middle of Capital City, rivaling the castle of His Majesty on the hill. But that wasn't my main concern at the moment. Instead, I was much more worried about Lilly, and about everyone else caught inside.

I managed to get Lilly home, glad that I was with her. She seemed to be in a daze, letting me lead her along and not saying a word. She looked around her with an expression like she had never seen the world before. Once we were home, I got her settled into a chair and brought her a cup of hot tea.

"Are you okay?" I asked her.

She nodded. "I think so. It's …it's hard, Duke. I've been able to touch magic my whole life, ever since I can remember. That's how it works for a lot of us. It's something we're born with. But now, it's like…I don't know…like someone removed my sight, or hearing. It's hard to explain."

"No, you're doing fine. But the real question is, what can we do about it? How can we get it back?"

"I don't know. I really don't. I've never even heard of this happening to anyone. I told you that this was going to be bad."

"Yeah, you did," I said. "But we'll figure something out."

She didn't answer me. She only sat and sipped her tea quietly.

Of course, the first thing that I did was go to see Petal's people. They all adored Lilly and credited her with getting them away from Fogwell and his Fun Fair. When I explained to them that she was in trouble, they came up immediately and saw her.

"Pretty pretty lady hurt?" Petal asked her, and wrapped her tiny arms as far as she could around Lilly's neck. Lilly actually smiled at that, a little.

The Brownies looked her over and cast spells, singing in those rapid high-pitched voices that they have. I was sure this was the answer, considering the natural power that they have. But in the end, they had to admit defeat also. Through the translators that the Watch wizards cooked up, they told us that they couldn't even tell what was wrong, let alone how to fix it.

I thanked them for trying, and with many a backward glance and well-wishes, they returned to their home in the basement. Petal stayed for a while, sitting quietly on Lilly's shoulder, one hand wrapped around a lock of her hair. But after a time, she too left, and Lilly and I were alone again.

"Thanks for trying, Duke," she told me. "It was a good thought."

"It's only the first," I replied. "I'm not through yet."

But the truth was, I didn't know what else to do. If Death Knight magic could stump Brownie magic, where else could we turn? And if Lilly was cut off from her power, what chance did I have against that thing?

There were no answers, at least not tonight. It had been a long day, and a hard one, so despite our worries, Lilly and I turned in, hoping that the light of day would illuminate a way forward.

It didn't. Not really anyway. If anything, the light of day was pretty dingy. It broke gray and overcast, and we weren't sure if it was going to rain, or if it was due to the presence of the Death Knight. Either way, it was a yucky day.

We took a walk to the site of the watchhouse, hoping to see a change for the better. But if anything, it was worse. The keep was now fully solid, built of strong, dark gray stone, stacked high with tight joints. The gate was firmly shut, blocking any attempt to enter. When we walked around the block, the wall continued, all the way around it, tall and strong, totally supplanting anything that was there previously.

Above the keep, dark birds circled high in the sky, never venturing far from the tower that now rose up, silhouetted against the gloomy clouds. The keep itself was silent, but it wasn't peaceful, it was more a brooding, menacing kind of quiet.

"I don't know, Duke," Lilly said, after we circled the entire building. "I have no idea how we're going to get in there."

"Get in there? Why would we want to do that?"

"Because Sarge is in there. And all of my coworkers, and who knows who else. What about all the people in the other buildings? Since there's no sign of them anywhere, I'm betting that they're in there."

"Oh, of course. Yeah, good point. We do need a plan then."

We were standing there, still staring at the place when a voice came from behind us.

"To do that, you'll need your magic back, won't you?"

We spun around, ready to face a new threat, but there was no need.

The women gathered behind us were all dressed in black, each and every one. But the styles differed. Some wore long dresses, with high collars and full sleeves. Others wore much less, revealing a lot of skin, while still others wore what looked like actual shadows. And I recognized the one who had done the talking.

"Minerva!" I said, moving forward. "Or should I say, Exalted One?"

She smiled. "Minerva is fine, Duke. I only got to play the Exalted One. And while it's good to see you, and see you back to your charming self, it's really Lilly that we're here to see."

Lilly stepped forward and hugged Minerva briefly.

"It's great that you're here," she said. "But why?"

"There's a great misconception about witchcraft, or at least some of it," Minerva said. "Most think it's all black magic, and yowling cats by the light of a full moon. And while all of that is well and good, it's not our main purpose."

"It's not?" I said. "I mean, no, of course not."

"Nice save. But no, it's not. Our main purpose is to heal, in one form or another. We may heal a sick child, or the blight affecting a crop in some farmer's fields. Some of us consider righting a social injustice, or putting a bully in their place, a form of healing, albeit on a wider level. All of it, that's what witches do the best. The rest is just for fun."

"Are you saying you can heal me, Minerva?" The hope that I heard in Lilly's voice nearly broke my heart, and I waited with baited breath for Minerva to answer.

"Perhaps. We will try anyway. We felt it when this abomination rode into the city, and even more when he called his keep into being. We felt it like a hot iron in our brains when he severed your connection to your magic. It burns there still. Even if we didn't think so highly of you, dear, we would still try to do this."

"Thank you," Lilly said. "What do I need to do?"

"Come with me. We'll need to work away from here, away from this, his focus of power."

I moved forward, but two witches stepped up and took Lilly gently by the arms. Minerva put her hand lightly on my chest.

"No," she said. "This is for us only, Duke. Leave her with me. No harm will come to her, I promise. I told you once that it wasn't a bad thing to have the witches look kindly on you."

She smiled at me, and although every bone in my body wanted to follow and guard over Lilly, I had no choice but to trust them, and wait to see if they could do what even the Brownies couldn't.

While I was waiting, I examined the keep more closely. There was no way to easily get into the thing. Maybe we could get over the walls somehow, with the help of the witches, or even a rope…although those black birds spiraling high up in the sky looked like spies. Or maybe guardians, and they were bigger than they looked, being so high up.

Or maybe we could…

I didn't finish the thought, because the gates started to open. They swung out, making a terrific groaning noise that echoed off the remaining buildings. Buildings that were now mostly abandoned, since people fled the area. I watched carefully, waiting for some sign of the Death Knight to appear, but it never came.

Instead, Sarge came out.

But it wasn't Sarge either. Not the Sarge that I knew for all these years, and visited at home with his lovely wife. This Sarge was a twisted and corrupted version of the man. His eyes had a red glow to them that pulsed with every step he took. His face was twisted into a leer as he looked at me.

Always a big man, he appeared even more so now, as if his muscles were swollen, causing his Watch uniform to fight too tightly around him, so that it bulged, looking like it would rip any second now. He didn't have any weapons, but his fists were clenched and the sense of menace which came from him was palpable.

"Sarge?" I said, sure that it was him, but equally sure that something was horribly wrong.

His eyes flashed to me, and he lifted his head and sniffed, like he was testing the air for the scent of prey. Then he lowered his head and a horrible smile came over his face.

"Duuuukkke," he growled. His voice had changed too, becoming much deeper and more gravely.

"Sarge," I said, backing up, and putting my hand to my belt. "I don't want any trouble here. Let's stay calm and..."

That was as far as I got before he charged me, breaking into a strange loping run, which ate up the distance between us. I pulled my gun from my belt, raised it, and ...stopped. What was I doing? This was Sarge, regardless of what the Death Knight did to him. I couldn't shoot him!

My thoughts were interrupted by him running into me, or more accurately, running over me. He lowered his shoulder and rammed me. I went down immediately, and Sarge kept on going, stepping on my stomach as he ran past. My breath exploded out of me, and I curled up into a ball, just in time to receive a kick to my back.

I actually flew through the air, pain exploding along my spine. It had to be broken. That was my only thought as I hit the ground and rolled. The stars flashed in my vision, white and blood red, and the darkness that I was all too familiar with these days crept in around the edges again. I lay in a heap, waiting for Sarge to finish me off.

But he didn't. Instead, I heard a guttural laughing noise, and when I raised my head, I saw Sarge, still standing where he knocked me down. He was holding something in his hand and staring at it, laughing. It took me a second to realize what it was. Sarge was holding my gun.

I climbed to my feet, groaning at the sharp pain that went up my back. But I could stand, I could move. I wasn't broken yet.

"Put it down!" I yelled, the anger at the sight of someone else touching my Ultimate Weapon rising through me, shouldering aside the pain. "Right now, Sarge! Put it down!"

He looked up, pointed the gun at me and said, "Bang!" Then he laughed again, and took off running for the door of the keep.

I ran after him, ignoring the pain that stabbed through me with every step. Before he could reach safety, I tackled him, or at least tried. Sarge was tough as old shoe leather, even before the Death Knight changed him. Now, he had all that old toughness, plus whatever evil sorcery was on him.

But he also had my gun, and that would not do.

I attacked with a strength I didn't know I possessed. I jumped on his back, wrapped my legs around his and tripped him up. When we went down, I shifted my weight so that I fell directly on him, digging my elbow into his kidney. This time, it was his breath that exploded out of him, and I scrambled up and aimed my own kick at his head.

But he was quick too, and been a feared street fighter in his day. He was ready for it, and rolled to the side, so my boot barely made contact. Surging to his feet, he swung around toward me, growling.

There are times as a Nuisance Man that you need to get to someone, and someone else will be in your way. A relative, or a friend, convinced of the innocence of the person you're trying to eliminate. A lot of times, that's this person's only crime. There are plenty of Nuisance Men who wouldn't hesitate to remove them too, but that was never my way. Instead, I used a non-lethal way to get past them.

I still kept it on me, although I didn't use it very much anymore. A stout piece of wood, about ten inches long and an inch around, worn smooth by being carried in my belt for all these years, it had rapped the heads of more than a few. If you were good with it, and I was, a sharp knock was enough to put down most, and they'd wake up with a headache, while I'd be long gone.

I pulled out my head-knocker and held it in my right hand. The trick now was going to be to get close enough to Sarge to use it, without getting mauled by him in the process. I feinted to my left, but he was too experienced to fall for that, and moved slowly toward me instead, his eyes watching the stick of wood in my hand.

His approach was relentless, methodical. My gun was laying in the street, back where I took him down, but it wouldn't do me any good even if I could reach it. Not unless I was willing to shoot him, which I wasn't. Not yet.

I let him come in, his hands hanging low, fists opening and closing. I could take a punch and was pretty sure that I could even handle one from Sarge. But Sarge in his present condition? That might be a different story, and I preferred not to find out.

I stepped in, swinging toward his head, but then spinning and lashing out at his knee at the last moment. It took him by surprise and my head-knocker cracked into his leg. He howled and jumped back, and I followed, swinging for all I was worth. I couldn't keep it up, but he had nothing to block with other than his own arms.

I hit him again and again, fast, without pausing. It was the only way I could think of to stop him from getting to me. Finally, he dropped his arm after I got in a solid blow on his elbow, and I had my opening. I whacked him in the skull, harder than I would have at any other time. There was a hollow sounding clunk noise, and his eyes rolled up into his head, and down he went.

Panting, I bent and put my hands on my knees, sucking in great gasps of air. If it lasted too much longer, I would have been done for, and Sarge would have finished me. Still, as I looked down at the unconscious face of my friend, I was sad that it came to this.

I needed to keep him down, and out of the keep. Now that he was out of there, there was no way I was letting him waltz back in to the Death Knight. Hopefully, when we killed him, Sarge and anyone else in his thrall would return to normal. If not, I was confident that Lilly would find a way to fix them.

Holding onto my back, which was now screaming at me, I limped over and picked up my gun. I closed my eyes and sighed, then tucked it back into my belt. While I did this, the gates to the keep closed of their own accord, but not before I was sure I could hear the Death Knight's laughter from within.

I found some rope, which seems to be plentiful in Capital City, since the place is almost always under construction, and tied Sarge securely. The area was still deserted so I wasn't too worried about some do-gooder coming along to free him. I rolled him to the side of the street, into the shade, and sank down, my back against the wall beside him.

I hoped Lilly would be back soon, all charged up and full of her awesome power.

By the time she did come back, Sarge was awake again and raving. He spouted nonsense words in a guttural voice, spitting and slathering the whole time. While I tried to remember that he was under a spell, it still got wearisome.

Lilly arrived in the company of Minerva and a couple of other witches that I didn't know. She looked better, and happier, than I saw her since the Death Knight arrived at the gates of the city, and I was hopeful that the witches had done it.

"I'm back," she said to me, and her voice was full of her normal confidence and surety. "And I'm ready to go kick that thing's behind."

"Well, good," I said, climbing slowly to my feet. "And as you can see, I've had my hands full here."

Her face softened as she looked down at the restrained figure.

"Oh, Sarge," she said. "What did he do to you? Minerva, could you...?"

Minerva moved forward and studied Sarge. Then she did something weird with her hands, which I've learned means that some sort of magic is coming, and Sarge's voice cut off. His mouth continued to move, but only silence came out of him. He continued ranting and raving for a minute, then looked confused, trying to shout, but having nothing emerge. Finally, he glared at Minerva with his red eyes, and settled down.

"That's the best I can do for now, Lilly," Minerva said. "But we can bring him back with us, and see what sort of spell is on him. Maybe we can break it. Maybe not. But we'll try."

"Thanks, Minerva," Lilly said, and the two of them embraced. Then the witches moved off, Sarge floating along behind them, twisting and turning in the air as he went.

"Wait," I said to Lilly. "They're not coming with us? Why not? They obviously have some power over that thing."

"No, not really. They're all about healing, which is the opposite of what the Death Knight does. They were able to reconnect me to the magic, barely. If I wasn't attuned to it, and could help myself as I got close, it probably wouldn't have worked. But here, in his focus of power, they'd be no match for him."

"But you are?" I said.

"Yes," she said, looking at me with the light of battle in her eyes. "I am. I may not have thought so before, but oh yes, I am."

I believed her. Lilly never gave me reason to doubt her, and I wasn't about to start now. But still, when I looked past her, at that dark keep, it was hard to keep the feeling of hopelessness at bay.

"Let's go," she said, and marched resolutely to the gates of the keep.

She pounded on them, her fist making a hollow booming sound.

"Open up! I'm not asking three times!"

To my amazement, the doors opened, swinging outward slowly, causing us to step back. I readied myself, trying to ignore the pain in my back, waiting for whatever it was that would come out of there.

But nothing did. Instead, we got a clear view into that desolate courtyard that we saw before. Somewhere, a crow croaked once, and then there was nothing but silence.

We entered, looking around carefully, ready to be ambushed as we came through, but nothing moved other than the wisps of fog crawling along the ground.

"Don't let it get to you," Lilly said to me. "He's trying to scare us."

I swallowed hard before I replied. "And it's not working, right?"

"No, it's not." Then she turned to me. "Listen, Duke. This is my area. I'm not going to ask you to stay out here, because I know you won't. But short of killing innocent people, there probably isn't much you can do. Let me handle it. You can watch my back, but if I need help, I'll ask for it."

"You sure about that?" I asked. "That thing seemed awfully powerful."

"He is, and I'm not saying this is going to be easy. It's just that…well, I'll explain more later, but let's say for now that I see things differently."

"Lead on. I've got your back."

She leaned in and kissed me, then smiled at me, and on we went.

Across the courtyard was the entrance to the keep itself. Also made of dark stone, it rose up into the sky, a high, square, ugly tower. At the top, a red light pulsed softly into the clouds.

"He's up there," Lilly said. "So that's where we're going."

Of course, we were. How hard could it be?

The door to the keep opened without Lilly even having to knock, and we entered. The fog that clung to the ground outside was in here as well, flowing along the floor, and glowing softly in the light of the torches that were hung on the walls every few feet. The corridor led away in front of us, with arched doors leading off to the left and the right about halfway down. At the far end, another arch led to what looked like a staircase heading up.

We walked slowly along, waiting for someone, or something, to come out of those side passages and attack. Nothing did. When we reached them, I looked in, and wished that I hadn't.

The chambers within were worse than the nest of gargoyles that we discovered on the second floor of Magnus' temple. That at least was the work of predators. Evil and vile, yes, but predators nonetheless. What was in these two rooms though, was the work of a sick and demented mind. Now we saw what became of some of the occupants of the buildings that disappeared when the citadel came into being.

Our tempers flared, and we went on, moving more quickly.

"Hold on," Lilly said, after a moment. "This is what he wants. He put those rooms there on purpose. He wanted to make us mad, so that we'd be less cautious. We can't play into his hands."

I nodded, trying to slow my breathing and heartbeat. I agreed with what Lilly was saying, but still, it was hard to not run up the stairs, so we could kill the Death Knight and end this all the more quickly.

The stairs spiraled up, also lit by torches, and also with that strange fog coiling at floor level. We passed a second floor, then a third, and the stair ended at the fourth level. It was identical to the first, including the two arched doorways on each side.

We slowly moved along, looking into those rooms to the same type of scene that we saw downstairs. The damage that was done to those people turned my stomach, and I looked away.

At the end of this hallway, the stairs continued, spiraling up again. We passed another two levels, and then they ended once more. Again, the hallway that led away looked identical, and again, the two doorways opened onto scenes of unspeakable depravity. I wondered how many people the Death Knight tortured, and if he did it all himself, or forced others in his control to do the work.

After we walked by these two rooms, heading for the stairs again, Lilly stopped, a frown creasing her face.

"Wait a second," she said, and turned back. She drew in a deep breath and looked more closely at one of the rooms. Her face trembled as she took in the details, but after a few seconds, she turned back to me.

"Come on," and we climbed the next set of stairs, again, stopping three floors above. This time, Lilly stopped fully at the doorways on the sides of the hall, and studied the scenes within.

"Son-of-a…" she muttered. "It's the same. Duke, all these rooms are exactly the same. We're not climbing past more and more of them, we're passing the same ones."

"No," I said, "We've been climbing the stairs this whole time."

"Yeah, too far up at once. I should have felt it, but there's probably a magic gate at the top of each one. It brings us right back here, to the first floor again. Come on."

This time, we did move faster, but we only took the stairs to the second floor, and when we passed the doorways, the torture chamber was gone, In its place, was pure temptation.

On one side, beauties lounged in various stages of undress, looking at me with come-hither stares and beckoning me to enter; on the other, the equal measure of men, strong and well-defined, eyeing Lilly as if she was a piece of candy.

The Death Knight should have done his homework. Lilly and I looked at each other, burst out laughing and moved on. Put a never ending tap of ale in one of the rooms and maybe I'd be tempted, but there wasn't one of those visions that could compare to Lilly. Luckily, her eyesight wasn't good, and she felt the same way about me.

We climbed again, to the third floor this time, and now the hallway changed. There were no arched doorways leading away, but there were also no stairs at the end of it. There was, however, a large window, showing a night sky outside of the tower that we were in. The fog still clung to the floor and moved in wisps about our legs.

"Now we're getting somewhere," Lilly murmured.

We were half way down the corridor when the rumbling noise started behind us. We turned, and saw the opening that led to the stairs closing up. The stones were moving of their own accord, much as when the Death Knight called this place into being, shutting off our escape.

Lilly nodded. "Yep, now we're making him nervous."

Then there was another noise from the other end of the corridor, and the window widened, becoming a doorway that led to a much longer hallway. The other end was far enough away that I could only barely make it out. And it was lined with door after wooden door, square and strapped with iron, like in a dungeon.

"I think it's going to get interesting now," Lilly said. "Remember, you watch my back, but other than that, let me handle this."

"You got it," I said, and hefted my head-knocker to show her that I was ready.

As if that was a cue, the doors opened, and they stepped out. I didn't know if the corpses in the torture chambers on the first floor were real or an illusion, but now we found the rest of the people from the buildings in the area. All of them changed much as Sarge was, only not quite as completely. Even with red, pulsing eyes, bulging muscles, and maniacal grins on their faces, they retained more of a semblance of their humanity. As one, they turned and looked at us, and then, with an ear-shattering howl, they came.

From behind, I could see Lilly's hair rise in a corona around her head, and the sparks popped and crackled among her fingers. Her eyes would be jet-black now, too. She gestured, and the first few possessed people dropped, and laid perfectly still.

She moved again, walking forward, and the next in line flew back, crashing into several others, and landing in a heap, where they all struggled to get up, seemingly stuck together now as a mass.

For the next few, she threw her hands wide apart, and they were suddenly themselves again, standing and blinking in the torchlight, unsure of where they were.

"Here!" she yelled. "Get behind me! Now!"

Even in their confusion they heeded the sound of her voice, and I would have too. It was full of command, and there would be no denying it. They ran forward, passing around her, and I directed them down the hall, toward where the stairway had been a few moments before.

But there were several still left, and I knew that wielding magic was tiring.

"Lilly," I said, "let me take some of them."

"No, this is my fight, Duke!"

"I know, I know. But you have bigger fish to fry. Let me take a few of these, then you can be ready for the Death Knight. I can't beat him, but you can!"

She sighed, and stepped aside, gesturing me on.

I ran forward to the attack, knowing that I wouldn't have long. I struck about me, getting in a few lucky blows here and there, and taking a few myself. Lilly watched as I fought, and if I looked like I was about to be overwhelmed, she'd deliver a spell that would clear the way for me, and give me a second or two to reset.

I've often bragged that I'm a good fighter, and it's something that I consider to be a fact and that I'm proud of. But I never fought like that before, and never wanted to again. I couldn't use my gun, and even a sword would have been out of the question. Instead, I used a short piece of wood, and fought and fought to knock out people possessed of a strength and ferocity that normal folk didn't have.

By the time it was done, I was exhausted. My back was screaming at me, and I was panting and bleeding from a hundred nicks and scrapes. I'd knocked people out, broken bones and smashed teeth. When they were all down, Lilly cast one final spell, and they all, including the ones that she turned back to normal, fell into a deep sleep.

"Are you alright?" she asked me.

"Yeah, I think so," I answered. "What about you?"

In spite of the exhaustion and pain, I was glad we did it this way. As it was, Lilly cast a lot of magic during that battle, and she looked as tired as I felt.

"I'm beat, to be honest. But we're not done yet. Are you ready?"

I nodded, hoping that I really was.

We continued forward, to the end of the hallway, and the final door, made of black wood, that was still firmly shut.

It was locked, and all of my attempts to open it, including kicking it, failed. Lilly stepped forward, chanting a spell and laid her hand in the middle of the door.

The wood began to rot. From where she pressed her hand, it started to soften and slump. The rot ran out from there, slowly at first, but picking up speed. The door itself started to sag against its hinges as it lost its integrity, and soon was nothing more than a pile of rotten wood on the floor that we could easily step over.

Beyond, was yet one more set of stairs, spiraling away overhead, with no end in sight.

We looked at each other, already exhausted and shared a smile. If nothing else, the Death Knight could keep you guessing.

The way up was long and arduous. We stopped several times and sat on the steps, one of us keeping an eye out below, and the other watching overhead, but nothing attacked us, or even showed itself. Finally, after what felt like weeks of walking, we came to the top.

The stairs opened into a large chamber, high ceilinged and supported by dark stone arches. Large windows opened onto the night sky down the length of it, and the ever-present fog curled up the wall, and out, into the air.

At the far end was a throne, made from bones, where the Death Knight sat, still fully encased in his black armor.

"You have brought Griefmaker to me," he boomed out. "How considerate. And you, necromancer. I see you have found your way back to the magic. For the moment."

"You're done," Lilly said, her voice matter of fact. "You never should have come here. I don't know who you once were, or how you got this way, but your time is over."

The Death Knight laughed, that same evil, skin-crawling laugh that he used before.

"Indeed, it is this city's time that is over. I am only the beginning, and now that I am home, I will rebuild all of my works."

Lilly began walking forward, and the Death Knight stood and stepped down from his throne.

"You challenged me once," he said, "and lost then. Why would this be any different?"

In answer, Lilly raised her arms, and called up her magic faster than I ever saw her do it. The same buzzing, invisible spell that she used before flew from her. Last time, it hit the Death Knight in the back, taking him by surprise, and barely moved him. This time he was ready for it.

He raised his hand, almost casually, and moved as if to swat her spell away like a bothersome fly. But the effect was entirely different. Even though I couldn't see it, I could see the aftermath. The spell went straight anyway, and cut into his armor, opening a gash in his stomach. There was nothing underneath, except for complete and utter darkness.

The Death Knight cursed, and fell back, stumbling against his throne.

"Impossible," I heard him mumble. Then, louder, "This will not stand! I am the master of death, and you are nothing!"

"No," Lilly said, "you are *not* the master of death. No one is. Death will not be denied, not by you, or anyone. At the most, it can be postponed. Yours has been, long enough!"

He climbed back to his feet, and drew his sword, which was black like everything else about him. It seemed to suck in the light, and made the whole chamber appear dimmer. He swung it, and the darkness came out of it, in a solid wall, and sped toward us.

Lilly stopped, swept her own arms in a circle and stood firmly, chanting. The blackness hit in front of her and parted, sweeping away on each side. The Death Knight continued to hold his sword, point straight up, and the blackness continued to pour from it. Lilly stood, her shield still strong, and her voice rose until she was screaming her incantation.

It must have been taking a lot out of her, but she held firm.

The Death Knight gave first. He faltered, his sword dipped, and the flow of darkness ceased. Lilly's shoulders slumped and her voice lowered, the chant stopped.

"You are finished," she growled.

She gestured again, and the fog began to bunch up, rising into small towers across the floor of the chamber. The towers turned, formed, and took on the vague appearance of people, with hollow faces and gaping mouths.

"What is this?" the Death Knight said, sounding for the first time, unsure.

"Death," Lilly said. "It's death come for you!"

She screamed again, and I clasped my hands over my ears. The fog people rushed at the Death Knight, flowing over him. I saw them slide into the visor of his helmet, and into the gash that Lilly made in his stomach. They wormed into any seam, or crevice in his armor.

And now he screamed. But where Lilly's was full of rage and anger, his was of fear, and despair. The same feelings that he invoked in others were revisited on him a thousand-fold.

The noise went on, and the Death Knight writhed and convulsed. Finally, it cut off sharply, there was a clatter, and his helm fell to the floor, empty and looking like a battered old helmet. Of the fog people, and the rest of his armor, there was no sign, and Lilly started to collapse.

I caught her, of course. I told her that I had her back, and I meant it.

The tower started to shake, so I grabbed Lilly, picked her up, and ran. Luckily, it was easier going down the stairs than it was going up. Plus, they didn't seem nearly as long. I ran and jumped down them, trying to stay ahead of the tremors that were chasing me. I made it back to the long corridor, where the people we fought were awake.

"Run!" I yelled as I sped by them, and they joined me. Some of those I had hurt were being helped by others.

We made it, all of us, and watched as the keep started to disappear. It flowed back, down and in, until finally, the watchhouse stood there again, flanked by the buildings that were there before the Death Knight came.

"Put me down, Duke," Lilly whispered. "I'm okay."

I doubted that, but did as she wished, and she stayed on her feet, although she did lean against me. With the way I was feeling, I think I was leaning against her as much.

"We did it," she said, sounding surprised.

"You did it," I replied. "And you have to tell me how."

"Later. For now, I want to make sure Sarge is okay, and then go home and sleep."

I nodded, more than happy to agree with her. But as we left the scene, I noticed two strange things, which I didn't mention.

The birds that were circling the tower earlier were still there, flying high in the sky, staying in the same pattern they were in before.

And there were two men watching us from across the street. They were dressed in black, although not like the Death Knight. One wore what looked like a wizard's robes, while the other was dressed in black pants and shirt, finely cut. They didn't appear to be menacing, but were definitely interested in what we were doing.

Whatever it was about, it would wait. It had been a long few days, and Lilly was right. We needed to sleep.

## PRIDE AND PUNISHMENT

Capital City doesn't have many holidays. Or, maybe I should say that it has very few officially recognized ones. Really, there's only the birthday of the current ruler, the date of which changes depending on when said current ruler was born. For that, people take the day off from work and celebrate, usually by eating like gluttons and drinking like fish. I think the day after should be a holiday too, since nothing really gets done as everyone nurses their hangovers.

Then, there's the rare occasion of a special event. Something like a child being born into the Royal House. That's also cause for at least one, if not more, days of celebration. But that doesn't happen very much, especially these days. The current ruler, His Majesty, had his daughters years ago now, and showed no signs of wanting others. And, from what I understood, he was also in excellent health, so there would be no change of date for the one official holiday any time soon.

What could also qualify as a special event, as we were to find out, was the visit to the city of a powerful enough foreign dignitary. So, when it was announced that for the first time in centuries, an emissary from the Elven kingdom was coming, it was big news, and we all assumed that meant a couple of days of free-flowing drinks and platters of meat filled to the tipping point.

"I don't know why you think this is going to be such a big deal," Lilly told me. I have to admit, I might have gotten a little excited when I mentioned it. The thought of free ale does that to me.

"Because it's huge!" I said. "The Elves are coming!"

"I never took you for an Elf fanatic."

"I'm not! I could care less about them. But, Lilly…free ale! And lots of mutton!"

"Like you need more ale. Or mutton for that matter. Come on, Duke, there's still whoever's been attacking the city to think about."

I was crushed, stricken a mortal blow by the lack of excitement on my beloved's part. Well, maybe not that bad, but a little enthusiasm would have been cool.

"Alright," I said, sitting back down in my chair. It was evening, and Lilly and I finished dinner and were reading the newssheets by the fire. She defeated the Death Knight only yesterday, and we were taking a couple of days to recuperate from the ordeal. When you added on the fact that I also took a beating in Underworld only a couple of days before that, it was much needed.

"Still," I said, "you have to admit, it'll be nice to have a day or two where we don't have to do much."

"It would be. If I thought that would really happen. But I don't."

"Why not? Do you think that another attack is coming that soon?"

"I'm not convinced the last one is over yet," she said. "What about those weird birds? You said they were still there after the Death Knight's tower was gone. And those two guys who were watching us."

"The birds are strange, I admit that. But those guys didn't act like they were a threat. More like they were spectators or something."

"Pfft. Spectators hanging around a Death Knight's keep? I don't think so."

I frowned. The fact was that Lilly was right, as she almost always was. Even after defeating the banshee, the pipers, and the

Death Knight, we were no closer to knowing who was responsible for any of it. I didn't think the Dokkalfar down in the Deep were an actual attack, just bad luck on the dwarves' part.

But still! Two days of ale flowing freely from every tap in the city, all paid for by His Majesty's overfull coffers. I could sit on a bench at the Draugr's Garden and quaff gigantic mugs of ale, or go to the Barman's Choice and drink in a more refined atmosphere. Or…or…why, the possibilities were almost endless, and I think my eyes glazed over thinking about it.

And then another thought hit me. What if the elves had ale? What if they brought some with them, as a cultural exchange kind of thing? I tried dwarven ale, and it was pretty tasty. Orc brew, not as much, but passable. Elven ale, though? Something told me that would be truly magical.

I pulled it back together, went to the kitchen to get a mug of ale of my own and returned to my seat. Lilly must have noticed my face when I took a swig. It was good, but not *elven* good, I was pretty sure of that by this point.

"What's wrong with you tonight?" she asked.

"Nothing," I answered, looking down into my mug as if I could will it to transform by merely wishing it. No luck.

We settled back into the newssheets, but I couldn't focus. Besides the upcoming visit, there was actually something else on my mind.

"Lilly?" I finally said.

"Mmm?"

"How did you beat him? I mean, when you came back from being with the witches, you said you could, and you did. What changed?"

She set the paper in her lap and looked into the fire, her brow furrowed a tiny bit.

"It might be kind of hard to explain," she said. "But I'll try. Minerva, and some of the others, taught me a different way to look at it. The magic, I mean. Well, more my relationship with it. Before,

I always kind of envisioned it as something that I wrestled with, forced to do what I wanted it to."

She stopped and looked at me.

"But that's not what they do. For them, everything is connected. They are connected to the magic, and the magic is connected to them. It doesn't need to be forced, any more than your legs need to be forced to walk. You don't think about it, you just do it. That's what they do with their magic. Oh, it takes practice, but the more powerful ones, like Minerva? Duke, she is wickedly powerful. She can perform magic by simply thinking about it."

"But I've seen her use her hands and stuff," I protested.

"Sure. It might help her focus, or it could be left over habits from when she needed to do that sort of stuff. Don't get me wrong, it's not like every witch can simply think about turning you into a rat, and poof! you're a rat. When they're younger, they need to do the hand gestures, and the chants and all the rest. But it's only a tool to get *to* the magic. Once there, they use it as easy as we use our hands to pick up this paper."

"Then why couldn't Minerva come in and help with the Death Knight?"

"Ah, I kind of wondered that too. See, the Death Knight really was a sort of master of death, regardless of what I told him. Or at least of death magic. As strong as Minerva is, that thing was still stronger, and would have cut her off from it like he did me. At best. Worst case, he would have killed her, and then turned her against us. We couldn't take that chance."

"But he couldn't do that to you?" I asked.

"Oh, he could have tried. But once Minerva and the others showed me what they did, I saw that I could do it too. I could reach out, and feel the magic as part of me, rather than something separate. Once I had that...well, he may have been a master of death, but he wasn't counting on one important thing."

"What's that?"

"I am, too. But unlike me, he continued to wrestle with the magic, bend it to his will. Me, I sort of asked politely, and the death magic did what I wanted. It's still tiring. You still have to use your own strength to power things, but that one element, of fighting your own magic all the time…that was gone. And that's what gave me a leg up on him."

I tried to absorb what she was telling me and was finding it hard to do. If I understood right, my soon-to-be wife was now more powerful than a Death Knight. Something I never even heard of until two days ago, and that was apparently even more powerful than the Brownies in our basement.

"Sooo…Petal and her folks?"

Oh, that's different entirely. Think of it like this. If the witches, me, the Death Knight, the wizards and whatever else all use magic, then the magic uses the Brownies. They have a more natural relationship with it than anything else in the world, and for them, it's there like air, or the rain. But still…it's different. Hard to explain."

I shook my head. That was more of a magical education than I had ever received in my life, and it served to emphasize how far over my head it really was.

"I don't get all that," I said, "but I'll take your word for it. I'm glad you're here and the Death Knight is gone. And we'll get back to work on who's responsible for all of this soon. But in the meantime…"

"Yeah, yeah," she said, rolling her eyes, "I know. The elves are coming."

I nodded happily, encouraging her to go on.

"And free ale," she sighed.

We stayed put and took it easy for the next day too, but by the day after that, we were starting to get cabin fever, and needed to leave the house and do something. My back was doing much better, Lilly was fully recovered from her efforts, and we decided it was time to go see Sarge.

We hadn't been back to see him since he was possessed by the Death Knight's magic, and neither of us were sure if he would remember what happened, or how he would feel about it if he did. So, it was with some degree of trepidation that we walked into the Watchhouse.

"Sarge," I said, to keep things normal.

"Duke, Lilly," he said, glancing up from his ever-present newssheet. "I'm guessing you've heard the big news."

"Elves," I said, glad that everything seemed to be back to normal. "Yeah, imagine that. I didn't think they ever left their own lands."

"Not often, from the little I know," he said. "But then, why would they want to?"

"To come here, of course! To see Capital City and all that it has to offer."

Sarge looked at me, his face twisted into a grimace.

"Yeah," he said, "I'm sure that's what they're coming here for. Maybe they've heard of you and want to give you the Elven Medal of Being an Outstanding Guy or something."

"Could be, could be," I said. "Or…maybe they want to give the Award for Biggest Sh…"

"That's enough, boys," Lilly said. She walked around the corner and stood on her tip toes to give Sarge a peck on the cheek. "Glad you're with us again."

With that, she disappeared down the hall that led to her work area, leaving the two of us alone.

"Hey," Sarge said, not looking at me. "About that…I…"

"Forget it," I said. "You'd have done the same for me."

"Sure would," he smiled. "Let me know when I can crack you in the skull."

I grinned at him, rapped on the counter and headed over to the Board.

Not that I was in any hurry to take a nuisance, but I felt I needed to get back in the game, or I was going to get too rusty. There wasn't much there, and hadn't been the last couple of times I looked. Maybe the attacks were keeping the random criminals from getting too bold. But that didn't mean there wasn't anything. Some people couldn't behave no matter what else was going on.

I couldn't believe what was posted there, amid all the goblins, gnolls, and couple of Unhoused orcs. An honest to gods minotaur. One of the only ones I ever saw posted. With honor being a major bone of contention for these guys, it was rare that one went bad. Instead, they lived by strict military standards, and were in much demand as mercenaries across the world. To the best of my knowledge, there weren't even that many of them here in Capital City. Most of them lived out on the plains somewhere, in vast companies, waiting until someone needed them to kick the tails of another army.

There was nothing for me to do but take the notice, of course. I looked at the picture of the hulking beast, with its huge curving horns, and large black eyes. He looked fierce, as minotaurs tended to, there was no denying that. But I had an Ultimate Weapon, so I wasn't too concerned with his appearance.

"I'm taking this one," I told Sarge. How often does a guy get to chase down a minotaur?"

"Be careful," he told me. "Those things are dangerous."

"Yeah," I said, grinning at him again, "so am I."

The notice said that this minotaur, Dabney by name, was last seen in the East Gate neighborhood. He was accused of assault on three teenage boys, and I had a suspicion that the Watch hadn't checked this one out very well. The boys were all human, and no Watchman was going to get that close to a riled-up minotaur if they could help it. Not when they could leave it to someone like me instead.

The neighborhood was called East Gate because, at one time, the wall there had a gate in it that led to the east. Makes perfect sense, but that was long ago, and since then, it was closed up, leaving only a small door, big enough for one person at a time to come through. It was rarely used, but still guarded in case someone on the outside tried to get cute. Not too many people even remembered it, because at this point, I think it mostly led to a pretty barren stretch of dirt that lay in that direction.

Then again, it could lead to the Gardens of Paradise for all I knew. I hardly ever left the city, and when I did, it was with a particular destination in mind, and a firm commitment to be back inside the walls as soon as possible.

East Gate was pretty nondescript, with all of the usual components that make any neighborhood tick. Plenty of houses, interspersed with shops, restaurants, and taverns, set off by a square with a fountain, and some street vendors' stalls around the edge. Nice but nothing special.

I saw no sign of Dabney, or of any other minotaur for that matter. But I found the street where the three boys lived, and went to the house belonging to one of them, the one who filed the complaint.

A middle-aged man who had seen better days answered my knock. Most of his hair was working its way off of his head and down his back, and he had a respectable paunch going on in the front. He was dressed in a stained undershirt, and didn't look pleased to see me standing on his step.

"Yeah?" he asked, and then paused to process a large belch. "What do you want?"

"Mr. Winchell? I'm Duke Grandfather, Nuisance Man."

"Congratulations. What do you want?"

"You posted a notice at the watchhouse. About a minotaur named Dabney who assaulted your boy, and two others. I'm here to take care of it."

He glared at me for a second, then turned his head and shouted into the house.

"Ronnie! Get your ass out here!"

A moment later a young, sullen looking teen-aged boy appeared.

"What?" he mumbled, not looking at either his father or me.

"Did you post something on that stupid nuisance thing they got? Something about getting your tail kicked?"

"No," he said. "Gerald's mother did. But they're going away for a few days, so she put our address on it. I told the stupid cow not to!"

Ronnie's father swung a casual, meaty paw around and cracked him on the back of the head, hard enough to make him lurch forward, and almost tumble down the steps.

"Watch your mouth, boy," he said. "You mind your elders."

Then he turned his attention back to me.

"There you go, Mr. Nuisance Man. I didn't post it, so I ain't paying."

I shrugged. "Suit yourself. I can always find something else to do."

I turned to leave, but stopped when I heard Ronnie say, "Wait, ain't you gonna do something about it?"

"No money in it," I said.

"Huh. You're going to let some cow-head push around our good human boys?" Mr. Winchell said. "Well then, I guess I'll round up a few of the fellas and we'll take care of this ourselves."

He was serious too. Winchell was the type that felt helpless in his own life, so he dealt with it by bullying those who were weaker. That was obvious by the blow he casually dealt Ronnie. And by the way Ronnie took it, it wasn't unusual either.

I wasn't worried about the minotaurs. If Mr. Winchell and others like him attacked any of them, they'd find out why they were one of the most respected fighting forces out there. But, if that happened, Ronnie and a few others would be growing up without a dad, and there was too much of that in this city already. So, while my opinion of Winchell wasn't very high, I didn't want to see him try to make good on his threat either.

"Alright," I told him. "I'll check it out. In the meantime, you leave it alone. If I don't deal with it, you have my blessing to get yourself slaughtered, if that's what you want."

He snorted and closed the door in my face. From inside, I could hear him shouting at Ronnie, the sound of another blow and what sounded like a young body hitting the floor. I swallowed my anger and walked away. Later perhaps, I'd be back for Mr. Winchell, but the city was full of injustices and I couldn't take them all on.

Since neither Mr. Winchell or Ronnie had been any help, I started scouring the area. I walked along, half window shopping and half keeping my eyes out. The thing about minotaurs is that they're huge, almost on par with ogres, so if one was around, chances are I was going to notice.

I did eventually, although it turned out I passed them by a couple of times already. Not just one mind you, but three of them, none of them Dabney. They were in the last place I would have thought to look, in the guard shack by the door that was the remains of the East Gate. It never would have occurred to me to check there.

"Hello boys," I said, walking to the shack. They looked down at me with bored expressions on their faces. Then again, their heads really do resemble cows, so I wasn't sure what any other expression would be.

"Help you?" one of them said, in passable common.

"I hope so. I'm looking for Dabney. Seen him around?"

The three of them looked at each other, then back at me. Guards all over the place always react the same, whether they're dwarven, human, or minotaur.

"Maybe. Who are you?"

I played them the same tune that I went through with Winchell. They perked up a little at my name, or maybe it was at my profession. Then they went into a sort of huddle, and whispered among themselves.

The one who was doing all the talking came back and said, "Come with me."

To my surprise, he led through the door in the wall, and outside of the city itself, where there was what looked like an honest-to-gods fenced in military camp, right there in the shadows of the wall.

It wasn't huge, at least not my untrained eye. It was laid out in neat orderly rows, with low, wooden buildings all lined up, and tents pitched in precise formations on the far side. I'm sure my jaw was scraping the ground as I followed the minotaur to the entrance of the camp.

There, two more minotaurs stood guard, sharply at attention. They barely glanced at me as we walked between them, and I was led to the first building inside the fence. It was a spotlessly clean and well-maintained building, made out of sturdy wooden logs. Inside, it was no different, clean, organized, and well laid out.

In front of me was a desk, placed so that anyone coming through the door would see it, and be seen by the minotaur who sat there. Yet, it was far enough out of the way that anyone in the closed office behind it would be able to make it from their door to the exit in a straight line.

My guide took me to the desk and mumbled something quietly. The minotaur who was sitting there nodded, looked at me, and then went to the office door and knocked. A rough voice from within called out, "Enter!"

A moment later and the desk minotaur reappeared, followed by the largest minotaur I ever saw. His arms were like tree trunks, bulging through the sleeves of the military style uniform he wore. He walked over, stopped in front of me, and crossed those massive arms over a chest that was big enough to serve as a dining room table. His large eyes gave me the once over from beneath huge horns that could have gone through me, with room for two more bodies on the other side.

"What do you want with Dabney?" he rumbled.

In spite of his size, I wasn't too concerned. Unless this was the rare rogue, he was going to maintain his discipline, and not gut me unless he was given specific orders. I didn't think there was anyone present who outranked him to tell him to do this, so hopefully, I was safe.

"I don't know that I want anything with him," I replied. "At least not yet. But someone put his name up on the Nuisance Board at the watchhouse. I took it."

"And you expect me to lead you to him so that you can kill him. Think again."

"No, actually I don't. The complaint was that he attacked three human kids, but I've already been to see one of them. I'm not so sure that I believe it. Now, I want to get Dabney's take on it."

"What did you say your name was?"

"Duke Grandfather."

"Huh. Yeah, I've heard of you. I'm not impressed."

I didn't bother replying to that. In my experience, it was either bravado, or they truly weren't. Either way, the results ended up the same.

When I didn't reply, he pointed at a chair near the desk.

"Sit there," he told me. Then he turned to the one who escorted me in. "Watch him."

With that, he stalked out of the room, his footsteps falling heavily on the wooden floor.

I sat, twiddled my thumbs, and waited. Then I waited some more. I tried to engage both my escort and the minotaur at the desk in friendly conversation, but they both ignored me and concentrated on their jobs without a word in return. Minotaur discipline, indeed.

Finally, the huge one came back.

"Come with me," he said, which I was beginning to learn was a polite invitation from a minotaur.

He led me across the compound to a larger building, complete with a flagpole out front. At the top hung the flag of Capital City, showing the crest of the Royal House. Below that was a red flag, with a large, black bull's horn, dead center, surrounded by a white circle. I assumed it was the flag for whatever group I was in the midst of.

The building that I entered was much like the one I just left, only with a few desks and offices. One of them was open, and the huge minotaur I was following led me straight into it.

The minotaur waiting for us was sitting calmly behind his desk. He was large too, as all of them are, but not nearly the size of my guide. But he had a certain something about him. A certain aura of confidence and poise, that made you feel this was someone that you would follow into battle, even if it meant storming the gates of hell.

"Mr. Grandfather," he said, his voice a deep rumble. "Please, sit. That will be all, Captain Darvish. Dismissed."

The larger minotaur saluted, gave me one last glare and then left the room, shutting the door behind him.

"I'm General Daken. What's this about a complaint being filed against Cadet Dabney?"

I told the General the story, from the time I took the notice off the Board, to my chat with Ronnie and his father, and finally to my arrival here. When I was finished, he asked if he could see the notice.

He snorted when I handed it to him, and then gave it back to me with a strange expression on his face. "Looks more like Captain Darvish than Cadet Dabney."

I would have to take his word for it. Other than size and coloration, minotaurs truly did look remarkably similar to me.

"If I could speak to him, General, I might be able to put this whole thing to bed. Would that be possible?"

"It might. Before that, let me ask you a question, Grandfather."

I sat back into my chair. "Sure, go ahead."

"What do you know about us? The race of minotaurs, I mean."

"Not a lot," I admitted. "What everyone does, I guess. You're considered to be some of the best troops around, honor is everything to you, and people pay you a lot of money to fight for them."

He considered me. "Interesting," he finally said. "An entire race, boiled down to a few fragments of ideas. But still, for all that, not entirely wrong. Excuse me for one moment."

He stood and went to the door of his office, opened it, and spoke quietly to someone outside. Then he returned to his seat.

"We do value honor, and discipline, it's true. And those things form a large cornerstone of our culture. But don't make the mistake of thinking that we fight for anyone who can pay us. We also have to believe in the cause. It's why we're here. Your ruler has allowed us to set up camp, create a new home, and in return, we'll help keep the wolves at bay and the enemies from the gates."

"Oh, yeah? Then where were you a few days ago when the Death Knight brought those gates down?" I asked.

"Here, unfortunately. We were as surprised as anyone else when that happened, and had no advance notice that he was arriving. Still, we should have been there. Shameful, really."

I could respect that. Not only did I fully believe that the Death Knight was able to slip past them, but I admired the way the General didn't make excuses about it.

I was about to reply when there was a hesitant knock on the door. "Enter!" the General called out again, and yet another minotaur came in.

If this was Dabney, or Cadet Dabney, as the General referred to him, then I could see why he got that strange expression when he looked at the notice. Did I say that I couldn't tell minotaurs apart? Well, in this case, I could. Easily.

This one wasn't all that much bigger than I am. Closer to Sarge's size really, so only that of a slightly larger than average human. His arms were thin, and his legs bent in an unusual angle, so that walking looked painful. His horns were undersized, and instead of coming to sharp points, were rounded off at the ends.

"Reporting as ordered, sir," he said, and his voice was too high-pitched to belong to a minotaur. He saluted as he said this, although it wasn't nearly as sharp as Captain Darvish's.

"At ease, Cadet," the General said. "The is Duke Grandfather. He's a Nuisance Man. Do you have any idea why he's here?"

Dabney sort of gawked at me when I was introduced. "Gosh, no. I don't know. A real Nuisance Man? Wow."

"Yes Cadet. A real Nuisance Man. He says that there was a complaint against you. Do you know anything about it?"

"Against me? No, I don't know nothing…" But he hung his head as he spoke, his eyes searching the floor.

"Dabney?" the General pressed, but his voice was gentle, yet firm.

"It wasn't my fault, sir. I wasn't doing nothing wrong. I wanted to see what was in there. Through the door, I mean. That's all."

"What have we said about that?"

"Not to go by myself," Dabney muttered. "I'm sorry."

I glanced at the General, silently asking if I could cut in. He nodded at me.

"Dabney," I said, "did you attack those three boys?"

"No! I didn't! I was looking at things, and then one of them threw a rock at me. I thought they were playing at first, so I threw it back, but then they all started doing it. They threw rocks, and…and…other things. That wasn't fun anymore, so I told them to stop. Then they came over and started pushing me, and wouldn't let me get away. I was scared…"

He stopped and looked at the General. Then he straightened up.

"I mean, I got angry," he said. "I put my head down and charged. To get away, I mean."

He looked so miserable and ashamed that I felt bad for him. I was sure the General would give him a dressing down for his actions, but he didn't.

"That will be all," he said. "You can go, Cadet."

Dabney saluted again, and left the room.

When the door closed, the General sighed and looked at me again. "Satisfied, Grandfather?"

"Yeah," I said. "I am. He seems like a good kid. He's your son, isn't he?"

"What gave it away?"

"He didn't keep calling you sir, and you let it go, for one. Also, the way you look at him."

"He is my son," the General said, looking back at the closed door with a sigh. "His mother died giving birth to him. Since then, it's been the two of us. He's one of the reasons I brought this outfit here."

"Why? So that he could get an education in the city or something?"

"No, so he could live."

The General noticed the expression on my face.

"In the old country, anyone born as Dabney was would have been left out on the plains, food for the wolves. If they were undersized, or born with twisted limbs, or whatever. Some even used it as an excuse if they had a female, but really wanted a male child. But when I lost Dabney's mother…well, he was all I had left."

"While here…" I mused.

"Here, we rule ourselves. The rest of the companies don't matter. We've made a better life for ones like Dabney, and try hard to make them part of our society."

"You're a remarkable person, General," I said, and meant it. It's not an easy thing to buck a lifetime of tradition and make a new start of things. I rose to my feet and stuck out my hand. "I've got everything I need. I'll take care of the notice and let the Watch know that Dabney is innocent. Maybe have a talk with those boys, too."

The General rose and shook my hand. "Thank you, Grandfather. Visit again sometime."

It was one of those polite things that someone says without meaning, like "how are you?" No one really cares, and he didn't want me to come and hang around, but it beat saying, "great, now get out."

On the way home, I went through the East Gate neighborhood again, but didn't see any sign of Ronnie Winchell. For today, I'd head back to the watchhouse and tell Sarge what I discovered. Tomorrow was another day, and maybe I'd come back and have a talk with Ronnie, and then a whole different discussion with his father.

That night at dinner, I told Lilly about my day. She hadn't heard about the minotaur camp, but wasn't overly surprised.

"The King's doing a lot of things like that," she said. "Not only the whole social openness that he's got going on, but I've heard that he's trying to make sure the city stays secure at the same time. It's not a bad thing for him to have an elite fighting force that's loyal to him for more than money."

Lilly always seemed to have the answer to all the "why" questions.

The next day was gloomy, the clouds rolling in and threatening rain and wind. Not a day to be out and about, looking for nuisances, but I was still feeling cooped up, so I went in anyway. The Board was full, telling me that most of the other Nuisance Men felt the same way about the weather as I did, only they listened to themselves and stayed inside.

An Unhoused orc was on the Board who was accused of shaking down kids, and stealing their lunch money of all things. But that wasn't the end of it. Once he did that, he was forcing them to show him where they lived and breaking in. He'd stolen money and goods, and in at least a couple of cases, hurt the kid pretty badly.

My thoughts went back to Ronnie from the day before, and I resolved that when I was done with the orc, I'd pay a visit to the Winchell house.

The orc was operating outside of Orc Town, which was pretty gutsy on his part. The family units had no use for those that were Unhoused, and even an organization like Tollerson's would have gladly ended him on sight. That alone told me that this one thought he was really tough and untouchable.

I set my gun to "orc" on the way there, and tried to time my arrival to when the kids would be heading to school. Sure enough, I saw groups of them walking along, most with a father or two hovering over them. Word got around.

But no matter the danger, some people had no choice but to work, and couldn't be there. Those kids all banded together, walking along, looking over their shoulders. I followed a group of them, staying on the other side of the street, so that I wouldn't startle them. It wasn't long before an absolutely huge orc jumped out of an alley, and grabbed the kid in the lead.

I fired as I ran across the street, pointing the gun up, so that the little, metal ball would hit the building behind the orc, and I wouldn't accidently shoot any of the kids. Everyone jumped at the loud noise and the orc saw me coming, dropped the kid, and took off back into the alley.

I ran after him, lowering my gun to take him in the back. I didn't even feel the need to talk to him, not after what I saw. I'd take him out, go claim the money, and then let Sarge know that one more true nuisance was off the street.

The orc was quick, and I hustled to stay with him. He dodged and weaved as he ran, getting through the alley, and bursting out into the street at the other end. To be honest, he was much faster than I was, and I was thinking that I might lose him, and have to start hunting him down, when someone stepped directly in front of him, blocking his way.

The orc ran right into the new figure, and they both went down in a tangle of limbs and a muttered oath. I ran up, grabbed the back of the orc's shirt, and dragged him up and off of the unfortunate who got in his way. He snarled and snapped at me, spinning around and wrenching his shirt from my grasp.

But now I was ready, and it was child's play to point, aim, and pull the trigger. The little, metal ball took him in the forehead, and he went down, dead before he even hit the pavement. No more kids were going to get hurt because of this guy.

It was only then that I noticed who it was that stepped in front of the orc. Dabney was picking himself up from the ground, brushing the dirt from his uniform and smiling at me.

"Did I do good, Mr. Grandfather? Did I help?"

I could only stare at him, my mouth hanging open.

"Dabney?" I finally managed to say. "What are you doing here? Why…"

"I came to help. I'm going to be a Nuisance Man, too!"

"You can't…I mean…does your father know you're here?"

He looked down at the ground, his smile fading. "No," he muttered. "He thinks I can't do it. But I can! I can be a Nuisance Man! I helped you!"

I rubbed my eyes. "Dabney. You can't burst in like that. You could have gotten really hurt. That orc was dangerous!"

"I know. That's why I helped, so that you wouldn't get hurt. That's what Nuisance Men do, right? We watch out for each other."

"You're not a Nuisance Man, Dabney," I said, trying to be patient. "Maybe someday, but not yet. Now, go on home."

"Awww…man," he said. "Can't I stay with you and do some more Nuisance Man stuff?"

"No! Dabney, you need to go home!"

"Aww," he said, and kicked at the ground. Then, with a last sullen glance in my direction, he turned and went.

I collected my reward, and several thank-yous, for taking care of the orc and returned to the watchhouse. I let Sarge know that the job was done, and asked him to tell Lilly that I'd see her at dinner. Running into Dabney like that threw me off, and I forgot all about going to see Ronnie Winchell.

The next morning, I woke to a pounding on the front door. It was ridiculously early, and Lilly and I were still asleep when it started.

"You get it, Duke," she said, rolling over. "It's probably one of your messes."

I couldn't argue that. Anyone Lilly dealt with knew better than to come knocking this early.

I opened the door to find a massive figure filling it. Even in my still sleep-addled state, it only took me a second to recognize Captain Darvish.

"Grandfather," he rumbled. "General Daken would like to see you. Would you come with me?"

"What? Why does he want to see me?" Then I remembered yesterday's events. "Oh, crap. This is about Dabney, isn't it? What's he done now?"

"I have no idea why the General wants you, or if it concerns Cadet Dabney. Will you come or not?"

I rubbed my hands over my face, and looked down at myself, still in my pajamas.

"I'll be there shortly," I told him. "I was still sleeping, so let me wake up and get dressed. Have a mug of coffee, then I'll be there. That work?"

He gave me a baleful look, then glanced at the sky, which was starting to lighten. The implication was clear. I was a lazy slug who wasted a good part of the day lying about, and should consider adopting a stricter code of behavior. On most days, he would have a point, but today, it was really early!

Finally, he gave me a quick nod, then turned on his heel and stalked away. I watched him go, feigning nonchalance, but actually feeling somewhat worried. I was sure the General wanted to see me about Dabney, but why? Although my curiosity was peaked, I didn't want to show Darvish that. His holier-than-thou ways were starting to get on my nerves. Or maybe it was that I was bound and determined to show him that I wasn't intimidated by him. No matter how big and fierce he was. No, sir. Not me.

I didn't dilly-dally as I was getting ready. I went back to the bedroom and put my normal street-clothes on, telling Lilly that everything was fine and to sleep for a while longer. I didn't even bother with the coffee, although I was sure I'd be regretting that decision pretty quickly.

It wasn't too much longer before I presented myself at the door in the East Gate wall, and was taken without hesitation to see General Daken. He was seated behind his desk again, and his aide admitted me, and left immediately, shutting the door behind him.

"Grandfather," the General began, "thank you for coming."

"No problem," I replied. "What's this about?"

"Dabney, as I'm sure you've guessed by now. He's gone missing."

I grimaced. "I knew it was going to be something like that. Since when?"

"We're not sure. He was gone yesterday, but came back later in the afternoon, very excited and eager to tell me about his adventure. He said that he was out helping *you* and that now he was a Nuisance Man too. At first, I was quite upset, and my inclination was to come find you myself and ask what the hell you were thinking."

He stopped, looking down at his desk for a moment, but then continued.

"Then I remembered that it was Dabney, and that he always had a…how shall I say it…an active imagination? I wasn't so sure it happened exactly as he was saying. He got upset when I told him that I was going to talk to you, and that he was grounded to the camp for the night. After he stormed off, I let him go, intending to speak to him later. But when I got to our quarters, he wasn't there. Neither was his battle axe."

"Damn," I said. "You were definitely right about one thing, though. I did run into him yesterday, but it didn't happen exactly like he told you."

I filled the General in on what happened the day before, and how I sent Dabney home, telling him that no, he was not, in fact, a Nuisance Man.

"I haven't seen him," I said, "so he didn't come to me, not that I think he knows where I live. He might be somewhere in the city, looking for what he thinks are nuisances. That could be bad. There are some dangerous people out there. But, on the positive side, at least he's got a weapon. That plus the reputation your people have, should help. At least, I hope so."

"Maybe. But reputation isn't going to stop an angry ogre, or worse, a troll. Even Captain Darvish would think twice before taking one of them on by himself. And his weapon? It's not…it's not real. It's a toy for young minotaurs to play with before being given the real thing."

"Oh, boy," I said. "But Dabney thinks it's real."

"Yes. Plus, he's convinced that simply being a Nuisance Man means that you're nearly invincible. It's all the stories he's heard since before we even came here, including about you."

"I'm assuming you have men out looking for him?"

"Of course. But there's been no report yet. I was going to ask you if you would simply keep your eyes open, and if Dabney came to you, to please bring him back to me."

"I'll do more than that," I said. "I'll actively search for him. I don't want to see him get hurt either."

"Thank you, Mr. Grandfather," the General said. "That's kind of you."

We shook hands again, and I headed back into the city, wondering how in the world I was going to find one solitary minotaur, who didn't want to be found.

Being a Nuisance Man does have its advantages, and one of those is working closely with the Watch. Some of us work better with them than others, but since Sarge and I were actually friends, I was confident I could ask him to have his officers keep on the lookout for Dabney. Being engaged to a high level necromancer employed by the Watch didn't hurt either.

I stopped by the watchhouse, told Sarge what I needed, and then stopped down to see Lilly and fill her in. Ever since my adventure in Underworld, we both got better at keeping each other informed when we could.

Then I hit the streets again. I had no specific destination in mind, other than wandering around, hoping to stumble on him. It wasn't a very good plan, but I did some of my best thinking when I was concentrating on something else. In this case, that meant not getting trampled by the varied and vast amount of people on the streets.

I dodged and weaved my way through the foot traffic, stepping aside for the occasional horse-drawn carriage or coach that passed by, and thought. Dabney wanted to be a Nuisance Man, and to him, that meant he needed to go after the bad guys. But, he was brought up outside of the walls, and presumably didn't have much interaction with those inside until recently. So, what would be his idea of a bad guy?

He saw me not only chase an orc yesterday, but actually shoot it and kill it. It could be that he would think that all orcs were therefore criminals and head for Orc Town. But that didn't feel right. It seemed like too much of a jump for him to make, plus there were plenty of orcs that didn't live in Orc Town, both in large groups and smaller, more intimate family units.

No, I didn't think he was purposely heading there. But what else? Then it hit me. What if he was now convinced that those boys who harassed him, Ronnie Winchell and friends, were actual bad guys? It was conceivable that he would try to bring them to justice. And with only a toy for a weapon...

Now, a minotaur with a toy weapon is about the same as giving a human man a semi-dull sword and telling him to go at it. Their toys weren't soft and cuddly. When the General said that, he probably meant that it was smaller than a real minotaur battle axe, and sort of, kind of, dull, instead of razor sharp.

This meant that Dabney could still do an awful lot of damage to those boys. And if that happened, Mr. Winchell and some of his buddies were going to have something to say about it, and Dabney was going to pay in kind, at least. Which would lead to the General coming in for his retribution, and so on. It would be a mess.

I hurried up, trying to get back to East Gate as fast as I could.

It took a few minutes for the door to be opened to my furious pounding on it. When it did, I saw Ronnie looking out at me through a huge shiner covering his left eye. It was swollen and mostly closed, and looked painful. Regardless, he studied me with the same sullen expression as the last time I'd seen him.

"Yeah?" he said.

"Ronnie," I began, then I stopped, unsure of quite how to ask this. "That minotaur, from the other day, the one your friend's mom posted on the Nuisance Board? Have you seen him today?"

"No," he said, and started to shut the door.

"Wait a minute." I stopped him from closing it and moved nearer. "If you didn't, where'd you get the black eye?"

"None of your business!"

"Ronnie," I said, lowering my voice. "I can help you. Get you out of here or something."

"I didn't ask for your help!" he spat. "And I haven't seen that stupid cow-head either! Now get out of here!"

I opened my mouth to say something more, when I heard Mr. Winchell's voice from inside.

"Who the hell is it, Ronnie? Do I need to get up because you can't handle answering the door?"

The fear on Ronnie's face was enough to make me step back. When I did, he slammed the door, blocking off whatever was going to happen next. I stood there, facing the solid wood, and fingered the gun at my belt. I could kick the door open, go in and...but no. I couldn't. I could tell Sarge, who might or might not know someone who could come and get Ronnie out of here. Or, I could walk away, and hope that my visit didn't cause him any more problems.

I walked away, feeling like crap.

If Ronnie hadn't seen Dabney, there were still the other boys. The one was still out of the city with his family, and I fared no better with the other. While he wasn't bruised and defensive, he still hadn't seen any sign of Dabney, and seemed almost sorry that they pushed him around.

Back to square one.

I spent the rest of the day roaming the city, trusting to pure, dumb luck that I would stumble upon Dabney. I tried Orc Town, and the areas around it. I walked back to my house, and to the watchhouse, but nothing there either. Finally, as the shadows started to lengthen, I admitted defeat and returned to the minotaur camp, and to General Daken.

"Sorry," I told him, plopping down in the chair across the desk from him. "I spent most the day looking, but no luck. Wherever he went, he's doing a good job hiding."

The General opened a drawer in his desk and pulled out a bottle and two glasses. He poured a small measure of a golden liquid into each, leaving one less full than the other. That one, he slid across the desk to me.

"Thank you for trying," he said, and raised his glass.

I was an ale drinker and not a huge fan of the harder stuff, although I would sip at it now and then. This stuff though, this was like drinking liquid fire. It reminded me of a slightly less powerful version of the potion that Lilly gave me after the banshee incident. But, unlike that one, this had a sweet, almost honey-like flavor to it as well.

I coughed after taking a sip. "Smooth," I choked out. "What is it?"

"A drink from home. Made from flowers that grow on the prairies. Do you like it?"

"It's not my usual," I admitted. "But yeah, it's not bad."

I took another sip and settled back, asking the General about his homeland. I listened while he talked of the wide open fields that minotaurs lived in, setting up their camps and then moving on when conditions, or simple restlessness, compelled them. About how the gatherings of the companies, with the mock battle and contests of strength that came with them, occurred twice a year. It was obvious that the General missed his home.

"Why don't you go back there?" I asked. "I know you told me what would happen to kids like Dabney, but you could say, 'no, we're not doing that.' But still get all the good out of living there again"

"It's not that easy. The companies are ruled over by a council, one that's respected and obeyed. To buck them would invite censure, and the wrath of all the other companies. The council agreed that I could take my troops here, endorsed it even. If I was to suffer abominations to live, better that I was far away."

"I think that's a damn shame…" I was starting to say, when there was an urgent rap on the door, followed by it opening before the General could say anything. Captain Darvish entered.

"Sir," he said. "Pardon the interruption, but we have him. He's home, sir, in the infirmary tent."

General Daken surged to his feet. "The infirmary tent? What the blazes is he doing there?"

"He's in bad shape, sir. Someone roughed him up pretty good. A couple of my men found him near the East Gate. We think he managed to make it back that far before collapsing."

The General rushed from the room, Darvish on his heels, and I started to follow when the Captain wheeled on me.

"Where do you think you're going?" he rumbled, looming over me.

"Let him come, Captain," the General said over his shoulder. "He might help find out who did this."

Darvish sneered, and then spun on his heel to follow the General. This time, when I fell into line, he didn't say anything.

Someone had beaten Dabney badly. His eyes were mostly swollen shut and one of his horns was broken off, leaving only a stump. There was blood covering his snout, which flowed from his nostrils and mouth. It looked like one arm was broken, and was being carefully wrapped. He was completely unconscious and lay in the bed without moving.

The General knelt down by the side of the cot. "Dabney. Son. Can you hear me?"

There was no response.

"Find out who did this, Captain." His voice grew cold. "Use whatever resources are necessary. I want a full report, and give it to Grandfather here as well."

Darvish didn't like that. "Sir, I don't think we should share our information with…"

"You have your orders, Captain. Or do I need to give them to someone else?"

"No, sir." Captain Darvish saluted, turned and left the tent without another word.

"What can I do, General?" I asked.

"Help Captain Darvish find out who is responsible. Bring them to justice if this was malicious. If not, and it was Dabney getting in over his head, find that out. Either way, I want to know."

I nodded, and left a father to his grief.

Outside, I saw Captain Darvish talking to two other minotaurs. When I got closer, I could overhear that these were the two that found Dabney.

"How did he make it that far?" Darvish was asking as I drew near.

One of them made to answer, but stopped short at a nudge from his partner, and a glance in my direction.

"Go on," I said. "The General has given his orders that I'm to be included in this. Please, go ahead and answer."

The two of them looked at Darvish, who reluctantly nodded.

"We don't know," one of them said. "We saw him coming, reeling like he was drunk. Next thing we saw, he keeled over. We ran over, saw that it was Cadet Dabney and brought him back here as quick as we could. Other than that, we didn't see anything."

"Anyone else around?" I asked. "You know, paying particular attention, or looking like they recently stopped running. Anything?"

"No," the other one said. "Like we said. We saw Cadet Dabney, and that was it."

"Well, Grandfather," Captain Darvish said. "You're supposed to a hot shot. Let's see you solve this one."

"I'm working on it," I said, and walked away.

Truth be told, I had no idea. Until Dabney woke up, I didn't see how I was going to figure it out. The city was full of ogres and trolls, either one of which would could beat Dabney to a pulp, to say nothing of other individuals teaming up to do it. It could literally be almost anyone.

Regardless, I did head out to where the minotaurs said they found Dabney. Sure enough, there were blood stains on the street, but not much else. The East Gate area isn't known for being the most genteel neighborhood and blood stains aren't that unusual. No one was paying any attention to it.

I back-tracked the trail, following as it led me through the winding streets, finally ending in an alley not too far from the edge of the East Gate neighborhood. There, I found signs of a scuffle, and more blood. Whatever Dabney encountered, he ran into it here. I picked up his broken battle axe, its head loosely hanging off the shaft.

But that still told me nothing. I knew where he ran into trouble, but not with who, and certainly not the why. It wasn't much, but I returned to the General, with the axe, to tell him what I learned.

When I got there, Captain Darvish was in with him.

"It was those three human boys again," I heard him say. "The same ones as before. We think Dabney went looking for them, to regain his honor, and they got the best of him. They beat him badly, but now they're all hiding in their parents' houses, afraid to come back out."

What? That obviously wasn't what happened. Dabney was nowhere near that area when he was attacked, and besides that, one of those boys was still out of town.

Why was Darvish lying to the General? Perhaps he wanted to be the one to solve the mystery before I could, to appear efficient in his general's eyes. Or maybe…could he have something to do with it?

I stepped back outside the building and slipped around to the side, where I waited. A few minutes later, I heard heavy footsteps, and watched as Captain Darvish strode away. Then, I returned to the General's office.

"Grandfather," he said, as I closed the door behind me and took a seat.

"General. There's no easy way to say this, so I'm just going to spit it out. Darvish is lying."

"What are you talking about."

In answer, I showed him Dabney's broken axe.

"Where did you get that?" he asked me, reaching across the desk to take it from my hands.

"In an alley, where I believe Dabney was attacked. Out of the East Gate neighborhood. Not only that, General, but those three boys couldn't have done this."

"And why is that?"

"Because one of them isn't even around. His whole family is out of town."

The General was silent for a moment, gazing down at his son's broken toy in front of him. "Then why would…"

"I have an idea," I said quietly.

He looked up at me, his eyes flashing. "Are you accusing Captain Darvish of attacking my son?"

"Yeah, I am. I don't know why he did it. But I'm pretty sure he did."

"It would be your word against his, you know. And I've known Captain Darvish for years."

"I know. But there may be a way to get to the truth."

"Such as?"

I looked around to make sure the door was still shut.

Later that evening, word began to circulate through the camp that Dabney was coming around, and would name his attackers. I was there, off to the side, standing in the shadows when the gigantic figure of Captain Darvish came into the tent. Any notion that he was there to wish Dabney well was dispelled by his furtive movements, and by the huge battle axe he held at the ready.

He moved to the bed and looked down at the still unconscious figure, then raised his axe high overhead. I stepped out of the shadows, gun drawn and aimed at his heart.

"Don't do it," I said. "You know me, Darvish, and you know what this gun can do. I'll blow a hole right through you if you move that axe an inch."

He froze, staring at me, hate in his eyes.

"Now, drop it," I said. "Right there, behind you. Let it go."

I was mildly surprised when he did it, but he did have other weapons; his great strength for one, not to mention those two wickedly sharp horns on his head.

"Leave," I told him.

"Just like that? You're letting me go? Why?"

"Who says I'm letting you go? I only told you to leave."

He dropped his hands, sneered at me, and walked out of the tent, and into a ring of fire made from torches stuck into the earth. Inside that ring, stood General Daken.

"Why?" was all he said.

Darvish looked around at the torches, and at the faces outside the ring, watching.

"Because you suffered that freak to live!" Darvish spat. "You brought us here, away from our home, made us weak and dishonored us! You aren't fit to lead!"

"Prove it then," General Daken said. "If you're right, you can take the company back to the plains. If not…then you won't have to worry about it."

Captain Darvish snorted, put his head down, and charged without another word.

I can fight, and I've had my share of tussles with those that are bigger and stronger than me. There are ways to do it. Don't stay in one place, stay out of arm's reach, punch and move, move, move.

But I've never seen anyone move the way the General did. Every move was precise, calculated. He stepped to the side, avoiding Darvish's charge, and his fists came down on the back of the bigger minotaur's neck as he went past. Darvish went down, but bounced back up with a bellow, and moved in again.

If he swung, Daken wasn't where the punch landed. If he charged, Daken dodged, and got in a blow that would send Darvish sprawling. If he tried to grapple, Daken grabbed and twisted limbs and fingers, causing Darvish to howl in pain.

Finally, Daken stepped in, delivering a flurry of blows to Darvish's stomach, then a vicious uppercut to his chin when he bent over. Darvish went down on his back, and Daken sprang on him, lashing out again and again, rocking Darvish's head from side to side, until he stopped moving.

Daken stood, breathing heavily, and looked down at his defeated opponent. The whole fight only took minutes and Darvish never laid a hand on him. My esteem of the General went up another notch.

"Anyone else?" he asked, turning to the others gathered around. "Anyone else dispute my right to lead?"

No one said a word.

Later, I sat with the General in the tent where Dabney still lay unconscious. He had brought the bottle, and I drank a little more of that floral liqueur.

"Will he wake up?" I asked.

"Oh, yes," the General said, smiling. "We're tough. Even Dabney. He'll recover, and I'm sure he'll name names. He's a good boy, despite his sometimes overactive imagination."

"Names? Like more than one?"

"I believe so. I'm not convinced that Darvish was the one who actually attacked him. But I'm equally sure it was on his orders. There may be other malcontents. We'll find them out. If Dabney can't tell us anymore, we'll get it out of Darvish, over time."

I nodded and finished up my drink.

"I wish you luck, General. It's been an honor to meet you."

"You as well, Mr. Grandfather."

As I walked home, it occurred to me that the elves were due to arrive in two days. I was ready for a holiday.

And beyond that? Well, there was still a mysterious figure sending attacks into the city, and even more importantly, for me, a wedding coming closer by the day.

# THE ART OF DARKNESS

The day before the elven delegation was to arrive, Lilly and I took the day off. Our wedding was less than two weeks away, and we still needed to find a place to hold the reception. She didn't like my idea of simply finding a tavern that appealed to us and going in. In her mind, it needed to be an event, with a pre-set menu, and perhaps a signature drink, whatever that meant.

The ceremony itself was going to be held at Father Magnus's temple, and I couldn't have been happier about that. Although I, myself, didn't prescribe to any one particular train of thought when it came to the gods, I did greatly admire Magnus, and firmly believed that if he were to bless our union, it would indeed be holy. Plus, there were a few unconventional guests attending, and by that I mean non-human, and since all were welcome at Magnus's Temple of the Good God, that helped too.

I wondered how Lilly's family would react to those other guests, but she assured me that it wouldn't be a problem. For all of their money and breeding, she swore that they were remarkably open-minded when it came to things like that.

Lilly heard of a new thing here in the city, which was what was making my idea of simply stopping in to a tavern unappealing to her. She said it was called the Rose Petal Room, and was bound and determined that we were going to check it out. After a hearty breakfast, and an extra cup of coffee, I felt fortified enough to brave it with her, and arm in arm, we headed out.

With a name like the Rose Petal Room, it sounded like it would be too…well…foo foo…for me. When we got there, I was surprised. It was even worse than I thought. The outside of the building was covered in ornate stone work, with glass fronted lanterns placed on each side of the door. Huge windows occupied the second floor, although there was only more Capital City to see from there. And true to its name, there was an abundance of rose bushes in pots, arranged along the front of the building. I was amazed that one of our more decorative minded citizens hadn't made off with them.

Lilly was enchanted, and stopped to smell several of the roses as we walked to the entrance, insisting that I do the same. They were nice. She gave me the fish eye when I said that, like I was some sort of barbarian who wandered in from the mountains and tracked mammoth dung all over the floor.

Inside, the place was a riot of flowers, and paintings on the walls of babies with wings holding bows and arrows. There was a small desk, tastefully lit by a small lamp, and a few couches and chairs placed around, obviously meant to never be sat upon.

"Helloooo! Welcome to the Rose Petal Room! I'm Mister Charles, and you must be Lilly! Oh, it's so wonderful to meet you!"

The voice preceded the man into the room, but not by much. Mister Charles appeared through a side doorway, popping into view like he was hiding there, waiting for his moment. At first, I thought perhaps he had been standing very still when we first came in, blending in with the floral arrangements. He was a short, thin man, wearing a jacket that hung past his knees, brightly patterned like the petals of a rose. His pants and even his boots were the same. While it was all a bit much, I did admire the artistry of whoever painted them.

He smiled at us with genuine warmth, and shook my hand with a firm grip. His black goatee wagged up and down as he took Lilly's arm, leading her deeper into the Rose Petal Room, chattering away the whole time about what a lovely bride she would be, and every now and then tossing over his shoulder what a lucky man I was.

He didn't have to tell me, but I had to give him credit. The place may have been new, but he was an old pro. Lilly's eyes were already glazing over happily as he regaled her with visions of the ultimate wedding banquet.

"Hold on there, Mister Charles," I interrupted. "How much is all this going to cost?"

I thought it was a perfectly reasonable question. I already heard mention of not one, not two, but three wandering minstrels spread throughout the building and the garden behind to entertain guests. There was talk of the bar, and what it should be stocked with, and what types of food should be out for the early arrivals to nibble on before the main dinner was served. Then there was the question of flowers, what type and where they should be placed.

That was what drew me out of my own daze and made me ask the question. Flowers? They were all over the place already! And we were in a place called the Rose Petal Room, for Pete's sake!

The look that I got from Lilly when I asked about cost was entirely different than the one I got from Mister Charles.

His said, "Ah, you're one of those, are you? You can see how much your dear one wishes for this. Nay! How much she *deserves* this. One day of perfection, just for her. But, I suppose if that's too much to ask…"

Lilly's look said, "Really, Duke? Money? At a time like this?"

I decided to do the wise thing.

"Well, I just mean I'd like to have an idea, you know…so that I can make sure I have the right deposit and so forth…" I coughed, and the two of them turned away and walked on, discussions of lighting and time of day going on without me.

I trailed along behind, trying not sneeze from all the flowers.

I awoke the next day with mixed feelings. The first was that today was the day! Our elven visitors were due to arrive mid-day, which meant that shortly before that the taverns would be open and dispensing ale, courtesy of the Crown. That thought was enough to make me want to jump right up and get moving.

The other feeling was one of being much lighter in the coin purse. Mister Charles finally got around to naming a figure for our big day, and it was all I could do to pick my jaw up off of the floor, smile weakly, and give him ten percent of it as a deposit. The elves were here for three days. After that, I'd need to get a few big nuisances off of the Board fast. Yikes.

But, that could wait. Today was the day! I bound from the bed, full of energy and eagerness. Since it was an official holiday, I slept in, but Lilly was up and moving for some time. Although she said that the visit didn't matter to her, I think my mood actually infected her. She was singing when I came down the stairs and into the kitchen, but even that couldn't sour my outlook.

"Good morning!" I said, grabbing her around the waist from behind and planting a sloppy kiss on her neck.

"Eww, gross," she said, but snuggled tighter into my embrace. "Happy today, are we?"

"Very. You know what day it is."

"I know, I know," she said. "You know I'm not going to sit in taverns all day with you, so you better find Jessup. I'll join you for an ale of two, but then I've got things to do."

"Suit yourself," I said, and let her go, so that I could pour myself a cup of coffee. "It's your holiday too!"

"I would like to go down near the gates and see them come in. Will you join me for that?"

"What? I thought you didn't care about the elves? Besides, it's going to be mobbed down there."

She turned to me, and that was it. I never could refuse Lilly. Hell, I shelled out a small fortune for what was basically a tavern with a bunch of flowers in it. Braving the crowds to see the elves enter Capital City for the first time in years was child's play compared to that.

Last time we headed for the gates, we had to fight the crowds also. But that was different. Then, everyone was fleeing the innate fear of the Death Knight, and we were moving against the current the whole way. Today, the crowd was all heading toward the gates, and in a much more festive mood.

The rubble of the old gates had been removed, and dwarven and orcish artisans worked hard to fashion new ones. They were huge things, made of solid wood, a good foot or more thick, crossed with heavy iron bands, and anchored into new, formidable stone pillars. Anyone who was still naysaying His Majesty's plan for inclusion in the city should come take a look here. Impressive.

The gates were thrown open, and people lined the streets and spilled out onto the roadway leading in from the countryside. The Watch had men stationed all along the route, keeping the viewers from blocking the road and watching for trouble-makers. There were even Watch wizards stationed here and there, keeping a careful eye out. Lilly told me that since the mystery of who was attacking the city wasn't solved, they were taking no chances.

The necromancers were given the day off to enjoy the holiday, but remained on call in case the attacker showed himself, and proved to be undead, or some other denizen of the night realms.

Lilly and I worked our way to the wall, and then up the same steps that we took the day the Death Knight came. There was Watch stationed at both the bottom and top to keep most people down from there this morning, but since Lilly was a member of the Watch, and was…well, Lilly…they let us go up.

There were a few important type people lingering on the wall, watching into the distance, passing drinks around and being attended to by their servants. It had the air of a festival, and I was more than ready to join in the fun.

The sun rose higher and the excitement began to build to a fever pitch. The crowd pushed forward, jockeying for position to see along the road, and the Watch had their hands full trying to keep them to the sides of the street.

Suddenly, a shout went up from someone on the wall, further down from where Lilly and I stood.

"There they are! I see them!"

Every head turned, every neck craned, and sure enough, there in the distance was a cloud of dust rising into the air. Soon, it resolved into several figures on horseback, still some distance away, but steadily closing.

When they neared, it was easy to see the horses for the magnificent creatures they were. Huge, and ideally formed, even a born and bred city boy like myself could tell that they were perfect. And those that sat on them were equally as grand.

The elves were tall and thin, with a certain grace about them, in the way that they sat astride their horses, or turned to talk and jest with each other. Six of them wore robes of brilliant colors that flashed and sparkled in the sun. Their hair was worn long, and hung in silver, gold, or black tresses down their backs and over their shoulders. These were the ones who were laughing as they rode.

Around them rode others, maintaining more serious demeanors. There were an even dozen of these, and they wore full armor, shining in the sun as well. They wore no helmets, and their hair was bound behind them, out of the way in case action was called for. Where the others talked among themselves, these rode with their attention on the surrounding countryside, their eyes flashing to the city walls and the crowds awaiting them. Obviously, they were the bodyguards.

When they neared the new gates a horn sounded, and from the street behind us a delegation rode out. There were high ranking members of the King's own family in attendance, as well as representatives from several of the other races housed in our city. To my surprise, Ivar Ivarson, the head of the NHLF was among them. He had risen far indeed.

The crowds quieted as words of friendship and mutual respect were exchanged. Then, one man from the city rode forward. I vaguely recognized him, and nudged Lilly.

"The King's brother," she whispered.

"Welcome," he began. "I bid you welcome to our city, and ask your leave to accompany you to the Palace, where His Majesty will be most glad to receive you."

One of the robed elves rode forward also. They were all stunningly beautiful, but she even more so. The last time I stood there, it was as if I was staring down into a cesspool, full of all the vileness the world could contain. Now though, now it was like looking from above at a summer's afternoon, full of promise and light. For all the darkness and decay of the Death Knight, this was its antithesis.

I glanced over, and Lilly was standing struck and silent as well. For once, her face wasn't calculating or watchful. She simply seemed at peace.

"I thank you." The elf's voice floated up to us, and we could hear her clearly. It sounded like a sweet song, a clear melody. Next to hers, all other voices sounded raspy and crude. "We would be honored to go with you, and look forward to seeing more of your remarkable city."

My chest swelled with civic pride at that. Our remarkable city! Indeed it was, too. We were enlightened and cultured, and if *she* could see that...why, it verified what I already knew.

With those words, the other elves moved forward and were joined by the representatives of Capital City. Hands were clasped, smiles and words exchanged, and then they all moved back through the gates, and began the trek to the palace. During all of this, I couldn't help but notice that the bodyguards stayed apart from the pleasantries. They did not exchange greetings, but stood near their charges, their eyes constantly in motion.

They passed out of sight, deeper into the city, accompanied by the sound of the crowd overcoming its collective daze and beginning to cheer. Down at the gates, people began to mill around, talking in loud, excited voices, and dispersing to their various amusements. Up here on the wall, it was much the same, but more refined.

I turned to Lilly and said, "Well, that was fun. They are something, aren't they?"

She nodded. "They are. I can see why they could be so dangerous. That's a serious glamour they've got going on."

"I guess," I agreed, trying to downplay the effect on me. "Anyway, time to head for a tavern?"

She smiled. "Sure, Duke. I'll join you for a couple as we head back. Then you're on your own. Holiday or not, I have to go in to the watchhouse tomorrow, so I'm done early. Deal?"

"Absolutely." I kissed her, took her hand, and down from the wall we went.

The holiday turned out to be everything that I hoped for. Our local taverns were handing out the free ale as fast as you could ask for it, and I ate at least three plates of mutton at the Barman's Choice. Lilly stayed with me for a while, nursing a wine or two, then cut out, leaving me in the semi-capable hands of Jessup.

When I woke up at what was still technically morning, I was feeling better than I had any right to. Stumbling down to the kitchen, I found a note from Lilly, saying that she had gone in to work and would be home in time for dinner. She fully expected me to be out and about, but asked me to meet her at the Barman's Choice.

Off I went to another afternoon of free ale, good spirits and fun. But I kept myself under control so that I would remember my date with my fiancé, and turned up there in plenty of time, and in reasonably good condition.

When Lilly came in, she had an odd expression on her face.

"What's up?" I asked her, as she sat and I signaled to the serving girl for a wine and another ale.

"It's strange..." she began, but then stopped.

"Yes?"

"Do you remember when that female elf said at the gates that she wanted to learn more about our city?"

"Sort of," I mumbled, now vaguely embarrassed by my reaction to it.

"I guess that meant that she wanted to be shown around, by someone local and *not* an official of some sort."

"Oh. Does that mean she could come waltzing in here?" I said it in jest, but then looked more closely at Lilly. "No, really? Did you spot her heading this way?"

"No, not yet. It's more that I've been asked to..."

"You? You're going to be her tour guide? Why you?"

Lilly's eyes flashed at that. "Why *not* me?"

"No, no. I'm sorry. I didn't mean it like that. I just meant, how did you get chosen?"

"I have no idea. My boss told me as I was leaving. She wants to start seeing the city tonight, so I'm to meet her at the watchhouse in an hour."

"Wow," was all I could think of to say as I started to drain my mug.

"Put that down," she said. "You're coming with me."

"But..." I was starting to protest when two men came up, pulled out chairs and sat at the table without so much as a word. I was stunned. No one did that to me, and absolutely no one did that to Lilly.

They were both dressed in black, head to toe, and it took me a moment to realize where I saw them before. They were the same two men who were watching us at the Death Knight's keep. One was dressed in black wizard's robes, the other in black shirt and pants.

"Lilly Deerborne." The non-wizard said. "We'd like to speak with you for a minute."

"Now hold on there, friend," I started to say, but the wizard looked at me. His eyes were completely black, like Lilly's are when she's casting a spell. He opened his mouth, and his words sounded almost hollow, like they were being spoken from the void.

"Peace, Mr. Grandfather. There is no cause for alarm."

It was all well and fine for him to say, but the alarm bells were going off loud and clear in my head. I tore my gaze away from him, and looked over at Lilly. Ah, my Lilly. She showed no sign of surprise or discomfort. She merely picked up her glass, sipped at her wine, and said. "I'm Lilly. What can I do for you?"

"Do you know who we are?" the non-wizard asked.

"I have an idea," she answered, which was news to me. I had no clue who these jokers were.

"Good, then we can dispense with that. Tonight, you have an assignment, one that His Majesty is most eager to have go well. We were sent to help ensure that this would be the case."

"I see," Lilly said. "Only, I don't need help. I can handle it on my own, thank you. Besides, if there is any trouble, and I can't handle it, Duke will be with me."

The man glanced over at me, but turned his attention back to her almost immediately.

"Be that as it may, the responsibility is yours."

Lilly raised an eyebrow. "Are you trying to tell me how to do my job?"

"Certainly not. But there may be more at stake here, for you personally I mean, then you realize."

"Really? Like what?"

I could hear the ice in her voice. Lilly didn't take well to being threatened, no matter how powerful the person doing it was. And these two radiated power like they were made out of it.

"Please," the man said. "Nothing like that. I simply meant that if things are handled well this evening and tomorrow, it may lead to an…invitation."

Lilly stopped with her glass halfway to her mouth.

"I see you realize what I'm talking about," the man said, rising to his feet in a smooth, fluid movement. "We'll be going then. Good luck with your assignment, and I'm sure we'll meet again soon."

With that, they moved away and disappeared into the night.

I took a sip from my ale before speaking. Then, "What the hell was that all about?"

"Interesting," Lilly said, sipping at her wine again. "I always heard they existed, but..."

I waited a few moments, but she said nothing else.

"Who existed? What's this about an invitation? Who were those guys? What's going on?" The questions spilled out of me, one on top of the other with no space between them.

Lilly set her glass down. "Have you ever heard of the King's Secret Guard?"

"The King's Secret Guard? No, can't say that I have. Are they like the Palace Guard?"

"No, they're much more...secret. They've been rumored for years, but not that many believe they really exist. They're the very elite, most powerful and good at what they do. Wizards, fighters, swordsmen, whatever. The King supposedly only calls them out in times of actual emergency, or in cases where the realm itself is threatened."

"Then where were they when the Death Knight came to town?"

"I don't know. There could be two reasons why they weren't around that I can think of. One, they weren't ready yet, and we beat them to it. Or two, and this one kind of frightens me, is that the Death Knight wasn't a big enough threat to call them out for."

I swallowed at that. I'd seen and been involved in a lot, and that Death Knight was the scariest thing I ever encountered, by far.

"But this invitation," I said. "What's that about?"

She shrugged. "Maybe they're going to ask me to join them." Then she laughed and finished her wine. "Yeah, right! It's probably going to be an invite to come speak to them about that Death Knight or something. Then they can tell me how I could have done it more easily."

"I'm not so sure," I said. "It wouldn't surprise me if they did want you to join them. What will you say if that is the case?"

"I have no idea. For now, let's get through showing this elf around the city."

A short while later we arrived at the watchhouse. Word was sent that the elf lady was coming here, so the place was cleared out, except of course for Sarge, stolidly behind his desk as he always was.

"Duke, Lilly," he said as we came through the door.

"Hey, Sarge," I replied, matching his casualness.

"Calm down, Duke," he said. "You're all atwitter."

So much for matching his coolness.

A few moments later there was noise outside the door, and then they walked in. The elven woman from the gate led the way, every bit as stunning as she was before, but even more up close. Behind her came her two bodyguards, who scanned the room, glancing at Sarge and Lilly, before their eyes landed on me.

As one, they moved forward, hands on the hilts of their swords and stood in front of me. The one said something in what must have been their own language, which managed to sound both melodic and threatening at the same time. The woman said something in return, and then repeated it with a sharper tone. The two stepped back, their stares never leaving me.

They were all tall, much more than I, but not quite on par with General Dakin and his bunch, or with some of the ogres and trolls around the city. They were thin, not to the point of being unhealthy, but rather lithe and nimble appearing. The woman had long blonde hair, very close to Lilly's own color, while the two bodyguards had dark hair, almost a perfect black shade.

Instead of the armor and swords that her bodyguards wore, the elf woman wore a long gown that flowed to the ground, and covered her slender arms. It was blue, I think, but then sometimes seemed green, or purple, when she moved. She smiled as she walked forward and extended her hand to Lilly.

"I apologize for Katashi and Masuyo. They are overly cautious at times, I'm afraid. I am named Tomoni, and I am happy to meet you, Lilly."

Lilly shook her hand and smiled. "It's fine. Duke's a big boy. It's nice to meet you too, Tomoni."

Tomoni turned to me and extended her hand a second time. "I am pleased to meet you, too."

"Duke," I said, as I shook her hand. "I'm with Lilly."

She cocked her head at this, as if she didn't understand.

"He's my fiancé," Lilly explained. "I hope it will be okay if he joins us?"

"Ah, you are to be wed? How wonderful! And yes, please join us. Now, can you show me some of this amazing city?"

Again, I felt that unreasonable sense of pride flare up in me as she said this. Why was I getting all giddy? It's not like I had anything to do with the place, other than getting rid of a nuisance here and there.

Lilly started the tour right there in the watchhouse, first introducing her to Sarge, who didn't seem awestruck one tiny bit. She showed her the Board and left it to me to explain to her how the system worked, and my role in it. She asked if she could see my gun, and I slowly took if from my belt to show her. The twins, (as I determined to call the bodyguards), shifted slightly and put their hands on their hilts as I did.

Tomoni took the gun and examined it, peering closely at it as she turned it in her hands.

"It is very old," she said, handing it back to me. "Even by our standards, it is ancient. It is a very special weapon, and I hope…well, it is special, that's all."

Huh. I didn't realize it was all that old. It didn't look it. It was clean, not banged up much, and worked perfectly, except that one time with the Death Knight. Now this was twice that someone…otherworldly, if you would…. recognized it.

"Thanks," I said. "Does the name Griefmaker mean anything to you, by chance?"

"No, should it?"

"No, I guess not. Just something I heard recently."

We finished there, and after answering any more questions, left the watchhouse. Lilly suggested a stroll to Silver Tree Lane, which would lead us through some typical working-class neighborhoods before hitting the mansions of the wealthy.

"See you later, Sarge," I said on my way out. "Don't wait up."

"You're like a little girl, Duke. Show some dignity, would you."

He was jealous. I could tell.

Tomoni looked around with what seemed to me to be genuine interest and happiness as we walked along. People stopped what they were doing when we passed, to stand and stare, but none of them braved the imperious glares from the twins, so we moved on unmolested.

For my part, I thought the bodyguards' constant vigilance to be unnerving. After all, what did they think was going to happen? Then, I remembered the recent events in the city and realized that they were absolutely right to remain on guard. I resolved to do better myself. After all, it had been made very clear to Lilly that the success of this venture was wholly on her shoulders. And while I was sure the twins were more than competent, I was the one that was familiar with the city and would know if something was out of the ordinary if I saw it.

But still, I liked to listen as Tomoni told stories of her homeland and asked questions of both Lilly and I. For someone so high up in the Elven Nation, and she was, she was remarkably down to earth. She asked questions about what the shops that we passed specialized in, how people made their living, and how the inclusion of so many different races was working out. And more impressively, she actually listened to the answers.

Finally, she asked if we could perhaps try some local food and drink, which was of course, my specialty. I knew the area that we were in, and ahead was a tavern of not too ill-repute, the Swinging Jug. While not quite as nice as the Barman's Choice, it would give Tomoni a good look at real life in Capital City.

Lilly went in first, followed by one of the twins, Masuyo, I think, then Tomoni, then Katashi, and finally me. Before I went in, I took a moment to smile at those who stopped to gawk. But then, across the street, something caught my eye. Like I said, I was more equipped to notice something out of the ordinary.

Most of Capital City is lit at night by street lamps: tall posts with an oil reservoir and wick at the top of them. The city employs an army of young men and women to go around at dusk and light them. Because of that, the streets are fairly well lit at night, and you can see pretty well.

But across the street was a patch of darkness and I saw that one of the street lamps wasn't lit. That was a little odd, since those same lighters are paid to make sure the oil well is full, the wick is trimmed and so on. But still, it does happen.

It wasn't a big deal, really, but it was something out of the ordinary that I noticed. I chalked it up to my remarkable perception skills, and then entered the Jug, to introduce Tomoni, and maybe even the twins, to the joys of ale. If I was lucky, they'd let me in on the mystery of whether or not there was truly elven ale, and if so, where I could get it.

Tomoni was a hit inside the Jug. A few people vacated a table when we came in so that she could sit. Before doing that, she said something to the twins and they moved off to stand near the wall at opposite ends of the room, where they tried, unsuccessfully, to blend in with the woodwork. Lilly and I sat down with her.

I gave her credit, she tried an ale, but didn't have the taste for it, which didn't bode well for my wish for elven ale. Instead, she drank a wine with Lilly and continued to chat like they were old friends. Several people made their way near the table, under the watchful eyes of the twins of course, and she engaged with them all. She was charming, pleasant, amusing and approachable. If the Elven Kingdom's wish was to have an ambassador that would entrance the masses of Capital City, they couldn't have picked a better one.

After a while, it was time to move on. Tomoni beckoned to her bodyguards and we left. I noticed that the light across the street was re-lit, but saw that one further down the street was now out. Cute. Someone must be playing games.

We discussed it in the Swinging Jug, and decided that we would end the tour for this evening, and pick it up again tomorrow. Tomoni expressed a desire to see the First Quarter and Underworld, as well as some of Orc Town, so it was going to be a full day.

As we started back to the watchhouse the street light that was out was in front of us, on our left. I happened to be looking at it when it suddenly came back on. No one relit it, or was even near it, when it flared back into life, burning merrily as if it had been lit all night.

Which was when the light that we were passing under went out. There were plenty of street lights around us still blazing away, so it wasn't as if we were plunged into sudden darkness. But there was a pool of inky shadow around us, and it was only when I spun around to look at the light that I saw the glint of the knife blade.

It was moving by itself, a shining, sharp edged dagger, rushing quickly toward us from the rear. It rose in the air as if an invisible arm was wielding it, raising it to strike, and then it plunged downward, directly into the back of Katashi.

Or at least, it would have been into his back if I hadn't seen it coming and pushed him. As it was, my actions were barely enough.

The knife cut through his armor like it was made of paper, ripping it open and cutting into the flesh underneath. It plunged into the elf's shoulder, and then rose again, dripping blood. I yelled and moved forward, drawing my gun, but as suddenly as it went out, the street light flared to life again, and the knife was gone.

Katashi was down on one knee, his right hand held over the rent in his armor, blood streaming from between his fingers. Masuyo had drawn his sword, and kept Tomoni at his back, walking slowly backward until she was near a wall, and he stood guard in front of her.

I reached down to help Katashi to his feet. He accepted the help for a moment, and then shrugged me off with what sounded like a curse. His eyes blazed as he searched the area, finding nothing, and no one, to vent his fury on.

For her part, Lilly was already in full action mode. She was chanting, her hair wild around her and her eyes black marbles. She scanned the street also, but she was doing it in ways that neither the twins nor myself were capable of. After a few minutes, she stopped, and returned to normal with a sigh.

"What was that?" she asked me.

"I don't know," I replied. "But it came when the street light went out."

"Let's get Tomoni back to the watchhouse, and then we can get a coach to get her back to the Palace. Stay on guard."

"Please," Tomoni said, pushing past Masuyo, "first let me make sure that Katashi is all right."

She went to him and they spoke in their own language. Tomoni inspected the wound and touched it, making soft sounds as she did. Whatever it was she was saying, it must have had some effect, because some of the pain went out of Katashi's face, and he breathed easier.

"All right," she said then, "let us go."

Lilly led the way, with Tomoni sandwiched between the twins, and I brought up the rear. I kept an eye on the street lights, but none of them showed any sign of going out. At least not until we neared the watchhouse.

We were right down the street from our goal, a mere block away, when every light on the street went out, casting us into much heavier darkness than we were in before. I looked around wildly, but didn't see any sign of that knife. I kept one eye on Lilly, and one on Tomoni, ready to charge over and get them out of the way should I see it appear near them.

There was a cry, and I spun around to see Katashi raise his sword in time to block a jab from the knife that appeared in front of him, and stabbed toward his stomach. His sword flicked out, caught the dagger and forced it up and away. But it immediately circled around, slashing toward his face, and it was only his remarkable speed and agility that allowed him to block it again.

Masuyo moved in, cutting at the air, where the arm that wielded the blade should be. His sword made a peculiar noise as it went through the area, like the sound of fabric ripping in two. The knife dropped to the ground and disappeared, and all of the street lights came back on, their flames dancing in the night air.

There was no sign of the dagger on the ground, or anywhere else around.

We all stood, breathing hard. The whole attack lasted mere seconds, and I was impressed at the cool-headedness and speed of the elven bodyguards. Tomoni was unharmed, if a little spooked, and other than the original stab wound in Katashi's shoulder, no one was hurt.

"Come on," Lilly said, "hurry!" and we all moved quickly to the watchhouse. We covered the remaining few yards without encountering any more attacks, and rushed inside, glad of the bright lights burning in the lanterns.

For one of the only times that I ever saw, Sarge was actually surprised.

"What the hell..." he began, when all the lanterns in the room went out, casting us into darkness once more.

Now that we were inside, there were no other sources of light to glint off a blade hovering in the air by itself. Now it could take its time and strike unseen.

"Lilly," I shouted, "we need light! Can you do something?"

In answer she started chanting again, and the sparks that always danced around her fingers gave off some illumination. Not enough, not yet, but better than nothing. We surrounded Tomoni, Sarge included, and tried to watch everywhere at once.

There! The knife came slashing in, heading toward Lilly's face. But she was more than ready for it, and with a word, it hit an eldritch shield around her and bounced away, sparks flying as it did. It disappeared again.

I jumped forward, stamping down as it came in low towards Masuyo's calf, trying to hamstring him. When my boot came down on it, it felt real, and there was a metallic sound as it hit the floor. Again, it disappeared.

We all stayed on edge, staring into the darkness. Lilly began working on another spell, calling into existence a ball of light that spit and crackled with energy, like the one she tried to throw at the Death Knight. The darkness began to ooze away from her.

"Inside or out, I haunt the darkness. None escape my knife once it has been given the name. It has yours now, Lady Tomoni. You shouldn't have come here to our city."

The voice was hardly more than a whisper, and came out of the air all around us. It was dry and cracked, like words spoken by something that should have been long dead and in its grave. Then there was a chuckle, a low, drawn out sound, and the lights flared to life once again.

"Lilly?" I said.

"No idea," she replied. "But I'm getting really tired of this."

We stood in a group, weapons drawn and waiting, but the lamps stayed lit, and there was no sign of the knife, and no more words issued in that dry, rasping voice.

"Lilly," I said, "can you make some sort of light that will last?"

"No, that's not my specialty. The Orb of Disintegration that I called up is probably the brightest thing I know, but I can't maintain it for long. Not even with everything Minerva taught me."

"We're going to need something. I don't think this is over."

Sometimes, I swear I have the gift of foresight, and should learn to keep my mouth shut. No sooner did I said that, then the lights were gone, the blackness descended, and we heard Masuyo cry out. The lights came back almost immediately, but the damage was done already. The elven bodyguard was bleeding from his side, where his armor was punctured. His already pale face was growing even more ashen, and with a groan, he sank to the ground.

"Masuyo!" Tomoni cried, and rushed to him, pushing past Katashi.

The lights went out again, there was a scream and the sound of something heavy hitting the floor. There was another grunt, and the lights came back on.

Katashi lay on the floor, blood pooling from his back. Beneath him sprawled Tomoni. As soon as she tried to move to the stricken Masuyo, Katashi had thrown himself on her, taking the blow that was surely meant for her.

His breath came in labored gasps as Sarge and I gently rolled him off of her. Lilly helped Tomoni to her feet and kept her close.

Katashi stared up at me, his vivid eyes becoming duller by the second.

"Watch out for her," he whispered to me. "Help Masuyo keep her safe…"

And he was gone. The knife found its mark accurately, even if it wasn't on the body that it was aiming for.

The lights went off again, and I sprang to my feet, putting my back to Sarge's. I heard Lilly chanting, and saw a soft glow surround both her and the elven lady. But peer as we might, there was no sign of the knife.

"That's one of you gone," the voice came again. "He was nothing, an inconsequential annoyance. I would spare the rest of you. Leave the elf woman to me, and go. Or I will kill you all, one by one."

The lights came on again, and we all looked at each other. Tomoni's eyes were wide and frightened, and she clung to Lilly, who made soothing noises as she checked the room for any sign of the knife.

For the next several minutes, the lights stayed on, and we got Masuyo to Tomoni, who helped him the way she had Katashi out on the street. She must have had some sort of innate healing ability, but I didn't know if that was special to her, or to elves in general.

I moved to Lilly.

"What is this thing?" I asked her. "I don't even have anything to aim at, let alone know what to set the gun for."

"I don't know, Duke. I've never even heard rumors of anything like this."

"Now what?"

"We have to keep Tomoni safe, at all costs. If we don't, it could mean a lot of trouble. She's the Elven King's family, and if she were to be killed here, I don't think they'll be happy."

"Do you think this is part of the attacks?"

"Probably," she said. "But that doesn't help us know what it is."

"Someone's got to go get help," I said. "If we can get one of the guys in black here…"

"Yeah, they might come out for a potential international incident. But who goes?"

"Has to be Sarge. Masuyo's not going to leave Tomoni, and I'm not leaving you. It's got to be him."

I called Sarge over and told him the plan. He wasn't happy about it, but saw the logic behind it. "I'll be back as quick as I can," he said, and ran out the door.

He was only gone a moment when he stumbled back in, bleeding from his shoulder.

"Bastard was waiting," he grunted. "Soon as I went out the door, the street lights went out, and he got me. I barely managed to block it and get back in here."

Again, the lights went out, followed by the sound of that dry chuckle.

"No, no one will leave here alive. Not unless the elven woman is left to me. Last chance. The next time the darkness comes, so comes your deaths. Think carefully."

The lights flared back into existence.

"What now?" I asked.

"No idea," Lilly said. "But if this creep thinks he's getting to Tomoni, he's got another thing coming. I can hold him off, for a long time if I have to. He won't get through my shield. The only problem is…I can't do anything else while I'm maintaining it. And I can't extend it any further, either."

"We're on our own, is what you're saying."

"Yeah, I'm afraid so. But Duke, if he starts getting the upper hand, I'm going to…"

"No," I interrupted her. "You're not. Regardless of what else, you hold that shield and get Tomoni through the night. Tomorrow, you can get her outside into the daylight."

"Duke."

"Not up for debate, Lilly. Besides, this thing's not going to take us."

I wished I felt as brave as my words sounded. I managed to keep any trembling out of my voice, but the truth was, I had no idea how I was going to stop this thing. In order to save Tomoni, and to avoid a war with the Elves, Lilly might be forced to watch Masuyo, Sarge, and me all get cut to pieces in front of her. And while I didn't want to be a filet of Nuisance Man, I also didn't want her to have to see that.

"Masuyo," I said quietly, "your sword worked on it before. It made it drop the knife, whatever it is. Can you still fight?"

He was leaning against the wall, bent slightly with his hand pressing the wound in his side. But now he straightened and looked at me. "Yes, I will fight," he said, in broken but understandable Common.

"Good. Sarge, how about you?"

"Not sure what I'd be swinging at Duke, but you know better than to ask."

"Alright then, here's the plan." And I outlined what I thought we could do. Lilly approved, as much as she could of anything at the moment, which was good. A large part of it hinged on her ability to maintain her shield and keep the thing away from her and Tomoni.

I drew my gun and whispered to it. Then, the three of us stood back to back, and waited.

The lights flickered, flashed, and blinked on and off, the flames disappearing and reappearing each time. Every time it happened, we tensed, held our breaths, and waited. It was playing games with us, making us think that it was coming, but then pulling back, letting the fear build to a fever pitch. We held steady.

Then, the lanterns went out and stayed out. There was a flash of soft light from around Lilly, and I saw the globe that surrounded her and Tomoni blink into a quick existence as the knife struck at it. But with a noise like the screech of metal on glass, the knife slid off of it, and disappeared back into the darkness.

It attacked again, trying from a different angle, and then again. But each time, it was stymied and slid away into the darkness. Lilly stood calmly, but I could see the strain on her face. Tomoni touched her shoulder and spoke softly, and I saw some of that strain ease. Now she could do as she said, and they were both safe.

There was a long, drawn out hiss from the darkness. Rather than the chuckle from before, this was a sound of frustration and annoyance.

"Necromancer," came the voice. "You play with the forces of death well. I cannot breach your defenses, nor can my knife. You leave me with one option. Lower it, give me the elf woman, or I will gut these others."

This time, the lights stayed off.

"Not a chance," Lilly said. "You're not getting Tomoni, so you might as well take your little toy and go back to whatever hell spawned you."

The chuckle sounded again. "Brave words. Foolish words. You will have cause to regret them."

The knife suddenly appeared and darted in at Sarge, who barely got his sword around in time to deflect it. It pulled back, hovering in mid-air, and then struck again, getting past his guard, and scoring a hit on his forearm. Sarge cursed, and his blade lowered for a second, but then snapped back into guard position.

Masuyo flowed around to confront the knife, giving Sarge a chance to drop back. The blade tried a flurry of attacks, diving in high, low, and in the middle, moving faster with every strike. But Masuyo was as fast, and although his breath began to come in gasps, and the sweat broke out on his brow, he held his own.

Sarge grunted, and I glanced over. He was looking at his sword, and the notch that the knife cut in it. I'd never seen such a thing, and it made me look more closely at Masuyo's. It was hard to see when it was moving, but every time he blocked the knife's blow, another small piece of his sword was cut away. Soon, very soon, it would be cut in two, and then the fight would be over.

He tried to reach beyond the knife, strike where the arm that wielded it should be, or the body behind that. But the knife blocked every attempt, no matter how skillful the elf fought. And every time, another small shard of metal was shorn away.

But he was doing the job and holding it at bay. Sarge ripped a strip from his shirt and bound the cut on his forearm. He moved up next to Masuyo and started to attack also. His efforts were no more effective than the elf's. The blade blocked every attempt to get past it.

I stepped off to the side, to where I could shoot at what should be the things body, and not risk hitting anyone else. I raised the gun, pointed at the area behind the knife and fired.

The little, metal ball that came out seemed to sail through the air in slow motion. It glowed as it exited the gun, and flared brighter as it went. The room was suddenly filled with light, and there was a horrible scream that split the air.

Behind the knife was a man of average height and build. He wore a black cape over a white, frilled shirt, and black pants. His face was sallow and pale, clean shaven, thin, and framed by stringy, black hair. His eyes were bloodshot, with very dark irises. It was he who was screaming as the light washed over him.

I fired again, and the next metal ball did the same, illuminating him more fully. The knife wavered, and Masuyo jumped in and plunged his sword through the man's torso. While the wound looked horrific, there was no blood, and the light seemed to pain him more.

He dropped to his knees and covered his eyes, the knife still held in his right hand. I took careful aim and fired a third time. This time, the ball travelled slowly, hit the knife and exploded into a brilliant glare.

We all cried out and flung our arms up to protect our eyes. When the flash cleared, we stood blinking, tears streaming from our eyes, in the normal, suddenly dim seeming light of the watchhouse lanterns. Of the strange man and his wicked knife, there was no sign.

"Good job, Duke!" Lilly yelled. "What did you set the gun to?"

"Darkness," I replied. "I told it to kill the darkness."

"And that worked?"

"Yeah, I guess it did," I said, and looked down at the gun in my hand. "I think there's a lot more to this thing than even we thought."

Lilly lowered her shield and ran to me. We embraced and stayed that way for a few minutes, enjoying the familiar solidity of each other. When we broke, Tomoni moved to Sarge and helped him with the gash in his arm.

"Thank you," she said, but then her face became sad as she looked over at the body of Katashi.

Sarge went and got some of the Watchmen who were on duty out on the streets. They fashioned a litter for Katashi and carried him with great respect to the Palace, followed by Masuyo, Tomoni and us. I had never been to the Palace before and didn't really want to go now. But there was no way that I was going to let Lilly out of my sight, even if it meant having to present myself to the bigwigs on the hill.

As it turned out, it didn't matter. We approached the gate and were met by the two men in black who visited us earlier in the day, along with several members of the Palace Guard. Neither of them were happy to see Katashi's body.

"Your mission was a failure," the non-wizard type said, a note of disappointment in his voice.

Lilly didn't bother responding. Instead, she turned and hugged Tomoni. The elf hugged her back, squeezing her tightly before she let go.

"I will never forget you, Lilly. Nor you, Duke. Nor Sarge. You have the gratitude of the Elven Nation, and my own personal thanks. I hope to see you again, and perhaps I can show you my homeland."

The two men in black shut their mouths and seemed to be reconsidering their opinions. Neither Lilly nor I cared. We said our goodbyes, even getting an earnest handshake from Masuyo and headed for home. It was a long, exhausting night, and I was ready for bed. I didn't even care if the taverns were still open, I'd had enough.

We got home, slipped into bed, and I reached for the light on the bedside table to extinguish it. Then I thought better of it, glanced at Lilly, and lay down, leaving it to burn throughout the night.

## TO KILL THE MOCKING BIRDS

After the elven delegation left the city, the excitement died down and things went back to normal. There was no mention to the world at large, through the newssheets or by any other means, of the mysterious attacks on Lady Tomoni, or of our role in staving them off. On the other hand, there was also no mention of the Elven Empire being angered and threatening ruin and destruction to us all. In fact, if anything, they painted the visit as a rousing success of inter-kingdom goodwill.

While I was glad that Tomoni didn't hold the attack on her life against us, I was still smarting at the disappointment that elven ale apparently did not, in fact, exist. Or if it did, none was offered to me, despite my best attempts to display my interest in it. Oh well, not everything in life turns out the way we want it to.

There were also no more visits to Lilly from those serious men dressed in the black clothes. We discussed it and decided that they probably didn't like the way Lilly handled her assignment, and were rescinding their mysterious invitation.

"Fine with me, Duke," Lilly said. "We've got a lot going on anyway, and I don't want my whole life to revolve around the King's secret business. I like our life."

Hearing her say that gave me a nice warm feeling inside, but at the same time I wanted to march up to the palace and demand to know what they were thinking. How anyone couldn't see that Lilly would be a boon to any organization was beyond me. They were probably all afraid that she'd end up taking over and telling them all what to do before the year was out.

But she was right in that we had a damn good life together. Our work was interesting, even if she was tied to a particular office every day, while I lived a more freewheeling existence. We had friends, Lilly had family, and most importantly, we had each other and a big day to prepare for.

The details of the upcoming wedding were rapidly coming together, although it always seemed like there was one more question to be answered, or opinion being solicited. Although if you were to ask Lilly, most of my opinions were in the nature of, "sure, looks good, either one." The problem was, to me, it did all look good and I didn't really care which flowers were in the temple and which were at the Rose Petal Room. As long as Lilly was actually going to show up that day, I was good.

I took a nuisance from the Board the day after our ordeal with the darkness. While I felt like staying in bed and sleeping the day away, getting back out there and doing my job was going to be the best thing for me. I pulled an ogre, which was a rarity for me.

There was a time that eliminating ogres off the Board was my bread and butter. With my Ultimate Weapon, and the intelligence levels of most ogres, it was pretty easy money. But now, I came to realize that that same lack of intelligence that made them so easy to outwit, was also the reason that most of them shouldn't have been on the Board in the first place. As a group, they were very easily manipulated and drawn into doing the dirty work for those that really should be on the Board.

But being stupid doesn't mean you also can't be mean and rotten to the core. And from all apparent signs, that was the case here. This particular ogre, Bucket, started out as a leg breaker for an orc family. One who shall remain nameless, but since become much more respectable. When they did, they didn't have as much need for Bucket's services and cut him loose.

Bucket wasn't too happy about that, and I'm sure he didn't know any other way to make money, so he started preying on some of his past victims himself, demanding they pay him, or suffer grievous bodily harm. Some did, others tricked him, and still others took the beating, which is never a good idea with an ogre. Those few successes, either the pay, or the beatings, went to Bucket's head.

Those types of people that Bucket visited when he was employed by the orcs were usually not the type to call on the Watch for help. Many of them were in debt from some sort of shady activity in the first place. If Bucket simply stayed with them, he might have lasted a while longer.

But instead, he got greedy and branched out. He attacked a human shop keeper, breaking both the man's legs and destroying his bakery. After that, he demanded money from the dry goods store next door. By the time he crossed the street to the butcher's, the door was locked, and the butcher himself was running to the Watchhouse as fast as he could.

Only to have his complaint taken off the Board by me, out for some money and to prove to myself that after a night of terror, I still had it.

I did. I located Bucket, tried to talk to him, and discovered that he wasn't interested in listening, learning, or changing. He demanded money from me instead, and when I tried to explain the error of his ways to him, he charged me. An ogre charge is a fearful thing to behold, right up there with a minotaur, only with more rage sounds and fist swinging. He didn't even get to within ten feet of me before I stopped him cold. Bucket wouldn't be preying on anyone again.

"What an idiot," a voice said.

I looked around, but since we were in a respectable part of town, there was no one on the street while I dealt with Bucket. Instead, they all watched through the windows of their homes and shops. The only thing around was a large, black bird, with a heavy beak, scratching at the cobblestones.

"Umm…did you say something?" I asked, feeling foolish.

The bird cocked an eye at me and blinked. "I said, 'what an idiot'."

Talking bird. That was a new one, but this was Capital City after all. We had about everything else, so why not a talking bird?

"Ogres aren't the smartest," I said, still glancing around, half expecting to see some joker enjoying himself at my expense, and half hoping that no one noticed me talking to a bird.

"What makes you think I was talking about him?" the bird said.

"Cute. Don't you have somewhere to flap off to?"

"Could be. But I was enjoying watching you make an ass of yourself. Hee-haw for me, would you?"

"Scat!" I said and aimed a kick, but the bird simply hopped back away from me, out of range.

"Stupid *and* slow. It's a wonder that woman's going to hitch her wagon to your star. Headed straight for the gutter, you two are."

I glared at it, and it sat staring back at with me jet-black, round eyes.

"Good comeback," it said, and issued a harsh caw, which sounded suspiciously like laughter, opened its wings and jumped into the air.

Too late I remembered the inherent danger of birds on the wing, and jumped back, only to feel the splat of something wet hit the top of my head. I put my hand up to wipe the filth away with an oath, and glared up into the sky. But the bird was already flapping its way over the rooftops, another harsh caw splitting the air behind it.

I looked down at Bucket, then back into the sky. Stupid bird.

I don't mean to say that Lilly laughed at me when I told her what happened, but she did chuckle. She swore it wasn't at me, and only at the situation.

"No, I've never heard of a talking bird before. But from what you say, it was most definitely still alive, so there's really no reason I would have. But come on, Duke. Given where we live, is it really that remarkable?"

"Maybe not, but it was...it was such an...I mean..."

"Aww, was the birdy bad to you? Being a bird doesn't mean it couldn't be a jerk. If you see it again, pluck it. That'll teach it, when it has to run away from cats on the ground."

Lilly has a scary side at times.

But we had things to do, and after I washed the reminder out of my hair, I forgot about my encounter with the bird. Which goes to show either how weird life can be in this city, or how busy Lilly was keeping me these days. Maybe both.

I spent the next day running around doing more errands for the wedding, but this time, it was something that I had complete and utter control over, and actually enjoyed doing. Lilly made me responsible for picking the ale that would be served. I was to go to various taverns and choose the one that I thought the largest number of people would enjoy. Now this was a task that I could get behind.

"There's a lot of them," I told her. "And I might get confused as to which is which. I may have to ask for a few samples."

"Knock yourself out," she replied. "As long as you pick a decent one and make the arrangements to have a few barrels delivered to the Rose Petal Room that morning. Mister Charles will handle it from there."

Ah yes, Mister Charles. For what we were paying him, you'd think he would go pick the ale up himself and carry it to the Rose Petal Room on his back.

I was heading to my fourth tavern to get a sense of what they have, when I noticed the bird sitting on a nearby barrel watching me. It was either that same, large, black bird from the day before, or one identical to it.

"Glug glug glug," it said. "Keep drinking, rummy. Maybe you'll manage to fall in a gutter and drown before you ruin that poor woman's life anymore."

"Get out of here!" I waved my arms at it, hoping to scare it off.

"Oh, scary. You're quite the hero. What does she see in you anyway? I mean other than a hired killer with a work ethic problem."

"What's your deal? Why are you hanging around here, insulting me? Did I do something to you?"

"Pfft. Like you could if you wanted to. Grandfather, you're minor league. I say these things not to hurt, but to educate."

"Go away. You're annoying."

"I'll leave. You keep on drinking, buddy. It's part of your charm."

And again, with a caw that sounded like laughter, he took off. This time, I watched him go, and dodged as he circled above my head. The splatter hit the cobblestones, not me. Small favors and all.

I looked at the tavern I was about to enter, and stopped. Suddenly, I wasn't as thirsty as I was, and my enthusiasm for my task waned. It wasn't as if I believed what the bird said, but it did make me question if others actually did view me that way. I mean, I knew that Lilly was way out of my league, but I didn't really want everyone else thinking that. Maybe a little, but not *way* out.

The Barman's Choice would be great, I thought. It was a good ale, and a popular place, so it should fit the bill. For the rest of the day I could head home and…I don't know…dust the shelves or something.

When Lilly got home later that evening, she was in a towering rage. Her lips were pushed tightly together, her fists clenched, and a cold fire seemed to dance in her eyes.

"Uh-oh," I said. "What's got you all in a twist?"

"That damn bird!" she exploded. "Do you know what it said to me?"

I was tempted to give her the same response that she gave me yesterday, but I opted not to. For one, I knew how infuriating that bird could be, plus, I was really hoping for a nice evening with her. And, honestly, I was relieved that someone else had run into it, and I wasn't alone.

"What did it say?" I wasn't sure I wanted to know, but there was a morbid curiosity.

She told me, and I was horrified. The bird had upped its game apparently. It even made me mad, hearing it secondhand.

I went to the door and opened it, hoping to see it perched nearby. Then we would see what a well-placed shot from my gun would do to it. Yes, I was that mad, that I was ready to kill it for what it said. But no luck, it was gone, or at least hidden out of sight.

We spent some time consoling each other, and managed to salvage a good evening out of it after all. Lilly even brought me a mug of ale out of the kitchen herself, telling me that the bird was an idiot, and if she had a problem with my consumption, I'd know about it.

I went with Lilly to the watchhouse the next morning. Since the wedding was running up some bills, I thought I would spend a few days taking nuisances and earning some cash. Better to get it paid for now and out of the way, than have to deal with it later on.

"Hey, Sarge," I said, as we came in.

"Duke, Lilly. Who's your friend?"

He pointed behind us with an amused expression on his face. The bird was back and following us in the door, waddling along behind as if it were a lost puppy hoping to follow us home.

"Get!" I said, and lunged at it.

It made a sad sort of noise and cowered, as if it were afraid of being struck.

"Duke!" Sarge's voice rang out, reminding anyone in earshot why he was called that. "What do you think you're doing? I won't stand for cruelty to dumb animals!"

"What? Do you know what this thing has…" I started to protest.

"Don't care. It's an animal. End of story."

I didn't realize that Sarge had that kind of empathy for the natural world, and judging by Lilly's face, neither did she.

"Sarge," I said. "You don't understand. This thing has been following us around for the last couple of days, saying the nastiest things."

"The bird has. Saying things. Right, now I get it. Very funny, guys. You two sure put one over on old Sarge. Ha ha."

"Wouldn't be very hard," the voice said. Sarge's eyes widened as he realized that it came from the bird. Neither Lilly nor I were surprised in the least.

"What did you say?" Sarge asked, a laugh in his voice.

"It wouldn't be very hard to fool you, you great oaf. Even these two ignoramuses could do it."

"Good joke, Duke." Sarge said. "What'd you do, get Lilly to magic something up so that it seems like it's talking?"

"Are you kidding?" the bird said. "That bimbo couldn't magic up a ham sandwich, let alone something as complex as me." It cut loose with that harsh mocking laughter again. "What a collection of idiots. It's no wonder you all get along."

"Last chance, bird," I said, and put my hand on my gun.

"Go ahead, big man, pull it. Prove what a tough guy you are. Might as well do it that way, since in the sack you're…"

That was as far as it got before I pulled the gun, didn't even bother saying anything to set it, and fired. The little, metal ball would do terrible things to the bird all on its own.

A moment later, I was shaking my head, trying to clear the ringing, and wondering how I ended up in a heap against the wall.

Lilly lay next to me unconscious, and from what I could see through the ruin of the desk, Sarge was out as well.

Of the bird, there was no sign, but from what I could figure out, it exploded when I shot it.

Other Watchmen came running, first to Sarge, then to Lilly, and finally to me. They helped us to our feet, questions flying. I could only hear bits of them through the loud ringing in my ears. It took several minutes for it to fade enough for me to make out what was being said.

I answered them as best that I could, and Lilly backed up my story. Sarge did also when he came around. They summoned a Watch commander, but since it would be some time before he arrived, they grabbed chairs from deeper in the Watchhouse for us to sit and rest.

Slowly, I became aware of another noise, one that was quieter than the voices talking around me. It took me a minute to realize that it was coming from outside, but was different than the normal city noises that are always present.

I rose to my feet unsteadily, shook off the offer of help from a junior Watchman, and made my way to the door. I opened it, and looked outside.

Birds. Tons of them. On the rooftops surrounding the Watchhouse, on the backs of benches, or perched on barrels. Some on the street itself. All talking, all making that annoying coughing laugh. As one, they turned and looked at me with those jet-black eyes, and the noise that went up was a cacophony of laughter.

"Lilly," I said over my shoulder. "I think you're going to want to see this."

Lilly came to the door as well, not saying anything. Her appearance made the birds laugh all the harder. Then, one by one, they took wing and flapped away over the rooftops. Soon, they were all gone, except for one, sitting on a sign post, regarding us.

"Smooth," it said. "I like the burnt look. Next time, stand closer. It can only improve your faces. Both of you!"

With that, it too sprang into the sky and soared away.

"What do you suppose will happen when those things start talking to the orcs, or the trolls, or ogres that way?" Lilly said.

I swallowed hard. I didn't want to think about it.

It wasn't too long before we heard the first explosion. It came from the Stews, and we headed that way as quickly as we could.

Sure enough, a troll was lying prone in the middle of the street, his face and hands scorched badly. He groaned, which told us that he was still alive, but was in pretty rough shape. It was a testament to the power of these things that he was in the condition that he was. Trolls are tough and there isn't much short of an Ultimate Weapon that takes one down easily.

According to eye-witnesses, the troll was seen shouting at a large, black bird. That in and of itself was worthy of getting attention, since despite their reputation, trolls are actually pretty even-tempered. But what was really eye opening to the bystanders was that the bird was shouting back. They engaged in some back and forth, the troll getting more and more angry, until finally, he grabbed the bird and shoved it into his mouth, intending to eat his troubles away.

The next thing anyone knew, there was a loud bang, and the troll was lying flat on his back. Of the bird, there was no sign.

"This is just the first," Lilly said to me. "We were lucky that the troll tried to eat it. It limited the damage, but you know that's not going to happen every time."

As she was speaking there was another tremendous boom, and a cloud of smoke rose into the air a few blocks away.

"Come on," I sighed. "We might as well go see."

This time, there was destruction that led beyond the rock-hard head of a single troll. Several orcs were down and bleeding, and their store front was burning. They were a smaller family, running a clothes-cleaning business and trying to make ends meet.

No one was really sure what happened, other than a couple of people who were amused to see a black bird waddle through the door and into the shop like he owned the place. Trying to make ends meet or not, there aren't too many orcs who are going to take being insulted by a bird and not try to do something about it.

They paid the price. A couple of them were slowly coming around. But more were severely hurt, and two were gone. One bird traded for two orcs and a lot of damage. I shuddered to think of what was descending on the city as I remembered the sheer number of them outside the watchhouse.

"We need to figure this out," I said to Lilly. "If we can't kill them, what can we do?"

"I don't know," she replied. "Let's go back to the watchhouse. I'll talk to my bosses. Maybe they can get the Watch wizards involved and they can come up with something that will trap them."

"Don't you have something like that? That first time we met, you threw something around that weird unborn thing that you said should have stopped it."

"Good memory!" she smiled. "But no, like that thing, that shell only works on the dead. Ghosts, spirits, poltergeists. Things like that. These birds are alive, they'd fly right through it like it wasn't there."

"But the wizards have the same sort of thing for living things, right?"

She shrugged. "Who knows? But we can hope."

On the way back to the watchhouse we heard yet another explosion, way off in the First Quarter. I hoped that no one I knew, like Brindar, was caught in it. That thought led to another, and then an idea hit me.

"Hey," I said. "I'm going to go see Ivar. If we can't stop them, maybe the NHLF can get the word out to not engage the stupid things, no matter what they say."

"Good idea. I'll meet you at home."

I gave her a peck on the cheek and turned to go. But as I did, "Duke?"

"Yeah?"

"Don't get in an argument with any birds."

"Ha. Yeah, you neither."

We smiled at each other and headed off in our separate directions.

I had to go through the same annoying dwarven clerk that I always did when I came to see Ivar. It seemed that no matter what I did, he was always going to consider me the enemy. Whether that was because of my past, or simply because I was human, I had no idea.

"Look, numbskull," I said to him, my voice taking on a menacing edge. And also, "numbskull?" Maybe I was taking after the birds. "I need to see him. I'm trying to save lives here. Non-human as well as human!"

"As I said," he answered with infuriating politeness. "Mr. Ivarson is busy and can't be disturbed. If you would care to wait, please have a seat in our reception area. If you'd rather make an appointment, I can do that for you. But Mr. Ivarson is not available at the moment."

I seethed as I stood there at his desk. A part of me wanted to reach over and slap him right out of his chair. But Hock, and who knew who else, was around, and they'd be on me in moments if I did. Sure, I could pull my gun, put a couple of them down, and where would that get me? Besides, the days that I shot someone simply for being an officious little snit were long gone.

"I'm heading back there," I told him. "Call Hock, call a troll, call anyone you like. I'll make a fuss and disturb the hell out of Ivar anyway! So, you might as well go get him!"

He called my bluff and simply stared back at me, daring me to make my move.

"Alright," I muttered, "but this is on you."

I stepped back and took a deep breath. The clerk tensed, ready to jump up and run for help as soon as I moved. That gave me a small sense of satisfaction, glad that my reputation was still somewhat intact. Then, I made my move.

"Ivar!" I yelled it as loud as I could. "Ivar Ivarson! Get your short ass out here! Now!"

While Ivar's door didn't open immediately as I hoped it would, my shout did garner some attention. A door behind the clerk's desk slammed open and a huge, green ogre came charging through, large wooden club raised and ready to smash down on the troublemaker.

"Ivar!" I tried again. "It's Duke! You owe me! I saved your hide from the war golem!"

This time, the door to Ivar's office opened and the dwarf himself appeared, wiping at his eyes. His business that was making him unavailable was a nap!

"What is the meaning of this?" he groused. "Hock, stand down. You know Mr. Grandfather."

The ogre slid to a stop in front of me, his breath heaving down into my face, smelling of cabbage, old meat, and other less pleasant things.

"Mr. Grandfather," Ivar said, walking over to me. "Really. I would expect more of you. Why didn't you simply make an appointment?"

Outside, in the distance there was a boom and the sound of screams.

"That's why," I said, jerking my thumb over my shoulder. "That explosion."

I filled him in on the birds, the fact that they could speak and were purposely trying to get themselves killed, and that they exploded violently when they did.

"I was thinking that you could get the word out. To all those that don't trust the Watch, or pretty much anyone else. Tell them not to engage them, and definitely not to attack them."

"You came down here, demanded my attention, and delivered this warning. All for... what? A few non-humans don't get killed by exploding birds?" He looked a little incredulous as he spoke.

"Something like that. Why is that surprising?"

Ivar stopped and considered. "I guess it's not. At least, it's not any longer. I must say Mr. Grandfather, you have continued to surprise me since I first met you in that alley. I find myself glad that I know you, and even more glad to call you friend."

He stuck out his hand, and we shook. "Let Brindar know that I'll be in touch. Lilly is working with the Watch wizards to figure something out. I'm thinking I might go talk to the Witches as well. When we have something, I'll let him know so that he can help with the cleanup."

"Of course. And in the meantime, we'll put our resources on to the problem as well."

"Good idea. Stay in touch."

And it was. Although I hadn't thought of it, solving problems was not the province of humans alone. At this point, the more minds focused on this thing, the better.

"Slumming?" a voice said, as I exited the NHLF headquarters.

I expected to see one of the birds, beaking off again. But no, it was a different type of pest, larger and on two legs, but every bit as annoying.

"Raven," I sneered. "What do you want?"

"Want? From you? Nothing. I was sent to find you."

I chuckled at that. "Running errands now, huh? Best job for you. Who sent you?"

To my great amusement, he looked uncomfortable. "Lilly," he muttered.

Now I did laugh. "Yeah, I'll give you a pass then. She's hard to say no to, isn't she?"

"Whatever you say, Grandfather. I've done as requested. You're wanted back at the watchhouse, although why is beyond me."

"Maybe because I'm helpful, and I work well with others, while you're an annoying prig. Ever think of that?"

"One of these days, you're going to mouth off too much."

"Probably, but it won't be to you."

We started walking while still jawing at each other, but some of the actual rancor seemed to have gone out of our relationship lately. I didn't like it. Raven was an obnoxious, bigoted ass, and I didn't want to like him, or to work with him. And I was sure he felt an equal amount of disdain for me. But ever since we fought the gargoyles together, and I saw him donate his reward to Father Magnus, my vehemence had died down some.

Still, that didn't mean I had to let *him* know that, and we were still going back and forth when we walked through the door of the watchhouse, only to find Lilly waiting for us. With her was a tall, thin fellow, with a long grey bird, bushy eyebrows and startling clear blue eyes. He was dressed in a long robe that hung to the floor, bright blue with gold symbols stitched into it. Even if I didn't know what Lilly was working on, I would have known that this was a wizard straight off the bat. Some people scream the part.

"Enough, you two," Lilly said, and Raven and I both stopped our sniping. "This is Wulftin. He's one of the higher up wizards for the Watch. Be nice, or I'll ask him to turn you both into frogs."

"Oh, my. My dear Lilly. I couldn't do that. Not really. I mean, I *could* do it, you understand. Meaning I have the necessary power and knowledge for a transmogrification spell. But the intent, the will required to power such a spell, I don't think I could muster that. You see, magic, at least for those of us schooled in the brighter side of wizardry, is fueled by our own internal forces, by our souls if you will, or perhaps our own sense of being, if you won't. Therefore, we have to believe in the magic for it to work. In two senses, actually. First, that the magic will indeed happen. In this case, that these two gentlemen would indeed turn to frogs. The second would be in the necessity of the spell being cast, and in the rightness of it, so to speak. Since I don't know these men, and their only crime, if you'd call it that, would be their unconventional means of conversing with one another, I don't think I could believe in that segment of the spell. Therefore, it would fail. Meaning that I simply couldn't do it. Although I could, in other circumstances."

The three of us, four if you count Sarge cleaning up the ruins of his desk, stood and stared at Wulftin.

"Well, yes, okay then," Lilly said. I almost chuckled. This was the first time I ever saw her at a loss for words.

"Am I needed here any longer?" Raven asked, his voice cutting through the awkwardness.

"You're never needed anywhere, Raven," I piped up, earning a glare from Lilly.

"You don't have to stay, if you want to go," Lilly said. "But if you hang around you might learn something, and be of some assistance when we know what we're doing."

"Then, for you, I will stay," Raven replied, glancing at me out of the corner of his eye. The funny thing was, I had no doubt that he meant it simply as a show of respect to Lilly. With most guys, I'd be watching them like a hawk after a comment like that, but I honestly believed he meant no harm.

"Good," she said, "Now, Wulftin thinks he has an answer. Go ahead, Wulftin."

I flinched as she said that.

"Yes, yes. Well. Lilly has told me of the conundrum facing the city. That of the exploding birds and their unfortunate habit of goading others into setting them off, as it were. The problem, as I see it, and as I'm sure you do also, although I'm sure I shouldn't speak for you, you may have other views on the subject, is that when they die, they explode, causing great harm and damage. Well, die may not be accurate. We've yet to see one simply die. In every case that has been witnessed, the bird has been killed, struck down by some outside force, such as your gun, Mr. Grandfather, or the troll who tried to consume one. In any case, considering their ability to annoy and enrage those they encounter, it seems likely that no matter how many public service announcements are disseminated, there will still be those individuals who will cause the birds harm, thus causing them to explode, incurring harm to themselves, their loved ones, or others simply in the area. This, as I see it, is the problem."

That was a whole lot of words to explain exactly what we already knew.

"Yes, Wulftin," Lilly said, a tiny hint of impatience entering her voice. "We knew that already. The question is, how do we get rid of them, or how do we kill them without having them explode? That's what you said you might have an answer for."

"Ah, yes. I see. Well, the short answer is that you can't. Not kill them without having them explode, anyway. I see no way of accomplishing that. As far as getting rid of them, I'm afraid any method, such as employing trained hunting falcons against them, would either end in the same result, or simply drive them off for now, only to have them return later. No, I'm afraid what you ask is simply impossible in this particular set of circumstances. What we must do is find a way to limit the damage when they do, inevitably, explode."

"But can you do that?"

"Why…yes. That is…yes."

He seemed slightly put out at being held to such a short answer.

"Then let's go," Lilly said. "Duke, Raven, come on. We might need you if this is anything like I think it might be."

We left the watchhouse, watching the sky, and checking signs and other possible perches. I was sure that finding one of these things was going to be fairly easy, since I had seen so many. But Capital City was a big place, and when they had the whole city to spread out in, they weren't as obvious as I thought they would be.

We had been wandering around for about an hour, Raven and I occasionally exchanging barbs and being shushed by Lilly, and still saw no sign of any of the birds.

"Forget this," Raven said. "I've got better things to do than wander around half the city."

He started to walk off when Wulftin, peering into the sky, said, "Would it help, do you think, if I tracked one?"

Lilly and I looked at each other.

"Wait," I said. "You can do that?"

"Yes, well, I mean, theoretically. I'm not entirely sure it would work, and as I mentioned a short time ago, that is one of the primary focuses in getting a spell to work the way you would like it to. But, I also have a strong suspicion that the method I'm thinking of may in fact work, and therefore, any slight sign of success would boost my confidence that I was, in fact, correct, thus leading to a greater chance…"

"Wulftin," Lilly interrupted. "We don't need the whole explanation. But if you can track one of these things, please do it."

"Of course," he said, and stepped aside. He closed his eyes, bowed his head and then began chanting in a sing-song kind of way, his voice rising and falling. After a moment, his hand reached into a pocket and he pulled out a feather, which he tossed into the air in front of him. The feather wafted slowly toward the ground, but then stopped, as if an invisible hand reached out and grabbed it. Then, it began to revolve slowly, rising further up as it did. When it was even with Wulftin's head, it turned until the shaft was pointing away from him, and started to move forward. Wulftin walked slowly along behind it, allowing it to lead him.

It turned and twisted, making its way through the winding city streets, until it finally halted. I realized where we were; right back at the watchhouse, where we started over an hour earlier.

"Are you joking?" Raven said, but at that moment, we heard the harsh croak. It was distant, coming from far overhead.

Looking up, I saw them. There were three of the black birds, flying in a circle over the watchhouse. I watched them, a thought nagging at my mind, that this scene seemed familiar somehow.

Then it occurred to me. "Lilly, what does this remind you of?"

She watched the birds for a second or two, and then I saw the recognition in her face as well. "The tower. The Death Knight's tower. These are the birds that were circling it."

"Yeah, I think they are. But what does that mean?"

"I don't know." She shook her head. "But it they're associated with him, then they're bad news."

The four of us stood, watching the birds circling high in the air.

"Did you see that?" Raven said.

"What?" I asked.

"Open your eyes, Grandfather. One of them just disappeared."

There were now only two birds soaring in the sky. But where did the other one go? As I watched, another winked out of existence.

"What the...?"

"Huh," I heard Wulftin say. "They must be going into that gate up there."

We all dropped our stares and looked at the wizard, who continued to watch the remaining bird, his hand shielding his eyes.

After Wulftin made his announcement, I went into the watchhouse and asked Sarge to come out. Neither he, nor the two other Watchmen that he summoned were able to see anything other than the birds in the sky. As we watched, three more popped into existence, and then several more came and went. While none of us could see anything, Wulftin was adamant that there was some sort of gate in the sky that they were flying in and out of.

It soon turned out that as we watched them, the birds were watching us. There was a sudden brief rain of droppings, some of which hit their mark. While I wasn't pleased with their accuracy for myself, I did have to grin when I saw the pure disgust on Raven's face as a splatter marked his black-clothed shoulder.

"A rain of shit for pieces of shit!" One of them flew down closer, swooping overhead and taunting us.

Wulftin moved faster than I ever would have given him credit for. His hand darted into his pocket and came out with a clear glass marble. He held it aloft and cried out an unintelligible word. I saw Lilly's mouth gape in surprise, and assumed she recognized it.

Around the bird a clear bubble formed in midair. The bird kept flying, but when it hit the side, it bounced back, stunned, and fell to the floor of his prison with a croak.

"Mr. Grandfather," Wulftin said, "would you be able to shoot the bird with your wondrous weapon? The shell should hold him in place, but still allow for the passage of something that is not actually alive."

He kept his hands elevated as he spoke, but started lowering them slowly. As he did, the globe in the sky moved closer to us, bird and all.

"With pleasure," I said, and pulled my Ultimate Weapon from my belt.

But as I started to aim, I noticed that the bird wasn't looking very good. He was getting puffy, his feathers standing up.

"Oh, crap…" I started to say, but was drowned out by the enormous bang as the bird exploded.

We all picked ourselves up a few moments later, ears ringing and eyes watering. It was bad enough that it exploded, but the energy also escaped Wulftin's spell. He took the brunt of the blast and lay unconscious a few feet away.

"Well, that didn't work," Lilly moaned as she climbed unsteadily to her feet. Raven muttered something under his breath.

Raven and I picked up Wulftin and got him inside. After a few gentle slaps and some water, he started to come around.

"Well", he said. "Now we know. Even impeding their movements can cause them to explode. A fact that is good to know, even if in the learning of it we suffered a slight setback. Still, that shell that I conjured should have held back the force of the explosion. You see, since the bird is organic, and the shell is designed to contain any organic material, my assumption was that the..."

"We get it, Wulftin," I said. "But now we need to know what else we can try."

"Save me from intellectual eggheads," Raven muttered. For once, I secretly agreed with him.

A short time later, we sat in the watchhouse, upstairs in one of the libraries that made up the wizards' section. There was a long, highly polished wooden table, piled high with books, scrolls and papers of all sorts. We needed to move some to the side to see each other as we sat down.

"Well," Lilly began. "We know that we can't kill them, and we can't trap them, or else they'll explode." As she spoke, we heard another explosion off in the distance. "And in the meantime, these things are doing a lot of damage to the city."

"If only we could close that gate," Wulftin said wistfully. "Then the ones that were left here would be trapped. Possibly cut off from the source of their power. At that point, they may revert to being no more than simple birds. But that's a mere pipe dream at this point. The gate is throwing off an incredible amount of dark magic, too much to be countered by my magic, or anyone else that I know of in the Watch."

We all sat and waited for him to go on, but for once, Wulftin appeared to be satisfied with what he said, and sat staring at the table in front of him in silence.

"Wulftin," Lilly finally said, "what do you mean by dark magic?"

"Hmm? Oh, yes. My term for the branch of wizardry that is more concerned with the realms of death and the hereafter. Not that I consider the practitioners of such magic to be dark wizards, you understand. No, that would be giving in to stereotypes. Instead, I merely mean it as a descriptor of sorts, one that…"

"You do know that I'm a necromancer, right?" Lilly said. Interrupting Wulftin when he was getting wound up was becoming a normal part of conversation. He didn't seem to mind, which made me think it happened to him quite often.

He stopped and regarded Lilly.

"Why, that's right! You are! My, how did I overlook that? Why then, you should be able to shut the gate down, assuming you could get close to it. If you're strong enough, that is, and I've heard tales of you, Lilly. Now that I suddenly remember. Oh yes, I believe you have the necessary power."

"But if it's Death Magic, why can't I see the gate? I should be able to, shouldn't I?"

"One would think," Wulftin replied. "However, part of the magic is hiding itself. I can only see it due to my third eye."

Again, Wulftin dropped a statement into the middle of a conversation that would normally require a half-day's worth of explanation, and then moved on as if it were the most normal thing in the world.

"You have a third eye?" Raven asked.

"Well, not a physical one, as such, no. It won't open in the middle of my forehead or some such. Wouldn't that be a sight! No pun intended, I assure you. No. Instead, what I mean is that I was born with an ability to see certain things that remain hidden from others. My Solstina Day presents were never a surprise to me, and my friends refused to play hide-and-seek with me, since I always knew exactly where they were. I could see them, you understand, whether they were around the corner, or behind a barrel, or in another room entirely. So, while the gate that is allowing the birds entrance to our city is invisible to most others, to me, it stands in the air as a gash in the fabric of the sky."

Well. That was a new one on me. And while I could see how his ability to see hidden things would be very useful to a Nuisance Man, the thought of not being able to turn it off gave me the shivers. Some things are best left unseen.

"We have two problems then," Lilly said. "I can shut the gate down, supposedly. But I can't see it, and I can't get near it. Where does that leave us?"

"Nowhere," I said. "From what I can tell, we'll have to try to kill as many of these things far away from anyone else, or anything important, as we can. What else can we do?"

There was silence for a few moments as we each thought of various ways of doing this. For me, it meant having to be a pretty good shot to take the birds out from far off. Lilly could do the same, I was sure. But Raven? Him, I wasn't sure about.

"I suppose I could get you up near the gate," Wulftin suddenly said, with a thoughtful expression on his face. "I could make a floating disc. It's a small spell, usually. Useful for getting the sugar bowl down from a high shelf for your tea, perhaps. But I believe I could make a bigger one. One that would support you enough to get you to the gate. Then, if all things remain as we think they are, you could shut it down, Lilly."

"That's great!" she said, but then. "But, no, that won't work. I still wouldn't be able to see it."

"And you'd be unprotected," I chimed in. "Which means that's out of the question. Unless you can make the disc big enough to hold the two of us."

"Theoretically, there should be no limit to how large a disc I make. You see, it's simply a matter of visualizing…"

"Three of us, then," Raven said. "I'm going too."

"For what?" I asked, unable to keep the surprise out of my voice.

"Those things fly around fast, and who knows what else will come out of the gate. While Lilly is shutting it down, I'll help you protect her."

"Why are you doing this, Raven? What's in it for you?"

"It's my city too, Grandfather. Besides, even if I don't understand her horrible taste in partners, I happen to have a great deal of respect for Lilly."

This was getting weird. Maybe I really did need to keep my eye on him, after all.

"That's settled then," Lilly said. "You'll float the three of us up there, Wulftin, and Duke and Raven will keep any nasties away from me while I do what I can to shut down the gate. But, you still haven't answered how I'm going to see it."

"Oh, well, that's not hard. I'll have to be with you. If I maintain close contact with you, with all of you, you'll be able to see it. Again, the ability is one that I was born with, innate if you will. But by an application of magic that I developed some time ago, I'm can share my sight with others, to let them see what is hidden as I do. Therefore, when we near the gate…"

"Wait a minute," I said. "What happens if you get hit and knocked out or something while we're all on this floating disc thing of yours?"

"Oh, well, I imagine that we'll plummet to our deaths. Yes, I would think a fall from that height would certainly be enough to kill us. Most unfortunate, of course."

In the end, we couldn't come up with a better idea. In the course of our conversation, we heard no fewer than another three explosions from around the city. In spite of all the notices being put out by the Watch and the NHLF, people were still attacking the birds in anger. If anything, the frequency of them was getting more, not less.

We left the watchhouse, with Sarge promising to keep any lookee-loos away, and watched the birds circling overhead. There were several of them now, flying in a spiral, some disappearing, others popping into sight, and yet others leaving to flap their way to different parts of the city.

Wulftin took out a flat, circular metal disc and placed it on the ground.

"Mind your toes," he muttered, and then started chanting in that same sing-song way I heard him use before. The disc started to expand, flowing outward, and becoming larger. We all stepped on to it when it grew large enough.

Without stopping his spell, Wulftin gestured, and we rose smoothly into the air. I grabbed a hold of Lilly's hand, and felt someone grab onto my shoulder. Raven's face was whiter than normal, and his grip on me was like iron.

"Fear not," Wulftin said, "the spell is working perfectly. Whoops."

The last was when the disc stopped rising and dipped down quickly, causing us all to lurch. He began his spell again, and we climbed higher into the sky.

The birds began taking an interest as we approached them. They flew around us, spewing insults and curses like a ship full of drunken sailors. But none of them approached too closely, seeming unsure of what to make of the humans floating in their realm.

Wulftin's tone changed and the disc stopped rising. Still chanting, he reached out and touched Lilly, then myself, and finally Raven. His touch was like fire, or ice, that blazed in my head. It was hard to think, and my vision blurred.

But when it cleared, I could see the gate, as Wulftin promised. It was a swirl of clouds in the air in front of us, surrounding a hole that led to nowhere.

"I need to get closer," Lilly said, her hair beginning to stick out from her head, and her eyes going pure black. "I can feel it, but I need to be closer to shut it down."

Wulftin chanted and the disc move forward, sliding smoothly through the air.

Suddenly, I felt something strike my leg, and a bird rebounded off into the air. They were starting to attack. I drew my gun, sighted, and stopped. I couldn't shoot one. The resulting explosion might very well cause Wulftin harm, or even toss all of us off of our platform.

Instead, Raven and I stood guard, ready to jump in front of either Lilly or Wulftin as the birds came in. They were only birds after all, so their attacks weren't particularly vicious, but soon, both of us were covered in scratches from beaks and claws, and bruised from the birds simply flying into us. All the time, they kept up the litany of filth and depravity.

"By the gods," I heard Lilly say. I never heard such despair in her voice before, not even when the Death Knight stole her magic. I turned and looked straight through the gate, and felt the same crushing weight myself.

It was another world through there. Dead, wasted, and decayed. It was our world as it would be, if the forces of darkness won…and they would. They were too omnipresent, too overwhelming. Oh, we could push them back for a time, but they would return, over and over, wearing us down. And our world would become the same as that apocalyptic landscape that I saw before me.

The birds sat in the dead trees of that world, croaking raucously as they fed on the scraps of some unnamable and long dead creature. A river, clogged with debris, oozed sluggishly along, winding through blasted hills of barren rock and dirt. The sky was an ashen brown color, with ragged wisps of clouds scudding along, occasionally passing in front of a pale, cold sun. Gusts of wind picked up dust, blowing it into choking masses, covering the birds at times, who would shake the grit from their feathers and curse.

And there was a man, floating in the air as we were, only by himself, with no need of a disc. He sat in midair in the lotus position, legs crossed, and arms held casually in his lap. His eyes were closed and his thin lips moved as he chanted silently. He was thin to the point of emaciation, and his grey hair hung down in a limp curtain from a fringe around his otherwise bald pate.

"It's him," Lilly said. "He's the one holding the gate open. I need to get to him."

"Are you crazy?" I yelled. "You're not going in there!"

"Duke, I have to! The gate has to be closed down! Look at that place. The birds are only the beginning. You can feel that, right?"

I felt it from the moment I looked into that world. She was right, but I didn't care. Let the world burn, there was no way I was letting her go into that place.

"No!" I shouted. "I don't care, Lilly. I'm not losing you!"

She opened her mouth to argue, when Raven stepped in, cocked his arm and threw a knife. Knife throwing is a skill that takes a lot of practice to master, and Raven must have put in the hours. The knife flew through the air, through the gate, and seemed to grow smaller as it sailed into that other world.

But it found its mark. It buried itself almost to the hilt in the floating man's shoulder. His eyes opened with a snap, and he glared at us, and even more than the banshee, or the Death Knight, or anything I had ever seen, I saw what true evil looked like. Evil that exists because it is, because that's all it ever was, or ever would be.

He opened his mouth and screamed, but unlike Wulftin, it didn't affect his spell, and he remained sitting in the air with no apparent effort. Lilly threw up her hand and started a spell herself. The man duplicated her actions, and they locked in a battle of wills, her black eyes locked onto his solid gray ones. The air crackled between them with the force of their magics striving against one another.

Behind me, I heard a grunt as a bird hit Wulftin and the disc slipped slightly.

"Raven! Protect Wulftin!" I shouted.

"What are you going to do?"

"End this."

I pulled my gun and aimed at the floating man. I didn't know who, or what, he was, but I didn't care. The little, metal ball would do plenty of damage on its own.

I fired, and the ball sped forth, striking the man in the forehead. His head snapped back with the force of it, but he quickly recovered, growling as a thin trickle of blood ran down between his eyes.

"Do it again, Duke!" Lilly yelled.

I shot him again, this time taking him in the chest. And again, and once again. Each time, the little, metal ball caught him in a different area, and each time, Lilly pushed her spell closer.

Finally, she unloosed a howl and the winds swirled around us. The spell that she was using became visible, and it looked like a rope of sickly light leading from her to the floating man. The end of it wavered in front of him, not quite touching him. He held his own hands in front of it now, warding it off, bleeding from where I shot him.

"Once more," Lilly said.

I fired again, and got him in the same area as the first shot. This time, as his head snapped back, the rope of light lunged forward and attached itself to his torso. It started to pulse hungrily, like a snake consuming a mouse, and he screamed again, but this time, his scream was rage, fear, and disbelief.

Lilly chanted louder, and the rope of light pulsed more strongly, until finally the man on the other end of it began to sink in on himself. His cheeks collapsed in toward his mouth, his stomach toward his back bone. His legs fell out of the lotus position and hung limply in the air. He twitched and jerked at the end of the rope like a fish caught on a hook.

In the end, Lilly sucked him dry, and we watched as his corpse fell out of the air, plummeting down to that ruined land below him. The gate began spiraling tighter, the hole in the middle becoming smaller, until with a snap, it closed, and the evil, dead land beyond was gone.

When it was over, Lilly leaned over the edge of the disc and vomited. I held on to her while Wulftin changed his chant and we started to gently descend.

"That was horrible, Duke," she whispered. "Like the worst taste that I ever…"

"Yeah, but you did it. Again. You saved the city again."

"We did," she said, glancing at me, smiling slightly before she retched again.

I held her, watching the ground come closer.

Later, after we got some wine to wash Lilly's mouth with, the four of sat in a tavern.

"You did good, Grandfather. Sometimes you surprise me," Raven said.

"Same here, but for you," I replied, and lifted my mug in a salute. He returned it.

"You were right, Wulftin," Lilly said. "When the gate closed, the birds became ordinary birds again. How did you know?"

"Well, you see, it was all very logical when you think of how the energy must have flowed from that other world, to this one. Indeed, the conduit must have been…"

I lifted my mug and took a swig, glad that some things in the world are wholly good. Like ale, and Lilly, and hell, maybe even Raven. Everything is relative, right? For now, it was good to sit in a comfortable chair, drink my ale, and let Wulftin's explanation wash over me.

## THE LORD OF THE THINGS

The incident with the birds shook Lilly and I more than we wanted to admit at first. While it was great that we defeated them, (well, I say "we", but really it was Lilly), knowing that other cold, dead land existed preyed on our minds. The sense of evil and despair from it permeated our thoughts, and we were having a tough time letting it go.

"It's possible that the place we saw is really the origin of a lot of the evil we've been seeing lately," she told me.

"Do you think that someone, or something, in that place is behind the attacks, then?"

"Possibly. I really don't know." She fell silent and shivered. I could sympathize, and I only saw the place. Lilly actually connected with it.

She took a couple of days off work, and I didn't go to the watchhouse either during that time. Instead, we stayed home, spending time together, and trying to concentrate on our upcoming wedding, which was now only a week away. To me, things seemed to be pretty much set. We had the location for the wedding ceremony and the location for the party after; we had figured out what food was going to be served and when, and the ale and wine was being taken care of. Apparently, flowers were arranged for and being delivered to both Father Magnus' temple and the Rose Petal Room. As far as I could tell, everything was ready and we were simply waiting for the big day.

"When are you getting fitted?" Lilly asked me over breakfast.

My blank stare said it all.

"Duke, did you really forget?"

I nodded, my mouth full, almost afraid to speak.

"Let's go, then," she said, pushing her chair back from the table. I took one last swig of my coffee and rose to my feet.

"Sorry," I mumbled.

"It's alright. We've had a lot on our minds the last few days. I hope it's not too late."

Half an hour later we were at the tailors, where I stood in front of a mirror while a small, elderly man measured me in ways that made me think that perhaps I was really betrothed to him. But he was very kind and spoke almost exclusively to Lilly, asking her what my preferences were as to cut, color, style, and so on. Obviously, this was a man who serviced many a wedding.

I, on the other hand, only had the one partially under my belt, but even I knew enough to stand there quietly and let Lilly answer for me. In the end, I knew it was also going to be the best thing. She had a much more developed sense of style and taste than I did.

Finally, all the measurements were taken and jotted down, things were done being poked, prodded, and lifted and we were able to leave, with the promise that my wedding suit would be ready in two days' time.

"Well," I said, as we walked into the sunshine of a bright Capital City day, "that was unpleasant. What do you say we get some lunch and put it behind us?"

"A quick one. We've got some more errands to run today."

"What? What else could we possible have to do?"

"We need some stuff for the house," she replied. "My parents are going to be seeing it."

"Oh, right. I forgot."

After our very pleasant, but too short, lunch, we wandered down the street again, heading for the First Quarter. There, Lilly could find all sorts of household items, which she said would turn the place from being a house into a home...whatever that meant.

For me, it meant standing around, offering non-committal opinions when she asked for them, and waiting patiently while she picked up one thing, examined it, put it back, and moved on to another. Often to return to the first one after looking at several others.

It was during one of these times that I saw the strange, gross little slug, crawling along the street as if it owned the place and didn't have a care in the world. It was about an inch long and pink colored, covered with a layer of mucous that gleamed in the sunlight. That alone seemed odd. I always associated slugs and other such slimy creatures with damp, dark places. Places where you felt like you needed a wash after being near.

The sight of this gross little thing slithering slowly along amused me, so I watched it make its slow progress from cobblestone to cobblestone. And then it got stepped on, and my attention was torn away from it, and to the boots that squashed it.

Since the First Quarter is home to so many dwarves, it was perfectly reasonable that it was the heavy boots of one that smooshed my unpleasant little friend. Glancing up, I saw that it had been done without malice, indeed, without notice even. The dwarf continued on his way, unaware that he had snuffed out a life so casually.

Oh well. It was a slug. It was fun to watch for a minute or two, but really, it was a slug. Lilly was wrapping up her time inside of this particular shop anyway, and my carrying the packages service was being called upon. With luck, this would be the last one and we'd head home to relax.

But as usual, luck was not with me, and there was another place to visit. And another after that. There was even a grocer, where we picked up several expensive, delicious items that I was told were not to be eaten. They were for our guests.

It was no wonder that I spotted another slug as I plodded along under my increasingly heavy load of packages. My head was down, both with the effort of carting everything, as well as with the need to keep Lilly from seeing what I was sure was a pretty glum expression on my face.

It was moving along in the same manner as the previous one, slithering from cobblestone to cobblestone. When it would get in the gaps between the stones, it would either turn and move along the space between, or it would simply begin to scale the far side.

We came to what Lilly swore would be our last stop, so I dropped the packages to the ground to wait for her, and contemplated the little thing as it struggled along. I thought the first one strange to see, and now thought it even stranger to see a second, but, perhaps this was some sort of seasonal migration of pink slugs that I didn't know about.

Then, another appeared. I looked around the street, but didn't see any others, so it seemed that it was only the two of them. Blindly, they approached each other, both making toward the same cobblestone. For a moment, I wondered if something was drawing them to it, but I couldn't see anything that would account for it.

I was silently cheering them on, hoping that they would reach the cobble at the same time and bump into each other. Yes, I was truly that bored that I was excited by a day at the slug races. I wondered what would happen if they did meet. Would it be like two old friends having a chance encounter, or two enemies suddenly facing off in a duel? Or was I going to get a slightly nauseating view of what constituted a slug's sex life?

My wishes came true, for once, and the two little things did squirm to the same cobblestone at the same time. One slimed his way up from one direction and the other from the opposite side of the stone. They must have been able to sense each other, because they headed directly at one another.

When they met, they didn't stop moving, but ran, for lack of a better word, into each other. It was like a slow-motion collision of two horse carts. I kept watch, unsure if this was slug love or war that I was witnessing, and also slightly embarrassed by how engrossed in the encounter I had become.

And then they…well, they moved…but not really. It was a weird kind of blurry effect, and then the slug was moving again, down off the cobblestone and on his way to wherever. One slug. One slug that was about half again as big as either of the original two.

Huh…slug love, I guessed. That was certainly a weird way to breed, but nature does some strange things. Which was yet another reason that I chose to stay safely inside the city walls and away from it whenever I could.

Two days later I was taking time for a long lunch in the Barman's Choice, my favorite tavern in our neck of the woods. Lilly went back to work, but I was taking one more day to laze about and live the good life before I took anything from the Board. I was finding the bottom of my second mug of ale and contemplating a third, when Brindar came through the door.

"Grandfather," he said, plopping down heavily in the chair that I pushed out with my foot.

"Brindar. What brings you here?" I searched around for the serving girl, lifting my fingers to indicate two ales. I was nothing if not sociable, and it would have been rude to let my friend drink alone.

"Nothing, really. Patrolling, I guess you could call it. Ivar wants me to have more of a 'presence' in the city, whatever that's supposed to mean."

"Huh. Well, glad you're present here. Let's have an ale."

We shared the one and then another, and by that time, I was ready to get on my feet and move some.

"Let's say we take a tour around the city," I told him. "See if we can find any trouble to stir up."

In truth, I didn't really want trouble, and neither did Brindar. But it was a better thing to say to another male than, "Hey, want to take a walk?"

Off we went, strolling along, two bad-ass Nuisance Men making their way through the mean streets of Capital City. And trouble did stay away from us. Like it or not, (and I admit that I did), I had a certain reputation, and Brindar had developed one in a remarkably short amount of time. There were no muggings, waylayings, or chicaneries within our sight.

But we did come upon one of the most disturbing things I had seen in quite some time. We were walking along for a good while and it was getting to the point that a stop at another tavern seemed to be in order. On the other end of the alley we were passing was a new place, The Drunken Man, that I was eager to try. There was such a thing as truth in advertising, and I admired their candor.

I mentioned this to Brindar, and since he was game, we set off down the alley, the thought of the cool, frothy ale already making my mouth water. But that feeling quickly dried up when I spotted yet another one of those pink slugs. Only this one was much larger than the ones I saw earlier. It must have been a good foot long, and as big around as an ale mug. It oozed along the alley, hugging the wall, like it was hoping not to be noticed.

"Wow," I said, stopping and pointing it out to Brindar. "Look at that thing. I saw a few of them a couple of days ago, but they weren't even close to that size."

"Yeah, I've noticed them too. Nasty little things."

As we stood and watched, a rat squeezed out of a crack in the alley wall and sniffed along, heading for the slug. When it got close it stopped, its nose twitching rapidly. Then, it uttered a squeak, jumped, and turned, trying to flee.

But the slug was quicker. It threw out a long, pink, slimy tendril, which wrapped itself around the rat and pulled it to it. The rat squealed and tried to pull away, but the slug was stronger as well. As we watched, it pulled the rat to a spot directly in front of itself, and then flowed up and over the rodent, whose terrified squeaks faded away.

I watched the whole thing happen in horrified silence. Brindar did the same.

"That was disgusting," he finally said.

I agreed. "I hate nature," I said, and we turned to go.

We only took a step or two, when a new noise caused us to turn. The slug was moving again, only now it had four legs, and what looked like a long, pointed snout, wriggling about on the end of its cylindrical body.

It turned what passed for its head toward us, and then began to move forward. If I didn't know better, I would have said that it was on the attack.

It turned out that I did know better. The thing did the trick with the tendril again, this time the slimy, pink string attaching itself to my boot. Unbelievably, I felt it give my leg a tug. It wasn't strong enough to actually move me, but I shouldn't have even felt it.

Biter swung down and severed the string, causing it to snap back in both directions, some of it landing on my boot, the rest back on the once slug. Brindar stepped forward and swept his axe down again, cutting the thing in two.

There was no blood, or anything else that oozed out of the creature. It simply fell in two halves and lay still on the alley floor, two pink blobs.

"That got a whole lot grosser," he said, sliding Biter back into the loop on his belt.

"I think I need that ale," I said.

That night, I told Lilly about what we encountered.

"That's one of the more disgusting things you've told me about," she said.

"Yeah, but if I have to see it, then you get to hear about it."

She looked thoughtful. "You know, I'm thinking about the fact that it started to take on that rat's shape. That doesn't seem like something natural."

"No, at least nothing I've ever heard of. But who knows what weirdness nature has to offer up. It's why I hate leaving the city."

"You hate leaving the city because there's too many taverns here. This thing you saw concerns me, though."

"Why?" I knew what was coming, but I didn't want to face it. Not yet.

"I'm worried that it's another attack on the city. Imagine if you and Brindar hadn't seen and killed it. What was next? A dog? A person? And would it have kept growing?"

"Aw, come on Lilly. Can't someone else handle this one? We're getting hitched in a few days."

"You're right," she said. "We've done enough for now. I'll tell my bosses about it tomorrow and they can deal with it, if need be. For all I know, you're right, and it's some gross slug that's perfectly natural. Weird and icky, but natural. If not, let them handle it. I'm working tomorrow, and then that's it until after we're married."

I have to admit, I was shocked. It wasn't like Lilly to let someone else take responsibility for something. Shocked or not, I was certainly happy about it. One of the things that I love about Lilly is her ability to surprise me.


But things are never as easy as they appear. I was going to the watchhouse the next day to take one last job off the Board while Lilly was at work, so I walked there with her.

"Duke, Lilly," Sarge said as we walked in, his nose buried in his ever-present newssheets.

"Hey, Sarge," I replied, then kissed Lilly goodbye and headed over to the counter, rebuilt after the bird explosion.

"Almost the big day," he said to me, glancing up.

"Yep. You're going to be there, right?"

"Wouldn't miss it. It should be fun to watch you squirm."

"Squirm? Who's going to squirm? I'm happy as can be about it."

"Sure. Now. But when Father Magnus starts talking about being married *forever*? Well, we'll see."

"You're not getting to me, Sarge. Not about that anyway. I know when I've got it made."

He laughed. "Yeah, I guess you do, at that. Working today?"

"Yep. Anything good on the Board?"

"Not sure about good, but certainly weird," he replied, his mouth twisted into a wry grimace.

"What do you mean?"

"See for yourself."

I walked over to the Board, expecting that it would be mostly empty. Instead, it was full, with notices posted one on top of the other. There were plenty of the run-of-the-mill nuisances, like ogres out of hand, or goblins burning down someone's business. But mostly there were slugs. Tons of them. Descriptions varied from ones that were a few inches long invading someone's house, to larger ones who, as Lilly had feared, had eaten someone's dog.

"You're kidding me," I muttered.

"Nope," Sarge said. He followed me to the Board and stood looking them over with me. "Like I said, weird."

"Yeah, well, I'm not taking any of them. Lilly thinks they might be another attack on the city, and we're taking a break. Let someone else deal with them. Me? I'm taking this one."

I pulled a notice almost at random, and then glanced down at it. It was a simple goblin, wanted for trying to set fire to a daycare over near Silver Tree Lane. My opinion of goblin intelligence sank to a whole new level. Not only stupid enough to target kids, but to target rich kids? Pure idiocy.

"Well, that one should earn you some money anyway," Sarge said, returning to his newssheets. "But let me know what you find out about those slug things."

"I told you, I'm not doing those!" I protested.

"Sure, Duke. I know."

I walked out muttering. I wasn't getting involved. Not now.

The goblin was a piece of cake. I talked to the complainant, got paid, and headed for the daycare. The goblin was still there, trying hard to light fire to a stone building with a flint and steel. It was almost pathetic, but the problem with goblins, especially one like this, was that they couldn't take a hint. I did what I needed to, and eliminated the nuisance. I surprised him, and didn't even need to set my gun to "Goblin". The normal little, metal ball did the trick.

Sarge was right. The money for this one was very good. The type of folk who lived on Silver Tree Lane could afford the best, which is why they got me.

I was heading home, winding my way through the streets and feeling pretty good, when I heard heavy foot-steps pounding along behind me. I turned and saw Brindar running after me.

"Grandfather!" he said, coming to a halt and taking a moment to catch his breath. "We've got a problem."

"Oh, no. *We* don't have a problem. *You* might have a problem, but I'm doing perfectly fine."

"Cut the comedy. I need you to come down to the docks. I need your help."

Dammit. That was hitting below the belt. Friends or not, it wasn't easy for Brindar to ask for help. It wasn't easy for me to do it either. If he was straight up asking, it must be bad.

"It's those stupid slugs, isn't it?" I asked.

"I guess you could say that. Not sure if they're really slugs anymore. Not after they overran an orc compound."

"Tell me it wasn't like with the rat."

"Worse. Much worse. But you have to come see."

"Hold on," I sighed. I located one of the messenger boys that inhabit the city like fleas on a dog and sent a message to Lilly, telling her that I might be late tonight after all.

But I wasn't going to tell Sarge where I was going.

I never knew Brindar to exaggerate and he certainly wasn't this time. What we saw the slug in the alley do was multiplied many times over by what we saw now. I don't know how they managed it, but there were several roughly orc shaped pink, slimy masses shambling around the dock area. What looked like arms, legs, or heads would grow out of the masses, be reabsorbed, and grow anew elsewhere. People scattered, and the slug-orc things had the run of the place.

"This is gross," I said, as Brindar and I stood in a nearby alley, peering around a corner.

"It's worse than that. They spit out those same sticky ropes that the little one did, only these are much thicker. See that big one?" He indicated one particular shambling mass, much larger than the rest. "That was an ogre. It fought like mad, but the thing pulled him in anyway. Look, you can see one of its arms."

Coming out of the back of the shape was what appeared to be a rough drawing of a huge arm, flailing around like it was trying to swat flies.

"It pulled an ogre in? That's not good. Have you tried to take one out yet?"

"No, I haven't been able to get near. I tried sneaking up close enough to use Biter on one, but it saw me coming. I barely dodged the rope thing it shot at me. Otherwise, you'd be seeing one with a big axe shape growing out of it. Think your gun can do anything?"

"I don't know. I can shoot them, sure. But since I'm not sure what they are, the little, metal ball is only going to do so much damage. If I knew what to call them, it'd be different."

"Well, try it anyway," he said.

I stepped out from the wall that we were hiding behind, pulled my gun, aimed and fired. I got off a quick three shots, and saw them all hit dead on. But to almost no effect. I saw three holes appear in the shambling mass, but they quickly closed up again. The only noticeable effect was that the slug-orc oozed around and thick, ropy tendrils of pink slime shot out at me.

I dove back behind the wall as the tendrils hit where I was standing a moment before. If I hadn't been ready for it, I would even now be getting pulled toward the thing. There was no doubt in my mind that if they were strong enough to pull in an ogre, they could easily do the same to me.

"No luck," I said.

"There's luck," Brindar replied, "but it's all the bad kind. Look."

Not only was the one that I shot heading in our direction, all the others were too. If they had some way of communicating, I couldn't see or hear what it was. But they certainly seemed to be acting as a unit.

As they neared, they drew closer to each other also, until the inevitable happened. Two of them bumped into each other. It was like watching the two little ones that I saw a couple of days ago. When they collided, they didn't move apart again. Instead, they flowed into each other, with a weird melting kind of motion. Their pink, slimy skin engulfed each other, and then they were one.

The new one was like the orc-ogre-slug hybrid bringing up the rear, but not quite as large. It had an arm that was sticking out of the top of it, and a leg jutting from its side. It moved in a jerking motion, that was half a stumbling walk and half a slide forward. Watching it was fascinating and horrifying all at once.

"Now what?" I said.

"What if you draw their attention, and I get close enough to take a swing? Maybe Biter can do some damage."

"What? I'm the bait?"

"Sort of, yeah. But move off enough that they can't get to you."

"How far is that?"

Brindar shrugged. His guess was as good as mine. We had no idea how far these things could shoot those ropey tendrils. But he had a point. The gun didn't do much damage, but it did draw their attention. And we couldn't let these things go, or they'd continue doing what they had been, absorbing more and more people.

I sighed. "Stay out of sight, and give me a minute."

I turned and ran off through the streets, circling around so that I could come back to the docks from the other direction. It took me a few minutes, but I came out behind the things, which flowed further up the way, toward where Brindar was still hiding.

I pulled my gun, aimed and shot one of them in what I hoped was the back, again getting off a quick three shots. No difference in the effect. The holes closed over, but the slug-orcs did turn back toward me, and started flowing in my direction. I fired again, at a different one this time, hoping that I was out of their range.

If I wasn't, then they weren't trying to snare me for some other reason. They didn't shoot their ropes at me, but did continue to shuffle and ooze toward me, odd appendages appearing in their bodies and disappearing.

Two more of them ran into each other, reducing the number of individuals, but increasing the size and danger of the ones that were left. It wouldn't be long until they all found each other and became a giant blob, intent on sucking up the entire city.

I fired, moved back, and fired again, keeping an eye out. When they all seemed to be fully focused on me, I saw Brindar sneak out from the alley where he was hiding. He walked slowly and carefully, Biter at the ready. As he neared the back of the rear most one, it must have sensed him, because it started to turn.

But Brindar was faster, and his axe came whistling around. It sheared completely through the slug-orc thing, cutting it almost perfectly in half. The top half slid to the side and then fell with a sucking noise. The bottom half stayed where it was, quivering. Like the slug-rat from the alley, no blood or other fluids ran from the wound.

Brindar carefully stepped around that one, and staying low approached the next. I kept firing at them to keep them focused on me. But as he moved forward, the two halves that lay behind him moved. Sticky tendrils shot out from both of them. Some of the ropes went toward the other half, and some of them shot toward Brindar, connecting with the backs of his legs.

The two halves began drawing themselves together, while the other ropes stopped Brindar in his tracks. He looked down at the backs of his legs in surprise. He was a professional though, and had been in plenty of sticky spots before this one. He kept his head, reversed his axe, and brought it down through the tendrils attached to him. Biter swept cleanly through them, and he sprang away before more could trap him. He took off running, gaining the safety of the alley before the two halves of the slug thing could reform.

I stopped firing, turned and ran, back into the streets, working my way around until I was with Brindar again.

"That half worked," I said. "But I don't think it's our answer."

"No, I don't think so either. Any other ideas?"

"Not without knowing what they are."

"How smart is that gun of yours?" he asked me.

"What? I don't know. What do you mean?" It never occurred to me that my Ultimate Weapon could have any sort of intelligence.

"Think about it. You've run into some pretty bizarre things and somehow the gun always knows what you mean when you name it. What if you don't have to have the exact name, but it will know what you mean anyway?"

"That's crazy," I began, but then stopped. What if? I mean, I told it to kill darkness and it did. Maybe there was something to that.

I shrugged. "Worth a try, I guess."

I stepped out from the alley, pointed the gun at the shambling masses and said, "Those things!"

I fired, and the little, metal ball that came out was a brilliant white color, and it left a trail of vapor in the air behind it. When it hit the slug-orc, it made a hole, but this time, it didn't close up. Instead, the edges of the hole turned a bluish, white color. The color began to spread throughout the thing's body and there was a cracking and creaking sound. Within seconds, the thing was frozen solid.

I looked back at Brindar, eyebrows raised.

"See?" he said.

I shook my head, turned back to the horde and continued to fire. One little, metal ball for each one was all it took. A few minutes later, the dock area was covered with what looked like disturbingly carved ice sculptures.

"Now what?" Brindar asked, coming up next to me after I shot the last one.

"Biter?"

"Let's see what happens now."

Biter shattered the first one, and we stood back to see what would happen. Nothing did. If the slug thing was still alive, it showed no signs of it. Brindar moved on, shattering one after the other. He seemed to be having a good time.

Soon, all of the frozen slug-orcs were destroyed, and icy pieces of them lay scattered across the dock area. We stayed alert, watching for any signs of them thawing, moving, or trying to reform. Yet, despite it being a fairly warm day, they stayed frozen, and when I worked up the nerve to try, ice cold to the touch.

Dock workers began to make their way back to the area, thanking the two of us for handling the problem. I looked at Brindar. "Ale?"

"Yep. Not that weak human stuff though. This time, we're going to go to one of my places."

That was fine with me. Dwarven ale is good stuff. The only problem is the ceilings in those places tended to be low, and I always banged my head. Luckily, I liked to sit down at a table to do my drinking.

Brindar led the way and I followed along with him, thinking of the peculiarities of my gun. For years, ever since I got it, I thought of it in the way that I had always known. Mostly, that I needed to specifically name what I wanted it to kill. But recent events, which all seemed to start when the Death Knight named it, made me think otherwise.

At some point, I was going to have to do some research into the thing. Maybe after the wedding Lilly and I could start looking.

My thoughts were suddenly interrupted by a tug on the back on my shirt. I spun around, half expecting to find a slimy, pink tendril attached to me. But it wasn't.

Instead, there was a small rat-man, who stood about waist high, looking up at me. He blinked in the sunlight, and rubbed his hands together in a nervous sort of way, while the whiskers on his snout twitched. It was unusual to see a rat-man during the day. They tended to do their business, whatever distasteful thing it was, at night. I think they saw better in the dark than in the light, but it also could have been because no one really wanted them around. Me included.

"You come," he said, his voice barely above a whisper.

"What? Come where? I'm not going anywhere with you."

My fairly recent change in outlook led to a much greater tolerance for those that were different from me. I drank with dwarves, ate with orcs and held conversations with ogres. I didn't even have anything against goblins, if I could find one that showed any sort of intelligence. Hell, I even stopped outright loathing Raven, and started to tolerate him.

But rat-men? They were different. There was something nasty about them, something dirty. There was always an odor that reminded me of garbage, or rotten meat. It wasn't strong, just enough to make you grimace. They did the types of jobs that no one else really wanted, like garbage collection, corpse disposal, and chamber pot emptying. And they seemed to relish those jobs. At least, I never heard of one complaining.

"You come," the rat-man repeated, reaching out to my shirt again. I drew back out of his range.

"No! Get out of here, will you?"

I turned from the thing and started walking off with Brindar again. The rat-man scuttled around us and got in front of me. I had no choice but to stop, or else walk over him.

"Please, come. You come."

"Persistent thing," Brindar muttered.

"Look, I'm not coming with you to whatever nasty hole you call home. For all I know there's a horde of your brothers and sisters waiting to roll me. Not going to happen. Get it? Do you understand?"

I made to move around him, but he shifted to get in front of me again. I sighed, pushed him none too gently to the side, and walked on.

"Please," his voice came from behind me, "he kills us."

Brindar and I stopped in our tracks and glanced at each other before turning back.

"What are you talking about?" Brindar asked.

"The man," the rat-man was looking at the cobblestones, his voice only a whisper. "He's does things, hurts us, bleeds us…"

Rat-man or not, my previous feeling of disgust went out the window. Maybe they were vile, repulsive little creatures, but if this one was telling the truth…well, no one should have to come to someone else with a story like this.

"You in?" I asked Brindar.

He nodded, still watching the little rat-man who stood before us. "Yeah, I think I am."

From the rumble in his voice, Brindar was as angry about this as I was.

The rat-man led us to a large hole covered by a grate on the side of the street. He bent down and struggled to pull the grate loose. Despite his size, and the very heavy iron grate, it started to shift. After watching the rat-man continue to struggle, Brindar bent down, and moved the grate aside easily. The gratitude on the rat-man's face was almost pitiful to behold.

He sat on the edge of the hole, pushed himself off, and dropped out of sight. There was a soft splash, and then a whispered, "come, come" from below.

Brindar stepped back and swept his arm out, inviting me to go first. I grimaced, but stepped forward and repeated what I saw the rat-man do. A moment later, I landed ankle deep in cold, stinking water, ten feet below street level.

"Careful," I called up. "It's a pretty good drop."

The light from the sky was blocked out as Brindar moved into position. I moved aside to give him room, and he dropped down beside me, splashing me with some of the water. I should have moved further away.

"Alright," I growled, wiping the water from my shirt and instantly regretting getting it on my hand. "Which way?"

"Come," the rat-man said. "This way. Quiet. Shhh. Come."

He took off with a scurrying gait down the tunnel of water that stretched off in both directions, his long tail hanging out of a rip in the ragged pants that he wore. The tunnel was made of vaulted stone, which wept cold droplets of water. It was illuminated every several feet by shafts of bright light coming down through grated holes like the one we came through, but in between those areas, it was inky black.

"I don't even have a torch," I muttered. "I don't suppose you have one of those lantern things, do you?"

"Nope," Brindar replied. "But it's not really that dark down here."

Maybe not for a dwarf, used to living somewhere like Underworld, and obviously not for our rat-man guide who scuttled ahead of us, but for me, it was like the middle of the night.

"You stay behind the rat-man," I said. "I can see you easier."

For the next several minutes, we were a strange parade as we made our way through the sewers. Finally, we came to another tunnel which met ours at a type of crossroads, sloping down to the left, and up to the right. Uphill, there was still the occasional spot of light from the grates, but heading down, there were no such areas.

"We're heading down that way, aren't we?" I said.

Neither the rat-man nor Brindar responded. They simply took the left turn and started down the slope, because of course we were.

I held on to the back of Brindar, reminding me of our time in Underworld. Only this time I wasn't as worried about something sneaking up behind me in the dark. Instead, I worried that I would step in a hole and find myself sinking into the stinking water. Which, I was dismayed to notice, was getting deeper, until it poured in over the tops of my boots, soaking my feet, and rose still higher, first to my calves, then to my knees.

It was bad enough for me, but even deeper on Brindar. For the rat-man, it was even worse. He must have been wading through water that came up to his chest, and even his neck in some spots.

Ahead of us, I made out a light, flickering in the darkness. It was a torch, shoved into a holder on the wall of the tunnel. While I was very relieved to see the light, I was also somewhat worried about who, or what, placed it there.

Our guide moved forward without hesitation. The water started to get shallower again as the tunnel first leveled out, then started a slight slope upwards. The water became no more than a trickle, coming down the middle of the floor, but leaving the rest slimy and slippery.

The perfect environment for those slugs, I thought to myself.

The rat-man kept on, with the torches flickering on the walls every twenty feet apart.

"Hey," I called out, "who put these torches here?"

"Shhhh. Quiet, quiet. Come," the voice came back.

Brindar glanced at me and loosened Biter in its belt loop. I did the same with my gun. While I didn't think the rat-man was leading us into a trap, you could never be too careful.

Finally, he stopped, and moved over so that he hugged the wet wall of the tunnel. Brindar and I did the same, although I grimaced at the thought of touching the tunnel wall. After a moment, the rat-man slowly peeked around the corner. I saw him release the breath that he was holding, and motioning us forward, turned the corner.

There were several other rat-men waiting there. When we appeared, one of them gave a squeal and rushed forward. Our guide opened his arms and the squealer threw herself into them. They hugged fiercely and nuzzled each other. Although I still found rat-men to be disgusting, it was a touching gesture. For all the world, it was like a worried wife welcoming home her husband after he completed a dangerous job.

The was a lot of chittering and squeaking noises, from both our guide and his significant other, and from the group gathered in front of them. I realized that they were talking in their own language, which was nice for them, but the high-pitched noises sent shivers down my spine.

"Look," I said, "I appreciate that you're the returning hero and all, but I'd like to get out of here as soon as I can. Go back to my lady? Understand?"

Our guide turned to us, holding the hand of the rat-woman.

"Down there," he gestured to a small side tunnel. This one wasn't made of arched stone, tightly fitted, like the one we were in, Instead, the stones were pulled from the wall at this point, and a rough tunnel was dug from the earth behind it. It sloped down steeply, and turned a sharp corner. The torches continued that way, telling me that whoever was down there didn't see in the dark like the rat-men.

If they were human, I didn't need to reset the gun, which I couldn't until tomorrow anyway. The normal little, metal ball did enough damage on its own for work like that. And if it didn't, Biter had no problem cutting through human flesh.

"We'll go see what's going on. Are you coming?"

The rat-man looked at his woman, who shook her head slightly and tightened her grip on his paw. I saw him hesitate, then turn to me and Brindar, and take a deep breath.

"I come," he said, and gently took his hand back. He hugged his woman, said something in their language, and walked over to us.

As we started down the new tunnel, I looked back. The rat-woman was watching us go, her paws clasped tightly together in front of her. The others stood behind her, looking equally as worried.

"We'll bring him back," I said gently. Hell, rat-men or not, I could appreciate the act of bravery it took for him to come with us.

We walked quietly down the slope, the rat-man back in front, leading the way. It took a sharp turn to the right, and as before, he hugged the wall and peered around the corner before continuing. There were no other turnoffs that I saw. Just more tunnel, always sloping down, leading us deeper into the earth.

Finally, we made our cautious way around yet another bend and came to level ground. The tunnel continued on for a good distance, making another sharp turn at the end of it. But here, for the first time, was a dark, gaping hole in the wall, out of which came a horrible stench.

"What do you think?" I asked Brindar.

"I don't know what that is, but I'm not keen on the idea of leaving something behind us," he replied.

"Me neither." I grabbed one of the torches from its holder on the wall and started toward the hole.

"No," the rat-man whispered. "Not there. Not there."

"Sorry, friend," I continued on. "I want to see what's in there before we go any further."

The rat-man stopped protesting, but stood, rubbing his paws together nervously again. "Nothing there. Nothing but death."

Brindar and I stepped through the gap in the wall, the torch held high in my hand, and my breath held against the stench.

I stopped short, the flickering light illuminating what was in that chamber. Brindar uttered a harsh curse in his own tongue.

Piles of rat-people bodies lay strewn across the floor. Most of them looked drained, their cheeks sunken in and their muscles loose on their frames. Eyes stared sightlessly up at the ceiling, and tongues lolled from their mouths. Some had been here for a long time. Others looked like they had been placed here recently.

"By the Gods," I whispered. My stomach revolted and I turned and let loose. Brindar grabbed my arm and pulled me back into the main tunnel, retching himself.

Once there, we both sank down, our backs against the wall. The stench was still strong here, but compared to being inside that chamber, it felt like fresh, spring air. This was almost a real-life version of the visions that the Death Knight had shown Lilly and I in his tower.

I looked at the rat-man and saw the tears shining in his eyes. "Death," he whispered. "He kills us."

I nodded, my sadness and nausea turning to rage.

"You're right about that, my friend. Death," I said as I stood up. "This time though, it won't be for your people."

Brindar rose to his feet also, his face clouded with anger. "Lead on," he growled, his hand finding Biter.

The rat-man nodded, turned, and started down the tunnel again. When he reached the corner, he stopped, holding up his paw to tell us to do the same, and very slowly and cautiously, peered around it.

He snuck out, staying pressed against the wall, and Brindar and I followed him. This new stretch of tunnel didn't lead very far. It continued for only a few yards before dead-ending at a door set into the wall. The door was of thick wood, bound by dark iron straps at the top and bottom and a heavy latch. But it was slightly ajar, and from within we could hear noise.

It took us a moment to realize what it was that we were hearing, but then it dawned on us. Laughter. Cold, maniacal chuckling that emanated from the room. Then there was a sharp squeal, like the sound of an animal in pain, and the chuckling got louder, followed by a high-pitched, cracked voice. "There, there, my little pet. It's not that bad. Soon, it will be over."

There was another squeal, and I felt our rat-man guide stiffen next to me. I put my hand down and touched him lightly on the shoulder. He looked up at me, and instead of the tears I was expecting to see, there was rage in his eyes.

I nodded, glanced at Brindar and took the lead, moving toward the door slowly and carefully, my gun now in my hand. Brindar pulled Biter out its belt loop as well.

When we reached the door, I held up three fingers, and slowly counted them down: three, two, one. When my final finger curled down, I slammed into the door, forcing it open and moving to the right with it as it did. Brindar came in immediately behind, moving to the left so we could both see the room and be ready for whatever was in it.

We weren't. Instead what we saw was a sight that would stay with me for the rest of my days.

There was a table in the middle of the room, with a rat-woman sprawled out on it, held down by ties crossing the table at her legs, hips, chest, and neck. Even her tail was lashed down tightly. The ropes bit into her, but compared to the other things the monster behind the table was doing with his knives, I was sure that she didn't even notice.

Around her were several clay and glass vessels, many filled with a deep, red fluid, which I knew was her blood. But there was so much of it, it couldn't have all come from her. It must have come from several rat-people. I now understood why our guide told us, when we first met, that "he bleeds us".

The man, if you cared to call him that, behind the table jerked up as we crashed through the door. He was middle-aged, at one time good looking. But his madness changed his features, and he stared at us with bugged out eyes, and pursed lips. His dark hair stood up on his head, glued into weird shapes by the blood and gore that was matted in it. He hadn't shaved in several days and a straggly beard covered his lower face.

But his clothes drew my eye more than the rest of his appearance. From what I could see they were, or had been, rich and luxurious. The type that only folks who live on Silver Tree Lane or even richer could afford. Now, they were also stained with blood and other filth, and were ripped and tattered in places. I thought perhaps he had stolen them from a human victim. A thought that was enforced when I heard the moan from the back of the room.

I moved cautiously, hugging the wall, while the madman watched both Brindar and I, his lips moving as he muttered to himself. Finally, I could see behind the table, to the man chained to the wall. He wore what was once a suit of brightly colored clothes, although now they were also dirty and stained. But more disturbing was the fact that this man was missing his hands. His arms ended in two roughly wrapped stumps, the bandages stained with old blood. He looked up at me, and I recognized him as one of the pipers who caused the city such problems a short time ago. In front of him, laying mockingly out of reach, was his pipe, the mouth hole packed tight with dirt and mud.

I turned my gaze back to the man behind the table, and watched as he continued to mutter to himself, his eyes taking in Brindar, me, the table in front of him, and sometimes the ceiling. He looked back at me and a change came over his face.

"Ah, gentlemen," he said, his voice suddenly becoming surprisingly deep and cultured. "How fortuitous that you have come. I've been awaiting your arrival."

Brindar and I looked at each other.

"Look, Crazy," I said. "I don't know what game you're trying to pull here, but it's over. You can either come with us now, or I'll kill you right here. And trust me, I'd much rather do the second."

He seemed surprised. "Come with you? Oh no, I'm afraid I can't do that. My work is much too important to be interrupted, you see. But if you return down the passageway, you'll find my store room. It's become a mess and I need you to clean it out. When you've done that, return here, and by then, I should have more refuse for you to dispose of."

The whole time he was talking, the rat-woman on the table in front of him writhed in silence. Now, she whined and tried to stretch against her bonds.

"Hush now," the man said, and brought the knife down.

"No!" both Brindar and I yelled, but it was too late. He knew exactly where to cut to claim yet another victim.

"Kill him," Brindar growled, and I raised my gun.

The man looked at us both again. "Kill me? How impudent."

With that, he swept one of the bowls of blood off of the table, and ducked down behind it. Before we could move, he tipped it, spilling the other containers that were on it, and breaking ones that were already on the floor. The blood flowed across the floor toward us, as well as several half-formed slug things, that wiggled for a moment, and then went still.

I heard what sounded like a door slam behind the table, and I ran around, avoiding the blood and dead slugs on the floor, only to find a trap door that opened into another passage that ran below this room. He had dropped down, and the sound of his footsteps running off echoed back up to us.

"Please, help me," the chained piper said.

"We'll be back for you," I told him, hoping that it sounded like both the threat and the promise that I meant it to be.

I dropped down into the passage, followed by Brindar. The rat-man followed, and at this point, I was no longer surprised.

The passage ran away from us and took another turn to the left. I didn't bother with stealth, but took off at full speed after the deranged lunatic. When I caught up with him, there would be no more talk.

I skidded around the corner and was hit with a large, slimy pink tendril. It was as big around as my leg, and got me in the right hand, hitting me so unexpectedly and forcefully, that it slammed the hand holding my gun into my body, and held it there. My gun was pointed off to the side, useless. I struggled to free myself, but the strength of the tendril was too great.

In front of me was the largest of the slug things I had yet seen. It took up a large part of the tunnel, and the arms, legs, snouts and tails of dozens of rat-people stuck out of the mass, were reabsorbed, and then appeared elsewhere.

The slug thing began pulling me in, my feet sliding along the tunnel floor. I was helpless against the strength of the thing. But Biter suddenly slashed down, severing the tendril, causing me to flop backwards from the recoil.

Brindar jumped back and to the side, barely escaping another slimy tendril that shot out of the thing at him. At the same time, another grabbed me again, this time wrapping around my right foot as I lay on the passageway floor. It pulled me toward it, as I struggled to free my right hand, and strove to hold on to the floor, the wall, or anything, with my left.

My hand was still stuck firmly to my chest, the barrel of my gun protruding from the sticky mess. The slug thing moved closer to me while it pulled me forward. I tugged at my hand, and while it may have moved slightly, I wouldn't free it in time.

Instead, I stuck out my left leg, ramming it into the dirt of the tunnel wall. I wasn't strong enough to stop the slug from pulling me toward it, but I did manage to make my body turn, enough that I could half roll, and pull the trigger. I didn't need to hit the thing dead center, anywhere would do.

The little, metal ball came out as it did up above at the docks. It left a line of searing pain across my chest as it went, but it did hit the slug thing. The effect was immediate. The same freezing process went to work, causing it to slow, then stop. The tendril was still attached to me, but it was no longer reeling me in. As I watched, the icy blueness reached the base of the tendril and started up. I wondered if the cold from it would freeze my foot as well, but didn't find out. Brindar brought Biter down again, severing the connection, and then walked forward and shattered the slug into a million pieces.

"Nooo!!!" we head a voice scream. It was the mad-man's voice, but back to the high pitched, cracked noise we first heard. "Not my Thing! You've killed it! My beautiful Thing!"

Really? This lunatic actually called these creations his things? Well, no wonder the gun worked.

Brindar helped me to my feet, and to get my hand unstuck from my chest. The stickiness of the mess that remained was fading, but I was still covered in a pink, foul smelling slime.

"Enough of this," he said.

I didn't even answer. We headed down the passageway to where we heard the voice, moving quickly, but more cautiously this time.

We needn't have bothered. The tunnel dead-ended, in an area that was still being dug out. Was the slug working on that very thing when we came upon it? Or were there other slaves that this guy had that we hadn't seen yet?

Regardless, I didn't ask him. He stared at us and ranted as we came around the corner. I heard something about the blood, more things to be made, and powerful friends. But as Brindar said, enough. The little, metal ball hit him at almost the same moment as Brindar's thrown axe.

I looked back at our rat-man friend, who stared at his tormentor's corpse with a strange expression. He looked relieved, but also sad. I understood. We stopped him, but too late for many of his kinfolk.

"We'll help you clean out that hole back there," I told him. Brindar nodded beside me.

"No, we do it. It our folk, our family. Thank you. Thank you."

He shuffled away, back toward the ladder that led up to the trapdoor in that horrible room above. Brindar and I followed silently.

We took the piper out of the room and back to the watchhouse, where Sarge locked him up. Since I was still covered in the remnants of pink slime, I broke my earlier vow and told him what we discovered.

"I'll send some men to get the body," he told me.

"Tell them to be easy on the rat-people down there," I said. "They've been through enough."

I parted ways with Brindar, telling him that I would see him in a couple of days for the wedding. Neither of us seemed to have much enthusiasm for it at the moment. It was a feeling that would pass, but right now, neither of us could get the images of what we saw down in the sewers out of our minds.

The clothes I wore would be burned, since there was no way that I was going to attempt to clean them. If any slugs still roamed the city, the Watch wizards would take care of them, using freezing spells and allowing Watchmen to clean up the rest.

I was done. I wanted to rest. A couple of days to do nothing but relax and get ready for the big day. The city could go on without me or Lilly for a while. It had Brindar, and Sarge, and even Raven. Not to mention a whole host of witches, wizards, necromancers, the NHLF and others. For all the times that Lilly and I stepped into some big emergency, they could handle it.

The way I figured it, they owed us.

## FOR WHOM THE WEDDING BELL TOLLS

There are some days that you can tell are going to be perfect, even as you open your eyes for the first time in the morning. The sun streaming through the window is the right brightness, and the sound of the birds singing in the trees or cooing from the rooftops is musical. Your eyes open, you take a moment to adjust to being awake, and then turn over to see the most beautiful woman in the world lying in bed next to you.

I looked at Lilly, still asleep, her face at rest. Today was the day that I got to marry her and there was a large part of me that still couldn't believe it was real. In a few hours, we'd walk into Father Magnus's temple, hold hands and say those words to each other. Words that...

"Ahhh!!! Duke!! No! Get out!"

My reverie was interrupted by a pillow being shoved into my face, followed by a hard push to my chest, which spilled me out of the bed and onto the floor. I lay there for a moment, stunned and not sure of what exactly was going on. While I did, I heard feet hit the floor on the other side of the bed, and go running toward the bathroom. The door slammed shut before I could get to my feet.

"What the..." I murmured, rubbing my backside where it hit the floor and putting the pillow back on the bed.

"Lilly! What's going on?"

"Get out! You're not supposed to see me today!"

"If I can't see you, how can I marry you?"

"Don't be an idiot! You know what I mean! You're not supposed to see me *until* the wedding."

"Then why were we both here last night?" I was honestly confused. At the moment, Lilly still owned her own house in that weird necromancer's place that you could only get to through magic. She never stayed there though, and we were planning on living here, at my place, after the wedding. Not least because this was where Petal and her people were. But still, if we weren't supposed to see each other this morning, she could have gone there.

I walked over to the closed bathroom door so that she could hear me through it without me having to shout.

"Lilly, that's an old wives' tale, right? What difference does it make?"

"Some of those old stories have real power, Duke. Do you really want to take the chance?"

"No, I guess not, but why didn't we think of this last night?"

"I did!" she cried. "But I fell asleep! I was going to slip out, but I couldn't stay awake."

"It's not the end of the world."

"Duke, please! Can you just go?"

"Where?"

"I don't know. Go get breakfast somewhere. Give me a couple of hours, then I'll be gone, and you can come back. As a matter of fact, you have to. Daddy, Bancroft, and Uncle Wally will be coming by, so you need to take care of them."

"What am I supposed to do with them?"

"I don't know!" For the first time since I knew her, Lilly was starting to sound frazzled. I got the impression that I wasn't helping.

"Okay," I said. "No worries. I'll make sure they're having a good time. Don't worry about it."

"Thank you. Now get out!"

"I love you, too," I yelled to her as I moved away from the door. "I'll see you at the temple."

I heard the door crack open behind me as I walked across the room.

"Duke?"

I turned back, ready to be told that she loved me too and she was sorry for shoving me off the bed.

"Don't be late," she said. "And don't forget your suit." Then the door shut firmly once more.

I never mind breakfast out somewhere. You can get a variety of eggs, breads, and meats without having to clean up after yourself. I went to the Barman's Choice, took a table near the open window, and ordered up a whole plate of morning goodness. I watched the life of the city flow by as I waited, and was happy to see that not a single emergency, or more than normal weirdness, occurred. Not even once.

My food came, and I took up knife and fork, cut into a nice thick slab of ham and realized that I had no appetite whatsoever. When I first came in, the smells set my mouth to watering and my stomach to gurgling. Now, my stomach was still making noises, but the thought of eating was making me ill. I put the fork down, pushed the overly laden plate away from me, and picked up my cup of coffee with a sigh.

Maybe Lilly wasn't the only one that was feeling frazzled after all.

I sat and watched the city, pondering why I would feel like this. Was it that I didn't truly want to marry Lilly? Or more likely, get married to anyone-ever? No, that didn't feel right. I was very happy about marrying her. I knew what I had in her, and that I was damn lucky...

There it was. I was lucky. And I felt somewhat like a fraud. I never tried to be anyone but myself around Lilly, and had no intention of starting now. But, I felt like I had still managed to pull the wool over her eyes somehow. And that feeling led to me thinking that at some point, she was going to wake up, realize that she'd been duped, and walk out the door. That…yes, that was it. That was what was making me feel this way.

But. What if she didn't feel fooled? What if she really did see me as a good guy, somehow worth being married to for the rest of her life. The fact of the matter was that Lilly was one of the smartest, most capable people I ever met. So how could I have duped her? It didn't seem possible.

Which meant…that I wasn't up to her level. Never would be. At some point, she would realize that. She'd come to know that she could have done much better than a not-so-humble Nuisance Man who liked his ale too much.

But then…

And around and around my thoughts swirled, while I sat and sipped my coffee. The perfect day that I envisioned when I first awoke was starting to fog over. Oh, the sun still shone down merrily on the streets, but in my mind there was a gray haze.

I sighed and sipped at my coffee, which was growing cold in the mug now. Then, the chair across the table from me was pulled out, and Jessup plunked down into it, a mug of ale in hand.

"I would have got you one," he said, "but Lilly would kill me if you started drinking this early today."

I smiled sadly at my friend. How could he possibly understand? He wasn't setting himself up for a world of pain, as I was when Lilly came to her senses.

"Oh, got the wedding day jitters huh? Well, get over it pal. You've got stuff to do before you get hitched."

"You don't understand…" I started to say.

"Yeah, yeah. Sure." His voice took on a mocking sing-song quality. "You don't understand. I'll never be good enough for her. She's soooo wonderful. Get over yourself, man."

My jaw was hanging open.

"What? You think you're the first of my friends to get married? They all say the same thing. But here's something to chew on. You're right. About all of it. She *is* too good for you. Any woman worth having is. I don't mean just you, I mean all of us. And they all know it, but they take us anyway. Be a good man, and a better husband, and live up to her expectations. Trust me, they're probably not that high for you."

He laughed and took a swig of his ale. I looked down at my coffee, set the cup down and reached over to take the ale from his hand. I took a swig, and passed it back.

"Thanks," I said, meaning for both the pep talk and the drink.

"No problem. But that's it on the ale for you, lover boy. You've got a suit to pick up."

I ate part of my breakfast, splitting it with Jessup, who was glad to finish what I didn't. Then, I took my leave, telling him that I would see him at the temple later on.

"Nope, you'll see me before that," he said. "I've been charged with making sure you're presentable and get there on time. I'll see you at your place in a few hours."

He winked, raised his mug to drain it and signaled for another one as I left.

The tailor had my suit ready for me when I got there. I tried it on, and stood for inspection. When he was satisfied with the final fit, he insisted that I remove it and put my normal clothes back on. As far as I was concerned, I was already dressed, so what difference did it make if I wore it now?

In answer to this, the tailor simply handed me a scrap of paper. On it was a message, which read: "Duke. Do what he tells you and don't give him a hard time! Lilly."

It certainly looked like her handwriting, and the tailor stood at his ease, waiting for me to comply with his, and indirectly, Lilly's, wishes. Moments later, I was back in my every day clothes and heading for home with the suit, carefully covered, hung over one shoulder.

Once there, I opened the door and shouted for Lilly, but there was no answer. I assumed it was safe to go inside now, so I did. Then....well, then I didn't know what I was supposed to do. I had been told to get my suit, take care of the male portion of Lilly's family, get dressed and get to Father Magnus's temple before 4:00 PM. It was only 10:00 AM now, and there was no sign of the guys.

I sighed, went to the kitchen and got an ale for myself. Yes, I know it was only ten o'clock in in the morning, but it was a good, heavy, dark ale, and I needed something to calm my stomach. Although Jessup had done a great job of helping me get rid of my doubts, I was still nervous. I comforted myself with the thought that it was probably normal to feel queasy on your wedding day.

I took my mug to the living room and sat in my chair near the hearth. It was a warm day, with no need for a fire. I picked up the newssheets, scanned them, and realized that I wasn't reading anything. I was simply staring at the words on the paper. I sipped my ale, and kept up the pretense out of sheer boredom.

Finally, after what felt like an eternity, but was really only about a half hour, I heard the sound of a coach pull up outside our door. Coaches aren't that common in Capital City, since most people can't afford them, and those that can don't take them to neighborhoods like this very often.

Before the knock even came, I was opening the door, to reveal Bryer, Lilly's father, Bancroft, her sister's husband, and Wallace Worthington, Bryer's business partner.

"Duke!" Bryer said. "It's good to see you again!"

"You too, Bryer. And you, Wally, and you too, Bancroft."

They bundled in, all of us shaking hands and asking about the trip, what was new, and so on. Before I knew it, Wally found the kitchen and returned with four ales, which he passed around.

"To Duke," he said, "who joins the family today. We welcome you."

I took a sip of my ale, but noticed that my three guests were intending to reach bottom, so I thought it rude not to match them. When it was done, Wally gathered the empty mugs, and made himself at home by returning to the kitchen, and coming back with four more.

"And that's your last one for now," Bryer said, indicating the mug in my hand. "Make it last."

I was glad that we were on the same page, since I had already determined that this would be it for now. No one even needed to say anything. I had no intention of showing up drunk for my wedding.

"So, Duke," Bryer said, settling into my chair. "Have you given any thought to possibly coming to work for me? I can make you an executive, like Bancroft here. He's taking care of our finances, and doing a bang-up job of it. I was thinking that you could be in charge of security, worldwide."

I nodded, surprised. It never occurred to me to go to work for Bryer's company. And worldwide? That sounded like a lot of time outside of the city, which didn't appeal to me in the least.

"Thanks," I told him. "But I think I'm going to stick with what I'm doing. It's not glamorous, I know, and we'll never get rich off of it, but I feel like I do some good sometimes. You know?"

"I do know, and Lilly said you'd say that. But you can't blame a guy for trying. You do good, Duke. Lilly tells her mother things, who then tells me. Trust me, any man that can win Lilly's heart must have something going for him. But you take care of her."

I sat back in what was normally Lilly's chair and smiled. "I'll try. But I have to say, I've never met anyone who needs taking care of as little as your daughter."

He smiled back. "Maybe not out there, on the streets. Or up here." He pointed at his temple, then reached out and poked me in the chest. "But in there, Duke. You take care of her in there."

I raised my mug to him. "Always," I said. He raised his back, and we sipped our ales.

Later the four of us went out to get lunch, where I watched with some degree of envy as they all drank a couple of ales, while

I sipped on water. I still didn't have much of an appetite, but managed to down some of my meal. Bryer made sure of that, telling me that there was no way he was going to watch me pass out in front of everyone and ruin his daughter's wedding. He was laughing when he said it…so I guess it was a joke.

It was one of the stranger days I have ever had, and that's saying something. At times, the day seemed to slip by, the minutes and hours flying past. Then, it would slow down, and when I was sure that it must be almost time to leave for the temple, it would only be minutes that had gone by.

Sometimes, I was fully into the conversation that was going on around me, and then I would realize that I had no idea what we were discussing, and that the talk had moved on to a totally different subject. The other three watched me with amusement written all over their faces, since they were all veterans of this, and remembered their own wedding days.

But finally, we were back at the house and the clock was nearing three. Jessup showed up, let himself in, and introduced himself to the family. He grabbed two mugs of ale, shoved one into my hand and kept the other.

"Let's go," he said. "Where's the suit?"

"In my bedroom, why?"

He put his hand on my arm and steered me in that direction. "Time to get moving, pal. Let's go."

"I don't need your help getting dressed, Jessup!"

"Nope, but I'm going to make sure you don't put your pants on backward or anything. You're not the smartest on your best days, Duke, and today your brain is mush."

I opened my mouth to spit out a clever retort, but nothing came to me. For the life of me, I couldn't think of a single witty, or even not witty, reply. Instead, I stood staring at Jessup, my mouth hanging open like a fish about to swallow a fly. Bryer and the others chuckled.

"Yep, like I said," Jessup said, and gently led me away.

I managed to get dressed all on my own and didn't need any help getting my pants on. Although, there were a few moments when I would pause, as it hit me all over again what I was about to do.

"Yes, Duke, Lilly is amazing." "Yes, she really does love you." "Yes, you're a very lucky man." These and others like them became a running commentary from Jessup, while he sipped his ale, then my forgotten mug, and watched to make sure I didn't mess up and embarrass both myself and Lilly.

Then, it was time to go.

The five of us walked from the house to Magnus's temple, a trip which took a good half hour on foot. We chatted as we went, or rather, chatter was going on about me and continued all the way up the steps and into the interior, where Father Magnus patiently waited.

"Duke," he said warmly, and shook my hand. I suddenly felt calm, and that everything was going to work out as it should. If Father Magnus was involved, and was giving our union his blessing, then it must be right.

"Father," I said. "Thanks again for doing this for us."

"Don't be silly," he replied. "I wouldn't have it any other way. Now, come with me. The rest of you, please take your seats."

He led me around the edge of all the long benches where people sat to hear him preach. Several of them were occupied already, and I couldn't help but take notice as I went by.

Minerva, Camelia and several other witches were there, smiling and whispering to themselves.

General Daken and Dabney were there, seated in one of the back rows, so that he wouldn't block the view of those behind him, I was sure. He nodded solemnly at me when he saw me notice him, and Dabney waved enthusiastically.

There were several members of the Watch, including a bunch of men and women in red robes that matched what Lilly wore to work, and near them sat both Gulston and Wulftin, the two Watch wizards that I worked with at times.

Ivar, the head of the NHLF, was there, along with Hock and some others. Nearby, were Jarl and Selvi, the orcs from the feuding clans that I helped some time ago. The same time that I first met Raven.

Speaking of…I looked around and spotted him. Trying to be mysterious and coming off merely as odd, at least to me, he stood off to the side, near where a few shadows lingered, trying to blend in. He spotted me also, and nodded, then turned away. He was only there out of respect for Lilly, and he wanted me to know it.

Up near the front was room for family, and Bryer and the rest settled there, leaving room for their spouses who were still with Lilly. Jessup planted himself there as well, and made eyes at some of the female necromancers and witches in attendance. More than one eyed him back, and I laughed to see it.

Brindar and Sarge were right up front as well. Sarge with his own lovely wife, who was making conversation with the dwarven Nuisance Man. It was nice to see.

And then they were gone, as Father Magnus led me around a corner into a corridor and gave me a good once-over, in case Jessup had missed anything.

"It's a good day, Duke," he told me. "A great day."

I smiled. "I know."

"Stay here until I call for you. Are you alright?"

I nodded and leaned against the wall.

"Was it necessary to bring that?" Father Magnus asked me.

I looked down to see what he was talking about. There, under the black over-jacket that I was wearing was my gun. My Ultimate Weapon. I hadn't even realized that I had strapped it on when I got dressed.

"I think I'd feel weird without it," I said. "It's like it's a part of me now."

"Hmm. Well, as long as it stays put away." He patted my shoulder and walked back into the main part of the temple.

There was music playing softly and I listened to it as I waited. But before I could get too relaxed, it changed, becoming louder and more dramatic.

I heard Father Magnus start talking, and call my name. I made sure my clothes were straight, tried to moisten my suddenly dry mouth, and walked into the temple proper. The benches were even more crowded now, with people that I didn't even know, but I assumed were friends of Lilly's or her family's. My eyes scanned over everyone, turning toward Father Magnus and back, looking for Lilly, but there was no sign of her.

But Magnus was smiling at me, so I kept going. He stopped me when I stood in front of him, and gently indicated that I should turn and face everyone. I did, with my heart beating in my ears. There was still no sign of her, and I was beginning to panic. My palms felt sweaty and I was getting a little light-headed. I knew it! I knew that she would come to her senses!

Father Magnus made a motion that I half-saw out of the corner of my eye, and the doors to the temple opened again, flooding the aisle with light. There was a figure silhouetted against that light. It moved forward, the doors were shut, and there was Lilly, walking slowly up the aisle, her eyes fixed on mine.

Did I say my mouth was dry and I felt light-headed before? That was nothing. Lilly has always been, and would always be, beautiful. But that day…that day it was as if the heavens themselves reached down and touched her. She was radiant, beautiful in a way that I can't describe, and most wonderfully, she was coming to be with me.

Her dress was long, and in the normal red that she wore, but much, much fancier and finer. It showed off her figure and set off her hair, and her eyes. She walked sedately along, glancing and smiling at those around her, but her eyes stayed mostly focused on me.

I smiled, because, despite the radiance and the almost overwhelming beauty, she was still my Lilly. Those eyes that I looked into so often were still the same and they were speaking to me as surely as if Lilly herself was talking. "What the hell are we doing here, Duke?"

She smiled back when she saw me do it, and that was it. Everything from that moment on was fine.

Father Magnus performed a beautiful ceremony, although I couldn't tell you a word of it. I said the right things in the right places, and so did Lilly. We held each other's hands and kissed when he told us to, accompanied by the sounds of cheering from those in attendance.

Then we walked out, and climbed into a white carriage that Lilly's father had arranged, which whisked us away to the Rose Petal Room.

We didn't do much talking on the way there, although we did occasionally come up for air, and to smile like idiots at each other. The ride was over way too quickly, so I asked the driver to take us around again. He smirked, but did as I asked.

Which meant that everyone was already there by the time we reached the Rose Petal Room and the party was in full swing. Mr. Charles insisted on introducing us as "Mr. and Mrs. Duke Grandfather!" which we laughed over for the rest of the day.

The party was a grand time, and Mr. Charles earned every penny of the money that we paid him. The food was amazing and there was plenty of it. The wandering minstrels kept our guests entertained, and knew when to pull back and perform quietly in the background. The ale flowed freely, and for those who enjoyed it, my choice of using the stuff from the Barman's Choice turned out to be a good one.

Both Lilly and I had mugs of ale and goblets of wine pressed into our hands several times, but we would usually take a drink or two, then set them down on a convenient table and forget them.

Don't get me wrong, I love ale, and normally would have drained every one of those mugs. But today, it wasn't important.

As the evening wore on, I noticed Brindar sitting at a table with Sarge. That didn't strike me as unusual, but the fact that Raven was also there, including himself in the conversation did. I walked over, leaving Lilly to talk with some of her childhood friends from the countryside.

"Grab a seat, Duke," Sarge said, and slid a chair out with his foot. I sat, and amazingly, Raven slid a mug of ale over to me.

"Congratulations," he said.

"Thanks." Then, to change the subject, turned to Sarge. "Hey, not that I want to talk shop today, but what happened with that piper guy you were going to send some men to get out of the sewer?"

"Oh, him. We've got him. He's still locked up, while some of the higher-ups are talking to him. From what I hear, he's being very cooperative."

"Any idea what his story is?"

"A little. Seems like he was in the employ of that crazy guy you fought off down there. He and his friends were hired to cause some chaos in the city, which you already knew. But when you and Lilly ran them off, he stayed, seeing if he could get more work. He did, and apparently, it was him who first drew those poor rat-people to that guy. But then, when he saw what was happening to them, he protested. Crazy guy told him that if he didn't like it, he could leave.

I guess he tried, but found out that he couldn't. He couldn't physically make himself leave the sewers. Instead, he went back to the guy who hired him and stood there, watching helplessly, while the guy cut off his hands. He said he could feel everything, and he could scream, but he couldn't move. Ain't that something?"

"Yeah," I said, looking down at the table, and remembering the piper the Palace Guard took. He was under a spell much the same. "It's something. And we think that guy we killed was behind all the attacks, right?"

"What guy that you killed? There was no one else down there except for some very scared, but grateful, rat-people, and that piper guy."

I looked at Brindar, who was staring back at me. "No, down under the torture room. In that other tunnel I told you about. We left his body there."

"We found the tunnel, Duke. But there was nobody, and no body, in it. Are you guys sure you killed him?"

"Positive," Brindar said.

"Well, he wasn't there. Maybe someone came and got him."

"Maybe," I began, but then Lilly came over.

"Enough shop talk, or whatever you guys are doing. Come on, Duke. Let's take a walk."

A walk with my new bride? Yes, please! And all thoughts of the rat-men, the piper, the missing dead guy, or even my friends went away.

For the next hour, we danced, we ate, we drank, and we had a great time. I saw Jessup dancing with Camelia, and watched as Sarge and his wife put us all to shame with their moves.

The evening was starting to wane, and Lilly and I were beginning to discuss how we could make a polite exit, when I noticed that I could see her breath as she was talking. Like on a cold, winter's day. Once I noticed that, I also noticed that the temperature in the room was dropping rapidly. People were shivering, and looking around as men took off jackets and draped them over the women they were with.

"Lilly," I said. "Is this something you're doing?"

"No, but I feel something…oh…yuck. Duke, it's like that day with the birds…foul…nasty."

There was a loud noise from the entrance of the Rose Petal Room, like the doors had been forcibly thrown open, or cracked right down the middle. Then I could hear what sounded like shuffling footsteps, interspersed with a heavy stomp.

The doors to the room we were in flew open with such force that they broke when they hit the walls behind. And there, framed in the doorway, was the crazy guy that Brindar and I already killed. But he was changed.

His one leg was huge and swollen, and he dragged it behind him as he moved slowly forward. His other leg made a loud sound when it hit the floor, as if he were heavier than he appeared to be. Death had come for him, there was no doubt of it when you saw the ruin of his face. His eyes were filmed over and his cheeks had dark splotches on them. His hair was falling out, and his tongue lolled out of his mouth as he looked over the room.

But most disturbing was the feeling that came over me. Lilly was right, it was like looking into that other world where the hideous birds came from. He had the same sense of wrongness, of decay and evil, that the floating man from that world did, only stronger, more intense. Here, that world had come through and invaded our own.

Before I could move, two huge battle axes hurtled through the air toward the intruder. One was Biter, and the other was General Daken's. Brindar and he took no time to wait to see what would happen, but their quick action did no good. As the axes reached him, there was a flare of sickly, yellow light, and both weapons dropped to the ground in front of him.

He looked down at them and chuckled, in a gurgling voice that sounded like he was drowning.

It was chaos after that. Minerva and the other witches stepped forward, casting spells that sizzled and spat in the air. The Watch wizards and necromancers threw magics at him that sounded like they would end the world. Raven threw his knives from the side, hoping, I'm sure, to find an unprotected vulnerable spot.

I fired my gun, although I didn't know who or what he was. I didn't set it to anything, hoping that I would find out what to name him later if need be, but it didn't matter. Lilly stepped forward and hit him with spells that made everyone's hair stand on end, not only her own.

All of it was for naught. The man, if that's what he still was, stood and laughed at us, while that pale, yellow light flashed with each attack, and drank in or deflected them all.

Finally, the room was quiet, as we all stood and panted, trying to catch our breath.

"Are you quite finished?" he said, surveying us with his milky eyes. "You cannot defeat what's coming for you. It's taken me, and promised that I should see its glory, and that I would have revenge."

He moved forward, taking one heavy step, followed by the dragging of his swollen leg. His eyes searched out mine. "Ah...there you are. Now, where is...?" And he looked around again, smiling when he spotted Brindar. "Yessss...time to pay the piper, eh?" He laughed at his own wit.

I raised my gun, determined that I wouldn't go down without a fight, but then he turned his gaze on me. My hand dropped to my side, and my fingers started to open so that I would drop the gun, but I fought him with everything I had, and although I couldn't raise my arm, my hand closed on my gun again.

"Hmph," he snorted. "It would seem that Griefmaker is attached to you. No matter, I'll take it when I take your hand."

I began moving toward him, unable to do anything else. Out of the corner of my eye, I saw Brindar do the same.

"No!" Lilly shouted and raised her hands in that manner that meant a big spell was coming. But the man glanced at her, snarled, and Lilly was thrown across the room, crashing into the tables and landing motionless on the floor. Her mother and Bryer ran to her, and I wanted to, so badly, but I still couldn't move.

"If you've hurt her..." I growled.

"What?" he said, mocking me. "You'll cry about it? Don't worry, Nuisance Man. There will be more to cry about than one dead necromancer soon enough."

His words sent ice through my veins. I heard Lilly's parents trying to speak to her, their voices becoming more urgent. My vision started to blur as the tears came.

"Good, good. Cry, little Nuisance Man. Misery and grief feed my masters."

The putrid light that flared around him with each attack started to pulsate now. It was radiating out from him, bathing all of us present in its glow. I felt sick to my stomach, and I heard someone behind me begin to vomit. I managed to glance at Brindar and saw the queasy expression on his face that I'm sure was on my own.

"Time to end this," the dead man gurgled. "Time to open the portal up all the way."

"No," a calm, deep voice said. "It's not. It's time to stop this nonsense."

Father Magnus walked forward, passing between Brindar and I, with absolute peace on his face, the pulsating glow not affecting him at all.

"Stop there, priest of a false god," the man spat. "Or I'll open it now."

Father Magnus looked at the man with pity and kept approaching. When the sickly light hit him, it reflected, becoming a pure, white shine that illuminated the whole room.

"Stay back, I say!" the man snarled, but moved back a step himself.

"I am sorry for you," Magnus said. "You bargained with powers that you didn't understand. Powers that cannot come here. Not now. Not ever."

He continued to walk forward. The man began to whimper.

"Go to your rest," Magnus said gently. "It's time for you to let go. I don't know what reward or punishment awaits you, but it's time to embrace it." He stopped, raised his eyes to the heavens, and whispered, "Thank you, Father."

There was a brilliant stab of pure, white light that enveloped the dead man, with a loud crack like the noise of a lightning strike. I closed my eyes, but too slowly, and when I opened them again, I couldn't see, but I could move. I blinked the tears away, and saw Father Magnus calmly looking at the spot where the man had been, and now nothing was. That horrible sense of wrongness disappeared as well, and the temperature started to climb back up.

I turned and stumbled across the room, trying to blink my eyes clear enough to see my way to Lilly. I tripped and banged into tables and chairs, but I made it to her.

"Lilly," I whispered, kneeling down next to her. She was so still, and her breath was shallow.

Her eyes opened, "Duke. What the hell was that?" Her voice was a mere whisper and blood flecked her lips.

"I don't know," I said, my voice thick. "But remind me not to get on Father Magnus's bad side."

I hugged her to me, and held her until Magnus came, and reaching down, took all of her hurt away. One moment, she lay in my arms, weak as a kitten. The next, he touched her shoulder, said a prayer, and she was looking up at me, full of the energy and power that was hers.

Magnus winked at me, then chuckled and walked off, grabbing a mug of ale off a table as he went.

I really liked that guy.

After an event like that, people will go one of two ways. Either they'll get out of there as quickly as they can, and distance themselves from what happened, or they'll stay, help clean up and provide support for one another.

I shouldn't have been surprised that our family and friends were of the second sort. Even Mr. Charles came out, tsked at the sight of his doors, and then had his staff start circulating with the food and drinks, as we all righted chairs and placed them around tables again.

Whatever Magnus did, Lilly said she felt better than she had in ages. I was very glad to see it.

Of course, there was a constant buzz in the air about what happened, and Lilly and I weren't exempt from it.

"Yeah, but who was he?" I mused. "I mean, why'd he have it in so badly for Capital City?"

"He was my brother," said a new voice.

I turned to the door and gasped. I had only seen him from a distance, but there was no mistaking the King, surrounded by hard looking men and women dressed totally in black.

"Well, one of them, anyway. I have a lot of them, and sisters, too. Dad got around in his day, I guess."

He walked into the room, stopping to shake my hand, and kissing Lilly's. We both stared with wide eyes.

"Please, everyone, pretend I'm not here." But his expression said that he knew that wasn't going to happen. "I've actually come to talk to you, Lilly. May we sit?"

"Of course," she replied, and they moved to a table. I walked with them, and at first, he looked as if he was going to protest, but then thought better of it. Which was just as well. After what we had been through, neither the King himself, nor a host of black-clothed baddies were going to keep me from her side right now.

Mr. Charles discreetly brought us drinks and slipped away, watched carefully by those in black. One of them stepped forward and tasted the ale before the King himself had a chance to.

"Thank you, Charles," His Majesty said dryly, then turned to Lilly. "I came to ask you if you would consider joining my personal guard. We could use someone with your talents."

Lilly and I glanced at each other in surprise. When we hadn't heard anything after the incident with the elves, we assumed that they weren't interested. I was thrilled for Lilly. Here was her chance at a big time that neither of us even knew existed until a short while ago.

"Thank you, Your Majesty," she said, and her hand found mine, our fingers interlacing. "But I think I need to pass."

Ha. That was Lilly. Turning down the King without a second thought. I picked up my mug to hide the smile that I was trying to keep off of my face.

"What if I offered the same to you, Duke," the King said to me. "We'll make it a package deal."

I lowered my mug without drinking, all thoughts of smiling gone. I looked over at those men and women in black. I could be one of them. One of the elite.

"Thanks, but no," I told him. "If I wanted a regular day job, I could have had one with the Watch ages ago." Then I did pick up my mug and take a sip, mostly to hide my nervousness. Lilly may be able to appear nonchalant turning him down, but I was having a tough time with it.

"I see," he said. His voice expressed a note of disappointment, but no anger. "Well, I can't say I blame either of you."

"If I may, Your Majesty," Lilly said. "What exactly do they do?"

"Pardon me?"

"Duke and I took out the Death Knight, and the Pipers, and the birds. He and Brindar stopped those nasty slug things, and if the banshee was part of it, we did that too. *And* we took care of the elves. So, what exactly does your personal guard do?"

The King smiled. "They keep *me* safe, of course. Now, is there anything I can answer for you? Anything. Consider it a wedding present to a couple who have saved our city."

"I'd like to know what the deal was with your brother," I said, horrified to hear my own voice asking the question.

"Ah. Well. He was one of the younger ones. No chance of ever getting the throne, even had I not had children. There are several older siblings in line before him. Like a lot of families, I'm afraid that those of us who were older weren't always the nicest to the younger ones. Picking on them and whatnot. Most of us grow out of it over time, of course, but for him, I imagine the scars ran deep.

He left here years ago. I, and some of my siblings, tried to find him again, to mend fences. But we never could. We heard rumors, but whenever I would dispatch someone to bring him home, he would have already moved on. Over time, I would assume his annoyance grew to a hatred, which grew to a desire for revenge. How he made a deal with whatever evil is in that other place, I don't know."

"Wait," I said. "All of this, everything that's happened, and everyone who's been hurt, is because of a spoiled brat who got his nose bent out of joint as a kid?"

The King took a drink of his ale. "Yes, Mr. Grandfather. I suppose it is. Now, I must take my leave, but I wish the two of you all the best in your lives together." He stood up to leave, but paused. "Oh, I almost forgot. I have something else for you."

He motioned and one of his men in black came over and placed two packages wrapped in brown paper on the table. On one was written "For Lilly" in an elegant script. On the other was simply, "Duke" in a neat print.

His Majesty bowed his head to us and took his leave, his personal bodyguard following behind. Lilly and I looked at each other, smiled, and turned our attention back to the items on the table before us.

"What do you think they are?" I said.

"Only one way to find out." Lilly picked hers up, and carefully unwrapped it, exposing a beautiful jewel, deep blue in color, held in a simple setting on a gold chain. There was a note with it, which read, "Dearest Lilly, May this gem bring you light in the darkness when you need it. I hope to return the hospitality that you showed to us. You and Duke are welcome to visit me at any time. Congratulations on your wedding. Your friend, Tomoni."

"How beautiful," Lilly breathed, and slipped the chain over her head. It could have been a trick of the light, but I swore I saw it flash brilliantly for a moment when she did. "How nice of her. We'll have to go visit soon, Duke."

I nodded, and picked up my own package. Under the paper was a wooden box, with a lid that slid off of one of the long sides. There was a note attached here as well, but this one simply read, "From one warrior to another. It will last longer than you think. Masuyo."

Inside the box was a small, brown, glass bottle, closed with a cork. I opened it, put my nose near to smell what was inside, and sat back, with a happy sigh.

"What is it?" Lilly asked me.

In answer, I slugged down the small amount of ale that I had left, and wiped my mug out with a napkin. I slowly poured out a measure of the liquid inside the bottle and took a sip. It was incredible. Better than I ever could have imagined. It was ale, but ale of such a nature that it took you away, made you think that there could never be anything as blissful as it was.

I slid the mug over to Lilly, who looked into it, then took a sip herself. If my expression matched hers, then I appeared very happy indeed.

"Is this…?"

"Yep." I reached to take my mug back, but she grabbed another sip first. "Elven ale. I knew it existed."

Masuyo's note was dead on. I wanted to share it with friends, so I found Jessup, and gave him a taste, then Brindar, Sarge, General Daken, Magnus, and even Raven. And still there was some left in the bottle. I put it back in its box after that, to be savored later on.

Finally, when the food was eaten and the ale drunk, it was time to go. Lilly and I said our goodbyes to friends and family, and took the coach back to our house. We disembarked and walked to the front door, but when Lilly went to open it, I stopped her.

"What…" she began, but I kissed her, swept her up in my arms, and crossed the threshold that way.

I'd always wanted to do that. Must be the romantic in me.

## THE END OF THE STORY

By the time Duke was done talking, the fire was lit in the hearth, and the lanterns were glowing on the walls. Meals were eaten, and ale drunk. The young man knew that his grandfather was tired, and his hand ached from writing so many notes, but he had a keen sense of satisfaction.

It was a long tale, but it was one worth hearing, and he thought that it would make a good book, too.

"So, the scroll, Grandad. What does it say?"

"Oh." Duke was nodding off now that the story was done. "Well, here, you can open it."

The young man took the scroll and carefully untied it and then spread it out on his lap. It was an official proclamation, signed by His Majesty, Robben the III, and it proclaimed that Duke and Lilly Grandfather were henceforth and forever citizens of note in Capital City, in recognition of services performed to the benefit of the city and its inhabitants.

"Wow," he said, "that's pretty incredible."

"Sure. That and a few silver ingols got me an ale."

"Doesn't ale usually cost a few…oh, I get it."

"Still," Duke said, "your Grandmother and I were pretty proud of it when one of the Palace Guards showed up here with it. Brindar got one too, as did Magnus."

"It was well deserved. I don't understand why there isn't a statue of the two of you in one of the squares."

"Ha. There isn't a sculptor alive who could do justice to your Grandmother," Duke said, with a twinkle in his eye.

"It's an incredible story, Granddad. Thanks for telling it to me. One thing though…"

"Yes?"

"When did you finish the Elven Ale?"

"Who says I finished it?" Duke got up from his chair, disappeared into the kitchen and returned with two mugs, and a small, brown glass bottle. He poured a small amount into each mug. "It refills itself every month. Truly a great gift."

The young man took a sip, and made the appropriate appreciative remarks. If he was to be honest, he wasn't much of an ale drinker, and while this was good, he thought it was somewhat wasted on him. But his grandfather was so proud of it, he didn't want to disappoint him.

"What about the elves? Did you and Grandmother ever go visit them? And Father Magnus, could he always do that stuff he did at your wedding? And what ever happened with the Dokkalfar down in the Deep? Did the dwarves have to worry about them again? And…"

"Enough," Duke laughed. "I've been talking all day, boy. That's enough for now. Maybe we'll do more another time. Maybe."

"Yeah, you're right. Let me go say goodbye to Grandmother, and I'll get out of here." He rose, gathering up his stylus and pad. "You know, Grandad, you've still never told me…"

"And now isn't the time either. Maybe someday, but for now, know that your Grandmother and I saved the world. Or at least this little part of it."

## IT'S TIME

Want to know how Duke got it? After all this time, he finally relents and tells his grandson the story of how he got his Ultimate Weapon. But it's not as simple as you might think. Read "Duke Grandfather Hears Voices" to finish the story

# AFTERWORD

Returning to Capital City was a lot of fun. After I finished the first book, Tales of a Nuisance Man, I knew that there were more adventures that I could relate, but I wanted them to be a little bigger somehow. Mean a little more to the world, rather than it being Duke fighting the monster de'jour.

It was time to put the city itself in danger. Attack it with some outside force, someone who had it in for the place. But not with an army, because that's been done a lot, and by much better writers than me. No, it was someone with a grudge. I won't say more than that in case you're one of those weird people who read afterwords before they read the book. If you're doing that now, then yes, I'm talking to you. You're weird.

For me, in the end, this book came out a little darker than the first one. There is no chapter that lines up with "The Witch's Broom" from Tales. But I like the adventure in it. I like exploring a little more of the different cultures, like the dwarven city right under Duke's nose, or the minotaurs, camped outside the walls.

Like the first book, it was a labor of love, that granted me hours of entertainment, and I hope does the same for you.

As always, I couldn't have done it without the constant support and encouragement of my lovely wife, Barb. She's my proofreader, my best friend, and my muse. Let's face it, she's my Lilly.

Also, I'd like to thank Judi and Marty again. And I'd especially like to thank my mother, Joyce. Her edits were invaluable to making this a better book.

And thank you for reading it! I hope you've enjoyed the visit to Capital City. Please take a moment to leave a review, visit my website, or check out the first book if you haven't already.

At some point, I'm sure Duke will be back. He's an old man now, but I'm certain he has more tales to tell.

Please, if you enjoyed this story, leave a review on Amazon. It's a HUGE help to independent authors like me. Thanks, and Happy Reading!

James Maxstadt lives in Burlington, NC with his beautiful wife Barbara and their old dog, Manny. When not writing, he's usually found reading, watching mindless TV, or performing a home renovation project. (Thanks, Dad!) But rather than read about James, he would much rather have you read the adventures of Duke Grandfather and his friends, or visit his website at www.jamesmaxstadt.com!

Made in the USA
Columbia, SC
07 December 2024

48674450R00167